Dearne Valley Blues

Sex and Coal and Rock 'n' Roll

Tony Lawrence

Lead in Yer Pencil Publishing

LEAD IN YER
PENCIL

Dedicated to the former coalmining communities of South Yorkshire, in which I discovered solid friendships, frank and fearless conversation and humour in abundance, and where the welfare of children and the elderly was uppermost in people's family life.

Acknowledgements

With my grateful thanks to Allen Ashley for all your professional guidance, critique and advice given to me during the writing of this story. To Ian, Mick, Paul and Terry for your patient reading of early drafts and for your comments, advice and contributions - I couldn't have written the book without your feedback gents, so many thanks for your input and assistance. And most of all to my wife Jacqui for your support and infinite patience in allowing me to sit in splendid isolation in my man cave, devoting countless hours of time trying to learn the craft of writing a tale. Thank you.

Chapter One

Barnsley, South Yorkshire, February 1989

In Winter, the chimney smoke from the Silverwood council estate mingles with the noxious gases rising out of nearby Monckton Coke Works and together they turn the cold damp night air into a pungent fog. This cloud then descends slowly over the Dearne Valley where the streetlights give it a yellowish, sulphurous glow, speckled by small flakes of soot drifting gently back to the ground like the start of a post-apocalyptic snowfall. After twenty minutes outside in this weather you end up with a face looking like a bad case of teenage blackheads and your hair smells like a bar of carbolic soap.

I'd just learnt these pearls from the taxi driver taking me to the Darfield Miners Welfare and Social Club from the Station Inn hotel in Doncaster where I'd arrived two hours ago. Through the car window all I can see is foggy darkness and the occasional dim streetlamp.

'First time in these parts, then?' he asked over his shoulder.

'Yes, it is,' I replied, cheerfully. 'I'm originally from Ontario, Canada but I'm living in London. I'm up here doing some weekend gigs. Darfield tonight, Brodsworth tomorrow and then Edlington on Sunday, before catching the mail train back home.'

'Bloody 'ell, tha's bein' brave visitin' them places. But I see thi've brought a weapon wi' yer though,' nodding at my guitar case.

I smiled. 'It's my axe. I'm a blues singer and guitarist.'

'Well, tha's seeing the Dearne in its best light lad.'

'But I can't see anything for the fog,' I replied. 'Plus, it's night and it's dark.'

'Aye. Means tha can't see all misery an' squalor that's surroundin' us.'

'So what do people round here do to enjoy themselves?' I asked.

'Drinkin', feetin', football and fuckin'…in that order. Oh and a chip-oil as well.'

'A what?' I asked.

'Chip-oil. Chippy,' he explained. 'Tha needs some snap inside thee when tha's enjoyin' thi sen.'

After another ten minutes we pulled off the road and onto an uneven and rough cinder patch of land in front of a single storey grey building.

'We're 'ere,' he announced, as I looked with dismay at my destination.

Discarded beer cans and litter lay amongst puddles of black water and a few tired and scrappy-looking cars were parked along one side of the club.

'Can you collect me at ten?' I asked, hopefully.

'I'll get my mate Terry to do it,' he replied. 'He's drivin' vomit-wagon round town tonight, so he'll be pleased to get a fare on way in.'

Taxis all settled, I opened the front door of the club stepping into a large foyer. It smelled of stale tobacco and beer and I could hear the raucous shouts and laughter of well-oiled punters. There were glass doors on my right leading into a snooker room, bearing the notice 'male members only on the table'. I wondered why they didn't use cues like everyone else. Straight ahead was another set of glass doors leading into a lounge or concert room and a serving hatch on the right gave a glimpse into a cavernous bar opening onto all sections of the club's interior.

On the left between the toilet doors was a tattered cork notice board. Pinned to it was a poster advertising the forthcoming star appearance of someone called 'Mervyn the Magnificent - Clairvoyant Extraordinaire' with a strip of paper placed diagonally across it bearing the hand-written message, 'cancelled due to unforeseen circumstances.' This wasn't boding well for me this evening.

A stocky middle-aged man with mutton chop sideburns and brylcreamed black hair leant against the hatch to the bar with a pint of beer by his hand. He wore a scarlet crushed velvet jacket and black bow tie with a crumpled off-white shirt which gaped apart between the straining buttons across his midriff.

'Who thi 'ell are you?' he asked gruffly.

'Good evening sir,' I said. 'I'm here looking for Mr Len Barrowclough, Entertainments Secretary. I've a booking to perform tonight.'

'Tha's lookin' at 'im lad,' he replied, glancing up sideways at a blackboard on the wall and on which several names had been written in white chalk. 'What's tha called?'

'I'm Jamie Martindale, from Ontario in Canada. I'm a blues singer and this gig was booked by my agent Henry Brownlow from London.'

'Ha, slimy Brown-nose,' he muttered, pulling out a piece of folded notepaper from his pocket. 'He rang 'ere yesterday and left me a message. Here we go, er, an American, name of Del Tabloose…ah think tha' needs a better stage name than that, lad,' he said.

'No,' I replied. 'I'm not American. I'm a Canadian. I sing American Delta Blues. My name is—'

'Well tonight thee's a Yank,' he interrupted. 'Name's Del,' he thought for a moment, 'Passo,' and promptly chalked it on the board. 'You're on at nine after Mavis, bingo and meat raffle, just before main comic turn.'

'Meat raffle?' I asked. 'What's that?'

'Butcher's tray of bacon, sausages, black pudding and kidneys for four - plus a joint,' he replied. 'Bloody nice prize an' all it is.'

'You raffle a joint?' I asked, bemused. Things may be looking up here after all.

'Joint o' beef for tha Sunday dinner,' he explained. 'Plus enough leftovers for three days snap tin.' Pulling out a pencil he asked, 'Now tell me what tha sings as I need to mek some notes to introduce thee later on stage.'

'Songs about the hardship and despair of down-trodden people. Classic blues from Texas and the deep South. I'm part of the great blues revival,' I added.

He stared blankly at me. 'Not in 'ere tha's not,' he declared. 'We don't do blue, only red. Barnsley play in red, we vote red and we only drink red,' pointing to the Wards Best Bitter signs on the beer pumps. 'Look out yonder lad,' he added, stretching out his left arm towards the front doors.

I followed his finger and could make out the illuminated colliery winding tower beyond the carpark. The metal structure was like a rusty skeleton rising out of the ground and bore a large signboard with the words 'NCB Darfield Main' in faded red lettering.

'That pit's bin 'ere since I wor a lad an' shortly it's gonna be shut down fer good,' he said. 'These lads in 'ere tonight will be outa work and on scrap 'eap. So wi don't need no talk of any bloody 'ardship – we've buckets of it an' loads to spare.'

I looked at him and wondered if I was in the right place. 'Now, mek tha mind up if tha wants the slot,' he said. 'It's fifty pounds or tha can sling thi 'ook an' I'll put on more bingo instead.'

'Just a minute,' I countered. 'Henry said it was a hundred. I've already paid him twenty pounds in commission.'

'He allers says that lad,' he replied wearily. 'It's fifty quid or it's nowt.'

Ah, the joys of being a professional musician I thought to myself. 'I'll take it,' I said. 'Now, where's the backing band and where do I get ready?'

'Brian and Roy are the resident duo – organ and drums – that's them playin' now,' he answered. 'And tha can get changed or tuned up in Gents,' pointing towards the toilet door.

I was quietly seething. Why had I agreed to come to this wasteland? Go North, Henry had said. There's tons of work in club-land for the likes of you. They're simply begging for musicians up there. Foolishly, I'd believed him and paid him to get me these gigs. Now I was regretting being miles away from my comfortable routine in South London. But I was also answering my own question as well: you're a musician and you go where the work takes you, so get on with it.

Just then there were several shouts and screams as two burly figures came bowling through the lounge doors locked together like wrestlers and trading punches, kicks and slaps with each other. It took me a moment to realise they were females, as the dark-haired one dragged her opponent by the ears through the front doors and they carried on laying into each other in the carpark.

'Does that happen often?' I asked, looking over at Len and worried at what I'd just seen.

'Not really,' he replied, scratching his chin thoughtfully. 'Ruby usually wins her scraps wi' Maureen but looks like she's on losing end tonight. They'll both be reet in a few minutes,' he concluded, wandering off into the concert room as I peered through the doors after him.

It was packed with people who crowded around formica-topped tables coupled with red plastic chairs and set out over a lacquered timber floor. Fluorescent strip lights hung from yellowed polystyrene ceiling tiles and shone though the haze of cigarette smoke to reveal the mottled red wallpaper and matching curtains drawn over the windows. A one-armed bandit flashed a multi-coloured display in the far corner. The bar over on my right hand side ran almost the full length of the room. It was four deep with thick-set men all with greasy hair and short brown curly teeth, shouting and laughing at each other.

On the small stage Brian and Roy, dressed in matching red frilly shirts and black bowties, were knocking out *Tie A Yellow Ribbon*, oblivious to their surroundings.

After a few minutes, Len returned to the foyer. 'Right then, I'm gonna be introducing Mavis, sorry, I mean Veronique, on stage shortly,' he advised. 'Then you can get sorted out with Brian and Roy.'

'What does Veronique do?' I asked, innocently. 'Is she a singer?'

He guffawed. 'She does a burly-esque act with her pet python. She used to be known as Mavis from Mexborough back when she wor a stripper but she's put a bit o' timber on since then.'

As if on cue, the Ladies toilet door opened and the figure of a large woman appeared. Dressed in a bulging red corset with matching head-dress, gloves and high heels and with a large docile-looking snake draped around her shoulders, she looked over at us and smiled. 'All set Len? Then let me just 'ave a fag first,' she said, lighting up.

Len nodded back and after a few moments he walked into the lounge, up onto the stage and signalled to the backing musicians. 'Now then, let's 'ave a big 'and for our very own Veronique,' he announced, as Brian switched on a cassette player at the side of the organ.

'Tha needs big 'ands to get 'old o' that lot,' shouted out a voice and laughter followed.

Mavis sashayed her way through the doors and started to parade around the room, gyrating her considerable bulk to the taped track of *Fever* by Peggy Lee. Nobody looked interested and I guessed they'd seen it all before, as they carried on with their own conversations. I watched as she stopped to stroke the bald head of one old man and as she did so her python nonchalantly leant over to the nearest glass, obviously feeling thirsty in this smoke-filled jungle.

'Get tha bloody snek out mi ale Mavis,' shouted the drinker, snatching his glass from the snake's reach. 'Tha don't know whee-er it's bin.'

'Places you'll never visit Bobby, but wish you 'ad,' replied Mavis suggestively, gently caressing the snake's head. Ribald laughter from the other drinkers cackled around her as she carried on.

I turned my attention to Brian and Roy who'd come into the foyer for a drink and walking over to them I introduced myself. 'Do you know any of these songs?' I asked, handing them my set list of seven plus one encore. They both looked at it before shaking their heads, doubtfully.

'It's no to number one, two and three,' said Roy. 'Number four I've heard of but can't play it and no to numbers five and six. Ah've never 'eard of number seven,

Texas Flood either. So, th'answer's no, lad,' he said, taking a mouthful of beer.

So much for a backing band. 'Well, how about any Stevie Ray Vaughan, or some Howlin' Wolf or BB King then?' I replied, hopefully.

'Never 'eard of them,' said Brian, dismissively. 'Only thing that's king round 'ere is coal. And I don't mean Nat neither, although we do know a couple of 'is songs.'

'So, what music do these people like?' I asked.

'Anything they can sing along to,' replied Roy. If they like it then they'll clap or they'll sing.'

'What happens if they don't like it?' I said.

'Tha'll soon know when tha's flying through front doors,' he answered. 'Do you 'ave insurance?'

'I'm more concerned about my guitar,' I said. 'It's a Les Paul. Cost a fortune and I'm still paying it off.'

'Meks no diff'rence whether it's Les Paul or Lyndsey De Paul to this lot,' said Brian. 'If tha's crap then tha'll know abart it pretty quick.'

I looked at their frilly shirts and bowties then glanced down at my black garb, boots and song-list and concluded that I was shortly about to die on stage. A radical re-think of my repertoire was needed and fast. Come on now Jamie, you're a professional, I said to myself. These things happen to the best of us.

I sat down at a corner table near the front doors and began to think and scribble out some possible song titles on a beer-mat. After a while I realised there was silence in the concert room. I thought I'd gone deaf then Len's booming voice yelled out, 'First one out, in wi' a shout, it's me and you, twenty-two.'

Bingo had begun. The previous laughter and banter had disappeared and the room was quieter than a school hall on exams day. I glanced up from my scribbling. Mavis had put her coat on over her working clothes and her python was wrapped around her shoulders like a scarf.

'Ave a good 'un luv. I'm off to Labour Club now, there's a better class o' punters over there. Ah might even be on wi' a promise for later on,' she said, winking at me as she walked out of the foyer.

Brian and Roy reappeared in front of me and I handed over the beermat to them. 'Here, I'm going to busk this lot the best I can,' I said, as they looked through the titles.

'Right-oh,' said Roy. 'I'll plug thee into th'amp on stage, it's all set up when we're ready.'

Before long we heard the shout of 'house' and general moans of 'not you again, by the bloody 'ell,' and the scraping of chairs as glasses were emptied and new rounds ordered noisily at the bar.

Eventually Len was back on the stage with the mike shouting out, 'Winning raffle number tonight is forty six,' and a small cheer went up in response. He cleared his throat and continued. 'And now, a very special treat for us,' he said. 'First time in Yorkshire and all the way from Ontario, Texas, let's give a big 'and to singing sensation Mr Del Passo…'

A smattering of polite applause went round the room as I took to the stage and looked out into the mist of ciggy smoke and expectant faces. 'Good evening ladies and gentlemen,' I said into the microphone. 'It's great to see you and be here with you in Darfield tonight. My name is Jamie, er, Del...Passo-Martindale and I'm—'

'Get on wi' it, yer southern gob-shite,' yelled a voice from my left.

'Thank you,' I replied. 'This is *Johnny B Goode.*'

I lowered my head and started the famous guitar solo opening with gusto, doing my best Chuck Berry impression and hoping to God that it's going to go down well here. Behind me Roy was keeping time with a four on the floor beat and Brian's doing a tidy boogie groove on the Casio organ. It's not exactly a rock and roll band, but it sounded good and I kinda liked it.

I started singing and risked a glance at the audience. A few heads were nodding and a fat guy was shimmying back to his table from the bar with two pints in each hand and a fag hanging out of his mouth, arms moving back and forth in time to the music. So far so good, no beer glasses heading my way and I went into the middle eight section.

As I reached the last verse I turned to Brian telling him to carry on whilst I moved seamlessly into *Roll Over Beethoven* followed by *Route Sixty Six*. Same key, same tempo…and nearly ten minutes had passed by before I needed to change tack.

The lucky recipient of the meat raffle was below the stage to my right. He'd reached inside the cling film cover and taken out a couple of sausages, beating them against his wife's arm like a pair of flaccid drumsticks. In response she cuffed his ear smartly and the table of drinkers around them were hysterical.

Behind me Roy yelled out to me to stop, as his 'bloody right arm is falling off' and as I finished the song I got some applause and a cheer.

'Thank you very much,' I said. 'Now, who want's some Glen Campbell?'

'I am the linesman for Notts County,' sang out a bloke from the side and started cheering.

I took this as an affirmative and launched full tilt instead into *Galveston*.

'Sharl-eston, oh Sharl-eston,' yelled my fellow singer. 'I can see thi' pit wheels turning…'

'Give order now,' shouted Len from the bar. 'Let the lad sing…'

Smiling, I carried on. Welcome to club-land. They're not exactly blues aficionados, but at least I was still on the stage and in one piece. After two more numbers they were applauding and whistling and I thought that they liked me. So I went into *The Wanderer* which had everyone stomping their feet and clapping followed by *Peggy Sue* and *Oh Boy.*

Then without thinking I announced, 'Here's a song that's pretty big where I come from, hope you like it.'

After the intro chords, I sang out the opening lines to *Working Man* and suddenly the whole room was singing along with me in full voice. Shit, I'd stumbled into the coal miners' anthem without realising…and they were loving it. Now there was a competition between tables as to who could sing the loudest. Arms were locked together with beer glasses swaying above their heads and ale spilled over each other, but no-one objected.

Brian was smiling and nodding and when I reached the end, well, it was back to the beginning for everyone and they carried on singing and swaying.

Time for a swift exit right I thought. I picked up my guitar, waved and sidled into the foyer to look for Len and my money.

'Here tha goes lad,' he said, handing me a bunch of five pound notes. 'Tha's dun all reet. Keep playin' them blues, tha'll go far…and preferably sooner,' laughing at his own joke.

'Thank you,' I said, counting out the cash before stuffing it into my jeans' pocket and packing up my guitar. 'Now, where's Terry and his vomit-wagon taxi?' I asked.

It was one down and two to go in my weekend debut in northern club-land.

Chapter Two

Stepping out of the club doors, with the raucous singing and cheering still ringing in my ears, the shock of icy cold air made me gasp momentarily. It was snowing and the small flakes jostled for dominance with the cloud of black coal dust whipped up by the night winds blowing across the colliery spoil heap. The combination of wintry blasts and dust set me off on a coughing fit and I wondered whether I'd choke to death or freeze out here.

Glancing at my watch in the dim orange door light, it was ten thirty. I peered over to the parked rusty vehicles in the slim hope that one was my waiting taxi, but no chance.

Inside the club the boozed-up miners sounded oblivious to everything outside their own small world. I pondered their oncoming fate as I looked at the pit towers with their top lights glimmering in the gloom, like searchlights in a prison camp watching over the inmates.

Any feelings of post-gig euphoria I had were quickly erased - not that I'd got many to start with. I'd been short-changed and shafted coming up here from London and after busking my way through a set of over-played rock 'n' roll standards, all I wanted now was a beer, a bite to eat and some sleep.

Whoever said being a professional musician was living the dream was either drunk, delusional or both.

Just then, the headlights of a vehicle rounded the corner and what looked like an armoured security van bounced and splashed its way across the cinders and puddles towards me.

'Are thee that Yank wantin' a ride inta town?' yelled a voice from the driver's side window.

I wasn't going to argue geographical semantics, so I simply replied, 'Yes.'

'Well then, 'op in lad an' quick abart it,' came the reply.

I slid the side door open and climbed aboard. 'Thanks for picking me up. You must be Terry.'

'Aye, an' you must be soft in yed for bein' in these parts,' he chortled. 'Still, tha's payin' for fuel inta town, so sit back and enjoy the scenery.'

As I couldn't see any scenery on account of it being pitch black, I looked around the van's interior instead, as Terry drove onto the narrow country road and away from Darfield colliery.

In the front passenger seat well was a bucket and small mop together with a couple of rolls of blue paper towels and a large plastic container labelled Jeyes Fluid. All the seats and floor were made out of rigid plastic and the side windows were fitted with reinforced glass.

'What is this vehicle?' I asked, curiously. 'Looks more like an armoured car than a taxi.'

'Used to be a cop mini-bus,' he replied. 'They 'ad 'em for miners' strike in eighty-four but sold 'em off cheap a couple o' years ago. Not exactly built for comfort but just the job for my weekend pick-ups. No chance of a brick comin' through win-ders nor anyone puttin' a knife in seats,' he added.

'But how can you see where you're going?' I asked nervously. The narrow road was un-lit and the mist and snowflakes swirled around the windscreen as we drove.

'Ah can't,' he replied. 'Just relying on no bugger else coming t'other way. Plus, if they did, well, they wouldn't do us much damage. Reinforced bodywork you see,' glancing round at me as he spoke.

I couldn't see anything in the darkness, so I just nodded.

'If tha feels unsafe, tha can always put a seat belt on, 'cept there aren't any,' he continued. 'Them Bobbies 'ad to move pretty damn quick back when they were feetin' wi' miners. Couldn't be doin' wi' seatbelts when they 'ad all that riot gear an' shields on,' he explained. 'So, sit back an' I'll have tha back in town in no time. Whereabouts you goin' to anyway?'

'The Station Inn Hotel.'

'That bloody doss-house. Ah wouldn't be seen dead in place. Mind you, neither would 'is missus. They reckon he killed 'er years back, you know, and got away wi' it.'

'Who did?' I asked.

'Landlord at the Station,' he replied. 'Harold Crofton he's called. Used to be a butcher in town before passin' shop onto his lad an' then buyin' th'otel on cheap. That were about fifteen years ago. Then 'is wife left him for a bookie she worked for and one night they both disappeared wi' out a trace. Never found 'em. Folk reckon that 'arold did the pair of 'em in, mincing 'em into sausages wi' pork an' black pudding at 'is old shop.'

'Charming,' I replied, not knowing if he was spinning me a tale or not.

'Aye,' said Terry. 'Ah'd stick to th'egg on toast for tha breakfast if ah were you lad,' he smirked. 'Moral of the story is if you're wed to a butcher, then don't go an' leave 'im for a bookie. Stakes are too 'igh an' you'll end up gettin' the chop,' laughing at his own joke.

I smiled back. The thoughts of food mingled with being holed up in a mad axe murderer's downbeat hotel ran through my mind and played out in ever-worsening scenarios. I realised my imagination was working overtime and instead tried to concentrate on looking out of the window. It wasn't easy in the darkness but eventually we reached the outskirts of town and then a few minutes later pulled up outside the Station Inn.

'Thanks,' I said, opening the door. 'How much do I owe you?'

'A tenner. And if tha needs mi agin call on this number,' handing me a card. 'But not tonight. I'll have me 'ands full wi' drunken women an' whatnots for next few hours. Si thi for now lad.'

I wondered what a 'whatnot' was as Terry drove off and I walked into the small hotel and found the lounge bar. It was occupied by a dozen scrawny old men nursing half-empty pints and clutching fags as they clustered around the tables murmuring to each other in hushed tones.

They looked up suspiciously at me and my guitar case, as if I was about to suddenly open fire with a sub-machine gun, all Al Capone style.

The landlord was pulling thick grubby curtains across the windows and behind the bar a bleached blonde-haired woman in her late thirties was wiping glasses whilst smoking a cig.

She looked up and smiled as I approached. 'Wi've just called last orders luv, but if tha's quick tha can 'ave a drink. What's tha want?'

'Er, a lager please and I'm a resident here,' I said, watching the landlord warily as he moved a large TV and video player on a stand into place at one end of the room.

'Are tha stayin' up for film-night then?' she asked, picking up a glass.

'What's that?'

'Bluey night,' she replied. 'We 'ave 'em wi' a lock-in for reg'lars, every so often.'

'Blues night?' I said, thinking she meant music.

'Bluey's...porno's,' putting my glass down and by way of explanation, she pulled out a small stack of VHS tapes from under the bar.

I glanced at them and then back at her. 'Er, will you be staying as well?'

'Naw, seen 'em all before,' she replied. 'Besides...' glancing at my guitar case and then back at me with a coy smile. 'I thought you might fancy singin' me a couple of songs instead.'

'Sure,' I replied. I recognised a pick-up when I saw one, even if I didn't quite understand the local vernacular. 'And where exactly would you like me to, er, perform for you?'

'My 'ouse,' she grinned, replacing my empty glass beneath the bar. Hell, I thought, can't I get a damned drink first?

'Come on,' beckoning me to follow her. 'I'm just knockin' off now.' Picking up her coat she shouted, 'See ya' tomorrow 'arold. Mi taxi's 'ere outside. I'll lock front door on way out.'

Harold just nodded in response and carried on with his TV adjustments. I followed silently and as we walked outside to the taxi, the snow was starting to settle on the roads.

'Just what we need,' she said. 'By the way, I'm Irene, but everyone round 'ere calls me Reeny.'

'Jamie,' I replied, as we got into the cab. 'But everyone round here calls me whatever they want.'

'Where to luv?' asked the taxi driver.

'Same place as every Friday – Wath.' Reeny pronounced our destination as 'Waa-th'.

'Then I'll be droppin' thee at Cross Keys roundabout, no further,' he replied. 'Got bloody robbed last time I went up there.'

'What's wrong with Wath?' I asked her curiously.

'Nowt,' she answered. 'It's a small pit village. Very peaceful...well it is on a Sunday lunchtime when everyone's in pub. Rest o' time it's like Beirut.'

'What, full of Arabs?' I asked puzzled.

'No,' she laughed. 'It's just dog-rough an' a proper shit-tip. Loads o' feetin' an' crap left everywhere. But ya get used to it.'

As the taxi drove off she looped her arm beneath mine and I glanced down at her hands...and her wedding ring. 'Er, is your husband expecting us?' I enquired.

'Our Bert?' she replied. 'Naw, he's on nightshift pit maintenance this wick. Would've gone to work for ten an' won't be home till mornin'. So, as long as tha's gone by six, there's nowt to worry abart. What you doin' round 'ere anyway?'

I told her my reasons for being in Doncaster and its surroundings plus a bit about myself, as the taxi made its way out of town. She nodded as I spoke, chuckling occasionally and twenty minutes later we pulled up outside the Cross Keys.

'That's a tenner,' said the driver. I wondered if all the taxi fares were a tenner round here.

As we got out and Reeny paid the fare, I looked at our surroundings. The snow had stopped but the wind still blew in icy blasts. The pub was in darkness and at one side of the building a couple of old men were arguing and swaying whilst trading drunken punches with each other. Over the road in the bus shelter, a couple of teenagers were

17

trying to copulate whilst both holding on to their bags of chips, no doubt anxious not to drop any post-coital nutrition.

As the cab disappeared down the road, I warily expected taxi-robbers to be lurking in darkened doorways, but none were to be seen. Instead, the neighbourhood chimney pots emptied their sooty smoke into the night sky and the thin layer of snow lying on the ground was turning to an ash-grey icy slush. I pulled up my collar to the cold damp wind, thinking I'm sure that line comes from a song, whilst Reeny took hold of my arm saying, 'Just up 'ere, won't tek us long.'

'Ok. Nice to get some fresh air and stretch our legs,' I said, struggling to make conversation.

A loud screeching noise made me jump and I turned round to see a diesel locomotive appear on the rail tracks across the road. It was pulling half a mile of coal wagons and heading for the huge coking works which I could make out in the distance. Following the direction of the train, I could see clouds of yellowish-grey smoke billowing from the plant chimney stacks and hear the clanging noise of industrial heavy metal.

The cold breeze blew the smell of phenol from the plant into my nose, making me feel that I was wearing heavy duty disinfectant as an aftershave. For a moment I was transported back to my old elementary school where the dutiful janitor would use something similarly repugnant to wipe the floor after a kid had thrown up.

We walked past a row of steel-shuttered shop-fronts then along a narrow street of derelict terraced houses. The roof slates had gone, leaving the trusses and beams exposed like the bones of a well-picked animal carcass. All the doors and windows were boarded up and garden fences had been ripped out leaving gaping holes in the ground.

Beer cans, broken bottles and discarded pushchairs littered the street and more rubbish was piled up against the concrete lamp-posts.

On one house, I saw that the words 'scabby bastard' had been painted on one of the walls in large white lettering. Puzzled, I was about to ask Reeny if this was a local reference to venereal disease but thought better than to risk spoiling the moment and romantic setting.

We turned a corner into a wider cul-de-sac of grey pebble-dashed, semi-detached houses, some with cars parked outside and others with light coming from the curtained windows. Over the top of the houses, I could see the dark outline of a large spoil tip and beyond it the lights of the colliery towers.

As we passed one particular house we heard the raised voices of a domestic in full flow accompanied by crockery smashing against the inside walls. I was alarmed but Reeny didn't bat an eyelid.

Welcome to Wath I thought. Even the combination of darkness and snowy winter weather could not disguise the truth of my feelings that this was indeed a fucking miserable place to be in.

'Ere we are,' announced Reeny, as we walked up the path to a semi with a car-port at one side of the house.

Opening the front door, I followed her into a small living room and she turned on a wall lamp. An open fire had burnt down to its embers in the hearth behind a rusting metal fireguard, but the house felt warm and welcoming with a lingering smell of tobacco and coal dust.

'Come on in an' put wood in th'oil,' she said, hanging up her coat on the rail by the door.

'What was that?' I asked, perplexed.

'Shut bloody door behind thee!'

'Ah,' doing as I was instructed. 'It's just that the phrase putting your wood in the hole has a different meaning where I come from,' I said, trying to explain, but Reeny just smiled.

Locking the front door she turned to me. 'Now, I only 'ave one rule an' that's cleanliness. I might live in a shit 'oyle but we don't have to smell like one. So upstairs now, run a bath for us an' get thi sen clean. I'll mek us both a drink an' join you in a minute. Beer or a whisky?' she asked.

I answered, 'Yes to both please,' propping my guitar case against the wall beneath a wedding photo of Reeny and her not so-beloved Bert as she went through to the kitchen.

I climbed the stairs and smiled as I realised that I was about to have my first bath in 'Waa-th' and my first encounter with a Mrs Robinson – well, kind of anyway. Still, it seemed a better option than watching pornos with the old gits back at the hotel.

*

Distant spotlights switched on as I heard my name being announced and I breathed in deeply, getting ready to walk out onstage at the Filmore East for my duet with BB King. Suddenly, my roadie was pulling at my arm, stopping me in my tracks, and I woke up to the startled voice of Reeny squealing, 'Get up now, quick,' as the sound of a vehicle pulled into the car-port downstairs.

'Hurry up,' she hissed. 'It's our Bert. He must 'ave clocked off early. He'll go round back to feed his pigeons first, so you can nip outa front door. If he sees thi 'e'll kill thee an' then me. Then 'e'll start askin' some questions.'

I didn't need telling twice. Leaping up from the bed, I pulled on my undies, tee shirt, jeans and boots and grabbed my jacket, all in one action. Reeny wrapped a bathrobe around her and peered out of the curtains. Bert had indeed walked round the back to his pigeon coop.

We raced silently down the stairs and she opened the front door to a biting cold wind. 'Here,' she whispered, 'Tek this wi' ya', handing me a black donkey jacket off the coat rack as she bundled me out the house. 'And go that way,' pointing to next door's garden. 'Go through ginnel back t' main road an' tha'll be reet. I'll see ya later at Station. I'm doin' lunchtime shift today, now go.'

Heart pounding, I did as I was told, leaving tell-tale footprints across the snow-covered garden, but I wasn't looking back. Pulling the rough overcoat on I realised it was about three sizes too big and it had a fluorescent orange band across the back bearing the letters 'NCB'. God, that husband of hers must be a huge bloke, I thought. Still, good job I got outa there intact and just in time...when suddenly, I stopped dead in my tracks. Oh Jesus, my guitar! It's still in the house and I can't go back for it now. Will Reeny realise and bring it to the hotel?

I shuffled along the desolate and deserted streets, cursing myself for being so stupid. It was five thirty in the morning, I was freezing cold and lost somewhere in Wath, minus my guitar. Plus, very recent events had now brought on a desperate need in me to empty my bowels.

Past the row of shuttered shops and across the main road, I could see some open space and a children's play area. A park, I thought, there's got to be some toilets there. Sure enough, a low grey concrete building stood on its own next to a car parking area and a patch of rhododendron bushes. However, any thoughts of comfort were soon dashed by the sight of the metal-barred gates locked firmly across the entrances.

Shit, it was going to be bush toilet time I realised, grabbing handfuls of leaves and creeping into the foliage.

I emerged from the bushes a couple of minutes later to be blinded by the headlights of a van being switched on in front of me and a gruff voice yelled out, 'Waz thar doin' thee'er at this 'our then?'

It sounded like a sing-song foreign language to me, so I just blinked and replied, 'Eh?' as a burly police officer walked up to me and shone his torch directly into my eyes.

'Fuckin' deaf as well are tha?' he shouted. Looking at my donkey jacket, he then declared, 'Ah! Tha's a flyin' picket, ain't tha?'

'A what?' I replied, completely baffled. I had no idea what he was talking about as he continued dazzling me with his torch.

'Davie, over 'ere mate,' he shouted and waved to his buddy to get out of the van. 'We're lockin' this bugger up right now.'

Gripping my arm tightly he said, 'I'm arrestin' thee now for loiterin', flyin', indecency, resisting, assaultin' an' being a general pain to society.'

'What? But I haven't done anything,' I cried, wondering how I could possibly be loitering and flying at the same time. 'And what d'ya mean by indecency?' I challenged him.

'Them bloody letters on yer back,' came the reply. 'I fuckin' 'ate picketing miners, 'specially your sort.'

I started to explain my circumstances but to no avail as he wasn't listening. Instead, I was promptly bundled into the back of the van and the door slammed against my shoulders.

I heard his colleague say, 'Four-five to dispatch, one male to bring in, bee and bee, over.'

'Dispatch, four-five,' came the squawky reply. 'Tek 'im to Roth'ram for booking, we've a full house here tonight. Over.'

'Tha's goin' to Roth'ram,' shouted Cop One to me over his shoulder. 'So, sit back and enjoy the ride.'

Turning to his colleague he said, 'That's us dun now for neet Davie, plus we'll get a nice breakfast aht of it too.' He glanced back at me again and added, 'Cheers for that, matey.'

I had no idea what he was on about and didn't care as I bounced around in the back of the van. Presently, we pulled into a yard outside a large redbrick building with the sign 'Rotherham Central Police Station'. I was led into a rear waiting room where a cleaner was mopping what looked like a combination of blood and beer from the linoleum floor. A polished wooden counter stretched across one end of the room and behind it a portly desk sergeant looked menacingly at me and the cop holding my arm.

'Caught 'im over at Wath Rec, Sarge,' said my arresting officer. 'Indecency, assault, loiterin', you name it.'

Turning me around so that the sergeant could see the lettering on my back, he added seriously, 'Plus, he's a flyer as well. Looked like 'e wor waitin' for some others to join 'im.'

The sergeant nodded and looked at me. 'Name, address and age and empty your pockets into this tray,' he demanded, slamming a metal dish on the counter.

'It's all in here,' I said, reaching for my wallet in my jeans' pocket and handing it over.

He peered down his nose at my Canadian identity card and then looked at the officer. 'He's a fuckin' foreigner as well. Pat 'im down an' put 'im in fourteen. I'll get a dayshift lad to process him later on.'

With that I was led away and down a corridor and shoved into a windowless and dimly lit cell. At least it had a toilet, I mused, staring at the steel receptacle in the corner. The door slammed and locked behind me. I went over to the small bunk and lying down I pulled the thin grey blanket around my head and over my eyes as I pondered my shit luck.

Back in London I'd heard the cops being referred to as the 'filth' and now understood it to mean the sly, underhand tactics that were used by some of them on innocent citizens such as myself. I couldn't see or understand how I had done anything wrong or committed any criminal offence.

If only I had chosen a lock-in and filthy vids at the Station instead of copping off with Reeny, then I wouldn't be here, stuck in an invidious cop station locked up by the filth. I turned to the wall next to the bunk and silently cursed that crap-head agent Brownlow for sending me to this miserable crap-heap of a place.

My thoughts turned to Reeny and how she'd beguiled me into going to Wath with her. Why hadn't I resisted and said no to her charms?

But it was too late now for regrets and more than anything, I was alone and parted from my beloved…my beautiful Les Paul guitar. Would I ever see her again in one piece?

Chapter Three

A succession of loud male voices and the rattling of metal keys in the cell door aroused me from my fitful slumber. As I opened and rubbed my bleary eyes, a bulky middle-aged police officer waddled towards me holding a metal tray, setting it down on the bunk next to my feet.

'Eat that then tha's gone,' he ordered. 'Sarge wants all cells emptied ready fer football yobs and we're buggered if we're gonna' be doin' all paperwork on you.'

I sat up as he continued with his instructions. 'So 'urry up an' you'll be released, with no charge for our 'ospitality,' he added, handing me back my wallet, watch and money in a small polythene bag.

I could smell the coffee but I didn't recognise the thick mass of greyish-brown substance spread over some toast next to the steaming plastic cup. It looked like it had been applied by a blind man using a trowel.

'What's this?' I asked, pointing to the tray.

'Toast and drippin'. What d'ya think?' he replied.

'Dripping what?' I asked. I had no idea what he meant.

'Cold, congealed fat an' jelly that's dripped off a nice big piece o' roast beef while it's bin cooking,' he answered. 'We calls it a mucky sandwich an' some fuckin' pit prop you are if tha don't know drippin'. Now gerrit down yer neck.'

My stomach heaved in response and so I drank the coffee instead. I reckoned that at least it hadn't been anywhere near a dripping dead cow.

The officer watched me then led me out of the cell and through a secure door into the front foyer. 'Now, fuck off matey,' he advised, quietly.

I nodded and walked over to where one of his colleagues stood behind a glass-fronted enquiries counter, scribbling on a pad.

'Excuse me sir,' I asked, as politely as I could. 'Where's the railway station please?'

Without looking up he said gruffly, 'Same place as it's allers bin. Next to railway line.'

'And where is that?' I persevered.

'Same place as its allers bin. Halfway between 'ere an' town centre,' came his answer.

I gave up. Looking around I spotted a payphone on the wall next to a notice board. Pulling Terry's card out of my pocket I walked to the phone, fed some change into the slot and dialed the number.

'Naw then, who's this?' asked a voice after four rings.

'Hello Terry, it's me, Jamie,' I wailed into the receiver. 'The Canadian guy from last night. Can you collect me please? I'm at the police station in some place called Rotherham.'

'What thi 'ell are tha doin' down there?' he asked. 'Was yer singin' that bad then?'

'It's a long story and I'll tell you when I see you.'

'Well, gimme about twenty minutes then to get over to you,' he answered. 'Be outside waiting for me.'

Relieved, I walked out of the entrance doors and sat on the low brick wall surrounding the police station premises. It was just after eleven thirty and the town was coming to life. People shuffled by me without a second glance.

Despite my appearance as a down and out druggie, I seemed to blend effortlessly into the scenery of a cold Saturday morning in Rotherham.

I breathed the crisp air deep into my chest, trying to rid my nostrils of the lingering smells of disinfectant and 'eau de police cell' before realising that it was actually me that was giving off the offensive odour. I plunged my hands deep into the pockets of the borrowed jacket, not so much to emphasise my state of desperation but more because I was shivering with the cold.

As a distraction, I watched elderly couples and shell-suited younger women amble into Tesco's across the street, whilst others emerged carrying bulging plastic carrier bags in both hands and paused briefly to light up a fag before continuing on their way.

The sight of all that food made my stomach rumble and groan. I realised that the last thing I'd eaten was a British Rail cheese and pickle sandwich from the train buffet on the journey up here yesterday. As dismal as it was then, I would have grabbed one now eagerly with both my hands. Then the thought of dripping dead cows came back to mind and I almost retched in response. That cop must have been having me on I reasoned, but I'd no intentions of going back into the nick to find out.

Groups of youths and teenage girls giggled and swore at each other as they walked past me, no doubt heading into the town for an afternoon's shoplifting. Down the road a large group of men dressed in denims and red football scarves were gathering outside the White Lion, banging on the doors to be let in and climbing on the stone sills to peer through the pub windows.

Then a car–horn beeped nearby, arousing me from my casual observations and I stood up and clambered into the sanctuary of Terry's wagon.

'What 'appened to thee?' he asked, concerned.

'I could tell you but first I need to eat something. I'm starving and I'm also in need of a shower, so don't get too close,' I advised.

'Right-o, you're the gaffer. It'll cost you mind. Meter's already on thirty quid for coming all the way down 'ere.'

I nodded back in silent agreement and peered vacantly out of the window, just pleased to see the back of the damned police station and its charming employees. I wondered if the phrase 'serve and protect' had ever been mentioned or discussed amongst the Rotherham constabulary.

'I'll take tha over to Cathy's Café on Parkgate Road,' announced Terry. 'They do a great pork pie an' peas an' just the job for you in your state,' he added, sympathetically.

'Big match on today,' he continued, as we weaved through the traffic. 'Barnsley v Donny in fourth round cup tie. Their own grounds aren't big enough for all crowds so it's being held 'ere in Roth'ram instead. There'll be some reet trouble goin' on when game ends, no matter who wins.'

I nodded back politely, but uncaringly and a few minutes later we pulled up in an area of old industrial mill buildings where Cathy's side-street café was already half-full as we entered.

A group of unwashed old men with three-day silver stubble and greasy greying hair sat around small formica-topped tables, scouring the racing pages of the *Daily Mirror* whilst hanging onto dog-end fags and slurping brown tea from pint-sized stripy chipped mugs.

As Terry ordered our food, I sat down on a wobbly chair, pushing the half-full ashtray to the side wall and wiping HP sauce droplets from the table top with my sleeve end. I fitted in perfectly with my fellow dining patrons.

Terry returned from the counter with two steaming dishes, each piled with a slab of meat pie surrounded by a sea of green mushy peas and a topping of thick lumpy gravy. It looked disgusting but smelled delicious and I tucked in with gusto.

'This is good,' I said. 'Thank you, it's making me feel human again.'

'Glad yer like it. 'Olesome proper food. There's nowt better when tha's 'ad a bad night – or a good one, come to think of it.'

As we ate, I gave him a potted history of last night's events, leaving out the more sensitive bits for the moment and he just nodded back at me through mouthfuls of pie.

'You see,' he said eventually, 'Folk round 'ere don't expect much. Men want a proper day's hard work with a decent wage to spend on the niceties of life - things like beer, fags, sex and food...and a wife an' some place to live,' he explained. 'Mebbe a bit of culture as well. Some footie, rugby or brass bands. Men 'ere need an 'obby to keep 'emselves occupied, you know.'

I nodded, thinking back about Bert and his pigeon coop.

'The women, well they just go along wi' it,' he said. 'It's allers been the case. So, they get bored and then they want some excitement. You wanna see 'em on a Sat'day night out in Donny. Like 'unting packs they are.'

'It's a bit of a one-sided lifestyle then, don't you think?' I said, sounding somewhat egalitarian as well as intellectual.

'Not really. So long as men 'ave work to do then we're all 'appy. But tek away our livelihood an' that's when trouble an' feetin' starts proper.'

He put his fork down and wiped his mouth on a paper napkin before continuing. 'You see, we're a proud lot up 'ere. Proud of what we still 'ave an' proud of our 'eritage an' what we've given to the world,' he declared. 'Round 'ere might look like a right shit-tip to you an' all them posh fuckin' Londoners, but it's our shit-tip an' that's what mek's the difference.'

I looked at him as he continued with his theme. 'D'ya think them lot down South would be proud o' livin' in somewhere like here, called Greasbrough, or whee'er I live in Grimey? That's Grimethorpe to you?'

I said I didn't know and carried on eating whilst Terry carried on talking. 'But the times is changin'. Pits are closin' and 'eavy industry is goin'. The world is moving on and we're not movin' wi' it.'

I detected sadness and regret in his voice. 'Work, home and leisure – those three essential parts of a man's life, are not the same anymore. Tek one away and the other two suffer, sometimes irretrievably. A man needs to be proud o' summat, otherwise you tek away 'is soul and 'is very reason for being alive,' he pronounced, solemnly.

'You're very knowledgeable, er, for a taxi driver,' I said, sounding a little awkward.

'That's because mi day job is lecturing at Barnsley Tech. Economics and Social History A Levels. Taxi-ing is just the weekend job. If anyone at College questions it, ah just say ah'm doin' field work research for my doctorate.'

'And are you?' I asked.

'No chance. Just tryin' to keep a roof over our 'eads. I've a high maintenance wife an' four kids to look after. Vehicle belongs to mi brother, who's, er, indisposed for the next eighteen months.'

I guessed he meant his brother was in jail, so I asked, 'And what did he do?'

'Got caught stealing,' came his bluff reply. 'Just tryin'' to 'elp his family out after losin' his job.'

He looked directly into my eyes as he continued. 'You see lad, we're on a downward spiral round these parts an' things 'ill get worse 'fore they get better, if at all. It'll be near on fifty year before this part of the world gets back on its feet.'

I listened intently as he carried on. 'But in the meantime we don't let it get us down. Life goes on whether we like it or not, so tha's better off likin' it than being a miserable bugger all time.'

I'd finished eating and as I put my fork down on the empty dish, my mind returned to the unanswered conundrum that had occupied it since the early hours of the day.

'Terry, I've got to ask. Who the fuck are the flying pickets?'

'They're a pop group,' he replied. 'Were in charts a while back wi' a right crap song.'

'What?' I exclaimed. 'You mean that I got arrested for impersonating a pop group?'

'Ha,' he guffawed loudly. 'Them cops must ha' thought you were a flyer – a striker goin' to picket someone else's workplace,' as I stared at him in disbelief. 'It's illegal see, they made it so back durin' miners' strike an' there's still a lot of bad feelin' around today between police an' them lads. It all makes sense now, what wi' you wearin' a Coal Board jacket an' all. Where did you get it from anyway?'

'Er, I borrowed it and I have to dump it,' I said.

Which reminded me, I also needed to recover my guitar. It was my love and my livelihood and it felt strange that we had been so cruelly separated.

Being out of my comfort zone up here in this bewildering place was driving me mad and I wanted to get back to London, if only to throttle my agent. For a moment I'd considered going straight to the train station. But I couldn't, I needed my guitar first.

'I have to get back to the hotel for a clean up and a few hours sleep Terry. Can you collect me at six to go to Brodsworth?'

'Sure enough,' he replied. 'I'll take tha back now along scenic route as main roads will be clogged full o' football traffic an' Sat'day shoppers. Then you can see our Dearne Valley durin' the daylight.'

We left the café and the delightful surroundings of Greasbrough, passing slowly through a succession of small drab towns with Terry gleefully announcing our arrival at each one: Rawmarsh, Swinton, Wath (been here already I thought), then Goldthorpe and Mexborough. They all looked the same to me with their rows of dismal grey streets, corner shops and vast estates of council housing.

I feigned interest as we drove through each one, my mind wandering back to Reeny. It had been a joyful experience right up to the point where I'd had to make an unscheduled and undignified escape.

I gazed out the window as the landscape changed sharply from the urban areas into stretches of open countryside and woodland. They appeared in stark contrast to the built-up streets we had just driven along and in themselves, were quite beautiful to look at. I was startled to see a pair of deer running across an open field to some trees and for a moment I was back in my rural childhood home in the middle-of-nowhere land in Ontario.

'Are those deer I can see in that field?' I asked, quizzically.

'Aye', he answered. 'They 'ave a big 'erd of 'em on Fitzwilliam Estate at Wentworth. Wi've just driven past entrance. Grand old place that is. Used to belong to one of the richest families in the Country at one time. Well worth a visit if only to see 'ow other 'alf used to live.'

Elsewhere the bare landscape was pock-marked with huge coal waste heaps, colliery winding towers and cavernous stone quarries. Lines of railway tracks and sidings criss-crossed their way across the valley bottom like badly stitched surgery scars. Even the farm fields were tinged brown and lacked any greenery to speak of, as if no self-respecting agricultural crop would dare to sprout up under such miserable conditions. But maybe I thought, that was also because it was still Winter. No doubt it would look different in the Summer months.

'Coal was king round here once,' Terry said, pronouncing it as 'coil'. 'Now it's disappearin' fast as an industry. Even Royalty at one time 'ad their coil from these pits to keep their arses warm down in Bucky Palace.'

'Is that right?' I asked.

'Not anymore though. These days we import coil from abroad despite there still bein' tons of it left 'ere underground. Meks no bloody sense to me,' he muttered.

I could see his point and realised I was a captive student, listening to one of his College lectures on the socio-economic history of the Dearne Valley, as we drove slowly through the changing landscape.

'Now then, 'ere's where a famous son of South Yorkshire wor born and brought up,' he announced brightly a few minutes later, as we passed a sign for Conisbrough. 'He's also in your game as well lad, worldwide singing star 'e is.'

'Who is?' I asked.

'Tony Christie,' he answered, as if I should have already known. 'He did them great songs like *Las Vegas* and *What I Did for Maria*. This is where 'e used to live before movin' to Spain.'

I looked out at the bleak mass of concrete pebble-dashed housing with chimneys already spewing out clouds of grey smoke which spiraled and gathered conspicuously in the half-light of the grim, misty Winter's afternoon. I wondered whatever had possessed Mr Christie to up-sticks and depart for such sunnier climes.

Driving out of Conisbrough, we crossed over the main A1 highway and eventually arrived back in Doncaster.

'That'll be forty five quid,' said Terry, as we pulled up at the Station Inn. 'If tha wants to include ride up to Broddy later on an' pay now, then we'll call it fifty quid all in.'

I paid him with the last of my cash and walked into the hotel. There was no Reeny and no guitar.

'Are there any messages for me?' I asked the landlord, hesitantly.

I watched him rummage through a drawer under the counter-top for my room key. 'Reeny's rang in sick today,' he said, giving me a knowing look. 'Said she'll drop tha guitar at Welfare Club tonight. She'll be there to watch show.'

I nodded silently in acknowledgement, but then his eyes narrowed as he stared menacingly at me. 'So she can't be that bloody sick then, can she?' he growled, holding up the key fob in his outstretched and meaty fist in front of me.

I said nothing and reached for the key, wondering whether he was planning on making me disappear as he had done (allegedly) with his wife. God, I hope she wasn't called Maria, I thought. The lyrics of the song ran through my head as I headed upstairs and unlocked the door to room five.

I felt refreshed and ready to rock when Terry collected me just after six for the drive to Brodsworth. It turned out that it wasn't far from where I'd been the previous night in Darfield and I recognised parts of the ravaged landscape and colliery wheels as the twilight turned into darkness.

'Who won the footie match Terry?' I asked.

'Doncaster, three-nil,' he replied sullenly. 'Bad news for Barnsley fans, which means anywhere on this side of the A1. Don't mention the match or the result tonight whatever tha does,' he advised.

A now familiar smell of coal fire smoke wafted into the van as we drove through Brodsworth village and towards the colliery compound. A collection of shabby brick buildings along with a large cinder car-park lay in front of the two winding towers. To the right hand side, a coach and several cars were parked next to a long single storey building, which I took to be my intended venue as it was the only one with any lights on inside. Sure enough, there was a sign on the wall declaring 'Brodsworth Miners Welfare Club'. From the outside it too looked like it was in need of some welfare.

'Call me if tha wants collectin' later on,' said Terry. 'Tha's good business for me.'

Too right, I thought, you've had sixty quid from me so far, as I walked into the club entrance and came face to face with a thin, worried-looking man.

He was dressed in a grubby grey suit, white shirt and red motif tie and nervously thumbing through the greasy pages of an address book with one hand, whilst balancing a packet of Senior Service in the other. He raised the cigs to his mouth and extracted one with his lips before fumbling in his jacket pocket for a lighter.

'Hi, I'm looking for the Entertainment Secretary here,' I announced.

'That's me, Cyril Sykes,' he replied. 'Are you our singer for tonight?'

Before I could answer, he lit up the cig and blew the smoke straight back at me. 'There's been someone askin' for thee,' he said. 'And none too kindly neether.'

'Who's that?'

'Bert Whittam,' he replied. 'Not someone who's known for asking after folk unless it was to mek trouble. He's not called 'Hit 'em Whittam' for nowt. D'ya know him?'

'Er, I think we may have a mutual acquaintance,' I replied, hesitantly. 'But no, I haven't met him in person before.'

'Well,' he continued, 'I need to mek some changes to our programme tonight an' bloody quick too,' puffing furiously on the cig. 'There's a lot bad feelin' inside, what wi' football result an' all. Plus, wi've got fish-yed's team an' their supporters 'ere today as well from Hull.'

'Fish what?' I asked.

'Fish filleters an' porters lads from the docks. They 'ave a rugby match wi' our apprentices every year. One year it's held 'ere an' then next over yonder in 'ull,' he explained. 'Bin like that ever since war an' we allers mek each other feel welcome at our venues. Friendly rivalry an' all that crap.'

He blew smoke in my face as he continued. 'But today's been a brutal one. Some o' their lads on field looked a lot older an' bigger than apprentices an' they've put a couple of ours in Barnsley General wi' concussion an' brokken ribs. Committee 'ill have to be told abart it an' so there's plenty o' blokes in thee-er not at all 'appy wi' things,' pointing over his shoulder with his thumb towards the concert room.

'So, yer gonna 'ave to get some goodwill goin' an' pretty fast,' he instructed. 'Ah'm putting you on as opener in ten minutes time before comic turn, whilst I try an' get mi hands on a coupla strippers. Not easy at such short notice,' he lamented, looking down again at his contacts book and turning the pages.

'Fine,' I replied. 'Do you know if my guitar is here?'

'Over there,' pointing to the case propped against a chair next to the small stage, where the distinctive red maple leaf emblem was almost smiling back at me.

'Thanks,' I said, with considerable relief. 'I'll go and tune up then. Where's the backing lads?'

'There aren't any,' he replied. 'Tha's on thy own lad. And remember, I want some 'appy, sing-a-long country an' western tunes to lift the mood up of this lot.'

'But I don't do country music, only blues,' I protested. 'Plus, there aren't any happy country-'

'Bloody well think o' some then,' he interjected loudly. 'Yer a singer aren't ya? Now fuck off outa mi sight while ah get these girls organised.'

My heart sank as I shuffled around the back of the stage to retrieve my guitar and I retreated into a small storage cupboard at the rear which doubled up as a changing room. Not for the first time I wondered if I was in the right profession. Maybe I should have gone into real estate development like my schoolmate Rory. He was riding high these days with cash in his pocket whilst I was still stuck in the pits and being mistaken for a picket.

Presently I peered around the changing room door. The lounge was heaving but there was no sign of Reeny, nor could I see any other women in the audience tonight. Instead, clouds of grey-blue cig smoke wafted up from groups of burly men who huddled around small tables and talked in hushed, urgent voices. Occasionally someone would bang a glass down on the table-top, followed by some virulent finger pointing and snarling glances were made towards the other tables of drinkers.

Unlike the previous evening, there was no laughter to be heard and instead a sense of brooding menace hung heavily in the air. Oh joy to the world folks, I thought; looks like I won't be doing my standard set of blues tonight.

As I made myself ready, I heard Cyril calling for order on the mike, but everyone ignored him. I was slightly relieved to hear my real name being announced, although nobody paid the slightest bit of attention as I walked onto the stage and plugged my guitar into the small amp before stepping over to the microphone stand.

'Good evening, good people of Brodsworth, and, er, beyond,' I said, trying to sound as cheerful as I could. 'Here's a little number you can join in with straight away and it's dedicated to someone I met last night. It's called Reeny, er, *Ruby, don't take your love—*'

'YOU!' boomed a loud voice from the back. 'Ah thought ah recognised that fuckin' guitar box.'

I stopped mid-voice and stared as a hulking brute of a man stood up waving his fist at me and then started to make his way to the stage, pushing through the crowd of seated punters around him. In his haste he tripped over a chair and fell full length onto the fish-yeds rugby team table, scattering their beer glasses and knocking some lads backwards off their seats.

'Tha's gonna fuckin' dee naw,' shouted one of their team members, as a fish-yed's right hook caught the big guy squarely on his chin and two more young men jumped on his back.

That was the signal for a battle to start and the room promptly erupted into a fury of shouting, flailing fists and flying beer glasses, as I stood rooted to the spot in mid-guitar strum. *Ruby* would have to wait.

The bar staff quickly pulled down the metal shutters over the beer taps and cowered below them whilst I gasped and gawped helplessly at the melee breaking out in front of me.

A pint pot sailing past my right ear soon brought me to my senses and I grabbed my guitar and case and fled off the stage. I glanced over my shoulder but no-one seemed to notice me and I wasn't planning on hanging around to meet Big Bert and discuss domestic marital arrangements and social pleasantries with him.

In the outer lobby Cyril was already on the phone, yelling into the mouthpiece. 'Yes, police, now, as many as you 'ave. It's fuckin' bedlam 'ere.' He looked up at me and wailed. 'Ah knew it. Ah just bloody knew it. Our concert room 'ill be wrecked now, an' ah've only just 'ad it re-decorated.'

'Where's my money?' I asked, urgently.

But he just stared back at me. 'Money?' he exclaimed. 'Fer what? You 'aven't sung a bloody note. If ah were thee lad, I'd get gone now an' bloody quick whilst tha's got both legs workin' an' they're still attached to thy bloody arse.'

I glanced back at the mass brawl taking place in the concert room. In between trading right and left punches, Big Bert had recovered his stance and was feverishly scouring the scene for any signs of me. I'd no intention of making his acquaintance. Cyril was right. It was now or never and, in the circumstances, now seemed to be the right choice.

Galloping through the front doors into the carpark, I realised that for the second night in succession I had been severely short-changed as a performer. This was no way to treat a professional musician like me I thought, somewhat superfluously, as I charged into the darkness of the Brodsworth Winter night. I'm definitely going to string up that agent I vowed to myself – if I ever manage to get back to London, that is.

In my panic I figured that I'd have more chance of hiding out in the darkened woods and open countryside rather than scurrying blindly around the desolate terraces of houses, so I ran as fast as I could towards some fields at the end of the village. Keeping low against a stone wall, I crossed a patch of ploughed land and headed up into a small, wooded copse. Sweating and panting, with my heart thumping away like a marching band bass drummer on speed, I stopped for a moment in the cover of the trees. Thankfully I couldn't see anyone in pursuit and I sat down to catch my breath and take stock of my situation, as the sound of sirens wailing in the distance wafted across to me over the empty fields.

I wiped my nose and face with my jacket sleeve. At one time that action would have earned me a cuff round the ear from my ever-doting and dutiful Ma. But she wasn't here. There was only me, miles from home and with a madman trying his best to kill me. I'd no cash left and I was wandering around the fields of a wild and foreboding land at night-time with a guitar and mud up to my knees. Still, at least I was wandering, I thought, making me think of a song. It's Saturday night and I ain't got no money – that sounded like another song to me but I dismissed it quickly. I desperately needed the safety of Terry's wagon to get me out of here.

After a few minutes my heart had stopped hammering in my chest, so I set off through the trees in the opposite direction and along the fields following the line of the drystone walls. I had no idea where I was heading but after about a mile I could see the lights of a building and as I got closer I realised it was a pub. It seemed quite smart-looking from a distance with a few cars parked alongside. At least I could call Terry from there, I thought.

As I climbed over the boundary wall and crossed the road to the front of the building, the front door of the Manvers Arms opened up and the figure of a large female filled the entrance. It was followed by a familiar voice who exclaimed, 'Now then luv, fancy seein' you 'ere.'

It was Mavis, the burlesque dancer from last night. God, was that only last night? A lot had happened since then.

'Oh, hi there,' I stuttered. 'I'm, er, in a bit of a rush...'

She looked down at my muddy boots and jeans and then back at my flushed face and said quizzically, 'And who from may I ask?'

I told her as quickly as I could about what had just gone on at the miners' club, minus the enraged husband bit.

'Nowt strange about that,' she said. 'But you look right nithered an' 'alf scared to death. I think you need some cleanin' up an' a large whisky down yer. Come on now wi' me, I live just round corner, five minutes walk, tops.'

How could I refuse such sanctuary? 'Thank you so much,' I answered gratefully, as Mavis linked her arm through mine and we walked down the hill, my breathing calming gradually to something approaching normality.

Chapter Four

Sitting on the sofa in the safety of Mavis's front room, I closed my eyes and felt like I was in another world. The glowing coals on the open fire warmed my toes and the whisky in my hand was warming everything else as I savoured each sip. This cosy stone cottage was indeed a haven from the havoc I had just been through and I basked nervously in its relative comfort. However, the thought of Big Bert on the warpath was ever present.

'Ah've put yer jeans on a fast wash cycle,' shouted a matronly voice from the kitchen. 'An' supper's in th'oven, so it'll be ready in abart 'alf an 'our,' said Mavis.

It made me appreciate my vulnerability as I sat in my underwear and tee shirt in a house belonging to a woman I hardly knew, in a place I'd never been to before. On top of which I was fleeing from a situation I hadn't encountered previously in my short life.

'Naw then, are you feelin' more like the livin'?' Mavis asked softly. She closed the kitchen door behind her and came to join me on the sofa, lighting up a cig as she sat down.

'Yes, thank you very much,' I blurted out. 'I hope I'm not putting you to any trouble.'

'No bother at all. It's nice to 'ave some male company that's, er, not 'ere for other reasons...' She trailed off, looking down at my bare thighs at the side of her.

'You have a nice place here,' I said, trying to turn her attention away from my legs and other parts. 'Have you lived here long?'

'Yes, for over twenty year now. Managed to keep 'old of it when I divorced that scumbag of an 'usband,' she said, pausing to take a sip of her whisky. 'He knew better than to try an' challenge me on that one.'

'Oh, I'm sorry,' I said, trying to sound sympathetic. 'I didn't realise…and have you been, er, on your own since then?' I asked, hesitantly.

There had been enough drama in my life already this evening and I didn't fancy the prospect of another drunken brute suddenly bursting through the front door and wondering why I was sitting comfortably in his front room, drinking his booze and chatting to his wife in my underpants.

'Oh yes. I've 'ad enough wi' men…well, bein' committed to just one I mean. I've 'ad plenty of male friends an' still have, but no-one is gettin' their feet under mi table again,' she declared. 'You see, me an' Den – that were 'is name, we 'ad lots of 'appy times at first,' she reminisced. 'But he 'ad a wand'rin' eye as well as a loose leg, an' eventually he ran off with this tart from Doncaster.' She took a sip from her glass and a drag from her cig. 'Should 'ave seen it comin' really, seein' that she worked for 'im an' he was allers takin' her along to races rather than me.'

'So what did he do for a living?' I asked.

'He were a bookie. 'Had a bettin' shop in town an' then used to run a trackside pitch at all the local race meetings – Donny, Pontey, Beverley an' York. Made a pretty penny at it 'an all, he did. Tell me now, 'ave you ever 'eard of a bloody poor bookie in all yer life?' she asked.

I shook my head as she continued. 'So I made damn certain that he wasn't kicking me outa th'ouse when he eventually buggered off.'

She took another drink and sighed. 'But that were some time back, near on twenty years ago now, an' after we got divorced, I never 'eard from 'im agin. Both 'im an' 'is fancy tart just disappeared. A friend of mine said she'd 'eard he'd sold up an' moved to costa del crime to escape taxman, or even more likely over to Lancashire, where he 'ad some relatives. Either way, I wasn't interested an' couldn't care less where the cheatin' sod 'ad gone.'

My recent brush with danger must have heightened my senses and caused my brain to go into overdrive. As I listened to Mavis telling me her story, my mind had been feverishly joining the dots and I realised that the said 'tart from Doncaster' must have been the wife of the landlord at the Station Inn…oh God, do I say anything to her or not?

Mavis crushed the remains of her cig in an ashtray and threw the butt into the fire as she took another sip from her glass, whilst I decided that silence was the better part of valour.

I needed to change the subject. Looking around the room, I caught sight of her python curled up in its glass tank. At least it was inside – I'd have been less happy to see the tank empty.

'So how did you end up with the snake?' I asked, pointing at the sleeping reptile. 'Did he come with the house?'

'No, he belonged to a friend of mine, Doreen, from way back. She'd got me into modelling an' then into, er, exotic dancin' an' suchlike. The snake wor part of her cabaret act along wi' her tassels-twirling an' fire-eating,' she explained, pausing to light up another cig.

'She'd called 'im Pythagoras after 'er booking agent. He wor a dodgy Greek bloke from Sheffield wi' a fondness for wantin' triangular relationships with his women clients, if you know what I mean.'

Reaching over to a cupboard next to the sofa, she took out a photo album and handed it to me. 'This was me an' Doreen – or Sheba as she was known professionally, in our younger days,' she said.

I turned the pages to reveal several photos and promo cards showing them both in all their seductive glam gear - as well as lots of naked poses. I had to admit that Mavis had been a stunner in her prime years and as my face slowly turned pink either through embarrassment or the effects of the whisky, I had to cross my legs uncomfortably in a vain effort to conceal my growing admiration.

'Very nice,' I said. 'I take it Den didn't mind your choice of work then?'

'Oh no, he encouraged it. He took all these pictures, then he was allers tryin' to mek a few quid on side by sendin' 'em off to men's girlie mags an' the like. But eventually, I 'ad to stop,' she said, as a note of sadness crept into her voice. 'Younger women wi' better bodies were takin' over strippin' game an' I kept gettin' upstaged by them. Doreen stopped performin' after her fire-eating tricks went wrong one night. She reckoned someone 'ad messed with her lighter fuel an' she ended up burnin' 'erself quite badly.'

'What did you do then?' I asked.

'Well, for last few years, ah've done three days a week at chicken factory in Goldthorpe,' she continued. 'Pullin' their innards out an' packin' 'em up for the shops. You'd be surprised where I can get mi 'ands when they're well-oiled up,' smiling at me as I instinctively crossed my legs again. 'Plus, I get a big bag of giblets free for Pythagoras each week,' she added.

'Then I still do an occasional burlesque routine at some o' the working men's clubs an' I, er, entertain certain select paying gentlemen here at 'ome on Thursdays an' Fridays. Nothin' too cumbersome though. I don't want mi neighbours to be thinking that I'm owt dodgy.'

I smiled at her self-effacing honesty. 'Seeing that we're in confession mode,' recalling my Catholic schooling, 'I'm a bit dodgy myself you know. I've over-stayed my visa here in England since coming to London a few years ago as a music student,' I explained. 'Originally, I'm from a very small farming town in Canada and thought the big city and bright lights was the place to be. So when I got the chance to study music over here I jumped at it.'

Mavis smiled as I paused to take a drink before continuing.

'Then, I started giving guitar lessons whilst studying and ended up getting a regular series of gigs around the pubs in South London. Officially, I'm still a student even though I actually left College three years ago. At the time I didn't tell the immigration folk and nobody bothered checking up, or if they did no-one told me about it. So that's why I'm still here.'

'Well, at least you're doing something you love,' she replied. 'That's a good thing to have in your life.'

'That's right, I am,' I replied, emptying my glass and feeling more relaxed. 'I'm trying to find a natural home for my love of blues music. It's the true expression of oppressed people's feelings, you know. Not only pain and anger, but also those of pleasure, joy and love.'

Mavis topped up my glass as I carried on in full flow. 'Throughout history, the blues has been a natural outlet for recounting life's hardships as well as a celebration at finding some justice in the world. It just wants to reach out to the common man and in my mind that makes it timeless and universally appealing,' I preached. 'For me, it's the music of your soul.'

I realised that the booze was making me talk bollocks.

'Then my agent booked me three gigs up here in Yorkshire, but so far it's been a disaster. I'd love to chuck him in with Pythagoras over there.'

'Well, we all do what we 'ave to just to get by,' said Mavis. 'You an' I are in the same business – we perform for money. Only diff'rence is that I'm at th'end of mi days an' you're at the start of yours.' She took a sip of whisky. 'But we're kindred spirits, so get used to bein' ripped off, short-changed, then 'eckled an' knocked back. That's showbiz, as they say,' she advised.

Putting down her glass, she stood up and walked across to pick up a framed photo from the mantelpiece. 'You remind me of my son Richie,' she said, as she passed it to me. 'He's about your age an' all.'

She leaned over my arm to look at the photo. 'He did an electrical apprenticeship wi' Coal Board, but I didn't want him going down pit all 'is life. So instead, he joined the Royal Engineers an' loves it. Been in Army now over five years an' calls me every so often to let me know where 'e is,' she said. 'He's in Cyprus at present, waiting to go into I-raq. Reckons it's all set to kick off there pretty soon.'

I nodded and made some comment about how he looked settled in his army life. We continued chatting then Mavis topped me up again and went through to the kitchen to check on supper, leaving me with her album and to think about what she had just told me.

I couldn't resist another look at her photos as I turned the pages and lustily admired her curves, before my guilty conscience took over. I closed the book and wondered if

Richie knew what mum had done for a living, then abruptly concluded so what if he did? It was none of my business. Mavis was right of course - we were both doing what we could to get by, so who was I to stand in judgement of her?

I'd heard and felt the warmth and sincerity in her words, just as I had with Reeny the previous night. There was no pretence or haughtiness about either of them and I realised that adversity in life didn't get people down in these parts. Whatever crap they found themselves in, they just dug their way out and carried on with their lives, smiling in defiance at the world around them. Pride, my taxi man Terry had called it and I was beginning to see what he meant.

I thought of some of the people I knew around my part of South London to whom adversity meant their local deli had run out of their daily supply of croissants. They couldn't handle half of what these northerners coped with.

'OK, supper's ready,' called Mavis. 'We'll be eatin' in kitchen, so come on an' mind yer arse when tha sits down, so you don't gerra a spell in yer cheeks.'

'What are we having?' I asked, as a delicious aroma filled my nostrils.

'It's only chicken casserole in a Yorkshire pud,' as she set down a steaming plate in front of me. 'I wasn't expectin' any guests tonight.'

'Looks wonderful,' I said, cutting a piece of the crispy, golden pudding, smothering it with casserole sauce and putting it into my mouth. It dissolved instantly, leaving my tongue feeling as if it was being caressed by angel's kisses. My taste buds tingled and yearned for more, stretching out like the necks of newly-hatched and hungry chicks in a nest. It was truly magnificent and I said so between forkfuls.

'Well, tha can't be in Yorkshire an' not 'ave our signature dish. Just wouldn't be reet. Normally we 'ave it on a Sunday wi' our beef, but they're just as good on any day o' week. I wouldn't be a proper Yorkshire woman if I couldn't make a decent pud, would I?'

I didn't want it to end. It was sensational – no better than that, it was sublime. I finished my plate before Mavis had got through half of hers and she just smiled at me.

'There's another in th'oven,' she said. 'Help thi sen, ah'm not tha mother yer know.'

I didn't need telling twice. 'Thank you. This is really delicious and I've never had it before. I've seen it in London but always thought it was a dessert, like a sponge pudding thing.'

'Some folk 'ill 'ave it as a dessert,' she replied. 'When I was a kid, grandad used to 'ave 'is on Sundays as a starter wi' gravy, then with 'is main an' then for 'is afters wi' some of this,' reaching for a tin of Lyons golden syrup from the worktop and handing to me.

I looked at it and repeated the words on the label out loud, '*Out of the strong came forth sweetness.*'

'Comes from the Bible,' she said. 'But I allers remember grandad insistin' it were written about us Yorkshire folk. Strong as wi are, sweetness is what wi bring to each other, he'd say to us and woe betide any bugger that tries tekkin' away our strength.'

I smiled. 'You must have had a happy childhood then.'

'Not really. We were a big family an' 'ad some 'appy times yes, but we also 'ad it tough, like many folk round 'ere.'

I could hear the sadness in her voice. 'Ah lost mi dad and older brother in a pit accident when ah were seven years old. It wor commonplace among minin' families an' we all used to pitch in and 'elp each other out best we could,' she said.

'Before that we used to meet up for a family dinner on a Sunday an' my job after church service was to go an' fetch grandad an' dad from the local pub,' she reminisced. 'Dad would lift me up on 'is shoulders as we walked back to granny's, then one day he wasn't there anymore,' gently wiping her eyes. 'After that I 'ad to grow up pretty quick. Mam took on extra work in the evenings an' I 'ad to look after my two little sisters.'

'That's too bad,' I said, wishing I'd never asked the question in the first place. I didn't want Mavis getting upset after she'd been so kind to me.

'But that's real life an' you've just got ter get on wi' it,' she continued. 'So ah did. Got married early on, didn't work out, got married again to Den then 'e buggered off. So sometimes all you can do is laugh at what the world chucks at you. If not, you'd probably die cryin',' she declared.

As I listened, I wondered how it was possible that some people could find humour from such circumstances in their lives and shrug off the negativity, as if it didn't matter. It even made me smile to myself when I recalled the recent events of the last twenty four hours and I suddenly felt brave enough to make another confession.

'You'll never guess what happened to me last night,' I started to say, when I was interrupted by a loud banging on the front door.

'Who thi 'ell is this?' complained Mavis, getting up and going to her front door whilst my heart leapt into my mouth.

I was convinced Big Bert had finally caught up with me. As they say in the musicians' bible, some people are discovered whilst others get found out and I contemplated making a quick run for it. What, without my jeans? Stupid idea, you idiot.

From the kitchen table I strained my ears to hear Mavis saying, 'No, not tonight I'm busy, I've got company,' to whoever was at the door.

But the caller was persistent. 'Come on Mave, it's only me. Ah've just got an 'our spare an' then ah'll be off,' said a gruff male voice…which I was sure sounded familiar to me.

I opened the kitchen door and peered down the hall. At the front door stood Terry, pleading with Mavis to be let into the house.

'Terry! What you doing here?' I shouted in amazement. 'I didn't call you.'

'What tha bloody 'ell you doin' here – and in yer undies as well?' he replied back, looking first at me and then at Mavis. 'Is this who yer busy with then?'

'Do you two know each other?' she asked quizzically as her head turned from Terry to me and back again.

'Yes,' we both answered in unison.

'Bloody 'ell, wi've got a right goin' on 'ere then,' she exclaimed. 'We'd all better 'ave a drink an' clear the air,' she added, as Terry walked sheepishly into the house, closing the front door behind him.

It left me very relieved that at least it wasn't someone else joining the party.

Looking over at me Mavis then said, 'I don't know how tha knows Terry 'ere luv, but what you probably don't know is that 'e's also my Richie's father.'

Chapter Five

It was Sunday morning and Mavis had let me stay the night in her son's room. After Terry's impromptu visit, he had left us to do his Saturday night pick-ups and Mavis had told me about how they had first met.

She had been 'life-modelling' for the evening art classes at the Technical College where Terry had just started teaching. Even though they were both married at the time, they became romantically involved. Then when Mavis fell pregnant she wanted to end their relationship, making her husband Den believe that he was the father of the child.

Richie was still a toddler when they subsequently divorced and was raised by Mavis as a single mother, never getting to know either Den or his biological father. Terry had continued to see Mavis when she divorced and had helped her financially to raise their son over the years.

However, Mavis would not allow him to break up his family and so they had kept their secret to themselves. Better to let sleeping dogs lie Mavis had argued and Terry had gone along with it ever since.

I wasn't sure why she had told me all this, but I reckoned both of them had always wanted to share their story in relative safety with someone at some point.

As I could hear movement in the kitchen I got up, washed, dressed and headed downstairs.

'Morning luv,' said Mavis, handing me a mug of tea. 'I've just given Billy at the Ravenswood a call to ask if you can play for tips over the lunchtime session. He's the steward there an' it should be okay as wi've known each other for years. I'll make you some breakfast an' then we can set off.'

'That's great, thank you,' I replied. 'You've been very kind to me.'

'Nonsense. Just bein' friendly to someone in need. It's the way we are round 'ere.'

After we'd eaten, it was a twenty minute walk to the club from Mavis's house. We strode briskly along the tidy terraced streets in the chilly but bright morning air and Mavis exchanged cheery greetings with other folks as we passed them.

Some had been for a newspaper and were chatting to one another outside the corner shop, whilst others were dressed in their Sunday finest and pulled small children by their sides on their way to or from local church services.

Across the street an old man in a flat cloth cap and matching muffler scarf wrapped over his threadbare jacket shuffled along the pavement, trailing a small dog on a lead behind him. He gave an enquiring shout of 'Ow did Barnsley get on?' to a similar-aged neighbour tending to his neat row of potted plants on the front window sill. I didn't have the heart to call out the football result to him for fear of causing him distress and upsetting his Sunday morning stroll.

We turned up at the Ravenswood a few minutes before noon. A crowd of people were already milling round the front doors, the men shuffling their feet and dragging on dog-end cigs whilst the women chatted cheerily to each other.

We went round the side of the building to the kitchen and Mavis hammered on the door. 'Billy, let us in,' she yelled. 'It's Mavis, 'urry up now, we're freezing out 'ere.'

The door opened and we were let in. Billy was about sixty five years old and looked as if he'd been drinking all his life, which he probably had. His belly hung out over his trousers like a badly filled sandbag and he swept his hands repeatedly through his combed-back greasy hair as he listened to Mavis soft-soaping him.

We were then beckoned into the lounge where the bar was being made ready for business and I gazed around the cavernous room. There must have been space for well over two hundred people seated comfortably, plus at the other side of the bar there was a games room equipped with a snooker table, dominoes and card tables and dart boards.

'Right lad, tha can do a spot, no more than twenty minutes between Maurice and bingo, just before Sandra's due on at two,' Billy said to me. 'If tha's crap, then tha'll be doin' two minutes, an' short un's at that.'

As I agreed and thanked him, he marched over to the front doors. Unlocking them, he pushed the handles forward to the waiting multitude with a cheery welcome of, 'Come on then you buggers.'

A deluge of people poured through the doors in response, filling the place up in a matter of minutes and bringing it to life. If only churches had memberships so eager then maybe I'd become a gospel singer and give praise to the Lord each week, I thought.

I stood to one side with Mavis to avoid the crush as men jostled around the bar shouting out their orders whilst their wives and pals made their way across to sit at their favourite tables around the room.

'No, tha can't sit thee-er, that's our Eadie's place when she gets here,' shrieked one woman, as her group of seven assembled around two tables, pulling them closer together as if to demarcate their family territory. 'And no, that's our Albert's seat. Now, go an' gi' Frank a hand wi' drinks,' she ordered to one of her brood.

Within five minutes the room was in full swing. There was plenty of laughter and banter going on as a light fog of grey cig smoke slowly rose above the heads of the happy punters. Everyone seemed to know each other and Mavis laughed and greeted some of them like they were long-lost relatives. The women cackled and waved to their neighbours and the men ferried trays of beers and shorts glasses from the bar to their tables like a well-oiled delivery service.

I watched the beer handles along the bar swinging back and forth like mechanical pistons as the barmaids pulled vigorously on them, repeating the orders out loud to their customers. Biceps bulged in competition with ample breasts nudging out from their flimsy nylon blouses.

'Put us three bags o' crisps on 'ere as well luv,' shouted one guy as he readied himself to pick up a large trayful of brimming pint glasses with both hands.

'What flavor?' asked the barmaid.

'Just taters,' he answered, and I watched as she balanced the 'ready salted' bags on top of the beers and plucked a tenner from where he'd held it between his teeth. 'Keep the change if tha's any left,' he advised, cheerfully.

It was non-stop action all along the bar as Billy kept a watchful eye on proceedings and the cash tills ker-chinged and rang out like the bells on the old-fashioned red buses back down in London.

Then Maurice opened up on the Hammond organ with *Una Paloma Blanca* and we were all heading for party mode and Spanish sunshine on a dismal grey lunchtime in South Yorkshire. I watched as people clapped and smiled with each other and sung along to the organist. They had no idea what they were singing about but that didn't seem to matter. They were happy and they weren't afraid of letting others know it.

As Maurice pounded away merrily on the organ keys, I noticed that he was wearing a surgical neck collar and I turned to ask Mavis if the poor guy had been in an accident.

'He 'ad a neck brace fitted a few years back after 'is wife brayed 'im wi' a fryin' pan for shaggin' one o' barmaids,' she said, nonchalantly. 'And 'e 'asn't looked back since,' she added, taking a puff of her cig.

She carried on chatting and bantering with Billy over the bar leaving me wondering whether to laugh or cry at Maurice's demise. I casually glanced over my shoulder at the bar staff and wondered which one he'd had his eye – and other body parts on. There was certainly plenty of choice on offer but the consequences of his indiscretions didn't seem to have affected his playing ability.

Then, before long I was being signalled by Billy to go to the stage and Mavis, God bless her, introduced me over the mike as I plugged in and steadied myself behind her.

'Now then every-wun, we 'ave a special treat today,' she announced. 'This young man's come up 'ere all way from London to see what proper folk are like. So mek 'im feel welcome an' put a tip in his glass 'ere,' holding up a pint pot and placing it at the edge of the stage.

'Ah'll gi' 'im a tip,' yelled a chap from the left, standing with a group of his pals. 'Fuck off back ta that London,' and everyone cracked a laugh.

'Hey, less of the profanity Smithy,' warned Mavis, 'or I'll tell everyone 'ere how small yer dick really is. Now let's see thi put a quid in his glass for yer bloody cheek an' quick abart it.' The man was shamed into delving into his pocket as his mates patted his shoulders and mocked him.

I smiled and mouthed 'thanks' to Mavis, launching straight into *Memphis Tennessee* and pretty soon I had a few hands clapping along and heads nodding. My guitar sounded good and even Maurice stayed where he was, providing some chord accompaniment on the organ for me.

I looked across at him and bowed in gratitude and he just winked at me with a smile. For a fleeting moment I wondered if he was trying to pick me up, but then I realised that he couldn't nod his head back, so I concentrated instead on my set and entertaining the crowd. After all they'd been told to tip me and I needed the cash. It was an opportunity to make up for last night's debacle and I was going to give it my best.

Mustang Sally was next as the audience continued with their weekly Sunday routine. I was background music to their social activity, but at least I wasn't getting boo-ed or having beer chucked at me, not that I could see these people wasting such a precious commodity. They were good-natured and in good spirits, pursuing a regular ritual of catching up with family and friends over a skin-full of ale.

The more I played, the more coins got tossed in the glass – I've just got to keep an eye on it in case any trouble breaks out, I thought. However, my initial fears were misplaced. This was a community at play and nothing was going to interrupt them from their cherished leisure time.

As I sang, I looked over at Mavis cradling a port and lemonade with a cig in her hand and holding court with some of the older members at the end of the bar. She could handle herself – and a crowd – that was for sure. I imagined her in another life, running an old-time western saloon and whorehouse in the days of the gold rush. She'd be the one in charge, the centre of attention, seeing that the girls were all in tip-top condition and encouraging the drunken prospectors to empty their pockets, and other things, at her establishment and nowhere else.

Looking at the crowd of men around her at the bar, downing pints as if a kind of modern Prohibition was about to be introduced, I realised that some things in life will never change. We all needed somewhere to regularly escape from the drudgery and hard slog of real life.

As I ran through *Pretty Woman* followed by *You're Sixteen,* the drinkers tapped their feet or knocked their glasses on the bar top, no doubt reminiscing about times past and loves no longer present in their lives. I wondered if Reeny had ever worked in here as no doubt she'd fit in well.

'Sing us some Tom Jones lad,' yelled a man, standing up from a nearside table.

So I gave them my version of *Green Grass of Home* and picked up a backing chorus of about a hundred voices along the way.

'Yes, we'll all come to greet thee, when tha's gone an' joined the Queen's nay-vee,' hollered out my companion in fine tenor voice.

'Sit down yer bloody fool,' shouted his wife above the laughter.

I finished my spot with *I Saw Her Standing There*, to whistles and applause and then I was offstage as Maurice filled in the gap whilst the bingo machine was wheeled to the front by a member of the club staff.

The jackpot for today stood at £250, a colossal amount for a Sunday Mavis had said to me earlier on. Presently the room fell into a deathly hush as the bingo numbers began and heads bowed around the tables as if in silent prayer.

Intense concentration on the cards and numbers in front of the punters took over from the chatter and banter.

I walked over to the bar and handed my glass of coins to Billy asking quietly if he'd please change them into notes and deduct any commission due to him. After a couple of minutes he returned, holding out a fistful of cash.

'Here tha goes, that's twenty five pounds an' fifty pence an' tha owes me nowt.'

'Thank you,' I replied, gratefully pocketing the money.

'That's not bad yer know for under 'alf an 'our's work,' he said. 'Much better rate than our coalface rippers are gettin' paid. Tha should consider doin' it for a livin' lad,' he advised.

'Thanks,' I replied. 'I will.'

Bingo ended abruptly with the cry of 'house' from halfway down the room followed by some enthusiastic applause all round with the over-joyed winner cheering happily at her good fortune.

As a rush to the bar ensued, I saw a couple of the club staff drawing the curtains over the windows along one side of the room. Some of the women were already getting up, gathering their belongings and giving firm instructions to their menfolk not to be 'bloody late fer their dinner.'

Then a few minutes later a disco soundtrack of *Bad Girls* started up over the speakers and the house lights were dimmed by Billy from behind the bar.

Mavis turned to me. 'Now, you've got a choice luv. You can either stay 'ere an' watch Sandra shek 'er tits an' ass for this lot or you can come back 'ome wi' me for yer Sunday dinner.'

'Er, will you be making Yorkshire pudding again?' I asked, expectantly.

Mavis just laughed out loud. 'What d'ya think? Tha's in Yorkshire lad.'

Linking my arm in hers she whisked me away from the bar as Billy called out after her, 'Eyup Mave, 'as tha pulled then?'

She waved back to him as a slim attractive brunette in fake leather lingerie shimmied past us with a beaming smile and made her way across the floor to the stage.

Chapter Six

Mavis had surpassed herself with her Sunday lunch and my stomach could barely fit inside my jeans as I sprawled lazily on her sofa. However, the clock was ticking and I knew that soon I would have to leave to get back to Doncaster, pick up my gear then head to Edlington for the gig, before heading back into town to catch the London train.

I'd become a taxi-driver's dream this weekend as I asked Mavis if I could borrow her phone to call Terry to make the arrangements. I did so and an hour later he pulled up outside, beeping the horn to alert us of his arrival.

I realised I was going to have an awkward and emotional farewell with Mavis as she had been so kind to me in my hour of need, despite not knowing anything about me. How many other people would have taken me into their house in the dishevelled state I was in last night?

However, before I could say anything she disappeared into her kitchen and returned holding a parcel in her arms.

'Here,' she said. 'I've made you some sarnies for your journey back South,' handing me the best part of a whole sliced loaf wrapped in silver tinfoil.

I gave her a big hug as I said my thanks. 'You're one in a million, Mavis.'

'Stay in touch,' she said, as we parted. 'But I know you won't. It's a big world out there an' a young man such as you 'as plenty o' time to see it an' enjoy all it 'as to offer.'

'You never know Mavis,' I replied. 'London isn't all it's cracked up to be.'

She wiped a tear from her eye as she waved and I got into the taxi.

I chatted absently with Terry as we drove into town and presently we pulled up again at the Station Inn. I wondered if Reeny would be here but there was no sign of her and the bar was empty and closed. I raced upstairs and threw my few clothes into the holdall and on the way back down I was confronted by the less than amenable Mr Crofton.

'Tha's 'ad a room 'ere fer two nights but not slept in it on either one,' he growled. 'What's thy bloody game then?'

'Does that mean I get a discount if I haven't used the bed?' I asked, optimistically.

'No, it bloody doesn't,' he yelled. 'An' checkout is at noon not bloody seven o'clock. Tha bill's seventy quid an' ah don't tek any cheques from foreigners neether.'

I gave him my Mastercard and he reached for the card imprinter and placed a paper slip inside it, swiping the device vigorously.

As I watched him I asked nervously, 'Er, is Reeny around today?'

'No, she don't work on a Sunday. Won't be 'ere till tomorrow evenin' when we open, that's if she's not sick again,' glaring at me as he handed over the credit card slip.

'Well, tell her I said hello and, er, hope she's alright,' I muttered. 'She lent me a coat the other night for the, er, cold weather and I've left it upstairs for her.'

Checkout all completed, I ambled back outside and into the taxi. 'How far away is Edlington?' I asked Terry, loading my bag on the seat next to my guitar and closing the side door.

'About fifteen minutes drive away, not too far,' came the reply. 'Not much to see there mind, 'cept for pit,' he continued. 'Place got 'eavily bombed one night durin' war when some Jerry planes on way to steelworks in Sheffield got intercepted by our lads from RAF Finningley. They 'ad to dump their bombs pretty quick to escape our boys, so Edlington copped the lot. Caused about ten quid's worth of damage all told.'

We crossed the A1 and then pulled off the main road and headed down along a smaller track. In the distance beyond the tight streets of terraced houses, I could see the now familiar twin pit towers and the collection of ancillary buildings comprising our intended destination.

'Here's social club on right hand side,' Terry said, as he turned the taxi round full circle and pulled up. 'Now then, I'm gonna call in for a pint 'ere later on, as ah know the Secretary. After that we can leave just after 'alf nine, as mail train leaves Donny at ten sharp on a Sunday night.'

I nodded my agreement and walked into the club foyer with my guitar and bag. As I looked around a voice shouted, 'Ovver 'ere lad,' and I was beckoned into a small office by a portly middle-aged chap with slicked-back silver hair and a pipe clasped firmly between his teeth.

'How-do lad,' he said. 'I'm Walter Bentley, an' the most important person you're goin' to be meetin' tonight,' he added. 'That's because I'll be the one givin' thee some brass – if tha's any good, that is.'

Before I could answer, he continued. 'Now, wi've a good crowd in this evenin' for our Sunday variety night an' a good line up of turns. You're due on at eight for thirty minutes before first session o' bingo. Come an' 'ave a look round in meantime,' guiding me out of the office and through the glass doors into the concert room.

The lounge was a replica of the ones I had already seen this weekend. Rectangular shaped, low ceiling, tacky red flock wallpaper and matching linoleum tiled floor, with a small raised stage at the far end. It was already full of people, their round tables crowded with beer glasses and large ashtrays and complemented by the obligatory steady plume of smoke hanging around the ceiling tiles and tube lighting.

At one side tucked away from the bar, I noticed a large group of youngish couples gathered together, all quite smartly dressed and chatting and laughing with each other.

'They don't look like coalminers,' I said, nodding over in their direction.

'Course they are,' he said. 'That's, er, our swappers club.'

I looked back at Walter, slightly bemused, but he simply continued. 'The men are all on afternoon shift next wick, meanin' they don't start work until two tomorrow. Happens every three weeks, so tonight's their big night out wi' their wives an' girlfriends,' he explained. 'Then, they, er, all get together afterwards, somewhere a bit more private like. Sing summat nice for em.'

'What, like *Stand by your Man?*' I suggested. I'd never been asked to do a request for a wife swappers' group before.

Walter looked at me and replied bluntly, 'Does tha want comedian's spot an' all tonight lad? Ah'd just stick to singin' if ah were thee.'

He puffed again on his pipe. 'We 'ave a nice atmosphere 'ere on Sunday nights – very relaxed an' easy goin', so ah want some nice folk songs to go wi' it.'

'Folk songs?' I said, alarmed. 'But I don't do those.'

'Bout time tha bloody started then. You're a singer aren't tha? Well, sing some bloody songs that folk 'ill like then,' he instructed, as his front teeth closed around the stem of his pipe. 'Otherwise, that strange sensation tha'll be feelin' round yer arse 'oyle will be mi right foot 'elpin' you through front doors.'

'Let me get a drink first,' wearily resigning myself to my fate.

'C'mon then, ah'll treat thi,' he said, as we walked over to the bar. 'I'll be knockin' it off tha fee anyway.'

'Thank you, I'll have a lager...no, a best bitter please,' I said, glancing at the beer pumps.

I was desperately trying to work out what I was going to sing tonight whilst the barman poured a pint and placed it in front of me on the bar top. I watched the contents of the glass swirling and slowly settling to reveal a golden amber-hued liquid, topped with a creamy foam head like a vicar's collar, as if to protect the fragile beer beneath it from any lurking impurities or contamination from the surroundings.

I raised the glass to my mouth and through the safety blanket of foam I savoured the most delicious ale I had ever tasted. It was smooth, rounded, not gassy or harsh and it gently caressed my tongue like an eager mistress.

'Wow, that's delicious,' I said, watching as the foam clung in rings to the inside of the glass as if it didn't want to be parted. This was nothing like the beer in London, I thought, which was twice as thin and twice as expensive and I said so to Walter.

'That's 'cos proper beer needs proper watter to start off wi', he answered. 'Watter that's pure and 'as filtered through these fine green 'ills of God's Yorkshire over thousands of years.' He paused as I nodded, taking another swig. 'Not like in London, where it's already passed through three people before ending up in a brewery. No wonder yon beer tastes like piss. What'd thi call it – *Courage*? Ha! Tha needs bloody courage to drink it,' he proclaimed.

He was right of course. Compared to what I was used to drinking, this was indeed heavenly stuff. 'Well in that case, I'll just have to have another one of these,' I said, draining the rest of the glass.

'Coming up and the usual for you, dad?' asked a young woman from behind the bar.

I hadn't noticed her before but now I did. She was slim and petite with shoulder-length auburn hair, deep brown eyes and a smile to die for. She waited expectantly for an answer as I gazed back at her.

'This is my daughter Jenny,' said Walter. 'Works 'ere on a Sunday night for some spendin' money. Trainin' to be a nurse, she is.'

He jerked a thumb in my direction. 'And this is, er, what is your bloody name any road, lad?' searching in his pockets for some notes.

I introduced myself to Jenny before Walter could say anything. Smiling, I instinctively stuck out my right arm to shake her hand, but in my haste I ended up knocking over my empty glass from the bar.

'Oops, sorry,' I blurted out. 'I'm not usually that clumsy.'

Jenny just smiled back and said, 'Pleased to meet you Jamie and I'm looking forward to hearing you sing.'

She pulled my new pint and placed it on the bar and began a fresh one for Walter who puffed on his pipe before turning to me.

'Now then, tek thi ale an' go an' sort yer act out with Ronnie and his trio over there,' pointing his pipe towards a corner where three guys were nursing pint glasses around a table. 'Stop faffin' abart an' get on wi' it, bloody quick.'

Well at least they had a band here, so I went across and made their acquaintance. We had an organ, drums and a bass guitar and they all seemed knowledgeable, friendly and pleasant lads.

'This guy wants me to sing folk songs and I don't do those,' I lamented to them.

'Don't tha worry 'bart 'im,' replied Ronnie, the organist. 'He knows folk-all about music. He's just a typical club Secretary. Has a menial day job at pit top but in 'ere the power goes to 'is head and 'e struts around like Napoleon looking for a shit-house,' he explained. 'As long as we've got this lot singin' or clappin' along an' swallowin' loads of ale then we're doin' alreet an' Walter will be 'appy. So, what does tha want to sing?'

That news perked me up and fifteen minutes later we'd worked out a set of seven pieces for me that they all knew. So far so good, I thought as I went to tune up my guitar and presently we were all settled snugly on the small stage ready to kick off.

Just then my attention was interrupted as a guy rushed across the floor in front of us wearing a white coat and struggled to balance a wide wooden tray in front of him held up by a canvas harness around his neck. For a moment I wondered if he was some kind of medic and then I noticed his lank greasy hair, thick bottle-bottom specs and the fake sovereign rings on his fingers and I changed my mind.

I learned over towards Ronnie for some clarification.

'Is that guy an ice cream seller?' I asked.

'He's the seafood man,' he answered. 'Prawns, cockles an' suchlike delicacies. Not so bad on a Thursday night when they've just arrived fresh from Grimsby boats, but a bit dodgy by now after three days cooped up in yon bugger's van.'

I watched bewildered as 'seafood man' moved quickly from table to table, handing out small bags of smelly crustaceans after first dousing them liberally with malt vinegar, whilst simultaneously pocketing the coins handed over to him with his other hand. His eyes darted in all directions as the people around him yelled out their orders and the women baited him with questions like, 'Has tha got some mussels on tha cock?' or 'How are yer crabs tonight?' accompanied by their ribald laughter.

No doubt he heard the same old stuff every night and to him the banter was just an occupational hazard and part of the territory. But crabs or not, the men rifled through their pockets for loose change and the guy was doing a roaring trade.

Even the swappers were stocking up, piling their bags of prawns in the middle of the table in an empty ashtray, no doubt in readiness for anyone in their party to help themselves whenever they felt like it.

'Right, let's get started then,' said an impatient Ronnie and after a count of four, into the opening bars of *Time is Tight* we went.

This was an instrumental track and it gave me chance to look around the room as we played. It was all going well – people were nodding as they tucked into their bags of smelly cockles or tapping their beer mats as they drank. We sounded good as an ensemble and my guitar and voice soared around the spacious lounge as we played *Route 66* and followed it up with the catchy beat of *You Never Can Tell*.

After some applause and a minute to catch my breath, I sang *Another Saturday Night* with some feeling, no doubt sub-consciously recalling my close encounter with the Beast of Brodsworth the previous evening.

Then we excelled ourselves, even if I say so myself, with *Twisting By the Pool* as Ronnie and his boys gave it some enthusiastic playing. We sounded like seasoned musicians, complementing each instrument and our individual song parts as a group, whilst avoiding the easy temptation of over-powering one another in the process. It was top drawer stuff by anyone's measure and I spied Terry cradling a pint at the bar and giving me a thumbs-up as we finished the song.

'Thank you very much,' I said into the microphone after taking a quick breather. 'It's great to see you all enjoying yourselves with us this evening. Now, for all the, er, romantic couples in the house tonight, here's a nice number for you by Dr Hook called *Sharing the Night Together*.'

I saw Walter giving me a quizzical look through the small cloud of pipe-smoke that he'd just emitted, but I was undeterred. The crowd seemed to like me and that was all that mattered, so away we went.

I finished my set with *Whisky in the Jar* to lots of cheers and whistles and gave a polite bow to my audience before unplugging and heading off the stage.

Behind me, Ronnie pulled out the bingo machine as a flurry of cards and pens appeared from pockets and handbags around the tables and silence descended across the entire room.

By now I was familiar with this routine so I walked over to the bar to join Terry for a beer. 'That's the spirit lad,' he said. 'As my old man used to say, always leave 'em wantin' more. Mind you, that's why he lost 'is job wi' Red Cross disaster relief.'

'I thought you were really good up there,' said Jenny, enthusiastically, as she placed a pint on the bar in front of me. 'Pity you're not doing another stint, I really want to hear you do some more songs.'

'Thank you,' I replied, and I was about to strike up a conversation with her when I was interrupted by Walter handing me an envelope.

'Ere tha go lad. Seventy five pounds weren't it? Less a tenner of course fer all th'ale tha's supped.'

At seventy pence a pint I couldn't work out how three beers amounted to a tenner, however, I'd passed the stage of arguing and besides I now had other things on my mind.

'Thank you,' pocketing my fee. 'You've got a beautiful daughter Walter,' I blurted out, watching Jenny as she pulled more pints for the customers further down the bar.

'Aye,' he replied, looking at me sternly. 'An' just remember, ah've also got a shotgun, a shovel an' an alibi. So, don't get any funny ideas lad.' I looked at him as he continued. 'Now, I've gotta go an' see to pies and comedian, so tha'll no doubt be gettin' on tha way 'ome an' sharpish, won't tha?'

He noticed Terry standing by my side.

'Now then Terry, 'aven't sin thee for ages. Thought they'd gone an' deed - an' wi'out payin' mi back for all drinks ah've bought thee over years.'

'No chance of me dyin' just yet Walter,' replied Terry. 'Ah'm still fair to middlin' an' tha's reet, tha did buy me a drink once,' nudging my arm. 'It were half a bitter back in 1973, so let me return the favour,' he chuckled and looked at me. 'Has tha got ten pence on thee, lad?'

I laughed back, but I was desperately trying to catch Jenny's attention. She must have been thinking the same because she came along the bar and said, 'Here,' slipping me a beer mat with a number written on it and I looked up at her.

'Call me sometime. After seven is good as dad will be down here and then we can chat. Got to go and serve now,' she said, smiling back at me.

'You were very good tonight lad,' Terry declared, as I put the beermat in my pocket. 'And this may be of some interest to tha,' pulling out a piece of paper from his jacket and handing it to me.

It was a job advert and as I scanned the text quickly, he continued. 'College are lookin' for a guitar tutor to join their Creative Arts Department. Says that some experience is necessary, an' ah guess you've got a fair bit o' that by now.'

I couldn't disagree with his reasoning as I read the advert again, this time more slowly.

'So why don't you fill this in now an' I'll drop it in for yer tomorrow?' he suggested, handing me a folded application form. 'Whether tha teks it any further is up to you, but you've nowt to lose by applyin' in first place 'ave tha?'

I nodded in agreement and especially when I saw the money that was being offered. It was nearly twice as much as I was scraping together doing gigs and lessons in London.

He handed me a biro and I retreated quietly to a side table. Fifteen minutes later I'd filled out all the necessary relevant details along with some additional artistic embellishments and I handed the completed form back to Terry.

Before long, it was time to leave the Club for the train station and so I said farewell to the backing band and shook hands with them.

Retrieving my bag from Walter's office, I finished my beer before picking up my guitar and waved to Jenny behind the bar. She waved back, making a telephone gesture with her hand against her ear and I nodded and grinned back, like the love-sick teenager I'd become. But who could blame me when she was so beautiful?

Outside, I rummaged in my pocket for the fare as I got into the taxi and we headed back towards Doncaster town centre. 'No, there's no charge for tonight,' said Terry. 'Tha's paid me enough fer one weekend.'

'Thanks Terry. And for everything you've done. You've been a great help,' I said. 'I don't know what would have happened to me if we hadn't met on Friday night.'

The traffic was predictably quiet for a Sunday evening and soon we pulled up at the railway station and Terry got out to give me a hand unloading my gear.

'Look after thi sen lad an' who knows, we might meet up before too long. Keep mi card in case tha gets locked up or arrested again,' he laughed, as we shook hands like old mates before he waved and drove off.

On the platform a group of postal workers were busy unloading their vans and throwing the sacks of mail into the sorting carriage. I walked past them and found an empty compartment and sat down heavily. Was I that relieved to be heading back to London?

I thought about all that had happened since coming here on Friday – was it really only two days ago? I thought about Reeny and about Mavis and then about Jenny, pulling the beermat out of my pocket and looking again at what she had written. Beneath the phone number was the message, *Call me after 7pm J xx,* and I smiled to myself in happy anticipation of a forthcoming conversation.

'Mind if I join you, young man?' asked a cheery chap, interrupting my reverie as he slid the compartment door open. 'Can't stand travelling on my own.'

'Sure,' I replied and watched as he placed his small case on the bench seat next to him and sat down diagonally across from me.

Raising his tanned face, he noticed the guitar case on the luggage rack above my head.

'Ah, a fellow musician? Have you been working locally?'

'Yes. I've just done some gigs at miners' welfare clubs over the weekend,' I said.

'Well, you must have done good then,' he replied in admiration. 'You're still in one piece and I can't see any cuts or black eyes,' looking at my face and smiling warmly.

'Not far off,' I laughed. 'But I have to say it was an experience though.' Outside the carriage, I heard the guard blow the whistle and the train pulled slowly out of Doncaster station.

'They're the toughest proving ground in the Country, these northern clubs,' said my travelling companion, as the train picked up speed. 'If you can conquer them you'll be an entertainment king in no time. It's where I started off singing some years back, so I know what it's like. They'll make yer or break yer.'

I looked over at his face and impeccable appearance. 'Have you been performing this weekend as well?' I asked.

'No, I've just had a quick visit to see my elderly folks,' he replied. 'But inevitably it always turns into an extended family gathering. I'm on my way to Southampton to join a cruise ship. Have to be on board by noon tomorrow so someone will be collecting me in London.'

He turned to flip open the locks on his case and pulling out a leather-covered travelling flask he asked, 'Fancy a drink? It's only Spanish brandy I'm afraid, but at least it'll keep the chill out.'

'Thank you. And can I offer you something to go with it?' taking out the pack-up from my holdall that Mavis had prepared. 'I'm sure I can spare one,' I quipped, as I unwrapped the tinfoil to reveal the colossal pile of beef and onion sandwiches.

He chuckled back and took one. 'Cheers,' he said. 'Oh, but hang on a mo, where's my manners?' Stretching his right arm towards me he introduced himself. 'Name's Tony Christie. I'm a singer. Now then, young man, tell me what you've been up to this weekend,' as he sat back and took a bite out of the sandwich.

After shaking his hand warmly, I smiled and took a sip of brandy.

'Well, Mr Christie, it's been like this...'

Chapter Seven

The Queen's Head in Sydenham was already half-full when I arrived around eight pm the following Thursday for one of my regular weekly gigs at this venue. The punters, as usual, consisted mainly of youngish people returning from their office jobs in the City. The men were dressed in over-sized double-breasted suits, their gaudy ties pulled askew as they relaxed over beers and the women all seemed to sport a similar range of shoulder-padded jackets and big perm hairdos.

Earlier in the week I'd managed to catch up with my errant agent Brownlow. After three attempts on the phone had all ended by going to the answering machine, I had stormed round unannounced to his shabby third floor office on Tottenham Court Road on the Tuesday afternoon. Although my initial anger from last weekend had subsided somewhat, I was still determined to give him both barrels.

'You sly, underhand sack of shit,' I'd bellowed. 'I lost money last weekend because of you.'

'Calm down kid before you do yourself a mischief,' he'd replied, sounding like he'd heard it all before. 'You know the deal. I get fifty per cent for all new out-of-town bookings and anyway, I got good reports back from up north.'

I just glared at him and remained silent. 'Except I can't get any answer from the Brodsworth Club. No-one up there is answering their phone for some reason. How did you get on with them?' he asked.

Before I could tell him that the place had most likely been wrecked over the weekend which would account for the absence of any phone response, he interjected.

'Tell you what, I'll give you back the commission you paid me,' handing me twenty pounds in grubby fivers. 'Now be on your way. I've got artistes waiting outside looking for work, so be bloody grateful that I'm still looking out for you,' he said. 'And call me next week. I may have some more bookings for you.'

It was a closure of sorts. Mr Christie had kindly given me a list of useful contacts in the entertainment business which thankfully didn't include the slimy creature sitting behind the cluttered desk in front of me. So I took the cash and left his office without saying another word. As I slammed the door behind me as a protest against being ripped off, the line of people sitting on the chairs in the corridor jumped in response and stared at me. 'That's showbiz,' I heard Mavis whisper in my mind, as I made my way back down the rickety old staircase and out onto the street.

Back here at the Queens, I was ready to take my place on the raised platform in the corner of the lounge, but before doing so, I wandered round the room listening to the chatter taking place amongst my audience. It all seemed to be about their latest jobs and money and about Epsom and money and about their cars…and more bloody money.

Giggling groups of young women puffed gently on cigarettes, tilting their heads as they blew smoke upwards as if in a self-congratulatory display of how good they were doing in public relations or over at the marketing agency.

I glanced over to the notice board by the pub entrance and to the printed poster advertising tonight's live entertainment. In bold letters, it was billed as celebrating the music of the real people - the Blues. But these folks were not real people I thought; they were merely imposters, seemingly riding high during the day and pretending to be down and dirty with the cool crowd of an evening.

To me the whole scene was as false as the stuck-on eye lashes of one of the women I'd heard addressed as Philippa. She sat with a small group of friends in a booth at one side of the room, cradling the stem of her glass of Chilean Casa Del Delores Sauvignon Blanc (dry white wine as they'd call it in Yorkshire, I thought) whilst her male companion Tristan shouted out for a pint of lager tops at the bar. They seemed fair enough and likeable as individuals, but they were as far removed from the struggles of ordinary people as you could get.

They weren't here to listen to me or to learn about the blues or to escape from their everyday life. Like everyone else in the room, they'd just come to a pub after work to boast about themselves to each other.

I tuned up and started playing, running through each of my numbers with the usual diligence. But I knew my heart wasn't in it and as the evening wore on, I failed to register any real and meaningful connection with my audience. Occasionally there was a smattering of polite applause over the loud conversations and drunken laughter, but no-one was remotely interested in what I had got to say musically, nor I in them. The whole experience served to reinforce the conclusion I'd come to earlier in the evening. It was now time to be decisive.

Before arriving at tonight's venue, I'd plucked up the courage to call Jenny. It was just after seven and Walter was safely down at his club, so we'd had a lengthy chat as if we were long-lost friends. She'd even called me back on the payphone when I ran out of change.

'I've been invited for an interview and audition at Barnsley College next Monday,' I'd told her excitedly. 'It sounds like a great opportunity.'

'That's fantastic news,' she'd replied. 'I'm sure you'll do great and they'll offer you the job. Then you'll be able to do more live gigs round here and make a name for yourself.'

'Well, I hope they do. It'll be a big step for me.'

We carried on chatting and bless her, she even offered to put me up for the weekend at their house. Walter would have to be informed about the arrangements, but mum was fine and she was already looking forward to meeting me, said Jenny. They'd make up the spare room and she'd meet me off the train, so there's nothing to worry about. Dad will be fine, you'll see, she had reassured me.

So the following morning I took my bag of meagre belongings and guitar and closed my bed-sit door for good, handing in my key to the landlady who lived in the ground floor flat. I stood for a few minutes on the pavement of Southfields Road and looked around at the crowded and decrepit Victorian houses, all of which had been converted into dingy bedsits. There were probably three hundred people living in close proximity to each other on this street and I wondered if any of them actually knew or spoke to their neighbours.

At my own address there were six of us, plus the landlady, in the one house and I'd barely spoken to just two of the other residents over the years that I'd lived there since arriving from Canada. These people around me seemed to live their everyday lives without knowing each other and without them having any visible sense of real community spirit or belonging. Where was the pride I wondered, as I looked at the street I had known for the past few years?

People came out of some of the houses and walked or jogged past me and each other without making any acknowledgement to one another. I realised with a shock just what an empty and hollow crap-hole I'd been living in without being aware of it. So I turned my back and walked briskly to the tube station some ten minutes away.

After reaching Kings Cross, I went straight to the main ticket office on the concourse. 'Second class single to Doncaster please,' I said to the clerk on the other side of the counter.

As I spoke the words and waited for my ticket, I realised that I was actually describing myself as a person. Still, second class living beats first class pretending, I thought.

Buying a cup of coffee and a sticky blueberry muffin from the take-away café, I walked down platform five, boarded the train and found an empty window seat, lifting my luggage up onto the rack to claim my space.

I thought about the journey ahead and recalled that Muddy Waters once sang, *You can't lose what you ain't never had.* Damned right you can't, I nodded to myself in agreement with the lyrics of the great bluesman. The whistle blew and I watched the northern suburbs of London go by as the train left the station heading to the North.

I had a job interview lined up for something I loved doing. There was no guarantee that I'd get the gig, but I had the necessary experience for it and how would I know for certain if I didn't give it a shot?

There would be a wonderful girl waiting for me when I got to Doncaster station in a couple of hours. It was early days in terms of a lasting relationship and who knew whether we would hit it off or not. But the signs so far were good and if she didn't like me then why would she be meeting me in the first place?

I'd recently met some lovely people in South Yorkshire who had made me look at things, including my own existence, from a different perspective. Even the slim prospect of running into Big Bert again could be avoided, especially if I didn't visit Wath or take up pigeon fancying as a hobby, I'd reckoned.

But what was beyond question were the things I had personally witnessed even though I had only been there for the briefest of time. I'd seen a true community spirit at work and at play, despite the immediate future holding some uncertainty for many of its people.

I had experienced the comfort and goodwill of complete strangers who didn't expect, nor did they ask, for anything in return. This was charity in action and if nothing else, I now had her two companions, faith and hope, firmly lodged at centre stage in my thoughts and aspirations for the future.

London had served a purpose and had provided a lot of experience for me since I'd arrived here five and a half years ago from the rural cornfields and backwaters of my childhood home. Whilst I was very grateful for my good fortune and for what I'd learned along the way, my heart was restless and yearned for something more meaningful. I'd come to the conclusion that I'd been living alone in a city of strangers and it struck me as being a very lonely and uncomfortable feeling.

Instead, I now wanted to be amongst real people, not pretenders. People who said 'how-do' to each other when they met in the street and meant it. I wanted to be part of a real community, to share in their joy in happy times and to feel their pain and anguish through tougher ones. I wanted to hear genuine banter and laughter and to hell with adversity and the harsh realities of working life. I wanted to play my music and to drink proper beer and love a Yorkshire woman.

Yes, I'd realised, I wanted to be a northerner.

Chapter Eight

'Now then lad, 'ow's tha gerrin' on?' asked a gruff male voice.

I looked up from the plate of baked beans and chips that I was wolfing down my neck in the bustling College refectory and into the beaming face of Terry. I'd only seen him in passing from a distance since starting my new job here and I smiled back broadly and motioned for him to join me.

'Hi Terry. I'm doing great, thanks. In fact, I'd go as far as to say I'm champion,' showing off my new-found knowledge of the local vernacular.

He sat down in front of me with a crusty ham and piccalilli doorstep and a cup of coffee, taking a big bite out of the sandwich as I brought him up to speed.

It was my fourth week living and working in South Yorkshire and my prior existence in London was becoming a fading memory. For the first time in my life I now had a regular job, a steady girlfriend and my own place to live in.

Yet deep down I wondered if it was all happening too fast.

Those three aspects of a man's life as Terry had previously described them to me - work, home and leisure - were now growing around me like wild brambles, threatening to curtail my previous footloose and fancy-free lifestyle, having no-one to worry about except me. It was all a novelty that I was enjoying so far, but it also gave me a weird feeling at times.

'So, 'ow's tha findin' the College then?' he asked, over the din coming from the surrounding tables of boisterous students.

'Going very well,' I replied. 'The Head of my section is a chap called Colin Wilson and he's a very pleasant guy.'

'Aye, I know him well,' answered Terry. 'Great bloke.'

Indeed he was. Colin, a middle-aged and mild-mannered gent, was a consummate musician who had practically welcomed me with open arms after my interview.

He'd told me that the two other candidates who'd turned up for the job were an unemployed punk rocker who couldn't play any guitar chords and thought that smashing up instruments was a modern expression of art and an aging country and western singer from some place called Hoyland Common, who only knew two songs from start to finish and both involved his banjo.

'He's keeping me on my toes with my tuition work,' I added. 'It's pretty full-on.'

Colin had lined up a heavy curriculum of music instruction for me. The job advert had said 'guitar tutor' but somewhere in the exceedingly small print he had added bass, vocal, and God forbid, drum tuition.

After group lectures, begrudging teenagers would turn up for their individual instrument lessons with me, each one going through a set curriculum of performance pieces and technical exercises.

Whilst Colin took care of the piano and string students, those few choosing brass or woodwind instruments had the luxury of a visiting teacher or a 'peri' as they were known.

This was short for peripatetic, a term I had not heard of before and it rhymed with 'very pathetic' in my mind.

'And I've got a nice young lady on the scene as well,' I said to Terry. 'Do you remember the dark-haired girl from behind the bar that night at the Edlington club?'

'Aye, I think I know who yer mean,' he replied, wiping some yellow sauce from his chin with a paper napkin.

'Well, Jenny's her name and I'm seeing her on a regular basis.'

'Don't know what a lovely bright lass like that would see in thee,' he joked.

As well as being good-looking and intelligent, Jenny was simply great fun to be with. Unlike me, she had a wonderful personality, always quick with a smile or a witty remark and I'd never seen her take offence at anyone or put on any airs and graces for show.

We'd been out a few times to local pubs and if she came across any of her friends, I was warmly introduced to them as 'mi bloke' by her. I had taken her for a meal at the nearby Berni where she'd insisted on going halves on the bill and I'd been to her house for Sunday lunch when her shift pattern allowed it.

Jenny was in the final throes of qualifying as a nurse and I often wished I was the one lying there in the quiet of her hospital ward at night as she drew the privacy curtains around us, before leaning over me seductively in her crispy white uniform and lacy stockings to administer a bed bath and tender loving care. I just wanted to see her more often – as well as to see more of her too – and then Terry interrupted my night-nurse fantasies.

'There's only two things to remember in College life,' he declared, slurping his coffee. 'Always be busy somewhere else whenever your Section Head is looking for you and don't break rule seven, or NFTS as it's known.'

'What's that mean?' I asked.

'No fuckin' the students,' came his blunt reply.

'Well, I could do with some of that,' I muttered, smiling as my lustful thoughts returned to Jenny.

We were working well as a couple but the one thing I wanted more than anything else just wasn't happening. I felt sure that the physical desire was shared between us and I'd been taking it nice and steady on the romance front, not wanting to appear over-bearing, but at the same time eagerly wanting the benefits that usually come from a steady relationship.

Instead, obstacles just kept appearing including the most recent and unexpected one. Jenny was currently working nightshifts at the hospital for a two month period as part of the requirements for completing her nursing qualifications.

When I was at work she was sleeping and vice versa, meaning we could never seem to be in the right place at the right time for long enough to have some decent, or even indecent, sex. It was driving me mad and talking of driving, not having any transport of my own didn't help matters either. This was something I'd have to work on and pretty smartish.

It had made me realise that I now envied drummers. Considered to be the lowlife of any band and the butt of everyone's jokes as being the people who hang around with real musicians, they had one advantage over the rest of us. Invariably, they needed a set of wheels to cart their gear about, thus giving them a distinct head-start in any post-gig romancing. A battered old rust-bucket van on its last legs could always double up as a passion wagon, even if it only possessed a smelly sleeping bag, a couple of cans of lager and a box of man-sized tissues as romantic accompaniments.

It was much better than trying to pick up girls after a gig when you were reduced to standing at a bus stop holding onto your guitar case. And that was the other bit that was absent so far in my new routine – my live performing.

'I'm missing doing my gigs though, Terry. The teaching is all well and good but it's not the same as being before an audience,' I lamented, finishing the last of my chips.

Usually, professional musicians do some teaching as a means of supplementing their income from gigs, but with me it was the other way round. Whilst the regular money was very welcome, I needed to find a way of balancing this out.

My quest to play my blues music in this part of the world had, from recent experience, not exactly been a success and so I had my work cut out to try and make some progress.

'Well, I may 'ave a solution for you there,' he answered. 'I've got a couple o' things to ask as favours. Any chance we can meet up for an early-doors at reference library later on today?'

'A what?'

I wasn't sure what he meant, nor that we had a reference library on site. I certainly hadn't seen one yet.

'A pint at the Corner Pin when they open at five thirty,' he explained.

'Sure, it'll make a welcome change from the usual harassment I'm getting on the way home.'

He looked worried. 'Who's harassin' you an' why? And where are you livin'?' he asked.

'Little place called Highfield,' I said. 'It's about five miles outside of town.'

'Aye, I know it well, just next to Goldthorpe. So, who's givin' you some hassle then?'

'It's nothing really. Just some factory women on the bus taking the mick,' I admitted, wishing now that I'd never mentioned it.

I travelled to work and back with my guitar on a number nineteen bus and it was a toss-up as to whether the top or lower deck was more hazardous to my well-being. In either option, groups of raucous women from the clothing factory on the edge of town occupied both decks on their way home and harangued me with constant banter about the big thing sticking up between my legs or asking if they could borrow my battery-operated boyfriend for the weekend. It was all good natured and filthy and whilst I just nodded and smiled, I wished I could think of something to say back instead of hiding red-faced, pretending to read my NME.

Terry just chuckled as I told him and said they're well known for it.

'Its 'ow them women are round 'ere. Tha'll get used to it. I'll catch tha later when we can talk.'

With that he headed off back to his Department and I did likewise for the rest of the afternoon.

I had a couple of hours of tuition to give then a bit of spare time to do some prep work as well as to write a letter to my folks back home updating them with my news and new address. As far as they were concerned, I was still in London.

*

There was a pint of Wards bitter already on the bar waiting for me as I walked into the Corner Pin pub and located Terry at the far end of the snug.

'Cheers,' I said, taking a mouthful of beer. 'That's nice. How did you know what I wanted to drink?'

'Ah didn't. Ah just saw you walkin' across street from Post Office an' figured any ale tastes better when someone else is payin' for it,' he joked. 'Plus, if tha don't like it then there's summat not right about thee.'

'It's very good, thank you,' I replied, pulling up a stool next to him and propping my guitar case against the bar as he made himself comfortable and explained what was on his mind.

'Firstly, we 'ave a debate comin' up in a coupla weeks wi' Sisters of Mercy Girls School over in Doncaster. Their upper sixth an' our final year economics students 'old one every year. It's intended to show that we have some integration an' co-operation across our local educational institutions. But really it's a chance for some o' girls who are destined for Uni an' 'igher things to practice their public speaking.'

'Okay,' I said, not really following where I came in.

'Each side fields a debatin' team, rest o' students listen, then they 'ave a vote to decide on winner,' he continued. 'Then they 'ave some supervised social time durin' which a recital, like a poetry readin' or a short play, is performed. I thought you might like to take some of your music students over to play as a group this year as our contribution.'

'It's a bit short notice,' I answered. 'But sure, I'll give it a go and see if I can put something together.'

He took a swig of beer. 'Great. I'll let Colin know you've said yes. Then I can drive you and your gear over in minibus. It'll save me havin' to put up wi' students an' their other lecturers who'll be goin' by coach.'

I wondered if he had a hidden agenda going on here, but I said nothing.

Taking another drink, he continued. 'Other thing is this. My eldest lad Mick is a Pit Deputy over at Barnstone. Funny enough, that's not far from where you're now living.'

I nodded as Barnstone was a couple of miles away going east from Highfield. 'Anyhow, he plays in their colliery band an' they're in a big competition soon, but they're a player short on their percussion team. So, he asked me if I knew anyone 'ere at College who'd 'elp 'em out an' I wondered if you'd fill in for them?'

I looked doubtful. 'What kind of band is it?'

He stared at me as if I was stupid. 'A brass band, what d'ya think it wor? An' a bloody good 'un an' all. Mick said it's not a hard part. If tha can read music an' hit a drumskin in right place, then you're almost there.'

This was a new musical departure for me and of all things, I was now being asked to stoop so low as to be a damned drummer. However, I couldn't disappoint Terry as he'd been so kind to me since I'd first met him. I took a long mouthful of beer and looked up at the ceiling lights as I pretended to ponder his request, but in truth it was already a done deal.

'OK,' I said. 'Let me have the details.'

He smiled broadly. 'I thought you'd say that,' delving into his shoulder bag and pulling out a large manilla envelope before handing it over. 'That's a copy o' sheet music an' a cassette tape of the competition piece. I'll tell Mick you're gonna be tied up until after the school debate, but that should still leave tha plenty of rehearsal time, a man of your musical calibre,' he smiled.

'Thanks. Flattery will get you everywhere, as you know.'

'Now, go over there on the Friday night next week at seven thirty an' they'll give you the rest o' details then. Plus, you can walk it from where you're livin' to their band room. Th'exercise will do tha good.'

I smiled as I finished my beer and ordered another round for us together with a pork pie apiece, which were warming in a glass fronted oven at one side of the bar and giving off a delicious 'eat me now' aroma. They certainly looked far more appetising than the jar of ghostly-white pickled eggs on the back shelf which appeared as if they had been floating there for several years, like formaldehyde specimens in a museum.

We continued chatting for a while and the pub gradually filled up with groups of cheery, older guys, many of whom were sporting red scarves round their necks.

'Last home game tonight for Barnsley,' explained Terry. 'I'm goin' to 'ave to go now as I'll be needed later on wi' taxi at Oakdale. So, I'll be seein' thi for now lad,' before standing up and draining the rest of his beer.

I followed suit and then looked around the pub for a payphone. I'd taken to calling Jenny each evening before her night shift began and rustling through my pockets for some change, I made my way over to the hallway at the other end of the bar.

However, I only got as far as speaking to her dad, Walter.

'She's gone in already, lad,' he said. 'Couple o' women on her ward 'ave gone into labour, so she went early to 'elp out. Tha can call 'er tomorrow.' Walter wasn't one for extended social chit-chat so I said goodnight to him and put the phone down.

Instead, I made my way outside and over to the bus station, passing through the groups of enthusiastic dads and lads heading down to the match. I reckoned that at least tonight I'd get a peaceful ride home on the bus, away from the rowdy knicker-stitchers.

Chapter Nine

The chatter amongst the bus passengers was all about the forthcoming Easter which was late this year seeing that we were already into April.

Winter was giving way to the brighter Spring days and the sunset above the roofs and chimney pots tinged the sooty grey clouds with shades of orange and vermillion, giving the illusion that I resided in a sunnier and warmer Mediterranean location, rather than in the depths of the Dearne Valley.

There was still some daylight left as I got off at my stop near the Spar shop and walked down towards Gladstone Terrace. Just tucked off the main drag, I rented a small mid-terrace home set amongst a huddle of similar houses and streets.

At this hour of the day the area was alive with shrieking kids playing football or doing wheelies on their bikes. I passed a pair of smiling teenage girls, pushing their prams and sharing a fag between them while taking the evening air on their way to the chippy.

Across the street, a trio of apron-clad older women were stooped over their sweeping brushes on the corner, laughing and joking with each other and as I walked by, one of them gave me a cheery, 'Hiya, y'all right then?' whilst pulling at her ginger hair tied back in a grubby headscarf.

I smiled at them and nodded politely.

Like all the houses around here, my place had originally been a two up and two down, built in the early part of the century to accommodate the influx of coalmining families who'd made up the majority of the local population and most likely still did. The rental particulars from the estate agent had described it as being 'compact with charming period features,' although so far, I'd been unable to find any.

At some point in the recent past, all these properties had undergone structural improvements whereby a downstairs kitchen was added at the rear with a bathroom straight above it, thus making redundant the small brick shed in the yard which had previously contained the outside toilet. Maybe this counted as a said period feature, charming or otherwise, but nowadays the locals seemed to be using theirs for storing coal or pigeons rather than for its original purpose.

The end of my back yard was bordered by a six feet high brick wall and timber gate which opened out into a narrow unpaved alleyway, or ginnel, running between the streets. This was just wide enough for the bin lorry to get down for the Tuesday morning refuse collections, but it also provided the local kids with an enticing skid-worthy surface and challenging width when using it as a racetrack on their bikes.

Highfield itself was more of a small hamlet, spilling over into the neighbouring larger settlements and punctuated on all sides by collieries. You couldn't get away from them and every time I opened my back bedroom window, I got a blast of coal dust sweeping in from the nearby pit stack. I didn't remember seeing that feature highlighted in the rental agent's blurb.

Any washed laundry that had been pegged out in the surrounding backyards during the early morning would have inevitably developed a greyish tinge by mid-afternoon and if it had been raining then all the windows on the houses would be streaked with black tears. The housewives across the road were constantly cleaning their front windows and I'd worked out why the launderette on the high street always seemed to be packed out with customers.

But my house was reasonably comfortable and more important, I had the place to myself. Unlike London, there was no more queuing for a shared bathroom to become free or trying to sneak in any unauthorised late-night guests past the prying eyes and ears of the ever-present landlady. Here I could wander around naked, scratching my arse to my heart's content if I wanted to and nobody would complain. The place was sparsely furnished with the basics and so I'd splashed out on some new bed linen, towels and a JVC television and video, paid for on a monthly instalment plan from the Rediffusion store in town.

As I reached my front door, a burly guy in a sweatshirt and jeans stepped out from a white transit van and stood in front of me.

'I've got some boxes 'ere to drop off for Mr Simms. Can tha let us in please.'

Simms was my landlord, whom I'd met when I first moved in and also saw when he, or one of his employees, came to collect the rent on a Friday early evening. He had told me to expect an occasional parcel delivery, as he was awaiting completion of a depot in Wakefield for his logistics and distribution business.

He'd struck me as being a bit of a shady character and I'd watched him make several house calls both in my street and in the neighbourhood on rent day, so I assumed that he must own a few properties in the area. He had also told me to leave my rent at the corner newsagent shop if I wasn't going to be at home on a Friday night and I supposed he also owned that place as well. However, he'd been pleasant enough with me so far and I hadn't got any concerns or complaints about my accommodation.

'Sure, come on in,' I said to the delivery guy and presently three packing boxes had been dropped in the back room.

'Someone will be along for 'em in a coupla days,' he advised, before leaving.

After stowing my guitar away upstairs, I watched him drive off before I went back outside, deciding that as I'd nothing better to do this evening I'd go for another couple of beers.

The Collingwood Arms was a short walk away and I'd previously dropped in there on occasion and found it to be a reasonable pub with chatty punters. But tonight it was emptier than usual, with just a couple of tables occupied in the snug and a group of four old men playing dominoes, whilst some pimply youths were occupying themselves on the pool table next door.

'Pint please and one for yourself,' I said, handing over a fiver to the young lady behind the bar who I hadn't seen in there before. I'd quickly learnt that round here a 'pint' meant a pint of best bitter and anything else required it to be called by its proper name otherwise the staff looked back at you for an explanation.

'Thanks, an' I'll 'ave a fifty pence wi' ya,' she replied, sorting my change and placing the coin in a small glass beside the till. 'Avent sin you before. Are tha from round here?'

'No,' I replied. 'Well, yes actually. I've just moved here from London. Well, from Canada, originally, I mean,' lifting my glass of beer in a vain attempt to cover up my rambling babble.

'What thi 'ell 'ave tha come up 'ere for then? Are tha workin' for Coal Board?' she asked.

'No. I'm at the Further Education College in town. I'm a music tutor,' I replied.

'Ah well, that's good,' she smiled. 'Tha can gi' mi some lessons then.'

I looked puzzled at her as she continued. 'I'm off to an open-mike birthday do at club on Sat'day an' we all 'ave to take a turn singin' summat. I like the song *Proud Mary* but I don't wanna show mi sen up. Do you know it?'

'Yes. It's a good song,' I replied, singing the first line of the verse back to her as if to reinforce my musical knowledge and credentials.

'You've a nice voice an' all…as well as bein' good-looking,' she added. 'We're quiet 'ere tonight as everyone's down at Oakwell for the footie. So later on for a lesson would be good for an hour or so, if you're free. How's tha fixed?'

This one wasn't backwards at coming forwards I thought and I was initially caught off-guard before answering her.

'Well, okay then, when do you finish work?'

'In about an 'our. I'm only covering early shift 'til nine. My other 'alf is workin' so I've got loads of time free…if you have,' she added coyly and dipped her eyelids at me.

'Sure,' I said.

However, I was mindful of what happened to me the last time I'd wandered off with a married woman and having come very close to grief then, I was determined to be more cautious this time round. After all, what was that old saying about being bitten once?

'Hang on, your husband isn't a miner is he?' I asked.

'No, we're not married, just together,' she said. 'And he's a Bobby, doin' nights this week. I'm Julie by the way.'

I introduced myself and smiled back at her.

I still wasn't convinced but I was definitely tempted. She was a slim and attractive brunette, aged around thirty and with a shapely figure and a bored housewife demeanour. Anyway, I figured that I'd moved here to meet new friends and settle into the neighbourhood, so what could be the problem?

'I live just round the corner on Gladstone Terrace,' I said. 'You could come there for a while, er, for a lesson, then afterwards I'll see that you get back home safely,' sounding very chivalrous. My seduction technique was underway.

'First time anyone's ever said that to me,' she giggled. 'Okay you're on.'

So shortly after nine, we left the pub chatting and walking together through the quiet terraced streets like old friends, as the smell of coal-fire smoke from nearby chimneys cut through the air and gently drifted up my nostrils.

The consumption of the last two pints had awoken the thoughts of sex in me and the possibilities started taking shape in my mind. If I had to give a singing lesson as a prelude to my supper, well, so be it.

However, the thoughts quickly vanished as we turned the corner and saw a police van parked near to my front door, which was gaping wide open.

A couple of my neighbours were peering curiously inside the house and shaking their heads at each other, whilst a uniformed copper was knocking on a front door across the street.

'What's happened?' I shouted, reaching the house and stopping abruptly as a policeman stepped out of my doorway and back onto the pavement in front of us.

'Is this thy 'ouse?' he asked. 'If so, tha's been brokken into.'

I nodded and leaving Julie where she was, I walked inside, turning on the lights and looking around frantically as he followed me round each of the rooms.

Upstairs, my guitar was still in its normal place, thank God, whilst downstairs the TV unit in the corner was untouched. Apart from a broken kitchen window, everything seemed to be in order. Then I noticed that the three packing cases had gone from the back room.

'There's some items gone belonging to my landlord,' I said. 'They were only delivered here earlier on tonight.'

He nodded whilst making some notes.

'Your neighbour next door called police after hearin' a window brekkin'. Said he's going to board it up for you, nice chap that he is.'

He beckoned me back outside to his patrol van.

'He saw a vehicle pullin' up here outside so he wrote down the reg an' I'm just gonna check on it now,' before picking up the radio mike and speaking to a control operator. 'I'll be able to give you a crime reference number an' all in a minute,' he added.

As he waited for a response, his companion returned from across the street and my heart sank as I recognised him. It was that obnoxious plod who'd previously arrested me on false pretences that fateful night after I'd been with Reeny over in Wath. However, as he looked up at us, he was clearly more interested in the woman standing at the side of me.

'What's thy doin' 'ere Julie?' he demanded. 'Tha should be at 'ome.'

'Er, I'm 'ere havin' a singin' lesson,' she answered, unconvincingly.

'A what?' he yelled back at her. 'Who thi 'ell gives bloody singin' lessons at this time o' night?'

'Well, I do,' I interjected. 'And what business is it of yours what I do and when I do it?'

He stared at me for a moment and then his face twitched as he exclaimed, 'You! Ah know thee, don't ah? Aye, you're that commie foreign agitator we locked up in Roth'ram a few wick ago. What the 'ell you doin' 'ere wi' my woman?'

I'd been called some things before now, but a 'communist foreign agitator' was definitely a first. However, before I could think of something to say, his partner called to him from the van window.

'Fletch. That plate, we know whose it is. Gang o' dealers from Leeds. They're on the system.'

Turning back to me, I saw that his top lip was curled aggressively, like a bulldog looking for a fight.

'So, you're a lowlife drug dealer are tha? Ah knew there were summat dodgy 'bout you from start,' he shouted.

My neighbours were still gathered close by and listening intently to the conversation taking place between us.

'I don't know what you're on about,' I said. 'My house has just been burgled, as you can plainly see and that's all there is to it.' However, I was starting to worry about this guy as we seemed to be going down a familiar path here.

'You're on my fuckin' patch now an' ah know where tha lives,' he snarled. 'I've got mi eye on thee an' I'll be back 'ere at some stage wi a warrant.'

He turned to Julie and muttered, 'Come on, we'll run thi 'ome an all,' as he took hold of her arm and guided her to the middle seat in the van. 'Singin' lessons, my arse.'

His colleague was a bit more amenable as he handed me a piece of paper. 'Don't worry 'bout him,' he said. 'He's always a bit 'ighly strung. Now, here's a crime number an' quote his name, PC Fletcher, Mex'bro station, in case tha needs it for insurance.'

I nodded but said nothing as he got into the driver's seat and Julie and the repulsive Fletcher were driven off.

As I watched them depart up the street, an old guy across the way walking a small dog gave a friendly, 'Ow-do Archie, 'ow've Barnsley got on then?' to an elderly chap putting empty milk bottles onto his front doorstep.

Probably much better than I have, I wanted to shout out to him. Win, draw or lose, at least they would have made it onto the pitch tonight and had a game, whereas I hadn't even made it to first base with flirty Julie.

I went back inside the house where I could hear some hammering going on at the back. The old guy from next door was in my yard, fixing a piece of plywood over the outside window frame and I unlocked the back door to speak with him.

'This should do yer lad,' he said, before tapping the wood panel into place over the window frame. 'I saw a couple of lads I didn't recognise hangin' around out back then I heard some glass brekkin'. So, I called the cops an' then watched from upstairs as the buggers marched outa yer front door, bold as brass, puttin' some boxes in a van. Little gits.'

'Thank you,' I said. 'I'll pay you for your trouble.'

'No bother, that's what neighbours are for. Now I need to get to mi bed as I'm up again in a few hours. But I'll get hold of a mate o' mine from across road who'll re-glass this pane for tha.'

I thanked him for his kindness as I realised I'd have to let the landlord know there had been a theft of his goods. But that could wait for now. Inside, I carefully picked up the larger pieces of glass from the lino floor and swept the remainder up into the waste bin.

So much for the promised singing lessons with the delightful Julie, as well as anything else that could have been lined up on the cards. Plus, that over-zealous psycho cop was back on my case giving me grief and now knew where I lived. After tonight's events no doubt word would get round the neighbours that I'm some kind of drug dealing scum. Just as I was trying to settle into the community and make new friends here. What a dammed mess, I thought.

Chapter Ten

The following morning, I made a point of searching out Terry. I'd had a restless night thinking about what had gone on and I needed his guidance. So just before eleven, I checked on his whereabouts with his department admin office and then caught up with him as he was coming out of a lecture room.

'Come on lad, let's grab a drink, ah'm parched,' he said.

We ordered some coffee at the snack bar and I told him about what had gone on the previous night. He listened and just nodded as I relayed the details to him.

'Well, if tha's not involved there's nowt to worry abart. It's a common trick.'

'What do you mean?'

'Dealers an' low life thieves are always splittin' their stash an' hidin' it away in unsuspectin' places. Other mobs will follow 'em an' then nick their stuff. Cops are always playin' catch up, never seemin' to be in right place at right time. It's a game really, but if you've 'ad nothin' nicked then it sounds like tha's no worse off.'

Reassured, I went off to find a payphone to speak with Simms. The answerphone kicked in on the other end so I left him a message quoting the crime reference I'd been given and outlining the basic details of what had happened.

Satisfied I'd done what was needed, I wandered back to the Department of Creative Arts where I held my tutorial classes.

Colin was on the phone in his cramped office and he signalled for me to join him, at the same time trying to tidy up the mess of papers and music scores on his desk. I gathered my thoughts on putting together a student band as he continued with his phone call.

I'd come up here from London wanting to play my blues, but so far, I'd been stuck with teaching scales, chords and curriculum set pieces, persuaded to play a set of God knows what yet for a bunch of schoolies and commandeered into helping out in a brass band.

Hey ho, it'll come right eventually though, I thought to myself as he said good-bye to the person on the other end of the line.

'The school debate should be okay,' he said, after I'd mentioned it to him. 'They tried it once before a few years back but the lads we sent pulled a flanker. Instead of playing some folk songs as they said they were gonna do, they did punk stuff like *Anarchy in the UK*, which didn't go down at all well with the Mother Superior, or whatever they call the Head Nun over at Donny. Anyway, she complained like mad to the Principal here, so I kept my head down and never got asked to send anyone again.'

I told him that I'd also been asked to help out at a colliery brass band competition and he seemed more interested in this news.

'What piece are you playing?' he asked.

I pulled out the envelope and sheet music from amongst my bundle of stuff.

'It's called *Journey into Freedom*,' I said. 'I've never heard of it. Sounds like some crap from a TV show,' I added, dismissively.

He sat back and his eyes misted over as he appeared to regress in time. 'You'll be surprised,' he answered. 'I think it's fabulous. I haven't listened to it for years, but just a minute…' Standing up and rummaging through the middle drawer of a filing cabinet, he pulled out a battered and faded booklet.

'Thought I still had it. This is the programme from when that piece was premiered in London back in 1967. I was there in the audience,' he said, proudly. 'Just listen to this for a quote from the composer, Eric Ball,' as he read out aloud from the booklet,

'…*whether or not they know, the amateur musicians competing today and the tens of thousands they represent are helping to keep open the windows of heaven in this harsh materialistic age. They focus on the unexpressed longings of the human heart, where mankind's greatest victories can be won. May they give us all hope and inspiration for these troubled times, as well as happiness and entertainment.*'

That certainly put me in my place and I shifted uncomfortably in the chair and silently cursed myself for opening my big mouth. 'Seek first to understand', yes, I was sure I'd heard that being said to me several times in the past by my high school teachers, but it seemed I had still not grasped its meaning and learnt to put it into practice.

Colin continued, oblivious to my rudeness. 'I remember that grown men were in tears when they listened to that piece. Not because it was bad music, but because it had the power to move them emotionally,' he said. 'At that time we were all scared stiff of a nuclear war breakin' out an' killin' everyone. The world was a violent an' confusing mess, with rioting goin' on all over the place in the West End and in other big cities.'

'I didn't realise you'd been in London,' I said.

'Yes, I was a student at the Royal College of Music,' he answered. 'After graduation I intended to stay there…before other things happened.'

He trailed off and blinked several times as I sensed there was something he didn't want to tell me and then he quickly changed the subject.

'Anyway, as a musician I think you'll appreciate it. Even if it isn't rock and roll or blues, it will definitely move you,' he said, leaving me suitably admonished.

'Well, first I've got to concentrate on this school gig,' I said. 'It's my neck on the block this time, even if I have to go and play there myself.'

'Good luck with that,' he smiled, as his phone rang again and I left him to his business.

*

I spent the next couple of days selecting the students who would form our College band for the debating gig, although this proved harder than I first thought. Despite most of them doing music courses because they seemingly wanted to take it up as a career, they suddenly became reluctant when faced with the prospect of playing before a live audience.

To make matters fair I'd originally asked for volunteers but deliberately didn't disclose where our venue would be. When that didn't work out, I persuaded some of the more able students that they might get better marks in their year-end exams if they were prepared to put themselves out a bit. I genuinely wanted us to put on a good performance. My sense of pride was at stake here and whilst I was prepared to be criticised for many things in life, delivering a crap show would not be one of them.

Eventually with me taking on vocals and lead guitar, I ended up with four students. Robbie was on supporting rhythm guitar, Benji on bass, Stevie on the electric keyboards and Woody (his real name was Stanley) on drums.

I was initially worried about his nickname until it was explained to me that Woody was so-called because he was as thick as two short planks and not due to any undue activity taking place in his trouser department. God, this English language was complicated at times.

However, thick or not, he was, like most drummers, unable to keep a basic caveman rock beat going steadily without speeding up. He needed a few concentrated sessions where I sat him in front of a metronome and got him to tap his hands and feet in tempo with the pendulum for half an hour at a time.

As he did so, he also nodded his head, like a novelty toy dog in the back of a car window, but if it was going to help him, I wasn't going to stop it. After a while the notion started to sink into his muscle memory and he became more comfortable at holding a steady beat. This was all we needed to get by on the gig.

From the sheet music library, I selected a list of fairly straight-forward numbers which would fill our allotted twenty minutes set and we began to rehearse them relentlessly. Then we had to come up with a name – the fact that the Barnsley College of Further Education Student Blues Band didn't trip too easily off the tongue. Eventually we settled on the 'Sharp Dressed Men' after our opening *ZZ Top* song.

I asked a couple of colleagues in Art and Design if they could run us up some sparkly jackets to wear over our tee shirts and denims together with a snazzy design logo to fit over the outside of the bass drum. They duly did so by delegating it as a project to some of their final year students. They come in handy sometimes, do students.

We then spent every spare minute plus the following weekend doing intensive practice on our set list and in the process we became more comfortable with each other and with the pieces I'd selected. Then on the day before the gig, I told them where we were going.

'Wow,' said Woody. 'I've not shagged a left-footer before.'

I wasn't sure what he meant, but rather than show my ignorance I simply said, 'We're all on our best behaviour whilst we are playing. What you get up to afterwards is up to you.'

After a final run through on the Thursday lunchtime, Terry came to collect us at two o'clock and we crammed the gear and ourselves into his minibus taxi. Here we were, just like a real rock and roll band, trundling down the A635 and jostling for position amongst the freight wagons and quarry lorries as we headed to our venue on the other side of the A1 in Doncaster.

As we drove, I leaned over from the front seat and read out the written agenda that I'd been given from Colin. It had been faxed over from the head teacher at the Girls School:

'*The visiting students from the College will be welcomed in the Assembly Hall where the debate will start at three pm. Each side will be allowed twenty-five minutes to put over their persuasive arguments for and against the motion that This House believes that a Capitalist Economy is morally wrong and ultimately self-destructive.*'

'Shit, what does that even mean?' asked Robbie.

I ignored him and continued:

'*Then we will take questions from the student audience before voting to determine the winning team. All students are invited to participate in the buffet tea during which time a recital by the school string quartet will be given followed by a performance from the College. Social mingling will be permitted, with all students to be off the school premises by six pm.'*

Everyone in the van guffawed loudly at me. Even Terry was laughing his head off as he tried to keep us on the road.

'What? What did I say?' I asked, bemused at their reactions.

Robbie enlightened me. 'You didn't say 'owt about the competition.'

'What competition?' I frantically re-scanned the paper in case I'd missed something important.

'There's always a competition to see who can 'ave a shag on school premises wi'out gettin' caught,' he said. 'Rules are simple. You've got to 'ave a used noddy to show off as evidence the day after.'

'A what?' I asked them.

'A durex,' they all shouted in unison at my ignorance.

I thought for a moment. 'Well, that doesn't mean anything does it? You could have, er, filled it on your own at home. How's that supposed to be evidence?'

'No, you don't follow,' said Stevie, as the other lads howled away at me. 'It's the girls who have the competition between themselves.'

They roared with laughter as they all dipped their hands into their jeans pockets and pulled out packets of three to wave at me. Except for Woody.

'Er, can you lend me one of them, Benji?' he asked, as the rest of them rolled about in hysterics. Well at least we had camaraderie going on here I reckoned and that was no bad thing.

Presently we drove through the school entrance gates and pulled up at the side of the assembly hall. A small door led onto the back-stage area and in the car park opposite to us two coaches had just pulled up and were disgorging the College's cohort of economics students and supporters, who predictably were all males. Just what we needed I thought: a bunch of testosterone-fuelled teenage lads put in a room full of repressed but sexually charged young women.

The hall was a large parquet-floored area with tall windows on either side and set out with rows of red metal and timber-framed chairs, which reminded me of my exams time back at high school.

The elevated stage stood at the far end with steps on either side and the back area was covered by two heavy full-length scarlet velvet curtains. As we loaded our gear through the backstage door, the figure of a tall elderly nun suddenly appeared in front of us. She peered down over half-moon specs at us in turn and I went cold just looking at her.

'Er, good afternoon, Sister, Mother, er…I'm not sure how I should properly address you,' I said, before hesitating. 'This is my College band, er, music group.'

I noticed that Terry had dodged out of the way, hiding deep in the stage side wing out of sight and all the other lads were looking down at their instruments or shuffling their feet, avoiding making eye contact with this ogre.

'Sister Agnes will suffice,' she barked at me. 'Are you in charge of this lot?'

'Yes,' I answered. God, I was feeling guilty already.

'Well, you've no doubt been told by your superiors what we are expecting from you this afternoon,' she said. 'We don't want any songs about promiscuity, sex or the taking of illicit or intoxicating substances. Nor anything to do with pursuing a degenerate or criminal lifestyle, even though you've come over from Barnsley.'

109

'Don't worry,' I said, trying to lighten the mood. 'I've deliberately not put *Highway to Hell* on our set-list.'

But she didn't alter her stare and continued with the stern lecturing.

'Our upper sixth girls are taught to be morally responsible and clean-living adults who intend to go into the wider world to lead constructive and fruitful lives.' She sounded as if she'd given this speech many times before and we all stood silently to attention as she carried on with her theme. 'Yes, at times they will have to encounter other less fortunate and lower order individuals, who no doubt have a different outlook on life.'

She peered at us in turn to reinforce the point that we were all lowlife creatures belonging to the unlucky degenerate masses.

'However, the rather shallow and dissident upbringing of such people is through no fault of their own,' she insisted. 'It's therefore our duty, and that of our girls, to help enlighten the less enabled by setting an example and showing them the right path in life, respectfully and with grace.'

I nodded at this wise advice, all the time thinking about the competition that would shortly be taking place. Or maybe I'd got it all wrong and the guys had just been having me on. After all, this dragon would put the fear of God into anyone even contemplating committing the slightest misdemeanour and I was fearful of what she may do next.

'Still, at least most of you look presentable this time around,' she said, as she studied each of the lads in turn. 'And what's this name you call yourself?' looking at the design on the bass drum head. 'What does that mean?'

'Cos all the girls go wild about sharp-dressed men,' blurted out Woody.

Before she could answer, I interjected. 'What he means is, that er, most young ladies would like to meet a respectable young man to, er, settle down and be fruitful with, er, in time, like you've just said,' I tried to explain.

Her grey eyes stared into mine with laser-like intensity.

'Are you of the faith young man?' she asked.

'Yes,' I replied, with all honesty. 'I come from a good Catholic upbringing back home.'

'And where is that exactly?'

I told her.

'Hmm, the Commonwealth colonies,' she muttered. 'I think that we may still have some schools there, even in that backwoods of the world,' before pausing. 'Well, no matter.'

She rubbed her hands together vigorously as if to dispense with the coal dust and deprivation that we'd brought over with us and casually dropped into her pristine environment.

'Now, after the debate has finished Sister Cecilia will be presenting her strings ensemble first and then you will follow them afterwards.'

I couldn't resist it and broke into song recalling the 'making love line' from *Cecilia* as I smiled broadly, trying desperately to break the ice whilst the lads just sniggered behind me.

'Shut up with the smut,' she snarled. 'Remember what I've told you. I've got my eyes on you, young man, and that goes for the rest of you. Mark my words well, boys,' she added, wagging her index finger at us before vanishing through the curtains back into the hall.

'That's you told lad,' said Terry, as he emerged smiling from the wings.

Out in the assembly hall the mass of students had piled in and after a few minutes they were brought to order and the debate got underway.

We got ourselves ready in silence behind the curtains, but as there was no chance of a doing a sound-check, I had to tune up the guitars individually back in the van and just hope that we sounded okay.

Eventually we heard a round of applause followed by the shrill tones of Sister Agnes again as she gave her thanks to the debating teams and invited everyone to get a sandwich and a cup of tea. Stringed instruments began tuning up and presently we could hear some gentle classical music being played over the hum of conversation coming from the students.

The lads started giggling but I told them to keep quiet. 'Show some respect,' I instructed. 'Music is music and they're doing exactly what you're going to be doing in a few minutes.' I sounded very grown up for all of my twenty-five years.

Then the soaring sound of high notes from a violin cut through the chatter in the hall and caught my curiosity. I peered round the edge of the stage curtain to see a tall, flame-haired girl swaying seductively as she played an arrangement of *Czardas*, a notoriously difficult piece which swept along feverishly in the style of a wild gypsy dance.

Her right arm guided her bow effortlessly and elegantly across the bridge of her strings as her companions plucked their cellos in time to the music and another elderly nun, whom I presumed was Sister Cecilia, thumped away on the piano keys in chord accompaniment.

But my Lord, this girl could play. As I watched and listened to her, I was captivated and forgot everything else around me. Her shoulder-length hair was tied back in a simple ponytail to prevent it straying across the strings and as she glanced back to the stage where I gawped like a peeping tom, she smiled, as if somehow knowing I was watching her and boy, she was a stunner.

Engrossed in the mood of her music, she moved and played like a woman possessed. Some of her classmates began to clap along in time with her whilst Cecilia kept up the tempo, nodding at the girl beside her on the piano stool to turn the music pages over every few seconds. Then she ended with a flourish and to rapturous applause from the audience as I thought, follow that.

Turning around and strapping my guitar on, I looked at my guys and said, 'Right, here we go.'

The stage curtains were wound open by Terry, who had somehow managed to avoid the post-debate pleasantries and chit-chat.

I tapped on the microphone in front of me before announcing, 'Thank you very much and good afternoon Sisters, ladies and degenerates…it's our turn now,' and we launched into our opening sharp dressed signature tune.

Considering that we hadn't had a chance to check the volume levels, we sounded good. I emphasised tapping my right foot on the floor so that Woody behind me would keep in tempo with the beat and he was doing fine.

In between the verses I traded twelve bar guitar licks with Robbie and he responded confidently, playing carefully and tight in response, just as I had taught him. No need for any prancing around on the stage, just let the guitar speak for itself and it was working a treat.

We may have something here I thought, as I looked round to each of them in turn, letting them have their moments as they enjoyed themselves and nodding my encouragement. 'This is it boys, this is rock and roll,' I mouthed to each of them, smiling as we played.

The students loved it. The lads whistled and clapped and the girls, well, they were something else.

It was of course broad daylight and from my elevated position on the stage I watched nervously as hips began to swirl around in the chairs and long legs seemed to grow out from slowly rising skirt hems. I'd been told there was no alcohol allowed, but I was convinced that small bottles and flasks were being passed around and poured surreptitiously into the paper tea- cups so as not to attract the attention of the watching staff.

At pre-determined intervals around the perimeter of the chairs, stood a severe-faced nun and together they made up a forward line worthy of a riot squad, no doubt intent on curtailing any signs of wayward behaviour. I realised that their numbers would have been augmented from the junior classes which would have finished an hour or so ago.

Now I knew how Johnny Cash must have felt when he appeared at Folsom prison. At least he only had convicted male thieves and murderers to contend with. In here, I could feel the atmosphere welling up with teenage lust and hormonal fervour, as any lingering thoughts regarding the perceived benefits or otherwise of capitalist economics had disappeared like melting snow. Dancing was definitely not allowed and any deviant girl risking it was immediately told to sit down by one of the attending Sisters patrolling the aisles.

We went straight into *Nadine* as our next number and this got some giggles and cheers when we discovered a student sharing the same name and she enthusiastically shouted out, 'Yes it's me,' at the relevant points in the song.

I made a point of looking at her whilst I sang the lyrics, my hand shading my eyes as I did so and the girls around her shrieked and pointed as everyone laughed and shared the joke.

This was good stuff so far. It was wholesome entertainment and I didn't think we'd offended the Mother Superior.

The students yelled out their encouragement as we carried on with *Rock And Roll Music* and then finished with *Pride and Joy*, giving me an opportunity to show off my bluesy guitar licks.

As we ended our set everyone applauded us and cheered like mad. The band guys all smiled and looked at me expectantly and I thought, okay then, here we go, as I nodded to Benji, whilst turning up the volume on the amps behind me.

He walked to the front of the stage and dug into the bass strings riff with gusto, nodding his head like a rock veteran and we stormed into *Roadhouse Blues* as our encore. This was a raunchy and gutsy track and I swear it would definitely not make Sister Agnes's desert island discs.

Out in the audience, the lads stomped their feet and played their air guitars whilst the girls were grinding their hips into their chairs and swiveling their upper bodies like Vegas lap dancers. I glanced at the ceiling above me, expecting to be struck down by a lightning bolt at any moment.

When I reached the line about ashen ladies giving up their vows, singing it in my most sultry, gravelly tone, the girls shrieked, cheered and yelled like mad and the nuns, well, they just looked ashen.

Everyone joined in with us singing the chorus lines to the end of the song. Then to screams and cheers the stage curtains were closed and we were done. The Sharp Dressed Men had just lost their musical virginity and looked very pleased about it.

'Well done guys,' I said to the lads. 'You all did great. I'm proud of you.'

'Let's go chase the fanny,' shouted Woody.

'Just a minute,' I yelled out. 'Pack the gear away and load the van first.'

I'd no intention of being left with having to do roadie duties whilst this lot went off to party with their new fans.

As we started to take down our stuff and pack it into the boxes, the face of a nun appeared between the curtains.

'Now then boys,' said a shrill-voiced Sister Cecilia. 'I want a word with you all.'

This is it I thought, brace yourselves. This is where we get both barrels fired at us.

'That was bloody great,' she said softly with a smile, as I breathed out audibly with relief. 'Music is the Lord's gift to us all, no matter how we decide to interpret it and you did very well, so may God bless you,' she continued. 'Now, I've got to go and join my Sisters and help round up the sinners and fornicators.'

'Who are they?' asked Woody.

'Everyone except you mate,' answered Benji, as they joked with each other.

I had no idea who'd won the debate and no intention of hanging around to find out. We'd done our bit and as the lads loaded their gear before going off to join their fellow students, I did a final check round on the back-stage area to make sure we hadn't left anything, before putting my guitar into the van and closing the door.

As I turned round, I was startled by the figure of a tall girl who I hadn't seen approaching and now she was in front of me and smiling. It was the violinist.

'Hello, I'm Rosalyn. What do I have to do to join your band?' she asked, in a soft, slightly lilting accent that had me melting on the spot.

She was even more gorgeous close up, with beautiful chestnut-brown eyes and a complexion of cream alabaster which was tinged in soft pink shades around her small apple dumpling cheeks.

I blushed in response as I struggled to get some words out.

'Er, I'm not sure,' I said. 'You play very well. Really, very well, in fact. Can you play the part to *Baba O Riley*?'

'Of course,' she replied, and I just knew she would say that. 'And anything else that you want me to play for you.'

'Well let me think about it,' I said, racking my brains on the spot for rock songs with violin parts and imagining that maybe we could do a cover version of *The Devil Went Down To - Barnsley*.

'Don't be too long about it then,' she said, handing me a folded piece of paper. 'Call me when you want me,' and then she turned to re-join her group of friends who were giggling and smiling at me.

I watched her perfect long legs and narrow hips swivel as she turned her head, coyly smiling back at me as she brushed her hand through her hair. Glancing down at the phone number in my hand, I breathed in deeply, catching a faint aroma of sweet lavender scent.

'Jamie!' yelled a stern-voiced Terry, bringing me back to reality. It was the first time I had heard him call me by my name. Any other time he just referred to me as lad. 'Remember rule seven.'

I put her number in my pocket as I smiled back at him and got aboard the taxi.

'Now there's the definition of unnecessary,' he said, looking out to the carpark and pointing at the two empty College coaches. 'All our lot will be off into Donny wi' them girls tonight. It's cheap night an' all on a Thursday, so I won't be expectin' many of 'em will be in tomorrow.'

I looked back through the assembly hall windows at the throng of excited young adults, some of whom were already spilling out in smaller groups and wandering off round to other parts of the school. I started to wonder what they'd be getting up to left to their own devices but then stopped abruptly in my tracks. Who was I kidding? I knew exactly what they were getting up to and I looked over at Terry.

'Does rule seven apply to the students of other Colleges?' I asked jokingly, although there was a hankering in me as I asked the question.

Sexual activity would likely be on the cards for some of this lot tonight and yet here I was, missing out again and the thought made me crave to be with Jenny.

Or perhaps Rosalyn.

Or even with Reeny, who would probably be working tonight at that crappy hotel in town where I'd first stayed at in Yorkshire. It couldn't be too far away from where we were right now and for a moment I thought about asking Terry to drop me off there, but he seemed to read my thoughts.

'Come on, I'll buy you a pint on the way 'ome. You did good lad. They'll be roundin' up them buggers for ages. With any luck they won't invite us again.'

I took that as a compliment and together we laughed and sang the *Roadhouse* chorus again as he drove us out of the school gates and into the early evening traffic.

I had the makings of a band here I thought and even though we'd done it for free, it felt good to be gigging again.

Chapter Eleven

The following evening was my scheduled appearance at the Barnstone Colliery band rehearsal. Terry had been right with his predictions about student numbers. Not many of them had turned up for the last day of the term so I busied myself during the morning and over lunch on the College percussion instruments, going through each of the bars of the sheet music for the part and making sure I could play all the beats on the respective instruments as required.

Despite the years I'd spent honing my musical skills and technique on both six and twelve string guitars, as well as a bass and a smattering of piano chords, not to mention singing, I reflected that I'd now been reduced to this…being a lowlife drummer, or a panel beater as we used to call them back home.

However, I'd made a commitment and I knew I'd have to stand by it, as it wasn't in my nature to let people down. So after getting back home and settling my rent with Mr Simms when he called round, I got washed and changed and was armed ready with a bag full of sticks and beaters that I'd borrowed from College, together with my sheet music copy. Checking I had everything, I was about to set off for Barnstone when there was a knock on the front door.

'Ow do,' said an elderly guy, dressed in a paint-splattered check shirt, corduroy pants and wellies and clutching a canvas bag of tools. He looked like a scarecrow short of a cornfield and I just stared at him, puzzled.

'I'm Archie Selby,' he announced. 'Ah'm 'ere to do tha window glass. Ronnie next door told me 'bout it.'

'Oh, er, thanks, but I'm just about to go out,' I said. 'How long do you think you'll be?'

'Don't worry, ah'll shut door behind mi when I'm done, tha'll be reet,' he said, stepping into the house uninvited and walking through into the back room.

'Are tha new round 'ere? Think ah might 'ave sin thi walkin' down street wi' yon instrument,' pointing to my guitar case propped against the staircase wall.

It reminded me that I hadn't put it in its usual hiding place in the bedroom this evening.

'Yes. Just moved in a few weeks ago. I'm originally from Canada,' I said.

'Bloody 'ell, that's a long way to come wi' a guitar,' he replied. 'Does tha do any singin' as well?'

'Yes, sometimes,' I answered.

'Does tha know any Shekkin' Stevens' songs?' he asked.

'Er, no, never heard of him,' I lied, unconsciously shaking my head.

'That's a pity,' he said, although I didn't necessarily share his sentiments. 'He's one o' mi favourites, along wi' that other guy, er, what's his name now…?'

He thought for a moment, looking up absently at the ceiling and scratching at the back of his neck with a long-handled screwdriver. 'Ah, got it - Alvin Sawdust,' he declared. 'We 'ad 'im up 'ere at Labour Club a few years back to perform at our women pensioners summer party.'

'That must have been fun,' I said, making a mental note to find out who the hell he was on about.

'If tha likes, ah'll let tha know when our next talent night is on,' he offered. 'We normally 'ave a country an' western theme for it each year an' we all go dressed up in cowboy gear. Tha'll feel right at 'ome,' he added.

'Mind you, last one were a bit tame cos we were banned from bringin' any shotguns wi' us after drummer copped a shin full o' pellets year before.'

'That doesn't sound too bad,' I mocked.

'Oh, it were,' he insisted. 'He 'ad to have his wooden leg replaced. Doctor even asked him if 'e'd been attacked by a gang o' woodpeckers. Bloke wi' shotgun reckoned 'e'd only bin aimin' at the singer's amp cos 'e wor so crap, but he woz too pissed to shoot straight an' so all pellets went straight through bass drum skin instead.'

I made a second mental note to avoid this event like the plague and felt sure that I would be booked somewhere else on that night, as Archie continued on with his tale.

'That's trouble when we 'ave clay pigeon afternoon on same day. Next talent do should be okay though, as Club Secretary's already said 'e's only allowin' 'atchet-throwin' contest durin' day, rather than target shootin'. So, no guns are allowed.'

'Well, give me plenty of notice about that one as well,' I replied.

'Sorry tha got brokken into,' he said, pulling out a new pane of glass from his bag and holding it up against the window frame to check the size.

'We don't get much thievery round 'ere, well, not from each other's 'ouses like. Mind you, it's better being fore-whatsit-ed, so tha should call in an' see dodgy Duggie when tha gets a minute.'

'Who's that?' I asked.

'Duggie Belton. He's an insurance bloke above the bookies on main street. We call 'im belt 'n' braces, geddit?

121

Anyhow, he'll sort tha some policy cover out. Just tell 'im Archie sent yer over.'

'Thanks, I will,' I replied, glancing at my watch. 'Well, I need to be going, er, Archie. How will I pay you?'

'In notes, when tha see's mi next,' he advised. 'Ah just live at top o' street, second door down an' it'll be twenty-five pounds. Usually, ah do paintin' an' decoratin' for mi day job so if tha wants any dildo rails puttin' up round walls just let me know. Ah'm a dab hand at slidin' them in.'

I didn't dare ask what he meant and instead, I gave him a cheery farewell and my thanks and left him to carry on with the window repairs. After putting my guitar out of sight upstairs, I headed out of the house and down the street.

Barnstone was about twenty-five minutes' walk away from my place and tonight was a pleasant Spring evening. Blackbirds perched provocatively along the tops of the hedgerows and in the woodland fringe and sung out in fine voice at me, as I followed the narrow footpath cut into the fields and waste ground lying between the coal mine compounds and the vast hump-backed spoil heaps.

Arriving at my destination, I found the band room across the main road, away from the cluster of pit buildings and about fifty yards further down from a corner pub called the Colliers Rest.

It looked a little like a church hall building and as I walked through the doors into a foyer area, a friendly voice shouted out, 'Ow do lad, come on in,' and an elderly bespectacled man dressed in a burgundy jacket and emblem tie and with a belly resembling a well-filled party balloon, approached me and extended his right hand.

'We're pleased to si thi,' he said, as we shook hands. 'I'm Charlie, the band secretary 'ere. Let me show you around,' and I followed him into the band room where there were already some half a dozen players energetically rehearsing their parts.

Charlie was an amiable chap, making me feel welcome and I took to him instantly. I met my other percussionist, an equally nice guy called Bill and then Terry's son Mick came over to introduce himself, before lifting out a tuba from a battered timber case.

It was a huge and fearsome looking instrument with yards of shiny silver metal tubing coiled in loops like snakes. He caressed and cuddled it with care, wrapping his blue-scarred forearms around it like a protective father holding his first-born child, before taking his seat in front of me.

With his big frame and stature, he reminded me of some of the farmhands back home when they man-handled their calves or hogs into their flat-back trucks.

By seven thirty the place was full and we were ready to go. Including myself, I counted a total of twenty-seven players, all male and of varying ages, some looking like they'd just come straight from the pithead showers, others like they'd been grafting without sleep for several days. We were warmed up by the conductor with a couple of traditional hymn tunes and then it was straight into our competition piece.

In my arrogance, I'd neglected to bother listening to the cassette tape that Terry had given to me, so I was unprepared for what came next. The combination of big, round, thumping bass sounds and cascading, trilling cornet and horn passages intermingled with gorgeous harmonies sent shivers down me.

I was metaphorically, like most of the instruments around me, blown away. These were sounds I'd never heard before and had not appreciated nor even considered, much to my shame as a professional musician. It was thrilling stuff and Colin's words of wisdom echoed in my mind as I listened and we played.

I watched eagerly as an active participant, as these guys around me concentrated their attention on their parts. Under the direction of the conductor, they played, stopped, repeated some sections, stopped again, tweaked little bits and then committed them to memory like seasoned professionals.

Never once did anyone question what they were asked to do and when the band stopped to go over a particular instrument's section of bars, or a solo passage, the rest of the guys remained absolutely still and silent. Their personal commitment, self-concentration and respect for each other was second to none and I was truly humbled and impressed to be part of it.

It took me some time to realise that all the men here were amateur musicians. They were simply pursuing their music as a hobby rather than as a living and doing so purely because they wanted to and loved it. But what a hobby – their dedication was nothing less than fanaticism and the quality of playing and musicality they produced was top-notch. Two hours of rehearsal time seemed to evaporate in a matter of minutes and I thoroughly enjoyed every moment of it.

Afterwards we all went down to the Colliers for a pint and I was introduced around and made to feel part of the crew. Charlie handed me a beer as Mick came over to join us.

'So what did you think then?' he asked. 'Dad says you normally sing and play guitar rather than do this stuff.'

'Yes, that's right. To be honest with you, I thought I wouldn't like it, but I was wrong, I'm converted,' I said.

'But I noticed all the musicians are men. Don't you have any women brass players here?'

'It's coming, in time,' he replied. 'There's lots of good women players around now. But so far we've managed to avoid it,' as he took a swig of ale. 'But don't get us wrong lad, we're all for diversification an' 'avin' some lumpy jumpers dotted around band room. Not everyone 'ere works at pit an' hell, we've even bin known to let some players in from Lancashire before now.'

I didn't understand the relevance of what he meant but when he offered to buy me a refill I nodded, emptying my glass.

As he walked to the bar, an argument broke out amongst three of the band guys in the corner and they shouted angrily and gesticulated at each other. I thought this is going to end in trouble.

'Don't worry 'bout them lads,' Charlie said, looking at my concerned expression. 'It's just our way of sortin' small things out. We may cuss an' swear at each other on occasion but come Sat'day on that stage we'll be as one, tighter than a duck's arse. You won't get a fag paper between any of us.'

Alerted by the shouting, the landlady had wandered round from the tap room side of the pub and putting down the bar towel in her hands she now made her feelings known.

'Oi, you three,' she yelled, in a voice that reminded me of industrial sandpaper rubbing against raw timber. 'Shut yer bloody 'oyles or tha can tek it outside right now.'

'Sorry Peggy,' one of them muttered and they all quietened down.

Peace was restored and their bluffness and no-nonsense exchange of sharp opinions had been reduced to meek adherence to the instructions dished out by this pint-sized lady. Instead, they concentrated on emptying their glasses.

'That's another reason we don't 'ave women in band,' said Mick, as he returned with the beers. 'Just too bloody outspoken on occasions.'

Charlie handed me some registration paperwork to fill in and sign for the forthcoming competition and I also glanced at the rehearsal schedule for the following week which I had been given. It was a demanding workload.

We would be rehearsing tomorrow during Saturday afternoon and then again same time on Sunday, so no chance of meeting up with Jenny then, I thought. After that, it was every night next week with the contest being held on the following Saturday in Sheffield.

This was a heavy load by anyone's standards and I was curious to know why. 'What's the competition for, Charlie?' I asked.

'Qualifying heats for the national championships,' he replied. 'Then the final is held in October in London. Have you been there before?'

'Been there? I've just come from there,' I laughed. I'd no intention of going back in a hurry.

'The nationals are held in the Albert Hall, have you ever been there?' he asked.

'No,' I said. 'But wait a minute. Do you mean The Royal Albert Hall in South Kensington?'

This was the world-famous venue where top artistes from around the world performed. My British guitar hero Eric Clapton had a week's residency there every year and I'd never been able to get hold of a ticket.

'You mean amateur bands like yours get to play there?' I asked, incredulously.

'Oh aye,' he said, looking at me as if I was stupid. 'It's not just some Sunday afternoon picnic on a fuckin' bandstand in Battersea Park,' laughing at my surprised reaction and I felt suitably cut down to size.

Before going back home I wandered off to find a payphone and call Jenny to tell her my news about the rehearsal schedule. Whilst I could detect regret that we'd miss this coming Sunday at her house, and I did like her mum's cooking very much, she was nevertheless excited for me and my new musical adventures.

'Well, we've got the following Sunday,' she said. 'Plus, I've got the Bank Holiday Monday off as well. So, we can spend some time together then on our own at last, with nobody bothering us, doing, er, things we want to…'

I felt sure she was thinking along the same lines as me and it gave me something to look forward to.

'That sounds great,' I said. 'Can't wait.'

Chapter Twelve

The rehearsals intensified over the weekend and during the following days as I became a brass bander and this piece of music burrowed itself into my brain like an earworm.

I was waking up during the night with parts of it repeating in my head like a stuck record. I'd never practiced something so intensely since I'd done my College exams some years ago. It was both refreshing and annoyingly irritating at the same time.

On the Tuesday evening, I was fitted with a band stage jacket, resplendent in gold and red braiding across the lapels and cuffs together with a plain burgundy 'walking out' blazer and tie from the spares wardrobe.

Charlie assumed that I already had the remainder of their dress code comprising a white shirt, with trousers, socks, shoes and a bowtie all in black. I didn't have any of these items but a quick trip to the market in town over lunchtime the following day got me sorted out for a few quid.

Our Friday evening rehearsal was scheduled to start and finish earlier than normal so that we wouldn't over-do it the night before the contest. This meant I wouldn't be at home when Simms called round for his rent, so I decided to take the other option and call in at the newsagents on the way back from my shopping trip in town.

I'd previously popped in on occasions to grab a local paper, but this afternoon I took my time, noticing that there was a fine selection of top shelf adult reading that I hadn't seen before plus a rack of videos for rental on the other side.

I selected a couple of suitable mags and rolled a copy of the *Barnsley Chronicle* around them before walking over to glance at the blockbuster videos, clutching my bag of clothes parcels in my other hand, whilst the shopkeeper served an elderly customer with some fags.

'Ah've got sum more round back 'ere if tha's interested in vids,' he called to me, when the customer left the shop.

'What do you mean?' I asked, looking over at him.

He was a man in his forties, I guessed, with unkempt tatty dark hair and a three-day growth around his chin that stood out like magnetised iron filings.

'Bluey's, all imports from continent,' he said. 'They're the proper stuff, an' reet popular round here,' beckoning me to come behind the counter.

As I did, he opened a storeroom door where a metal shelved cabinet was stacked out with porno vids, all neatly numbered with a small white label along each of their spines.

'And how much are these?' I asked.

'Well, that's thing,' he said, sweeping one hand through his greasy hair and looking back at me.

'I'm not licensed for sellin' such items. But there's nothin' stoppin' me rentin' 'em, on quiet I mean. So, first one you rent costs a tenner but then when you want to swap it just bring it back an' next one will only be a fiver. That way everyone in club gets a chance of seein' all new stuff as I get it in.'

'Well actually, I've just come in to pay my rent…but seeing as you're asking, go on then, I'll take this one,' I said, picking up a video cassette numbered thirty-five.

'Right oh. I'll need to write a chit for tha rent an' so I'll put yer details on your video club membership at same time. Here's your card,' handing me a wallet-sized ticket with the number one hundred and thirty-three on it.

'If I'm not 'ere when you come again then just show that card to the missus if you want an exchange. She'll sort yer out.'

He pulled a tatty-looking notebook out from under the counter and wrote in it with a biro. 'Right, you're member number one hundred an' thirty three an' you've rented vid number thirty five.'

I gave him my address with my rent money plus the rest for my porn stash and daily paper. It was all relatively neat and tidy although I doubted that such records were kept for the benefit of the taxman, more for the use of the dodgy Simms who I guessed was also in on this little venture. Still, that wasn't my problem and armed with my reading and viewing material tucked inside the newspaper, I headed for the door.

As I opened it, I turned to say bye and stepped outside without looking, bumping straight into an old guy who was about to enter the shop. The video tumbled out from its hiding place onto the pavement between our feet.

'Oops I'm sorry,' I said, noticing that the guy was actually Archie, who had fixed my window glass. 'Didn't see you there, are you okay?' I asked, as I bent down and retrieved the video.

'Aye lad,' he replied. 'Tha must ha' bin thinkin' 'bout summat else. Ah see tha's a member of dirty Dave's club,' he added, pointing at the tape that I was tucking back inside the folded newspaper.

I could hardly deny it, so instead I just quietly replied, 'Yes,' simultaneously feeling a bit embarrassed.

'I'm just poppin' in mi sen for one fer this long weekend,' he replied. 'Wife likes a bit o' blue goin' on while I get 'er greased up for some action.'

'Well, whilst we're both here, let me settle up what I owe you,' I said, pulling out my wallet from my pocket. 'Sounds like you'll be having your hands full then over the weekend,' I smiled, whilst I tried to put the thought of a naked Archie out of my mind by counting out some notes.

'Hands full? Are tha callin' mi missus a fat cow then?' he asked.

'Er, no, I was only just saying, er, you might be busy,' I stammered, blushing.

His wrinkled features broke into a wide grin. 'Only pullin' yer plonker lad, tha's no need to get thi sen flust'ed. Tha's gorra laugh an' enjoy life when tha can. Tha'll be a long time dead when it comes knockin' fer yer.'

I nodded and smiled as I handed him the twenty-five pounds for his handiwork as well as his cheek. 'Thanks for doing that job for me,' I said. 'It was very good of you.'

'No bother,' he said. 'That's what neighbours are for. Mind you, if tha wants to borrow wife for an evenin' I might 'ave to charge more,' he laughed, before entering the shop and I headed back home, a new member of Dave's local home viewing club.

*

I was up bright and early on the Saturday morning as I put on my new shirt and tie, taking several attempts to secure a proper knot in it, before setting off for Barnstone. Everyone was gathered with a keen sense of eagerness and anticipation and we left the band room on a coach at ten o'clock, arriving at the venue some fifty-five minutes later.

I hadn't realised that Sheffield was such a sprawling conglomeration of industrial buildings, main roads and hills of dense housing, but the City Hall itself was a dazzling display of neo-classical architecture. Standing in its own stone-paved square, it had huge columns and steps leading up to the front entrance doors and was surrounded by smaller streets of commercial offices, shops and restaurants. The place would have looked perfectly at home in central London.

We pulled around to the rear of the building where a collection of coaches were already parked along the pavement and bandsmen clutching large instruments and cases milled around in small groups, some having a fag, others chatting with their colleagues and supporters.

'What happens now?' I asked Bill, who was sitting next to me on the coach.

'Charlie goes inside for the draw. Numbers are drawn out of a bag which tells us what order and roughly what time we'll be playing. There's eleven in our section, so with a start time of twelve thirty, it should all be over and done with by about four o'clock.'

Sure enough, Charlie returned twenty minutes later and yelled out, 'Number seven.'

That meant we had over two hours to kill before our appearance on stage. However, there was a strict no drinking beforehand rule in place and so instead we retreated to a pre-arranged venue at a nearby church hall to put in some last-minute practice, before returning and changing into our stage uniforms on the coach.

Once inside the City Hall, we had to sign our names on a registration sheet before being herded together backstage, where we could hear the band before us undertaking their performance. Then it was our turn and when we got onto the platform, I looked out into the magnificent art-deco style auditorium.

The place was packed to the rafters and unlike the recent venues I'd played at in Yorkshire, here the audience was buzzy, but disciplined and intent, many looking at the music score laid out across their knees. The atmosphere was tense and hot as I took my place behind the array of percussion instruments at the rear of the stage alongside Bill and we got ourselves ready.

I'd been told that the two adjudicators were 'blind' as they were listening and judging the piece from inside a closed timber framed box with a curtained front and which I could now see located in the middle of the auditorium floor.

In this way they didn't know the identities of the bands in advance and so could only judge each individual performance by what they heard. Seemed fair enough, I thought.

Then an old guy in a dinner suit and matching bowtie was on the microphone at the side of the stage, announcing that, 'Band number seven is on stage and ready at your signal, Adjudicators.'

A football whistle sounded in reply, which meant it was our time to start.

Silence descended around the auditorium as the lights dimmed and intense concentration wrapped itself around us on the stage like an invisible cloak. Despite my years of performing in public, I could hear my breathing coming out in laboured bursts. My heart was pounding away and under my jacket I could feel that I was sweating buckets, even though I'd not even hit anything yet.

Off we went into the thumping opening bars and the next fourteen minutes or so was just a blur. I remember us reaching the end and the final thrilling chords with an intense feeling of emotion flooding through my chest.

In response, the previously placid audience went wild, cheering, whistling and clapping, as we stood to take our collective bow. I now understood what Colin had meant about grown men being in tears and I was close to them myself.

Many, many hours of intense rehearsal time had been reduced to a brief performance and now it was all over. I felt elated because of the reception we were getting from the crowd, yet at the same time deflated because they liked us and we had no encore to give them. We'd done our bit for them as well as doing all we could for ourselves.

The relief was palpable amongst the lads as we came off the stage, but the result of our efforts was out of our hands and had yet to be determined.

However, now we could relax and it was time for a gallon of beer. After loading up the coach and a quick change into our burgundy blazers, we all crowded into the venue's back bar. It was noisy and heaving with bandsmen and supporters and beer was disappearing faster than a brewery with major plumbing problems in its supply pipes.

I was enjoying the chat and banter immensely and presently it was my turn to squeeze through the thronging crowd and go to the bar to get a round in.

After being served, I clutched the four jug-handled glasses with both hands and turned round swiftly, inadvertently bumping the arm of a large guy in a black blazer. The words 'Brodsworth Brass' were emblazoned in gold on his breast pocket in my direct line of sight, whilst the best part of the pint he was holding spilled down his trouser legs due to my clumsiness.

'Oh, I'm sorry,' I said, as I glanced up at him, before then turning pale with shock.

It was the face of Big Bert, he of the Reeny husband connection, who I'd last seen fighting his way through a mob of fish-gutters in the miners' club, intent on finding out why my guitar had been left at his house overnight and no doubt wanting to express his opinion about my sharing the marital bed with his wife. But he was glaring down at the big stain appearing on his grey slacks whilst trying to wipe it off with his shovel-like right hand.

'Steady on lad,' he said, staring at his leg. 'That's good ale tha's wasting.'

My God, he hadn't recognised me I thought, and I so tried to keep up the pretence.

'Let mi get thee a fresh pint,' I said, in a terrible Yorkshire accent, turning my back to him and shouting out across the bar for another beer. 'Tek one o' these, ah've just gorrem in,' I said, sliding one of my glasses to the side without looking round as he continued mopping at his trouser leg with a bar towel.

'Thy band played well today,' he said, over my shoulder. 'Looks like you're fieldin' some good new players this year.'

'Aye,' I said, avoiding turning my head to him as my legs trembled away beneath me. I figured that he'd worked out who our band were because of our burgundies as everyone else here was dressed in black or navy blues, or in civvies.

'Any 'ow, better get back to me mates, I'll si thi...' I said.

I turned away from him clutching my round of beers as the glasses wobbled in my hand and I let out a big sigh of relief. I didn't know if I'd got away with it but I wasn't hanging around to find out. Still, I was sure that Mick and my new bandmates would come to my assistance if the worst happened.

Presently, word went round the bar that the results were about to be announced and so everyone emptied their glasses and traipsed back into the auditorium in excited anticipation. Only the top two places would qualify for the London final.

The elderly MC appeared on stage again with some papers in his hand and after giving his thanks to the organisers and the audience, he began to read out the results in reverse order.

Fifth, fourth, and third place were announced in turn as representatives from each placed band clambered onto the stage for their consolation prizes, bravely smiling for a photo and knowing that the cheque they were being handed wouldn't even cover the cost of their coach hire for today's event.

'In second place,' said the announcer, 'with a score of one hundred and ninety-four points, is the band who played…number seven, Barnstone Colliery!'

Shit, that was us and I was swept up by a roar of cheers and whistles from the guys all around me, as the audience clapped and yelled out their approval.

The winner was the apparent favourite, an outfit called Black Dykes, who contrary to their name, were all white men and this fact confused the hell out of me. One of these days I'll get the hang of this bloody English language. But right then, that didn't matter. We'd qualified and it was celebration time, so we downed more beer like condemned men waiting for the hangman.

After being kicked out of the City Hall bar to make the venue ready for an evening event, everyone clambered back onto the coach in very high spirits bound for the Colliers Rest.

'*We are going to Lon-don, we are going to Lon-don, da da da dah*'- the lads chanted as they conga'd and cheered, showing their bare backsides out of the coach windows to the disgruntled groups from Brodsworth, Huddersfield and other distant parts of Yorkshire.

I sat back and laughed at their antics, as we made our way out of the City and back towards the Dearne Valley villages. Here was a happy crew and they knew it. Their hard work had paid off and I felt honoured to be sharing in their celebrations even though I knew my head would be suffering in the morning. But so what?

Charlie was standing in the coach aisle, apparently about to start singing, but before he did so he leant over towards me.

'What did yer think then, lad?' he asked.

'It was an amazing experience, I have to confess,' I said. 'Do you think that one day your band will feature some electric guitars as well?' I asked, optimistically.

He looked puzzled for a second and then his face turned serious. 'Not in my lifetime it won't. It's bad enough 'avin' to put up with fuckin' drummers,' he said, before bursting into ribald laughter.

Chapter Thirteen

Thumping drumbeats banged painfully with relentless regularity against the inside of my skull the next morning. Lying on my sofa, I tried several times to rouse my body from a state of near death but without success.

It was nearly eleven o'clock and I'd told Jenny that I'd be round at hers for Sunday lunch, which religiously began at one. So, time to get shaping I thought, but for some reason my legs refused to work and I looked down at my feet to try and make some sense of why things were not responding as they should.

Jesus may have risen from the dead on this very day according to the Bible, but at least he didn't have to cope with having heavy duty gaffer tape tied around his ankles.

It had all been part of an initiation ceremony last night by those impish band lads back at the Colliers. At some point, way past normal closing time, the cheeks of my arse had been ceremoniously waxed with said tape, before they had trussed me up and dropped me off at my front door, still minus my trousers, which I last saw hanging over the pool table lightshade. If I hadn't been so drunk and laughing like a hyena at the time, I might have taken offence. But it was all good fun and they were a wild bunch of lads for sure when the mood took them.

I managed to crawl off the sofa and into the kitchen for a knife. Suitably freed from my shackles, I then swallowed a couple of pints of water together with four paracetemols before climbing into the bath upstairs.

Forty-five minutes later I was cleaned and preened and on my way to see Jenny, still with a hazy head but nevertheless looking reasonably presentable.

Jenny lived over the other side of Conisbrough, which entailed two bus journeys from my place in Highfield and I cursed myself again for not having a car. The sooner I got my own wheels the better life would become.

Her mum Dorothy was a lovely woman, very homely and comforting in her ways and so at the bus station in Mexborough I bought her some flowers as well as a chocolate egg for Jenny. On a bright sunny Easter Sunday morning it seemed to be the right thing to do.

I arrived at her parents' house and, as usual, Walter gave me his cautious, but distant, friendly greeting. We sat around the dinner table enjoying a delicious roast lamb and all the trimmings, with Yorkshire Puddings of course, and I regaled everyone about how we'd got on at the band competition the previous day, minus the loss of my trousers and beautician treatment bits.

Jenny and her mum were both thrilled at our success, but Walter glanced at me curiously as I supposed any father in his position would do. I figured he was a man suffering inner turmoil, with one watchful eye on his little girl who he wouldn't let grow up, even though she was now aged twenty and a fully-developed beautiful young woman, and the other firmly on me – a prime example of a lecherous, reckless and feckless wanderer, with intentions strictly dishonorable towards his precious daughter.

Both he and Dorothy naturally wanted the best for Jenny and for her to be happy in all aspects of her life. Jenny seemed happy enough being with me, as I was with her, but whether I was considered to be suitable material as far as Walter was concerned was clearly still open to question.

However, Jenny did look stunning this afternoon and I couldn't help just ogling her. She'd already told me that she was borrowing the car for the rest of the day and so we could go off and do our own thing.

'Are you at the club later on today Walter?' I asked, making some conversation.

I already knew the answer.

'Aye. It's family afternoon for members an' their kids,' he replied. 'So we've got games an' suchlike for them before the evenin' entertainment kicks off. Some nice country singer tonight. None o' that rowdy crap that you lot like to play.'

'But you said Jamie had done well,' interjected his wife. 'Said you wanted to book him again because the locals liked him.'

'Well, we'll have to see about that,' he muttered. 'I'll check on when we've got a free slot comin' up,' before changing the subject. 'An' mind 'ow you treat that clutch Jenny if you're usin' the car. Ah've just 'ad it replaced last week an' it cost a pretty penny an 'all.'

We finished eating and Walter filled his pipe from the tobacco pouch before going out into the back garden for a smoke, whilst I helped the ladies with the washing up.

Then at last we were on our own. I thanked Dorothy for a lovely meal and I sat back in the passenger seat as Jenny reversed the Austin Metro out of their drive.

'Where are we going?' I asked. 'There's always my place, if you'd like to, you know…?'

'Wait and see,' she said, teasing me. 'I want to show you some of our local sights and it's a beautiful afternoon for some fresh air.'

We drove through the winding lanes for about twenty minutes and eventually parked up at Wentworth. This was a glorious old stately house, surrounded by parkland and woods and where the spring flowers spilled out in a riot of yellow, pink and lilac colours as far as we could see. It gave anything in the posh parks in London a run for their money. We walked hand-in-hand past the colossal front of the building and finding a shaded area in the trees, we sat on the grass and I was all over her like a rash in a rush.

'Stop it,' she squealed. 'Someone will see us.'

But it didn't deter me and I continued my quest as I nuzzled at her neck.

'It's time I, er, you know, showed you how much I, er, feel about you,' I whispered, in between kissing and pecking at her shoulders as she giggled and squirmed slightly beside me.

Her legs were firm and slim and poked teasingly out of her denim skirt, beckoning me like a Venus fly trap, although I wasn't sure that was the most appropriate picture to have in my head at that moment.

'Time and a place,' she said. 'The time's maybe right, the place, well, I'm not so sure.'

Well, I was damned sure. What could be better than making love to my gorgeous English lady in the midst of this wonderful historic country mansion on a beautiful Spring afternoon? But just as I was about to launch full tilt, the sounds of children shouting and laughing made us both sit up and brought a sudden halt to proceedings. An Easter Egg hunt was under way and a family with a couple of kids ambled by about fifty yards away from us and we both realised that our romantic interlude wasn't going to work.

'Come on, let's go somewhere else,' she said, wiping bits of grass from her skirt as we stood up and walked back to the car.

We drove a short distance, up a small hill then she turned the car along a track into a wooded ridge overlooking the valley, but unseen from the road. I wondered how she knew about this spot and if she'd been here before, but it didn't matter in the overall scheme of things.

We both knew why we were there: no prying eyes and no noisy kids and so we got to passionate grips with each other like the overgrown lovesick teenagers we really were at heart.

Attempting to have sex in the confined space of a small car was a first for me and we twisted and turned and bent our limbs into all kinds of shapes to try and get things done. At one stage Jenny was laid across both front seats and as I climbed above her in order to hump her, as we'd politely say back home, I accidently knocked the handbrake lever beneath her thighs.

In response, the car lurched and then rolled backwards a few feet off the track. As we scrambled to get up from the seats, it collided into a tree trunk, knocking us both forward and making a loud crunching noise at the rear.

'Oh no,' she cried. 'Dad will go mad, now. What am I going to tell him?' as she reached down by the pedals to retrieve her discarded knickers and pulled on the driver's door handle at the same time. But the door wouldn't budge.

'Why won't this door open?' she yelled, pulling at the locking lever and the handle, as it remained firmly shut.

'Let me try from the outside,' I offered gallantly, trying to tuck my love tackle back into my jeans and getting out of the passenger door. At least my side of the car opened okay and I scrambled round to the driver side via the back of the vehicle. Oh hell, there was a big vee-shaped dent in the bumper where the car leant back against the tree and I realised that we'd need to get it back up onto the level ground of the track to be able to drive it away. I pulled furiously at the driver's door but it remained stubbornly firm.

'You put your feet on the panel from the inside and push and I'll pull from the outside,' I yelled.

She did as I'd suggested and I pulled on the door with all my strength. We heard a screeching, grating noise as it suddenly flew open and the weight pushed me backwards onto my arse. The door hung limply at an odd angle from the car body with me still clutching the handle and it became clear that we'd damaged the hinges in our efforts to open it.

'Oh shite,' shrieked Jenny. 'What have we done? I'm going to get killed now.'

I stood up, one hand still grasping the door handle, to take a closer look. What a mess. Why couldn't we have gone to my place as I'd originally suggested, picked up a bottle of wine and spent the rest of the day in bed? Even if I did live in the shadow of an unsightly pit stack and amongst a set of neighbours who didn't miss a thing, at least we'd have a car that didn't now look like a demolition derby participant.

Jenny was in tears as I tried to comfort her. 'Let's see if we can get the car back onto the track,' I suggested. 'At least then we might be able to drive it.'

She tried the engine, which started fine, but the rear wheels just spun deeper into the soft earth beneath them and the car remained stubbornly reposed at its thirty-degree angle, lodged firmly up against the tree.

'It's not working,' she shrieked. 'I'm going to have to call dad. Or a garage or something. But there's nowhere to call from round here. We can't leave it with the door hanging off in case some little shithead sets it on fire.'

'We could do that,' I suggested. 'Tell the police it was stolen and then someone's gone and set in on fire. That would probably work.'

'Stolen from where?' she asked. 'And then how did we get up here, you idiot?' Yes, she was right, that was me being plain stupid.

'I've got an idea,' I said. 'If you don't feel safe on your own up here, then walk down to the village, whilst I look after the car. Find a phone box and call my friend Terry. Tell him you're with me and that we need his help with his lad to pull the car back up onto the track. Then we can worry about the door.' It was not the best of plans, but in the circumstances, it seemed better than nothing.

Jenny reluctantly agreed and so I gave her the phone number and watched as she walked down the track out of the woods and then down the lane back towards Barnburgh village in the distance. I sat on the passenger seat cursing my bad luck and still contemplating setting light to the car, more out of frustration that despite my best efforts, I still hadn't managed to have any sex.

About an hour and a half later, I heard voices and was relieved to see her return. Terry and Mick were following behind her and they carried a tow-rope together with a pulley and some winching gear.

'Bloody ell,' Terry laughed, when he saw me and the car. 'She weren't kiddin'. What the 'ell were tha doin' lad?'

'Er, I was trying to practice my driving, not being used to this type of car and I accidentally reversed over the bank and then we couldn't open the driver's door and er…'

'A likely bloody tale,' smirked Mick. 'Now shift outa way an' gimme a bit of space.'

He bent down and threaded the tow rope through a hook at the front of the car then rigged up the winch and pulley block around a tree on the opposite side of the track.

He started winding on the winch and the rope became taut and Terry leaned inside the car to hold onto the steering wheel whilst I pushed from the rear. It creaked and groaned a little but then started to move and after a few seconds we had it back on the horizontal. Jenny looked and recoiled with horror at the dented wedge in the back bumper and the lop-sided door, hanging limply from the frame like a broken limb.

'Right,' said Mick, after he inspected the door hinges and making a quick scan of the rest of the vehicle. 'There's one 'inge that's bust its pin an' bushings and t'other's all bent. That's why the door won't shut. They'll need some work an' that dent should be able to get pulled out from th'arse end pretty easily. I reckon the garage I use in Thurnscoe will do it for about a hundred an' fifty quid all in an' it'll be ready in a few days.'

Jenny started to weep again at this news.

'It's not that simple,' I explained. 'It's her dad's car. He'll go mental and we can't tell him...'

Mick looked at us sympathetically. 'In that case, it's plan B and I can probably 'ave it ready by tomorrow mornin'. I'll do the work on it at fitter's shop at the pit this evenin' an' 'ave it back round to yours before I start my regular shift. Wi've got all the tools to straighten them 'inges an' deal wi' dent, plus some weldin' gear if we need it. There might be some minor crackin' on paintwork but as it's white we may 'ave a match. How's that sound then?'

'Fantastic. You're a life saver,' I said.

Jenny agreed. 'I'll have to phone mum and tell her that I'm staying at yours tonight,' she said. 'There's a chance I may even get back in the morning with the car before dad gets up. So he might be none the wiser.'

Smiling, she said, 'Thank you,' evidently relieved that plan B seemed a much better alternative course of action.

Terry just stared at me. 'Next time sort yer courtin' episodes out somewhere a bit more accommodating. That goes fer you too lass,' he said.

'Thanks Terry,' I replied. 'We will and in the meantime let me pay you something for coming out and helping us.'

'Nonsense,' he replied. 'Just follow us slowly down to pit yard now. If you think anythin' is dodgy on the car, flash the lights an' we'll stop,' he said, tying the driver door to the car frame with a length of twine. 'Bloody things I 'ave to do and on an Easter Sunday too,' he said.

We did as we were told and a few minutes later we were driving through the gates of Barnstone Colliery. We followed Terry as he drove round to the back of a corrugated steel workshop. Mick produced a bunch of keys and slid the door open before turning and guiding us into the building.

'Now, get thi sen off-site pretty quick an' especially you lass,' he said. 'Some o' older men are superstitious about seein' women hangin' around pit yard. It gives 'em a bad feelin' that summat's gone wrong.'

Turning to me he said, 'I'll work on the motor then drop it at your house. I know where it is an' I'll put keys through letterbox, as no doubt you'll be up to your taters, er, I mean you won't want to be disturbed,' he smiled, before looking over at his dad. 'The things I bloody 'ave to do as well,' he muttered.

'Thanks,' I said. 'I'll square up with you on Wednesday night at band practice.'

We left them with the car as instructed and walked slowly back towards Goldthorpe and Highfield as I held Jenny's hand and reassured her.

'They're nice guys,' I said. 'They'll do alright. It'll be fine, you'll see.'

I was now anticipating a night of passion for us and with Jenny not having to drive anywhere we stopped at a pub for some drinks whilst she called her mum. Then we dropped into the Spar for a couple of bottles of wine and picked up the take-away set meal for two with extra prawn crackers from the Chinese on the high street.

Settled back at home on my threadbare sofa, she seemed a bit more relieved with things and I went to put some music on as she arranged our supper onto plates. I picked up a Dire Straits tape, before thinking that maybe in the circumstances it was not the best named choice and so opted instead for some Eagles country rock. Eventually we were able to laugh about the events of the day.

'You really know how to treat a lady and show her a good time, don't you?' she teased, as we finished our food and chatted, gradually getting drunk on the cheap Frascati.

I kissed her gently as I whispered softly, 'Well, I do try my best,' before taking her hand and the rest of the wine and leading her upstairs.

'Now, where were we before I went and balls-ed up the car?' I teased, as she squealed at my touch.

It was time for me to give her my best intentions. And so I did, and more than once.

Chapter Fourteen

'Now, are tha ready to see what a real job looks like?' asked Mick, as he pocketed the cash.

I'd just paid him for fixing Jenny's car as he put his tuba back in its case and though he was reluctant to take any money from me, I insisted that he should, forcing fifty pounds into his meaty right hand.

He'd done a great job on the repair and whilst I did hear him push the keys through the letter box during the early hours of Easter Monday morning, he was correct in that I was otherwise occupied at the time.

A quick inspection of the vehicle in the daylight showed no obvious damage and the driver's door opened and closed smoothly. Jenny had been delighted in what the previous evening had produced - and in more ways than one.

'What do you mean?' I replied. 'I've got a real job. Well, at least one that suits me for the time being.'

College had finished for a couple of weeks for the Easter break, but I had a pile of material to get ready for the Summer Term and the end of year exams, so I was reasonably busy on stuff even though there was no tuition to be done.

'Ever been down a pit?' he asked.

'No,' I said, and regretted what I knew would be coming next.

'Well, if tha's not at College this week an' tha doesn't 'ave a second job drivin' taxis like mi dad, then come an' do a shift wi' us. I'm on afters from tomorrow so I'll take tha wi' me as a visitor. I'm allowed to do that as a Deputy, so long as you're supervised at all times. You'll understand a bit more about what it means to really work as a team,' he advised.

After what he'd done for us I was hardly in a position to refuse and so I agreed to his request, realising that I was going to be educated in his daunting and mysterious world.

The following day Mick picked me up from home shortly before lunchtime and we drove to Barnstone Colliery.

I was shown to the locker room and given a pair of boots and a hard hat plus a set of overalls from the spares cupboard to put on over my undies. Then I was taken to collect a head lamp, connected by a long lead to a heavy battery which fitted around my waist on a belt and Mick handed me two metal discs with numbers on them.

'Give the brass one to that guy when he opens the cage door for you,' pointing to a stocky, grey-haired bloke.

'Then give him the other silver one when you come back up. That way, if I'm not around for any reason, we'll know tha's not still wandrin' around somewhere down below like a lost soul.'

About thirty men all dressed as I was, harangued and bantered with each other as they crowded around the cage. This was a steel sided elevator attached to a cable which would take us down some seven hundred feet beneath where I was presently standing, quaking in my borrowed boots.

Despite my bravado, I was about to enter an alien, forbidding world where nasty things happened and quite frequently as well, and whatever possessed normal sensible men to do this job was beyond me. When I'd mentioned to Jenny that I was going underground she wasn't at all happy about it.

I gave my disc to the banksman as he patted me down to ensure that I had no matches or cigs and we crowded into the cage where the steel mesh door was then closed in front of us. A bell sounded and then we were being lowered – and fast.

My ears popped with the pressure changes and musty air whistled up around my face as we descended into the gloom. The men either turned their heads or looked down to avoid their lamps shining directly into the eyes of their colleagues as we grew accustomed to the darkness. Then the cage slowed and stopped and we got out at the shaft bottom into a tunnel entrance.

This wasn't so bad at first glance, I thought. The roof was well-lit by running lights on cables and it looked a bit like the tube tunnels back in London, with a wide thoroughfare leading off into the distance and a set of small rail tracks at one side, on which stood a line of metal tubs filled with coal.

'Now we 'ave to walk for about 'alf an hour,' said Mick.

'What? That's over a mile,' I said.

'Aye, that's where coil is nowadays. Any further an' they'd give us a little train to ride on like they do at some other pits. But 'ere it's Shanks's pony.'

'What, we have to get on a horse?' I asked.

'No, we 'ave to walk,' before I heard him quietly mutter, 'thick bastard,' to himself under his breath.

We passed through a couple of steel doors placed across the tunnel which acted as an air lock and one of them had to be closed before the other could be opened.

'That's to keep fresh air movin' through pit bottom,' Mick said. 'Stops any gas from buildin' up as well as bein' useful to us in other ways,' he added.

'Like what?' I asked.

'Helps us to keep breathin' for one,' he joked.

Jesus, how can you joke like that down here? We walked steadily and the tunnel height gradually narrowed as we came towards the end, whilst the noise, heat and dust grew more oppressive.

There was much less overhead light here and the misty yellow beams from our headlamps were speckled with coal dust as they bounced across the side walls and tunnel roof. The air tasted stale and smelled musty and I felt I was crunching on bits of grit, so I tried to keep my mouth closed.

We clambered up into an opening at the side of the tunnel, or driveway as I was told it was called, from which a conveyor belt was poised over several empty wagon tubs waiting to be filled. I tried to stand up straight but bashed my helmet against the roof.

The height was about four feet and I had to half-crouch and waddle as I followed Mick into the heart of where his operations and miners lay. It was pitch black, lit only by the beams of our lamps and we were crawling behind a long battery of hydraulic metal legs, lined up like a legion of Roman soldiers on an ancient battlefield. Steel ramps extended from each one and lay up against the roof. In front of them I could see a black wall of coal and a fearsome looking steel wheel with teeth, which was tethered to a mass of cables and ready to strike into action.

As we crawled, with me staring at Mick's backside ahead of me, I could hear small rock movements and as I twisted my head to the right, my lamp picked out a sight which made me gasp. Bits of the roof were falling off in clumps and I thought we'd be buried alive.

'Mick,' I yelled. 'The damned roof is caving in.'

'Relax,' he said, laughing and carrying on without turning round to me. 'It's supposed to do that.'

'But I can see it,' I wailed, terrified that I was about to be entombed alive.

He stopped and swivelled round on his haunches to face me. For a big guy in such a confined space, he was as agile as a cat and he lifted the lamp off from his helmet as he tried to calm my fears.

'Look over there,' shining his lamp at the coal face. 'As the cutter moves forward through coil seam, the chocks move wi' it an' support the roof. Then gradually we let it come down naturally behind us.'

He shone the beam over to my right side where pieces of the unsupported roof were breaking away and making disturbing cracking noises.

'It sounds daft but that's 'ow we mine coil these days an' it's a lot safer than it used to be, so just relax,' he added.

How could I relax when I felt I could be buried alive at any moment? However, my thoughts were distracted by sudden shouts coming from the far end of the section. They were followed by the roar of an engine starting up and rattling my eardrums as the steel cutter started to spin and shear through the coal, causing huge chunks to fall onto the conveyor belt beneath it.

Mick continued crawling calmly and sedately as if he didn't have a care in the world and I followed him through the horrendous din and the dust. As we neared the end of the chocks line, I heard a man's voice yelling out, 'Keep that fuckin' belt moving', above all the noise.

I couldn't see anyone in the darkness and instead Mick guided me down from the face into a clearing at the side. I sat crouched, terrified, just feet away from where the steel beast swept along the face shearing away at the rock and producing a mighty cloud of dust and mist from the water sprayer pipe above it.

It was like I was in hell. The sound was deafening and I couldn't breathe properly for the dust. Nor could I see anything in the near darkness and to cap it all they were letting the roof fall in around us. I tried desperately to quell my fear, but it was no good and I indicated to Mick that I needed to throw up, but he just laughed.

'Here,' he shouted, throwing me his canteen of water. 'Take a big swig followed by some deep breaths.'

I sat in sweaty panic trying to calm my heartbeat and breathing slowly for a couple of minutes as the machine worked its way back down the coal face and away from us before coming to a halt.

My ears were ringing and whilst I could feel the draught of forced air blowing out from a ventilation pipe above our heads, it was still like being in a sauna.

'Ave tha fetched a lackey wi' yer today Mick?' asked a burly guy in a dirty vest, his torso and face blackened with dust and his shoulders and arms glistening with sweat.

'This is Reevesy,' said Mick, looking over at me as he introduced us. 'He's the ripper in charge of this face. There's two other lads wi' him plus a fitter an' a sparky lookin' after 'lectrics on that machine. Whatever tha does, don't get 'im singin'. We'll never shut the fucker up otherwise.'

'Pleased to meet you Mr Reeves, er, well, I think I am,' I said. 'I'm just a visitor. And a brief one at that.'

The collier laughed.

'It's just Reeves, like in Jim,' he replied. 'Welcome to my world lad, the best five-star workplace tha can find. It gets much worse after this.'

We sat for a few minutes as I regained my composure and then I turned to Mick.

'How the hell do people put up with being down here?' I asked him.

'It's a lot better than it used to be,' he said. 'Before we had all this machinery, men would lie on their sides wi' pickaxes for hours on end, 'acking that coil out. And wooden props was all they 'ad to hold up the roof above their 'eads.'

I struggled to picture what he'd just described. To me, what I was currently witnessing was bad enough.

'If you think this is bad, imagine what mi granddad an' 'is generation 'ad to put up with when they wor workin' miners. They were men alright, a breed apart.'

I looked up from my vantage point at the shiny black seam. It had a rare beauty of its own, glistening in places where the water droplets from the cutter spray clung to it and sparkled like diamonds.

It resembled an underground river that had somehow been frozen in time and which called out to you seductively, drawing you in towards it like a siren. It reminded me of the stories we were told in school about the fabled Greek river of Styx connecting the Earth with the underworld, the boundary between the land of the living and the subterranean kingdom of the dead beneath it.

Whilst the tale had enthralled me as a child, now I knew it was no fable as I gazed up again at the coalface in front of me. I was living the story and it scared the crap out of me. I was in Hades or whatever the hell it was called these days and I just wanted to get back to the land of the living. But then, things got worse.

'Now, tha can make thi sen useful an' do yer bit for our production figures,' said Mick, handing me a short-handled shovel. 'They're gonna be movin' that cutter forward in a few minutes, so all the coal lumps that's dropped between these props needs shoveling back onto belt below it, double quick time. Here you go, follow me.'

I did as I was told. I couldn't stand up straight in the confined space and it was too uncomfortable bending half double, so I crouched on my knees behind the hydraulic ramps and tried to collect what lumps of coal I could see.

There wasn't enough room to twist fully round and I kept knocking my helmet off as it crashed against a prop or up against the roof when I tried to stretch my back. I cursed and after a couple of minutes I was panting like a prairie dog, my shoulders aching and crying out for me to stop.

Ahead of me, Mick moved along the face on his knees, shoveling away effortlessly, like he was clearing out a child's sandpit in his back garden.

'Come on lad, keep bloody shovelin',' shouted out Reeves behind me. 'Wife wants ter go to Spain this year for us 'oliday's an' rate you're goin', she'll be thee'er on her own.' He paused for a second. 'Mind you, that's no bad thing...might even insist she goes for two weeks this time.'

After ten minutes I could stand it no longer and I crawled back to the edge of the driveway, feeling coal grit crunching in my teeth and my eyes streamed from the dust and the sweat running into them. I was coughing and choking, so Reeves handed me his bottle and I took a big gulp of his cold sweetened tea. It was the best thing I'd ever tasted.

As I regained my breath, I looked down the driveway and saw two lamp beams dancing and swaying in the distance. Presently a couple of guys came up to us, one holding a box on a strap over his shoulder and the other carrying a wooden tripod.

'Bloody 'ell, it's balls-up Barry an' little Willy Walker,' shouted Reeves in a greeting. 'Ave tha cocked up on yer measurin' agin lads? We've gone decimal now tha knows.'

The two surveying guys just smiled and said they wouldn't be too long as they set up their gear and one shouted out that he'd be all finished in a couple of minutes.

'Aye, that's what yer wife's allers complainin' about when ah nip round an' see her,' replied Reeves. 'Good job she has me to fall back on.'

As he wandered back to the coalface he sung out, 'Move those sweet lips a little closer to tha phone,' before adding, 'and spread your legs a little wider for my bone…'

I smiled as I listened and watched these men banter and cajole each other as if to somehow turn their attention away from the horrible place they were in. It was indeed a world on its own down here.

Far above us in the real place I had grown up in and was used to, folk would be getting on with their everyday lives without realising that below their feet men like these sweated and toiled, as they had done for centuries.

Eventually the cutter was back in place against the seam and it roared back into life. Mick returned, made some notes in his pocketbook and we left Reeves and his crew to it.

'Now we've got two other stops to make further on up the next drive,' he said. 'These are in far worse condition so tha'll probably get a bit dirty.'

We walked on in the dim light down an incline for about four hundred yards. The air was hot and stale and I almost retched in response. I was going to ask Mick what the men did for toilet facilities underground as I hadn't seen any signs for 'Gents' but the smell answered my question.

We reached the end of the drive where three men were busy assembling a similar set up across the coal face, with a long conveyor belt stretching back up the incline where we had just come down. Mick spoke to them for a few minutes as I waited, trying to breathe in small gasps.

I could see that the coal seam here was much thinner than on the previous section we'd visited. Barely two and a half feet from top to bottom with about six inches of it lying in foul-smelling water which pooled at one corner. A mechanical pump chugged away to try and remove it, pushing the water along a pulsating canvas pipeline.

As I followed the pipe with my lamp beam, I could see that it led back up the incline where we had just walked down and where the water discharged itself in irregular spurts. I realised it would just seep away to eventually make its way back down here again. These guys were having to push water uphill.

'This face is nearin' run-out or what we call exhaustion,' Mick explained to me. 'See how it's just turning to shale and muck here,' as he pointed out the duller grey rock in the beam of our lamps. 'Just a couple more weeks left 'ere at best an' we'll 'ave to pull out of this section fer good.'

He handed me his note-pack and told me to wait as he crawled up the face to where I could see several other lamp beams in the distance. When he returned a few minutes later he looked like he'd been in a mud bath, panting to catch his breath as he paused to make his notes.

The motor was started up and once again my ears rang out from the noise of the deafening shearer. I thought I was familiar with loud noises by playing my guitar at full amp volume, but this was something else. The sound seemed to travel up through my bones and rattle against the inside of my skull.

I followed him around to the other parts of the pit under his watch for the remainder of the shift. Some sections had been abandoned and stood as eerily quiet and ghostly black chambers where he tested for gas, whilst others were being used as temporary storage places for machinery and props. Here he checked each of the roof supports before nodding his head and making some more notes.

Eventually we headed back to Reeves's section, stopping to let a line of coal tubs pulled by a small electric locomotive go past us. He made his final checks and notes then I was thankful and relieved to hear it was time to head back to the shaft bottom and out.

I questioned Mick as we made our way back along the tunnel to the cage, trying to understand why men would be willing to do this work.

'It's just in our blood,' he said. 'If you come from families or communities who 'ave worked in pits for generations, then you're just part of it an' it becomes part of you. It's a peculiar type of bond we all 'ave. In our world you don't live your life alone, you live it for and with other people.'

I nodded and thought about his words as we walked in the darkness.

'Minin' sounds a grim job, but it's a great feelin' when you've got a good set of lads around yer,' he said. 'I've worked in three pits round 'ere an' once you get to know the people you're with, there's nothin' like it. Even puttin' up with Reeeve's crap singin' all the bloody time.'

'I can agree with that,' I said. 'The grim job bit, I mean.'

'We've no airs an' graces an' everyone's up for a laugh an' some piss-taking. You've got to get on wi' folk because we rely on each other, sometimes to save our lives. But how long we will last for as an industry, I just don't know,' he said. 'Coil is in serious decline. We tried to stop it a few years back wi' big strike, but it just didn't work.'

'I remember seeing that stuff on the TV news,' I replied. 'It looked like one long pitched battle was going on with the cops all the time.'

'It wor a bad time then,' he agreed. 'But don't believe all of what tha saw on telly. We 'ad nothin' an' the dispute split families an' friends apart like nothing we'd ever known. It's 'ard trying to be comrades when you've no money coming in an' starvin' kids to feed.'

'That must have been a tough time for everyone round here,' I said.

'It wor,' he answered. 'We 'ad to collect food parcels from welfare club every week an' rely on mi mum an' dad for a decent meal on a Sunday.'

'How long did that go on for?' I asked, aware that I was treading on sensitive ground here with him.

'Over a year,' he said. 'We thought we'd win but we were wrong. Eventually we went back to work, still with our 'eads held high, but with our hearts beaten an' our pockets empty.'

'I didn't realise it had lasted that long,' I said. 'After going through all that, do you think you'd ever go on strike again Mick?'

'That's a good question,' he replied. 'We were proud to 'ave done what we did, an' always will be, but pride doesn't keep you alive when you're up to your bollocks in debt. As mi dad allers says, pride comes before a fall.'

He hadn't answered my question directly, but I could see how Mick got his philosophy on living from Terry, who had given me a similar account of what really mattered the most in life that morning he'd picked me up from the cop station in Rotherham.

'Well, having seen it for myself, I don't think I could do the job,' I said, thinking of my own folks and the labour they did back on the family farmland. Yes, they worked long days, especially in the summer months and for not a lot of reward, but at least they were out in the open all day long and I said so to him.

He just laughed. 'Aye, I can understand that. Lots of men like to 'ave creative hobbies that they can think about whilst they're down here. They'll do things like painting or, as you know, like me wi' band. We love our music an' it takes us to another place. Other lads like nature an' grow stuff on allotments or keep pigeons. Anythin' to do wi' the wider qualities of just being alive an' enjoying the fresh air.'

As we reached the pit bottom area, other miners on the same shift were gathering round, waiting for the cage to descend and when it did, we all huddled together inside it. The close scrum of dirty, sweat-stained and smelly men was enough to make me retch, but I held my breath as best I could and looked down and concentrated on my boots as a distraction.

We were winched upwards and the sudden appearance of the evening's summer sunshine made me squint as we emerged, whilst the fresh air was invigorating and I breathed it in deeply, immensely grateful to be out of the blackened depths of the earth.

I handed back my metal tally and my lamp and after a hot shower it felt wonderful to put on my normal clothes again, before we went across to the Colliers for a couple of beers.

'And yes,' said Mick, 'We do enjoy our ale. It's only thing proven to get that dust outa yer throat.'

I didn't disagree as I thought about the working lives of the men I'd just seen. Men who had done this job week in, week out, for years. I glanced out of the pub window as passing cars slowed down to turn right into the pit yard and I realised they were more miners coming in to do their night shift.

It also remined me that I hadn't had my dinner yet, or tea as they called it in these parts, and I was starving.

So after a couple of pints, I said goodnight and thanks to Mick for an interesting day and walked back home, grateful to be breathing in clean air before picking up my regular ginger chilli beef with fried rice and spring rolls from Wing Lees.

Eating my food in front of the telly, I started to nod-off despite it only being ten o'clock and then as I walked upstairs my legs and back ached in places where I didn't know I had muscles.

I tried to get comfortable in bed and lying on my side, I imagined holding a pick in front of me and chopping away at a coal face for hours on end in the darkness, all the time resisting the overwhelming feeling of being choked and smothered by the layers of rock above me. Even the bedroom ceiling eight feet above my bed threatened to close in and stifle me.

Eventually I had to get up, pulling the curtains back a little and opening the window by three inches. The cool night air smelled of coal dust but the comfort of the slight breeze against my cheek and the soft orange glow of the streetlight made me thankful that at least I was on the surface of the earth tonight instead of beneath it. Somewhere below me, hundreds of men toiled away in the hidden depths, enabling me to switch on the lights whenever I wanted to or watch the telly whilst eating my Chinese or turn up the amp when I played my guitar.

It made me think about how much I'd taken for granted in our modern world and how little I'd cared for people in those occupations which had made it all possible.

Without doubt, I was now in awe of their unremitting labour and sacrifice and I felt extremely grateful to miners everywhere for their contribution to making my life much easier.

Chapter Fifteen

College had started up again for the Summer Term and whilst the emphasis was on the upcoming end of year exams in June, the lads in the band were constantly at me to do some more gigs. I couldn't blame them as I was hankering for more live performances as well. So, one afternoon, I sat down at Colin's desk with the Yellow Pages and set about phoning all the places that looked likely to book us. After two hours ringing pubs and clubs, I came back with exactly zero.

'I thought people round here loved their music, Colin,' I said, when he returned later on and I lamented my wasted time on the phone.

'So why can't we get some bookings?'

'Well, it's getting near summer and people will be thinking about goin' away, not sittin' in smoky clubs and pubs,' he replied. 'Plus, no-one knows you yet. The bookin' agencies in Leeds or Sheffield handle lots of local artistes and you need to get in with those guys. Send them a demo tape,' he suggested.

That wasn't a bad idea and I silently cursed myself for not thinking of it before.

'Also, there's some practicalities you need to consider as well,' he said. 'It'll force you into makin' some important decisions lad.'

'What do you mean?' I asked, as he sat down and leant back in his chair and stretched his arms above his head.

'Well, firstly, in what we commonly call clubland round here, there are still plenty of opportunities going as they all want to see a variety of acts. That's the good news,' he said.

'So apart from them not liking foreigners, what's the bad news?'

He laughed. 'It's nowt to do wi' where you come from. It's all about speed and agility. They need a quick turnaround of acts. That works fine if you're a solo performer or even a duo, as you can get on and off the stage quickly and without causing any disruption. Many jobbin' artistes will do two or even three clubs per night in a particular locality and make a decent living that way.'

I nodded as he continued.

'For a group it's different, obviously. No one wants to see a bunch of hairy-arsed rockers, or whatever, trooping through a bingo session or interruptin' the act of another performer, just so they can set their gear up,' he advised.

'So that means if you're booked as a band then you're usually on first, but then you're stuck there for the night. You can do maybe thirty minutes or perhaps two spots, but that's it. To do a two hour show you have to be a well-known act, well-liked and 'ave a lot of material under your belt.'

He was making a lot of sense, I realised. My previous appearances at the miners' clubs had all been just me, utilising the resident backing musicians, if they had any.

'Which brings me to the third point,' he said. 'No one knows tha yet. Some of the clubs will hold open afternoons for new acts, or shop windows as they're called. It's a kind of an audition where local club secretaries will come along and listen. If you sound half decent then they'll approach you afterwards with their diaries for a booking. It would be worth your while findin' out when the next ones are scheduled and goin' to a couple of them.'

'Okay, thanks,' I said. 'I'll make some more enquiries.'

I felt a bit deflated but knew deep down that he was giving me sound advice as well as things to think about regarding my future aspirations as a live performer.

'So, you have to decide on what you want to be,' he said. 'A solo artiste will get more work, but after a while it will become repetitive an' you've constantly got to be changin' your material. Otherwise, you'll get bored, the audiences will get bored of seein' you and you'll end up wi' nowt.'

I nodded back as he continued.

'A group act also needs to offer something different. No point in just copying what you hear on the radio, as people can pay to go and see those bands for real when they come around on their tours.'

'So what would you do if you were in my place?' I asked.

'Well, if it was me, I'd be a bit different. You like the blues, but that style, in itself, is a bit of an acquired taste and doesn't have wide appeal. So, I'd think about combining it with other styles as a music fusion thing,' he replied.

'Or perhaps even bringing a bit of comedy into your band like a cabaret style act, although that's been done already.'

I nodded whilst I scribbled some notes.

'The point is, if you're different, then you'll get noticed as being entertainin' an' that's the key word,' he said. 'It's what hard-working folk want when they're relaxing over a bellyful of ale on a weekend. If they're not being entertained by them that's on stage then they'll entertain

165

themselves instead, an' you'll end up ignored, heckled or paid off. I've seen it happen lots of times with budding performers an' it can be cruel.'

As ever, he talked a lot of sense and it left me deep in thought over what I should do. I liked performing as a solo artist, but I also liked our band as well.

These lads were keen, if not yet proficient in their art, but they were enthusiastic and willing to give it a go. If only we could find a way of breaking through, then we'd have something to work towards and aim for the future.

Terry was a bit more supportive when I shared my thoughts with him the following day over lunch.

'Well, first off, get some o' th'art students to do you some A5 flyers and hand-outs,' he said. 'Then you can pass 'em round the bigger pubs and clubs. Practically every trade 'as their own club or boozer these days. Tha can put mi taxi phone number on 'em if you like and I or missus will take the messages an' do the admin for you – for a small fee of course.'

'Thanks Terry, that's a good idea. You're a real pal.'

I sought out one of the Art lecturers and charmed her into putting some designs together for our band. She took some photos of us in our snazzy jackets and a few days later she came back with her ideas.

Unfortunately, a typing error had changed us to the 'sharp pressed men', but the overall image was right and after making some amendments we presently had a promo flyer looking as it should and she printed out five hundred copies for us. Nice of the College to help us out with their resources, I thought, not that the management or accounting department knew anything about it, naturally.

Over the course of the next few days the band lads, plus Jenny and myself, set out to drop the flyers into every club and pub that hosted live entertainment. We scoured the local newspaper ads to find out who was appearing where and when and drew up a long list of places, ticking off each one as we dropped a flyer through the doors and hoping that Terry would get a phone call.

Meantime, we also had to put some serious rehearsal time in. We currently had enough material to cover a thirty minute spot without breaks, but that was it. Ideally, we needed enough songs to be able to pull off a two-hour gig if necessary, which meant a lot more work for us to expand our repertoire.

We were busy practicing on the following Monday evening when Terry stuck his head round the door and interrupted us. 'Good news,' he said. 'I had a call from a guy at Rebels last night. They're featurin' a local bands night on Friday's an' 'ave asked if you want to appear this week as their original bookin' has bailed out.'

'Great,' I said, excitedly. 'Er, where is it?'

'Sheffield,' said Stevie, unenthusiastically. 'It's a bikers' heavy metal club. Crap joint, full of scruffy headbangers.'

'Well, a gig is a gig Stevie,' I said. 'How much are they paying?' I asked Terry.

'Thirty. Plus a free beer each on the house.'

Shit, I didn't need a calculator to work out the maths. We'd already agreed to pay ten percent to Terry for organising the admin and phone calls, which would only leave us twenty-seven pounds. Out of that we would then have to pay him another twenty for use of his taxi. That left seven pounds to split between the five of us. Just about buy me a small beer and a bag of chips.

It made me question my choice of vocation once more. Those glossy and dreamy photos in the music press or on album sleeves showing wistful-looking guys with guitars slung over their shoulders and thumbing a lift by the side of the road aren't just done for artistic effect. No, it's because we really are skint most of the time. They'd be better off showing a bloke in a bus shelter on a miserable Winter's evening in November, trying to light a dogend cig in the pouring rain, minus the tanned and well-nourished appearance. That's more like the reality of the music business, but it probably wouldn't sell many records.

The guys were less than impressed and seemed to be disheartened after listening to Terry and his announcement.

'Look,' I said, trying to work up some encouragement. 'We need the exposure. The more we do, the more we'll get noticed and the more people will hear about us. It's how all bands start out.'

They didn't look convinced, but I continued regardless.

'The ones that have the commitment and the balls to soldier on are the ones that make it,' I said. 'The guys that give in at the first sign of struggle just end up stacking the supermarket shelves on night shift or pumping gas.'

'What's that?' asked Woody.

'It's an expression we use Woody. It means if you don't have ambitions and put up with some shit along the way then you'll end up in a deadbeat job, feeling pissed off with life.'

They all nodded, but I could see he wasn't won over.

'What I'm trying to say to you is that every musician worth his salt has had to start somewhere. Nothing is for nothing you know,' I said, trying to work out where I'd heard that before. I sounded very motivational for all of my young years even though I felt a little exasperated.

'Let's give it a go and see what happens. Tell 'em we'll be there, Terry,' I said, before turning back to the band. 'Now, back to this middle section on *Confidence Man...*'

The following day I decided to take old Archie's advice and get some insurance cover in place for my stuff. I'd nearly been parted with my beloved guitar when I'd inadvertently left it at Reeny's house and I didn't want to contemplate how much I'd have to fork out for a replacement if anything untoward happened to it again.

I was able to leave College at lunchtime and I found the brokers' office on a corner of the high street in Goldthorpe above the bookies, exactly as Archie had described it.

The entrance was via a fire escape staircase on the side of the building and the large but faded office sign read, 'Douglas D Belton Insurance and Clams Specialist', as the letter 'i' had fallen out from the fascia board.

A fat guy with bottle-bottom specs and greasy silver hair was thumbing through the racing pages of the *Daily Express* and looked up from his desk as I walked in.

'Hello,' I said. 'I'd like to take some insurance out for my guitar and other household items. Archie sent me here to see you.'

'Archie Selby?' he asked. 'Don't tell me he's damaged your place with his decorating.'

'Er, no,' I said. 'Quite the opposite.'

'Well, that's good,' he replied. 'It's just that I get a lot of clients claimin' on their policies for his crap work. He's colour-blind you know, which is not a good quality to 'ave as a painter an' decorator. Still, it provides me wi' commissions an' I count 'im as a mate. Tek a seat young man.'

I told him what I wanted as he scribbled down some notes before telling me he'd get a policy sorted out and that a cover letter would be sent out in the post in a few days. Then he leaned across the desk and looked carefully at me.

'Now, if tha's ever short o' money at any time, come an' see me first,' he advised.

'Why, are you a money lender?' I asked.

'Not exactly, although I've been known to run a book or two on the quiet from time to time,' he replied. 'No, it's just that I 'ave a little self-help scheme goin' that some of my, er, more discerning clients like to take advantage of from time to time, when they have the need, of course.'

'What's that?' I asked, intrigued.

'Well, it works like this,' he said. 'You agree to me brekkin' into your house one particular day an' liftin' some pre-arranged items, which I then store for you safely in my lock-up. Meantime you report the burglary at the plod shop an' get a crime number from them. Then you submit a claim on your policy, with my 'elp of course, to the relevant Insurer. Once it's paid out, we split the cash an' I return your goods intact. Everyone's 'appy and life goes on as normal.'

'What happens if you get caught though?' I asked.

'Caught by who?' he replied. 'Them insurance reps aren't interested in comin' out to this backwater of a place, scared stiff they might get their shiny shoes all muddied up. Plus, local plod round 'ere won't waste their time looking for a stolen bike or a telly, as they can't be arsed,' he added.

'Ah've been 'elpin' my clients wi' this for years now, but keep it to yerself, you know, I do have some professional standards to stick by,' pointing to a boxed qualification certificate on the wall behind him.

I glanced over his shoulder but was distracted by the framed black and white photograph next to it, which depicted a smart-dressed young man in military uniform with a guard dog by his side. 'Was that your father?' I asked, pointing at the picture.

'No, that was me in my, er, former service days for our Queen and Country,' he laughed. 'Back when I was still slim an' good-looking and before I, er, had to find a new career direction, pretty smartish. That's how I ended up in the insurance game. Still, I've managed to scrape a living as well as acquiring several stones in weight for my troubles.'

'Well, thank you, I know where to come if I need you,' I said, leaving him to his racing tips for now.

*

Back at College we carried on rehearsing like crazy for the following two nights and on the Friday evening, we set off with Terry just after seven, all fired up for the gig. We'd been told to do a forty-minutes set from ten o'clock onwards and if the crowd liked us then we'd be allowed one encore. Either way, we were to be off the stage by eleven and no argument because that's when the DJ started up with requests.

Rebels was located on the end of a run-down precinct in the City Centre, on what looked like the top floor of an office block building. We were directed round the back into a small courtyard which doubled up as a loading bay for the department store next door and where a tiny goods lift was available to get the gear up to the stage. But we, as well as all the punters, had to climb about seven flights of stairs in order to reach the actual premises.

'Ah'll be back for yer all by eleven,' said Terry. 'Might as well see if I can make a few bob wi' taxi whilst I'm 'ere in town.'

'Mek sure you've cleaned seats down if yer goin' up to Broomhill,' mocked Robbie back at him. 'I don't wanna be catchin' summat from them filthy women they 'ave up there.'

The venue was unwelcoming to say the least. We set up our instruments on a small stage overlooking the black painted walls and ceiling of a lounge smelling like an over-filled ashtray.

All the windows had been boarded over and even the skylights were painted black. The room was illuminated from a combination of rusty fluorescent tubes hanging precariously from the ceiling and orange-glow neon signs stuck around the bar area. The flooring was a mix of carpet and parquet timber, but it was difficult to work out where one piece ended and the other began. Every patch was sticky and coated with a tar-black layer of something obnoxious that had built up from years of spilled beer and cig ash.

A long-haired chap in a stained tee shirt and jeans came up to announce that he was 'Josh' and he'd be doing the mixing desk for us, so we had to use the amps that were already on the stage.

They were massive and even running through the sound-check with him made my ears ring. 'Do we need to be that loud?' I shouted over to him, as he waved and stopped us part way through *Jean Genie* to fiddle with his knobs.

'It wor fine for Def Leppard when they were 'ere last year,' he yelled back.

'Were they deaf before they came here then?' I asked, but he didn't answer.

'Looks like we need the cotton wool buds for this one guys,' I said to the lads, but they all just looked at me in bewilderment.

At nine o'clock the doors opened and we watched from one corner as the place slowly started to fill up. Stevie was right with his earlier assessment and most of the clientele looked like they'd come here from a motorbike rally.

Beer bellies, broken-heart tats and hairy armpits appeared in bulk quantities from ripped leather and denim jackets and they just belonged to the women.

Guys shuffled from the bar to their wall seats in grease-stained jeans and biking boots, trying to peer through locks of shoulder length hair which fell forward over their faces in untidy clumps and dangled into their pints of cider or lager. As they took their seats, some blokes tied bandanas around their heads before rolling dodgy-looking cigs from paper packets, no doubt to ensure that they wouldn't set their greasy hair alight when attempting to smoke and head-bang simultaneously.

I noticed that all the drinks were served in plastic pots and no bottles were allowed, which reassured me somewhat. If they didn't like us then at least we only had to cope with being soaked rather than glassed. Visiting the launderette was better than going to Accident & Emergency.

After listening to a steady stream of heavy metal records for nearly an hour it was time for us to get on stage. We kicked off without any announcement and right away we had a sound fault. One of the rear amps wasn't working and so we had to stop whilst Josh climbed up on the stage and threaded another cable through, all the while coping with the chorus of jeers and general abuse coming from the punters.

Then we were going again and it seemed we were okay. I'd been rehearsing the guys on some heavier numbers for this gig and we made a reasonable impression with our covers of *Deeper And Down* and *You Aint Seen Nothin' Yet*, which I had to admit sounded good on such big amplified sounds.

The crowd joined in with us on the chorus line, stamping their feet and nodding their heads as we played away to them. But I didn't want to overdo it. Nothing sounds more crap and is guaranteed to cause arguments than hearing a poor version of your rock hero's music and I wasn't going to risk this lot losing it with us.

Woody held us together without speeding up and seeing that I'd insisted there was no drinking before we played, there were no dropped drumsticks either. The rest of the guys did a good job and I tried to dazzle the audience with some guitar licks between the verses on each of our songs.

Despite my initial misgivings, we gave a competent account of ourselves as a band. The punters behaved respectfully towards us and when we finished the set, we got some whistles and cheers. So, we did our *Roadhouse Blues* for our encore just as we had done at the school. God, what a contrast in venues, I thought. Then it was all over as the thrashing sounds of heavy metal took over from the DJ booth.

We dismantled and packed up our gear and I sent the lads downstairs to locate Terry and the van, whilst I remained upstairs at the rear with our stuff, waiting for the goods lift to be unlocked.

As the noisy sound of *Paranoid* carried through from next door, Josh came across to give me our fee. I counted out the fivers and put them in my pocket, as another bloke about my age wandered up to me and leaned forward into my ear.

'Whose band is this?' he asked, loudly.

'It's ours, from the College at Barnsley,' I shouted back.

From a distance we looked like two deaf blokes yelling at each other.

'Well, I thought you sounded not bad at all,' he continued. 'Would you be interested in being on a televised local talent show?'

I looked at him as he continued. 'We're busy looking for some local bands to compete at the Leadmill here in town during August. The winner gets a cash prize and will feature as a support act for a major band touring round the UK and Europe during the Winter. Interested?'

Interested? Damn right I'm interested, what a stupid question! 'Yes, certainly we would be, thank you very much,' I said, politely.

'Great,' he replied. 'Only thing is, yer need to change your band name.'

'What do you mean?' I asked.

'Well, it looks like you're trying to rip off a rock tune an' that doesn't go down well in TV land. They're shit scared of being sued for copyright and suchlike. Call yerselves something like, I dunno, the Barnsley Bluesmen, or something less crappy than that.'

He handed me some paperwork. 'Fill this in with all yer details and get it back to me so that I can confirm your booking and the date. The sooner it's back with me the better.'

I expressed my thanks again and shook his hand before he wandered off back into the main room.

I'd heard of the Leadmill, which was an old industrial building that had been converted into a purpose-designed music venue and club and featured established bands as well as emerging talent. It sounded right up my street and my heart leapt as I realised this could be our ticket to something big. At last, some good news and I'd explain it to the guys once we were in the van, away from this din and where I could hear myself think.

As Terry got us back on the road I broke the news to the lads, waving the application forms in my hand and they all whooped and cheered like mad in response.

'Yeah, big time here we come,' shouted Robbie.

'Well, it means a lot of work and remember you will have finished College Term by then, so no going off on holiday,' I said, smiling at their reaction.

'Holidays? What's them?' said Benji. 'Sounds like you've been living down in that London for too fuckin' long,' and we all laughed back at him.

'Plus, we need a new band name,' I said. 'Something that's a bit more original than a song title.'

'How about 'Terry's All Blue'?' suggested Stevie.

'Cheeky young bugger,' replied Terry and we chuckled at his reaction, but I thought this was somewhere on the right lines.

'How about 'Red or Black' as a name?' I asked. 'Reminds me of playing roulette and betting all we've got on either winning big or losing the damned lot.'

They agreed and then we cheered ourselves again as we joined the M1 motorway heading back home. They were good lads and they had something about them as a group. After the hard work we'd put in over the past few weeks, as well as my years of living and working as an impoverished musician, maybe this was the real chance I'd been waiting for. It was certainly an opportunity to break onto the music scene in style and I just couldn't wait for it to happen.

Chapter Sixteen

Jenny and I had started discussing our plans for what we'd be doing over the Summer months when College ended. She had now finished her exams and was confident of passing them, plus, the hospital in Doncaster had offered her a full-time nursing position, which she was excited about.

I was also excited about the upcoming Leadmill event, feeling certain that my long wait to hit the big time was nearly over. When I'd told Jenny about it and that it would be on the television at some stage, she was thrilled and made some comments about hanging around with a superstar as she called me, before then saying she'd have to fight off the inevitable groupies.

'Let's worry about them when we have some,' I said, jokingly. 'When they turn up, I'll let Terry deal with them.'

This Sunday morning she was round at mine again having stayed over the previous night. If Walter hadn't come to terms with what was going on between us, then he never would.

Anyway, I did think a lot of her. She was fun to be with and I missed her when she wasn't with me. We were in love I suppose, although we hadn't actually said the words to each other yet. Her mum was pleased that Jenny was in a steady relationship and was always happy and welcoming whenever she saw me. Walter was still to be convinced, I guessed, but at least he hadn't discovered anything amiss with the car, thank goodness. I was considering asking if I could buy it from him and wondered if the transaction might sway the balance to him fully accepting me.

Jenny had been splashing about in the bath whilst I was lying on the bed strumming the acoustic guitar from College and singing *Poor Boy Blues* to myself.

'That's nice,' she said, as she appeared at the bedroom door wrapped in a towel with another one coiled around her hair. 'Sing it again for me,' she asked, dipping her head provocatively as she sat on the edge of the bed.

I sung it as sweetly as I could, telling the story about a young man's unwavering love for a woman which was now in peril as he had nothing useful or valuable to give to her, being a penniless musician. I knew how he felt.

'I know where you've got something useful,' she said, as she stroked my leg with her foot and reached up my thigh with her toes.

In response, I stretched out and slipped my hand under the towel and was just about to start singing again when there was a sharp knock on the front door. I jumped up off the bed and opened the window to look down into the street below.

'Some parcels for Mr Simms,' said the thickset guy looking up at me and who I recognised from previous deliveries. He'd never mentioned his name, so I didn't know what to call him.

'Hang on mate, I'm coming down,' I said, grabbing my jeans as I went downstairs to open the door. Presently there were half a dozen cardboard boxes lined up in the back room.

'Someone will be along later to collect 'em,' he said, before driving off.

'That's a strange carry on,' said Jenny, when I rejoined her upstairs in the bedroom. 'Why doesn't he get his stuff delivered to his work premises or to his own home?'

'I don't know,' I agreed. 'All he said to me was that he was in the middle of having some bigger premises done up ready for September. It's happened a couple of times now and anyway, it doesn't bother me.'

'Who's Rosalyn?' she asked, changing the subject.

'Eh?' I said, feeling my heart skipping a beat.

'There's a name and a phone number on this piece of paper,' she said. 'It was here on the chair when you picked up your jeans.'

I tried to disguise my blushes as Rosalyn had been on my mind frequently since I'd first met her at the school gig and it was true, I'd been carrying her phone number around in my jeans pocket like a lucky charm. Half of me wanted her to be in our band, but I didn't know yet how we could do this, although it might just add to the uniqueness that Colin had mentioned to me. The other half of me just wanted to be in her, plain and simple, but I couldn't admit that fact to anyone, least of all right now to my regular girlfriend.

'Oh, she's a student who was interested in joining the band, er, if we had a place, but I don't think so,' I muttered, trying to hide my embarrassment.

I needed to change the subject and pretty fast. 'Now, where was I up to?' I murmured, sliding my hand up beneath the towel. She giggled in response as we rolled around the bed and all mentions of Rosalyn were forgotten, for now.

However, as I walked into College the following morning, the thought of that auburn-flamed hair and gorgeous smile came back into my mind and the phone number in my pocket seemed to burn against my thigh. Could I introduce her into the band and give us a new twist on things? Would it work with the other guys? Most important of all, could I keep my hands off her and any romance away from Jenny?

These were serious considerations and there was only one way of finding out. I'd have to call her and meet up in person and I decided that I'd do just that before the week was out.

As far as my tuition was concerned, the remaining weeks of the Summer Term were all sorted out. I'd got all the exam material ready for my cohort of students and Colin was already priming me for the new academic year in September, saying that he wanted to introduce more music-based courses which in turn would increase my workload. Will it increase my pay though I had asked and he'd just laughed as if I was joking with him.

'Welcome to the world of academia my lad,' he'd said. 'It's a vocation don't you know? You do it for the love of teaching, not for the love of money.'

I was still pondering this thought over a refectory sandwich at lunchtime when Terry appeared and sat down opposite me. His face was drawn and he looked troubled by something.

'Now then Terry,' I said. 'You don't look so good.'

'No, I'm not,' he muttered. 'I've somethin' to tell thee, lad. You remember Mavis don't you, who lives out near Mexborough?'

'Yes of course I do.'

I hadn't seen her since moving up here, but I couldn't forget her kindness. The mention of her name made me feel guilty that I hadn't bothered to keep in touch as I'd promised to and I was about to say I would go and pay her a visit soon.

'Well, thing is, I 'ad to go an' see her last night,' he said. 'You see...' he hesitated, before taking a deep breath. 'She's lost her son, Richie. He was killed in an Army accident whilst on exercise somewhere out in Middle East. They're flyin' his body back for a burial on Thursday this week.'

I was shocked. 'Oh no that's terrible, poor Mavis.'

Then the penny dropped and I gasped at the enormity of what I'd just heard. 'But Terry, he's your son as well,' I exclaimed, remembering what Mavis had told me that night at her house. 'I'm so sorry for you.'

'Aye, he was the son I never knew an' tried to forget about,' he said. 'I only ever saw 'im from a distance an' even then, I don't think I ever actually said more than two words to 'im. Mavis didn't want any complications wi' my family, so I just went along with her wishes all these years.'

I nodded, remembering what she had told me. It had been a difficult situation for both of them and they'd had to learn to live with the consequences of their secret liaison ever since.

'Now listen, you're gonna 'ave to keep this quiet,' he said. 'I don't want word gettin' out an' especially to our Mick. He thinks a lot of you, you know, so don't go blabbin' or sayin' owt otherwise I'll 'ave bigger things on mi plate to deal with. He knows nothin' about Mavis or 'er lad, nor does my missus, an' that's the way it's gonna 'ave to stay.'

I nodded before tentatively asking, 'Are you planning on going to the funeral service?'

'Yes, an' that's what I wanted to talk about as well. I'll be there, but I'll stand away an' be discreet. Mavis needs to have 'er privacy and 'er dignity an' it's gonna be awkward, for the pair of us.'

I agreed, wondering how he would manage the situation he now found himself in.

'She's arranged for the service to be at four o'clock at St Mary's so that some of 'is former mates from pit can attend wi'out 'avin' to take a day off work. Then, there's a wake afterwards down at Ravenswood. When I saw her, she'd said as how you'd once done a turn there an' I told 'er that you'd now moved up here an' was livin' locally. So she asked me if you'd come along and play a song for him.'

'A wake? What's that?' I asked.

'It's a gatherin' that folk 'ave after funerals. Dates back to olden days when members of a family would keep a vigil over the deceased before burial. But nowadays it's a chance for everyone to share their grief an' memories, as well as some laughter about 'appier times,' he said. 'It 'elps us all to come to terms wi' what's 'appened an' move on wi' things.'

Oh God, this was a body blow. 'Yes, of course, I'll come along,' I replied. But I didn't know the poor guy who'd died. All I'd seen of him was his photo on Mavis's fireplace. And what could I sing that would be suitable and not offend folk?

After lunch I went to see Colin for his advice.

'Death affects different people in different ways,' he said. 'Some folk want to be remembered an' would want their friends an' family to enjoy a good piss-up in their memory, whilst others are more introverted. If he grew up in one of the villages around 'ere, you can expect there to be a large gatherin' of locals. It's how they'd want to show respect an' their support for his family.'

'Yes, I expect there'll be a large gathering. He'd worked at a pit before joining the Army,' I said. 'Lots of people would have known him and will no doubt want to say their farewells, I think.'

'Aye,' he replied. 'It's a far cry from when I said goodbye to my Gabriella. I was the only one there.'

I thought I'd misheard him. 'Sorry Colin, did you say…?' I asked, hesitantly.

He realised that he'd over-stepped his normal reserve and took a deep breath. 'Yes. Gabriella was my wife,' he said. 'But she was taken from me far too soon.'

'What happened?' It seemed an insensitive question to ask, but I just had to know the answer.

'She was from Bologna in Italy an' we met as students in London,' he explained. 'Then we got married in a mad rush in 1969, just after we'd both graduated. But she died shortly afterwards from a drugs overdose.'

'Oh, I'm so sorry,' I said. 'That must have been dreadful.'

'Don't be,' he replied. 'We were all into LSD in those days an' being stoned was pretty normal for both of us.'

I was shocked and didn't know what to say.

'One night she was given a bad mix from someone at a party. At the time I was doing a gig with my jazz trio an' when I arrived at the house later on, I was told she'd been taken off in an ambulance. If I'd been with her all night it probably wouldn't have happened.'

He paused at the painful memory. 'Anyway, she spent nearly three months in hospital in a coma before she passed away. Even if she had recovered the doctors had warned me that she'd be brain-damaged beyond repair.'

'I'm so sorry for you, Colin,' I said, even though I knew the words couldn't really give him any comfort.

'Her parents blamed me even though I wasn't at fault,' he said, quietly. 'But they were right. I was her husband and I should have been there to take better care of her.'

'That was a bit harsh though, blaming you,' I said. 'After all, it wasn't your doing.'

'Well, we were all into heavy stuff back then an' we were stupid without realising it. I put my music gig before her and ending up paying a heavy price for it,' he said, taking a deep breath. 'I wanted her buried in a local churchyard near to where we lived in Earls Court at the time, but her parents refused. They had her remains sent back to them an' I was banned from ever coming near any of their family again. To this day, I still don't know where she's buried.'

I looked at the pain in this man's eyes and couldn't fathom how this meek, inoffensive and kind guy could have been such a wild thing in his past life. It just didn't make any sense to me and I realised appearances can be deceptive and that folk around me who I regarded as being older generation had indeed gone through their own turbulent times in their younger lives.

'So after that I came back home to live with my parents just outside Sheffield. Then after a while and a couple of temporary jobs, I became a full-time piano teacher before being taken on at a school and eventually I joined the teaching staff here. Keeping busy an' teaching others has been my way of grieving an' trying to make up for the life we never had together and I vowed I'd never play in public again. You never forget, but time eases the pain,' he said. 'Anyway, that was my life. Yours is still in front of you, so don't fuck it up.'

It was wise advice and despite my carefree lifestyle so far, this was something that made me sit up and think. I could honestly say that the drugs scene was not something

I was into, despite its common associations with the so-called rock and roll lifestyle.

Yes, I'd smoked an odd joint here and there and beer and whisky were my favourite drinking companions, but that was about it. Was I missing out on something? Possibly. But could I cope with the aftermath of someone close to me, intimately close at that, dying prematurely as a result of our social habits? No, I don't think so. Whatever I did to myself was my decision, but to live with the guilt of having caused the loss of someone close, that was a heavy load for sure.

Colin's revelations were a shock to say the least. All this stuff about the social evils of today really was nothing new and it had been going around for ages. Maybe there was more of it now than in the past or maybe it just didn't get discussed as much back then, as any indiscretions or mishaps were probably over-shadowed by the horrendous loss of lives either during the war or occurring from occupational job hazards.

Since my trip down the pit with Mick I'd been reading about past accidents and explosions in coalmines around the Dearne Valley and they had been horrific. Just walking around my village streets had caused me to realise that I was never too far away from where many men and boys had previously perished below my feet.

Even a former King and Queen of England had at one time witnessed a pit disaster whilst on a local visit. They had broken away from a banquet to go and offer their comfort to the women trying to identify the shattered and burnt bodies of their sons and husbands, not that far away from where I was now living. Then, despite advice to the contrary, the King had gone underground with the miners the following day to show solidarity and support for them and I thought that must have taken some balls.

I was still bothered by what Colin had disclosed to me when I met up with Jenny that evening and told her about the funeral that I'd been asked to attend.

'It happens all the time,' she said, nonchalantly. 'Maybe not in the large numbers they used to see at one time, apart from the football stadium disaster the other month, but I see death most days at work and we just have to get on with it.'

I paused for a moment, recalling the terrible tragedy in Sheffield just a few weeks earlier. It had been all over the news as well as a main topic of conversation at College when the new term had started. Several of the staff and students had been at the match and had witnessed the events unfolding at close hand. I didn't know any of the people involved but to me it seemed a tragic waste of life for so many supporters who had simply gone along to watch their team in action.

I felt as though I was surrounded by the spectre of death and said so to Jenny.

'Well, it's just a natural part of the circle of life,' she answered, philosophically. 'Every single day people die and new people are born. What they do in between those two events is up to them and that's the part that really matters. Life is short when you look at the bigger picture of things,' she added.

I nodded in agreement with her as I brought my thoughts back to Mavis. 'I'm going to have to go to this funeral wake thing,' I said. 'But I don't know how it's going to be. I've never been to one before.'

'It'll be fine,' she said, reassuring me. 'His mum will be glad to see you and she'll appreciate that you've made the effort of turning up and showing your support.'

*

I remained apprehensive over the next couple of days but on the Thursday afternoon I made my way over to St Mary's. The little churchyard was already full of people congregating in small groups and I watched from the relative comfort of the pavement running alongside the stone boundary wall.

Several Army lads in their regimental band uniform played hymns outside the church doors as the mourners gathered. Then I saw two black hearses coming to a halt on the road and six more uniformed colleagues came and lifted out a coffin, raising it onto their shoulders before proceeding down the path into the church. Mavis got out from the other car and followed the coffin, comforted by her friends and neighbours.

I joined the congregation in the back pews where I noticed Terry sitting in quiet contemplation and he nodded back at me. I felt like I was an intruder, awkwardly clutching my guitar case, at what should be a private family service. When the army band began to play *Abide With Me* it became too much to watch and so I slipped outside and again stood at a safe distance.

Eventually the coffin was brought out from the church and laid to rest in a freshly dug grave. As the mourners dropped handfuls of the soil back into the earth, the Minister gave a blessing, the Army lads stood to attention and saluted and a bugler at the side of the grave sounded *The Last Post*.

The Ravenswood was just down the road from the church and the congregation made their way to the club, whilst I followed behind at a discreet distance. Inside, the games room had been reserved for the occasion and the snooker table had been covered over and laid out with an array of buffet food. I remembered the last time I was here in this venue when the atmosphere was very different.

Now, the conversation seemed quiet at first, stilted and awkward but gradually as the beer started to flow, it became more fluid and eventually I plucked up the courage to go over and give my condolences to Mavis.

'Oh, thanks for coming luv,' she said. 'It's good to see you again,' as she clung onto me. 'I'm just sorry it couldn't be in better circumstances.'

'Mavis, you've nothing to be sorry for, it wasn't your fault,' I said. It was awkward to find the right words.

'All his friends from his squad are 'ere plus some of the lads he did his apprenticeship with at the pit. They'll give 'im a good send off an' he'll be pleased they did so,' she said, wiping her eyes.

I set up in one corner to play a couple of songs. All week I'd been trying to think of something to play and sing that would be suitable for the occasion. I'd decided to bring along the acoustic six string so that I could strum and pick my way through some easy listening tunes which may pass as unobtrusive background music.

So, without introduction I began with the ballad *Simple Man* and hoped that the lyrics describing the advice given by a mother to her son would have some meaning today. Next, after a short gap, I followed it up with *Have You Seen The Rain*.

Then I played *Why Worry* hoping that I'd get it right, having spent most of the previous night practicing it. I also hoped that the lines about laughter always following pain in a natural and never-ending cycle would help to lift the mood of the assembled folks. But I looked around as I sang and played and I could see the tears in the eyes of the young men and for a moment I wondered if I'd chosen wisely.

However, Mavis came to give me a hug as I finished the song and everyone clapped as she turned to address them. 'Thank you everyone for coming this afternoon and giving your support. Richie would have been pleased to see you all.'

'Good on yer Richie lad,' shouted one of the pit lads and the rest nodded in approval.

Mavis smiled as she continued. 'Now we're here not to be sad but to remember a happy lad who's no longer with us. He wouldn't want us to be morose now would he, so let's 'ave some drinks an' recall some of the funnier times we all had together. And don't worry about me getting offended, I'm very broad-minded you know,' smiling, as she raised her glass to the mourners.

Someone shouted for a round of scotch chasers and that gave me an idea. 'Join in with me on this one,' I announced, as I went into *Whisky in the Jar* and presently we were all singing away like happy drunks on a coach party stag night.

The Army lads mixed in with the miners and they were chuckling at past stories and downing beer like it was about to go stale. A music system played a selection of Richie's favourite musical tracks and photos of better times were passed around as memories were recalled and past events discussed between his colleagues.

I went to get another beer and found Terry standing on his own at the bar. 'For God's sake Terry,' I said. 'Go and give Mavis a hug. He was your lad too. She needs you man, now more than ever.'

'Aye lad, I know. I will, in our own time,' he answered. I bought him a drink and we stood silently together for a while, both immersed in our own thoughts and deliberations.

Then the Army band lads got out their instruments and started to play and the miners and squaddies stood up, putting their arms round each other's shoulders as they sung *The Parting Glass* to their absent colleague. It was too much for me to bear and so I nodded to Terry and sneaked quietly out of the club and started to walk back home.

It was a warm Summer's evening with the sun low and lazy in the sky and the larks were joyful in their twilight song. The verges and hawthorn hedgerows bordering the open fields between the villages were a resplendent green and sprinkled with pink blossom as they bustled with the sounds of tiny birds chirping their way through the branches.

I took a short cut through the oak and sycamore woodland in full foliage and blokes walking their dogs gave me a cheery, 'Ow do' or a 'Grand evenin,' as they ambled passed, before I stopped at the top of the ridge for a breather and took in the panoramic landscape in front of me.

Despite my dark mood, the land had a surreal and calming beauty about it. Down in the valley bottom the river cut a gentle meandering pattern through the meadows where buttercups erupted in yellow clumps along its banks, whilst the rail tracks threaded their way like arteries as they ferried trains of coal wagons from pits to faraway power stations.

In the distance the scattered colliery towers were silhouetted in black against the setting sun and resembled the figures of soldiers on the Remembrance Day posters I'd seen in London, their headgear wheels gently leaning against the supporting ironwork like thoughtful heads lowered against rifles, as if in mourning at the passing of one of their own.

As I came into Goldthorpe high street, the large pub on the corner was in full swing and cheerful guys sitting on the outside trestle tables waved at me and shouted for me to come over and play them a song, but I just smiled back and walked on.

I stopped at the chip shop for something to eat but I wasn't really hungry and ended up giving the food away to a couple of cheeky kids who persisted on following me on their BMX bikes, yelling out 'gis a chip mister'. Plus, it's not easy trying to eat a bag of chips whilst walking and carrying a guitar at the same time.

Smiling neighbours were chatting to each other on the corner of my street and they waved and nodded as I walked past them. It was a reassuring sign that normal life was still going on around me and no doubt would continue to do so. The circle of life carried on regardless of events, I realised, thinking of Jenny's comments to me earlier in the week.

I got to my house and closed the door behind me, propping the guitar against the wall and poured a glass of whisky before sitting down. I thought about playing some songs to take my mind off things and tried to forget about Mavis and about Terry and how they had to cope with the things that life had thrown at them.

I reached across and took the guitar out of its case and cradled it like a child on my lap. Then I thought about the wake service again and inexplicably, tears began to well and I cried my eyes out for the memory of someone I had never known and now, would never meet.

It had been a sad day.

Chapter Seventeen

I was back at the Barnstone band room the following evening for their Friday rehearsal, but I could sense that all was not well tonight. Heated conversations and shaking heads were going on between some of the guys outside and worried looks had taken the place of the normally placid and joyful musicians I had come to know and respect.

My colleague Bill on the percussion team was already inside and so I asked him what was going on. 'They've announced the pit is shuttin' down in eight weeks,' he replied. 'End of August.'

Oh no, I thought, this is dreadful news. No wonder the men looked unhappy.

The conductor tried gallantly to muster up some enthusiasm amongst the band members as we started to play the first piece for tonight's rehearsal, but it was no good. Minds were focused elsewhere and after twenty minutes he decided to call a halt.

'Look lads,' he said. 'Let's take this evenin' off. Sort out what needs to be done first, then we can get back to concentrating on our music. There's not much more I can say tonight, except be strong and think about what you need to do for your families. I'll see you all next week.'

Everyone packed away their instruments and I followed some of the guys down to the Colliers, not knowing whether I could offer any consolation. 'Sorry to hear the news Mick,' I said. 'You must all be devastated at what's been announced.'

'Well, we knew it were comin' someday, but it's just a shock when it actually happens,' he said. 'It's not that we're unaccustomed to bad news. Every miner knows that at some stage 'is workplace will close when coil seams 'ave run-out or conditions become too dangerous. We're all used to that.'

'But I thought you still had plenty of life yet in this pit,' I said. to him. 'That's the impression I got from my visit underground with you.'

'Aye, we do,' he replied. 'And that's just it. When there's stacks o' coil left to be got at it meks no sense to us for a state-owned industry to be closed an' people put out of work.'

He paused to take a mouthful of beer.

'Mi granddad used to say how 'e rejoiced forty years ago when they nationalised the mines after the war, proudly declarin' that they were now being managed on behalf of the people. That's what was written on every fuckin' colliery signboard and they even put photos in the papers at the time to show everyone. Now look at 'ow they treat the people today. Cryin' shame that's what it is.'

I felt for his family, his livelihood and his colleagues. And yes, it didn't make any sense to me either, but what did I know? All I could see was that a thriving, hard-working community was being purposely deprived of their means of making a living and that didn't stack up in my mind as being a sound economic decision.

'Now it's just a waiting game to see what they're gonna offer us,' he said. 'Some o' older men will be alright. They'll get early redundancy on good terms an' will most likely move away an' buy a cottage at seaside or somewhere wi' warmer Winters. Rest of us, well, we'll just have to wait and see.'

I wanted to offer some suggestions and encouragement, but I couldn't find the right words. This was different to me trying to motivate my College lads to practice harder and become better musicians. These men didn't need any motivation to go to work. They wanted to be working and they were skilled in the jobs they did and now they all faced the very real prospect of being unemployed.

As far as I could make out, all they wanted was a fair crack at things and to be treated squarely by a Government that needed improvements made in all the state industries which it owned. No one was objecting to that as a point of principle.

However, I got the impression that the only thing these miners had received in recent times was injustice and you didn't have to be a genius to work out why communities like these felt hard-pressed and downtrodden at times. Despite us being in the decade of individual achievement and progress, as I seemed to remember lots of people saying back in London, it was clear to me that some parts of Britain were still moving at their own pace.

'Anyhow, moping about it isn't gonna change 'owt,' he said to the guys around him. 'Let's concentrate on summat else, like gettin' arse-holed,' as he ordered more beer. 'Tomorrow will still be good enough for making future plans.'

I felt that I was intruding on their personal space so I left them to it, realising that I also needed something else to take my mind off things. So instead, I went to the nearest phone box and made a call.

After three rings I heard an elegant male voice say, 'Good evening, can I help you?'

'Er, yes. Is Rosalyn there please?' I asked.

'And who is calling?'

'It's Jamie, er, just tell her I'm calling about our band,' I stuttered, as my explanation for being on the phone didn't sound plausible. 'We met at, er, a concert a few weeks ago.'

The line went quiet for a few seconds then the lovely sound of her voice purred through the receiver into my ear.

'Hi, I didn't know if you would ever call,' she said. 'How are you doing?'

'I'm very well,' I lied, into the phone. 'I was just, er, thinking about whether we could get together to, er, fit you into the band in some way,' turning bright red in the face as I spoke.

'Well, I'm in middle of revision for my A levels,' she replied. 'But we could get together tomorrow afternoon for a while if you like. I could do with a break from all the textbook stuff. Can you pick me up say around one pm?'

'I wish I could, but I've no transport of my own at the moment,' I said, hesitating and making me wish that I hadn't bothered calling in the first place. All week I'd wanted to speak with Rosalyn but it now it felt like it was turning into a bad idea.

'Well, no worries, come over here for lunch at twelve then,' she suggested. 'Have you got a pen there? This is my address,' as I wrote feverishly on my palm. 'We can chat then,' she said. 'Bring your guitar with you as well.'

'I'd love to,' I answered. 'Look forward to seeing you then. Got to go now,' I said, putting the phone down as my change ran out.

I stood silently in the phone box to think for a moment as I breathed out heavily onto the little glass panes and watched as they misted up as if to somehow conceal my presence from the outside world. What had I just gone and done?

I was due to meet Jenny tomorrow and now I'd arranged to go off and see another woman. I could hardly ask to borrow her dad's car for the afternoon to visit someone I fancied like mad and naturally I couldn't take Jenny along with me either. Nor could I not turn up at Rosalyn's having just agreed that I would. Shit, how was I going to talk my way through this one?

I put some more money in the phone to call Jenny. I explained what had just gone on about the pit closure news and that I was going to help Mick out tomorrow with some jobs at his house as a bit of a distraction, so could we just meet up on the Sunday instead. No problem she'd said and suggested I come over for their usual family lunch.

'Give my best wishes to Mick as well,' she added. 'It's a shame about what's happening.'

'Yes, I will,' I said, putting the phone down and realising that the shame was all mine. In my usual self-centred way, I was turning into quite a proficient liar as far as Jenny was concerned.

Just before noon the following day, I got off the bus near to Tall Trees Lane to the north of Doncaster and very nearly turned back to go home.

Rosalyn's house was beautiful. It was a large detached Victorian place with a manicured front lawn and no doubt the same round the back, fringed along the sides by high hedges and rose beds and dotted with silver birch trees. A BMW saloon car stood in one corner in front of a double-width garage. Her family must be loaded, I reckoned.

I gripped the handle of the guitar case as I took a deep breath and approached the imposing front door. After knocking politely, I noticed a push-bell button at the side and cursed myself for my stupidity.

Then the door was opened by a smart-looking middle-aged lady who said, 'Good afternoon Mr, er, sorry, I'm not sure of your name.'

'It's Martindale, but call me Jamie, or James,' I said, flustered.

'Come on in then James,' and she led me into a lounge room across the hall where a similarly elegant chap wearing a golf jumper with matching slacks was reading the *Daily Telegraph*. He put the paper down and stood up to greet me.

'Richard Carter,' he said curtly. 'Ros should be down in a minute. Please sit down,' motioning me to the sofa in front of the fireplace and diagonally across from his chair, where he studied me for a few seconds. His wife announced that she was getting the lunch ready and left us alone as he struck up a conversation.

'Now, Ros, er, Rosalyn, tells me you have some kind of a band, is that correct?'

'Yes,' I answered.

'And you want her to join it?' He was very precise and to the point and I wondered if he was a surgeon.

'Well, yes, er, maybe,' I said. 'We just need to sort -,' but he interrupted me before I could finish.

'Well, she's not,' he declared. 'No argument, no discussion.'

I was taken aback at this comment and looked at him a little confused. I wasn't expecting such a blunt statement but before I could respond, he continued speaking.

'Let me put it another way. Ros is revising for her A level exams due in the coming weeks. After that, she's a choice to make between Cambridge or Kings London, where she will read law,' he said. 'She will shortly be turning nineteen and needs to concentrate on the career ahead of her. She can spend some brief time in the Summer before we go to France for our family holiday if she wants to be with her friends or, with people like you, but that's as far as it goes. Her future is more important and that comes before everything else.'

'She's a wonderfully gifted violinist,' I said, trying to gain my composure. 'Do you realise that?'

'Yes of course we do,' he barked. 'We've paid enough for her lessons over the years and yes, she does have talent. But that will only serve to help in her future professional life.'

'I don't follow you,' I said.

'Being musical is good for the brain, we all know that for a fact,' he answered. 'But being a musician is no way to go through life and make a professional living. There's a clear distinction between the two.'

'Well, that's what I am,' I said, in a show of defiance. 'I'm a professional and I'm doing okay,' I lied.

'Precisely my point,' he said. 'Doing okay is not good enough. Following a rootless, feckless existence with a band of teenagers from College. How can that be described as being a solid basis for the future?'

I looked at him dumbfounded and I wondered if he was related to that awful Head Nun at his daughter's school as he continued lecturing me.

'Yes, you may have a job in further education, well, bully for you. But that could end at the stroke of a pen. Then what would you do?' he demanded. 'Go busking around the town centre streets for spare change? Hardly the definition of being a professional is it?'

'Well, I agree that busking is not very highly rated, but that's not the point.'

I tried to argue but I could see I was on a slippery slope.

'It's exactly the point. Ros needs a solid base for her future and the law will give her that,' he said, firmly. 'It hasn't done me any harm over the years and yes we have a nice lifestyle, but it didn't come without making some sacrifices. Her music, like my rugby when I was a young man, will always be there to enjoy as a pastime, a hobby. But that's all it is and all it ever will be.'

I tried to intervene again, but he cut across me before I could get the words out. 'Where are you from anyway?' he asked. 'You have an accent. Is it American?'

'No,' I said. 'My parents have a farm back in Ontario, Canada.'

'Hm, well, it's better us being straight with you from the outset. We make a point of being civil to all the friends and acquaintances of Ros's, even foreigners,' he added as a joke, but it didn't work. 'Her path in life is set out and she doesn't need, or want, any distractions from it at this critical stage.'

Just then, the lounge door opened and in walked Rosalyn. She looked radiant, dressed in a light floral summer dress and her smile lit up the room. I was smitten again as I stood up and said hello and I noticed her dad watching me carefully with one eye.

'Hi. I see you've brought your guitar,' she said. 'That's great. I was thinking about some songs we could work on this afternoon.'

'I've just been explaining to this young man here what your immediate priorities are, Ros,' interrupted her father. 'Just so that he understands how the land lies and doesn't get the wrong impression.'

'Well, what I wanted to ask Rosalyn and explore with her,' I said, choosing my words very carefully, 'was this. We've got a possibility to combine her talents with those of my band for an upcoming competition which will get some TV coverage. You never know it may just work.'

He wasn't convinced and pulled a face at me.

'And on the balance of probabilities, it won't. And even if it did by some remote miracle, how long do you think it would last as a sustainable career?' he asked.

God, this damned guy had an answer for everything and annoyingly, he seemed to be right each time. I thought he was being a bit too harsh and Rosalyn seemed to be dismayed by her father's attitude towards me.

As I nodded back politely in acknowledgement, but not necessarily in agreement with him, I looked from father to daughter and then again and wondered who was right. Was she correct in making her own decisions and life choices, which may of course include studying law, or was dad correct in channelling her into a pre-determined career path of his own choosing?

Mr Carter stood up. 'Now I've got to go,' he announced. 'I've an appointment on the first tee and your lunch will be ready, so enjoy your afternoon.'

He looked at me directly and said, 'For all the right reasons, I look forward to not seeing you again. I have made our position clear and would expect you as a professional, so you say, to respect it and abide by it.'

With that he showed us through to a dining room where his wife had laid out a meal of cold meats and salads.

What could I say? He had the knack of being pleasant whilst putting me firmly in my place. But his wife seemed more friendly and she beckoned me to sit down. As I did so, I looked at the talented beauty at the other side of the table and smiled and wondered if I was way out of my league here. Maybe I was, but I'd taken the decision to turn up and she captivated me.

Over lunch, her mum introduced herself as Katherine and asked me lots of questions about my family and my younger life back in Ontario. She was pleasant and friendly and I could tell from her accent and voice that she'd originated in Ireland. I got the impression she was used to dealing with people in a sensitive and caring manner and I began to feel more comfortable, even if we didn't talk about the band.

However, she did remark that she'd heard we had made a strong impression at the school. She didn't say if it was a good or bad one, but Rosalyn just giggled and her mum smiled, so I said diplomatically, 'Well, we tried to put on our best show, but we are nowhere near as good as Rosalyn.'

'Sorry if my husband gave you the third degree,' said Mrs Carter. 'He's always got his barrister's head on when he wants to make a point. He, well, both of us really, only want the best for Ros. I'm sure you understand that.'

'Yes, I do understand,' I answered. But that didn't necessarily mean that I agreed with them if their chosen route was not the same as Rosalyn's. It may have been, but I didn't want to provoke an argument by asking the question.

We finished lunch and Mrs Carter announced that she needed to pop into town for some things and would be back home at five.

'Will you clear the table please, Ros?' she asked.

'And let me help you,' I blurted out, as we gathered up the plates and cutlery.

I followed Rosalyn into the kitchen with my hands full and gasped. The room was bigger than the entire downstairs of my house and a large window overlooked the back garden and the flower beds in full bloom.

'You have a beautiful place here,' I said. 'All I can see from my kitchen is a dusty pit heap and dirty washing.'

She laughed. 'It's not the house or the view that's important. It's the people in it that determines how nice somewhere is.'

Presently, her mum left us to do her errands and we went through into a conservatory where Rosalyn already had some sheet music scattered around and took her violin out of the case to tune it up. I did the same with my guitar and then there we were, instruments at the ready, wondering what to do next.

'It's an unusual combo, violin and rock guitar, but it can work,' I said. 'There's songs like *Black Water* and of course *Baba O Reilly*, that have great violin solos in them. As well as this one. Do you know *Dust in the Wind?*'

She nodded as I started to pick the guitar strings and then she joined in with the haunting violin riff, partly playing from memory and improvising as she went along. It was such a difference from trying to bang basic chords into the lads back at College and as we played together, I looked at her in wonderment. She gazed back at me and we connected in a silent language, following each other on the melodies and the counterpoint and blending perfectly as she sung with me on the harmonic parts.

The lyrics of the song reflected both the fleeting moment we were in and how quickly it would end and yet at the same time how some things on a higher, spiritual level remained forever, untouched by the material things around us.

'That was beautiful,' I said, as we ended the song before adding, 'As are you.'

She smiled, put down her violin and came over and kissed me. 'Flattery will get you everywhere maestro,' she teased. 'You're not so bad yourself you know. Come with me.'

She took my hand as we walked back into the hallway where she checked that the front door was locked. 'Have to take some precautions, you know,' she said, leading the way upstairs.

'Er, but I don't, er, have anything with me,' I said.

'Shush,' she said, soothingly. 'Mum's a doctor. She's used to seeing lots of young women and men like us and takes a pragmatic view of sex and the world we live in. She sees too many of them making mistakes. Family planning is for when you want a family she says and contraception is for when you don't. So don't worry, I take the pill, just for the rare occasions like this.'

'But I thought the Catholics didn't approve of such things,' I said.

'They don't, so don't go telling mi dad, or he'll kill me.' I nodded back and smiled, thinking he'd no doubt kill me first. 'Plus, I'm only half Catholic anyway,' she said. 'Dad just wanted me to go to the Sisters of Mercy school because it has a good academic reputation.'

'I'm sure it does,' I murmured, watching as she slowly unbuttoned her dress in front of me.

'But I need something to brag about on Monday,' she said, letting the dress fall to the floor and stepping out of it towards me. 'Now, show me how you make love to your women back in Canada.'

'Well, I'd need a tractor and a couple of hay bales to start off with,' I joked, but then I held her close and we kissed passionately as she reached down and unbuckled my jeans.

'Just remember to call me again,' she whispered. 'I'm not getting shipped off to University just yet.'

How the hell could I forget? As the Summer sun shone through her bedroom window and warmed the back of my naked body, we played and loved and, for too brief a time, we forgot that the rest of the world around us existed.

Chapter Eighteen

My world was very much in existence by the time I'd got back to College on the following Monday. After grabbing a cup of coffee, I went through to retrieve any items left in my pigeon-hole and discovered an eagerly-awaited letter from the Leadmill. It was the agenda for the competition which was only five weeks away and I read through the contents with growing excitement as I sat alone in Colin's office.

There were going to be eight bands taking part, including ours. Starting in the morning, we each had a playing slot of fifteen minutes, so no more than three songs per band, which would then be scored by a panel of three judges.

The top three highest scorers would then be invited back to play one song of their choice, then the marks from both sessions would be added together to decide the overall winner, who would be presented with their prize at the end of the day.

The entire event would be filmed by a TV crew for a later broadcast but I was already anticipating the outcome. We were going to win. It just had to be my reward for all I'd done and worked towards over the years and I was convinced that we could walk it if we included Rosalyn in our line-up.

The thought of her brought back the memory of the weekend and caused a queasy feeling deep inside my guts that I knew I couldn't blame on the crap-tasting coffee in my hand.

After being with Rosalyn on the Saturday, I'd spent the Sunday over at Jenny's where I'd talked for ages about the pit closure and how it would affect all the guys and their families that I knew.

But she seemed uncharacteristically down-hearted and bothered by something else. I figured that it was due to me going on about the pit troubles, but she was also quiet at the table and didn't eat much of her lunch. She'd just said she was going into the hospital later on to do some extra hours and so would eat something there, midway through her shift.

She'd asked me about Mick and I'd said I'd helped him clear out his loft space in anticipation of him doing a conversion on the house, in the hope of it increasing in value should he have to sell it at some point. I'd said it had taken longer than we'd expected and the work had gone on into the early evening.

I hoped that Jenny would never work out that Mick's house didn't have a loft to start off with. To my shame I'd reeled off a series of lies with unnerving fluency and I wondered where it was all going to end. But I could hardly tell her where I really was and what I'd done during that wonderful Saturday afternoon.

Had I crossed a line being with Rosalyn? Well, we hadn't done anything that was against the law and it was only the one brief occasion, but I had a nagging doubt that other people would not see things in quite the same way. Maybe if I'd met her out in a pub one night and we'd ended up with each other afterwards, then the matter would seem a little less awkward, but it hadn't been like that. I couldn't escape the fact that we'd met through my job as a tutor, a position that in truth carried a degree of responsibility and care towards those under our instruction.

I tried to convince myself that Rosalyn didn't exactly fall within this definition, but I couldn't deny the fact that technically she was still at school, if only for a couple more weeks. I may not have broken Terry's coveted rule seven, but even I had to admit that I'd definitely put a dent in it and the thought that I'd let him down as my friend caused me some anxiety.

But more important, where was my loyalty to Jenny? I felt ashamed again, realising that it was about time I started putting other people's feelings before my own selfish attitude.

Just because I'd had a lonely existence in London, it didn't necessarily follow that I now had the right to take advantage of others whenever the opportunity arose. Jenny wouldn't see things that way if she knew the details, nor for that matter would Rosalyn's father. I wasn't so sure about what her mother would say, but before I could reach a conclusion, Colin interrupted my self-recriminations as he walked into his office and stared at me.

'Have you ever played cricket?' he asked.

'No,' I replied. 'Isn't that the game which lasts for five days before it's declared a draw because it starts raining?'

'Very funny…and no it isn't. It's a game of skill, guile and excitement, particularly so when it's a limited overs match,' he said. 'We are having one next week against the Council's Properties Department, up at the Woolley Colliery ground.'

'And?' I asked, thinking he wanted me to come along and cheer them on.

'It's a regular fixture that's been goin' on for years, our teaching staff against their officers and it's a great event.

But College pride is at stake. We haven't won for five years an' we need to get back on the scoreboard. We're a man short and we wondered if you'd help out and play in the team?'

'But I don't know the first thing about the game,' I replied.

'You don't need to,' he said. 'If you get the chance to bat then it will be right down the lower order, number nine or ten an' the rest of the time you're just fielding. Match starts at five, sixteen overs each side an' it's all done by eight o'clock. Then we have some beer an' a barbie afterwards an' everyone goes home happy.'

I'd no idea what he was talking about with overs, lower orders or fielding, but one thing struck me.

'Well, I'll play if my band can do a spot afterwards. I've just got the agenda here for the Leadmill competition,' I said, waving it around in my hand. 'It's challenging but I think we can pull it off and any chance we get to play in public beforehand will be good practice. Plus, it will give you the chance to hear how we sound as you've not heard us play yet.'

Now he couldn't really refuse.

'Okay then', he replied. 'I'll have to clear it with the committee guys at the cricket club first. They should be alright wi' it as long as them lads don't get pissed up an' start messing about. Also, you'll need to play some nice stuff that people will appreciate and listen to properly.'

'They won't and we will,' I said. 'They understand that they need to be on top form and ready for the competition and so we are all focused on getting that right.'

Now, could I introduce Rosalyn into this cricket gig as well to see if it would work musically for us?

Later on, I phoned Jenny and told her about being asked to play in the cricket match and that I didn't have a clue what I was supposed to do.

'Dad's a big cricket fan,' she said. 'He used to play for a local side. If you come over, he'll show you what you need to do.'

'Ok, that sounds good,' I agreed.

So she came to pick me up after College the following afternoon and drove me back to her house. Walter was sitting in the garden with his pipe and a beer at his side and he seemed to be positively glowing with enthusiasm.

'So, tha's gonna be playin' cricket then, eh lad?' he asked.

'I think so,' I replied. 'It's not something I'm familiar with as we don't have it back home. More of a minority sport, I think. Only thing we play with a bat and ball is baseball.'

'Minority sport?' he exclaimed, loudly. 'Wad ya talkin' about lad? It's only the greatest bloody game in the world. Wi've bin playin' cricket 'ere in Yorkshire an' knockin' 'ell outa any an' all comers long before thy bloody Country wor invented,' he said.

'Maybe. But I still don't understand it. How do you score some goals for instance?'

'Tha don't,' he said. 'It's all about runs an' it's easy to understand.' He relit his pipe and took a deep breath before continuing.

'Let mi explain,' he said. 'There's two sides, eleven men apiece. One's out in field, t'other's in. Each man in the side that's in, goes out. When he's out he comes in an' next man goes in until he's out.'

I was lost already. 'Goes in where?' I asked, perplexed.

'To bat, stupid. Then, when all men are out, the side that's out comes in and the side that's bin in goes out and tries to get those coming in, out. Are tha followin' mi, lad?'

'No,' I said. 'I'm totally confused.'

'Let me mek it simple for tha,' he said, taking a big puff on his pipe and emitting a cloud of smoke around us.

'When a man goes out to go in, the men in the side who are out try to get him out and when he's out he goes in and the next man goes out and goes in. Are tha wi' me?' he asked, as I looked blankly at him, shaking my head.

'No wonder your Canadian yankee lot couldn't get th'ang of it. Tha' can't follow a simple set o' bloody rules now, can tha?'

I now wished I'd never asked in the first place, but Jenny intervened saying that I could borrow Dad's old gear and he'd even give me some practice.

'Aye,' he said. 'Come on, I'll save mi breath for a more worthy audience an' get tha padded up for nets instead.'

'Nets?' I asked. 'Are we going fishing as well?'

'Are you tekkin piss now?' he asked. 'Here I am tryin' to do thee a good turn an' you're not tekkin' it seriously.'

I followed him and Jenny to the garden shed where, amongst the usual assortment of tools and pots, lay a battered old luggage trunk.

Opening it, Walter pulled out a pair of baggy white flannel trousers and handed them to me, together with an old cricket bat, some moth-eaten leg pads and a pair of thick padded gloves.

'Tha'll be needin' this thing as well,' he said, handing me something that looked like a birdseed scoop on a strappy holster.

'What's that?' I asked.

'It's for, er, protecting tha gulags...an abdominal guard. You might want to 'ave kids one day an' tha doesn't want to be spendin' rest of tha life soundin' like a boy soprano if tha gets nobbled by a fast bowler.'

Jenny giggled as her dad blushed bright pink.

'It's to protect your genitals he means,' she explained to me. 'It's called a box. First used back in 1874 and then a hundred years later they started using helmets to protect their heads. It took men that long to realise that their brains were just as important as their balls.'

'Jenny, there's no need for that,' said Walter. 'This is men's talk.'

'Dad, I'm a nurse,' she replied. 'I see men's balls as often as you see pints of ale. They're nothing to get that excited about.'

'Well, whatever,' he muttered, before turning back to me. 'You'll need it, so might as well 'ave this one. No bugger else will be keen on lending you theirs, plus you don't know where they've been.'

After taking the contraption from him and staring at it closely, I picked up the old cricket bat and swung it around in my arm. It looked like it had been pickled in brown vinegar for about twenty years and it stank like old fish bones.

'What's that awful smell?' I asked, wrinkling my nose up in disgust.

'Linseed oil,' he said. 'Best thing there is for rubbin' into your wood an' gettin' it to perform well.'

'I might try it one day,' I muttered, but he didn't get the joke, ordering me instead to get kitted up in his equipment.

The oversized trousers came up to my rib cage and after strapping on the leg pads and adjusting the abdominal guard to sit as snugly as possible over my valuables, Walter drove us down to the cricket ground at Edlington, not far from where I'd first met Jenny that night at the miners' club.

At the far end of the pitch, some netted-off areas were set up and several lads were batting and bowling to each other, if that was the right terminology. We found one that was empty and Walter set up the wicket stumps.

After showing me what a crease was and how to take a guard, he demonstrated the correct stance to adopt as a batsman, pulling and pushing my limbs with his hands as he spoke.

'Shoulders square on, chin in an' head forward, back straight an' lean slightly over like tha's diggin' an allotment,' he said. 'An' stop waving bloody bat around like tha's swattin' flies, it's not rounders yer know. Now, put them gloves on an' I'll bowl a few easy ones at you.'

I did as I was instructed, feeling very trussed-up and uncomfortable and thinking this was damned complicated for what was supposed to be just a friendly bat and ball game.

'This tek's me back to the days when I used to face fiery Freddie bowling 'is monsters at us,' he said to Jenny. 'By, what a time we 'ad then.'

Turning to me, he shouted, 'Are tha ready now lad?'

'Yes,' I replied and watched as Walter took several steps backwards, before skipping up and lunging a small red ball down the length of grass at me.

As I swung the bat to launch it back over his head, the right stump behind me flew out of the ground.

'Out fer a duck,' Jenny shouted and laughed.

'Keep tha bloody eye on ball, lad,' Walter yelled. 'Watch it an' tap it down, like ah've told yer to. That's all tha needs to do. By the bloody 'ell, the things I have to put up with.'

This performance went on for the best part of an hour before Walter gave up, claiming that his bowling arm and shoulder joint were playing up and giving him some pain.

Secretly I was glad, having been clobbered on the leg pads, ribs and arms, as well as picking up and replacing the stumps countless times and only fleetingly making contact with the ball.

This was not a game, it was a trial of patience and courage, neither of which I had in great commodities and my lower back ached like mad from standing in an unnatural semi-crouched position.

'Still, at least the genitals are okay,' I said to Jenny, tapping the rigid cover inside my pants as we walked back to the car. 'Want to find out if they are still working?'

'I already know they are,' she smiled, then her face flushed slightly before Walter intervened.

'Tha can keep 'em where they are, locked away in that bloody box if tha don't mind,' he said.

Chapter Nineteen

Back at College I told the guys about the Leadmill agenda and the cricket match gig and they were all enthusiastic at another chance to play in public before our competition appearance. But now I had to bring up another subject. 'How do you all feel about adding another player to the band?' I asked.

'Are you replacing one of us then?' asked Woody.

'No, I'm thinking of adding another instrument to our line-up. Might give us something different than the rest of the bands when we go to the Leadmill.'

'Playing what?' asked Robbie.

'A violin,' I replied. 'Which will be amped up to match the volume of the guitars.'

He seemed unenthusiastic. 'But we 'aven't got any violin players in College, 'ave we?' he asked.

'No. I was, er, thinking about Rosalyn. You remember her, from the girls' school gig?'

'Are you shaggin' her?' asked Stevie.

'No,' I lied. 'And anyway, it's the music I'm thinking about. She could add another dimension to our sound. Other successful bands have done it, perhaps we should.'

'But it won't be the same though, will it?' Robbie continued. 'This band is our creation, now you're adding in someone from the outside. Don't think it will work boss.'

'Well, the idea isn't to be the same,' I said. 'It will still be our band. I'm just looking for an edge over the others in this competition.' But I could see from their faces that they weren't convinced by this idea. 'Well, how about if we invite her up for one rehearsal, see how it goes and how we all feel?' I suggested. 'Then we'll make a decision. Will that work?'

'Well, how are we going to invite her?' asked Benji. 'We don't know where she lives or 'owt.'

'Er, I think I've got her phone number somewhere...' I mumbled, as I blushed. 'She gave it to me after the school gig. Just in case.'

'See, he is shaggin' er,' confirmed Stevie.

I could see that they weren't going to be persuaded tonight, so I decided to leave it for the moment. 'Okay, let's get back to work on this piece. Benji, from the top again.' It seemed that it would indeed be a *Cold Day in Hell*, before I could get the lads on my side on this one.

I continued pondering over the practicalities during the following days. Firstly, to get Rosalyn to a band practice, I'd have to call her. That meant dealing with her dad, a no-go area, or her mum, which may be a possibility. But then, she'd have to get across to us in Barnsley which meant her parents knowing where she would be. Next there was the tricky bit about how the guys would take to her. They hadn't shown a lot of enthusiasm so far and apart from them all probably lusting after her, which I certainly didn't want, what effect would she have on us as a group? Perhaps more than anything, how would I keep her separate from Jenny and if not, what would be the consequences if they did meet and started talking? These were tough questions and I didn't yet have the answers ready at hand.

But by the Saturday afternoon this matter had been playing on my mind so much that I plucked up the courage to call Rosalyn, just hoping that her dad would be out playing golf. I was right and she answered the phone, causing my heart to flutter a little as I heard her voice again.

'I'm stuck in here with my revising,' she said. 'Just two more exams to do then I'll be finished.'

'And how are they going?' I asked.

'Fine, I think. But I can't really tell.'

I told her about the upcoming gig at the cricket club and asked if she would like to come along and play with the band. I figured that if I sprung it on the lads at the event they'd hardly take offence and start kicking off in public. It was a risky strategy but if it didn't work then we still had our current line up to fall back on and I knew they wouldn't want to do anything to jeopardise our Leadmill appearance.

'It's possible,' she said. 'Let me just check on the calendar in the kitchen.' The line went silent for a few seconds as I wondered who had calendars on their kitchen walls, before she returned. 'Thought so. Dad's at a golf dinner that night, so I could probably get there,' she said. 'But I'd have to come over with mum. That's the only way it would work as then he probably won't suspect anything.'

'Well, it's at the Woolley Colliery Cricket Club,' I said. 'If you can make it that'll be great, if not there's no problem and I'll call you again when your exams are over. I'm playing in the cricket match they're having beforehand, if you wanted a laugh.'

'Well, I'd be laughing with you, not at you,' she said and again I felt my insides melting. 'I have an idea though if you're free tomorrow,' she continued. 'There's a nice park near me at Sandall and I could meet you around noon for an hour. I go there sometimes for some fresh air so my parents won't suspect anything if I take a break from my revision, as long as I'm back in time for lunch with them.'

Temptation took over as I realised that Jenny was doing a day-shift on the Sunday and I would be at a loose end. 'That sounds great,' I replied. 'Whereabouts shall I meet you?'

'At the boating lake. I'll be sitting on one of the benches, feeding the ducks,' she replied.

'Okay, I'll see you then. Don't work too hard and take care,' I whispered, as I put the phone down on the cradle realising that deep down, I was potentially getting myself into hot water. I might get away with a quick rendezvous tomorrow, but it was more than likely that Jenny would be at the cricket match and gig and if Rosalyn showed up as well, I wondered how I could keep them apart. I'd just invited her and so I could hardly now tell her not to show up.

It was an odd thought to have as I caught the bus to go over to Conisbrough. Walter was going to give me some more net practice before going off to his club for the evening, but I knew that my attention would be diverted elsewhere and not at his cricketing tips.

The following morning, I was up bright and early and after two bus journeys from Highfield over to Sandall Park, I wandered past the bowling green and down towards the boating lake, glancing at my watch as I did so. Weaving my way through the small crowds of families, I watched their toddlers screeching happily as they clutched their dripping ice cream cones and pointed at the ducks and geese. The kids were clearly enjoying being outdoors in the beautiful Summer sunshine.

Rosalyn was sitting on a shaded bench and waved as I approached her.

'Hi,' she said, standing up and kissing me as I returned her embrace. 'Glad you could make it.'

'Me too,' I replied. 'How have you been, er, since the last time I saw you?' I asked, awkwardly and my face blushed as the words came out.

She laughed. 'I'm fine. Our time together was wonderful and I hope it wasn't our last.'

'Yes,' I agreed, guiltily. 'Maybe we'll get some more time together before you go off to Uni. Do you know where you are going to yet?'

'Depends on my results,' she replied, as we started strolling hand in hand. 'Cambridge want straight A's but London is a bit less stringent. Either way, it will be a big change and very daunting to say the least. Can't say I'm looking forward to it.'

'Everyone feels like that,' I said. 'Just look at me, I moved countries to come here and study. You'll meet loads of new friends and have a great time.'

But she didn't look convinced. 'Maybe, but I don't have your confidence,' she replied. 'I'm more of a shy person around people. My friends at school will be going to Manchester or Liverpool, but I doubt we'll keep in touch with each other. I think my violin is my best friend.'

'Well, you need confidence to play it like you do,' I said. 'You have a gift and you wouldn't be able to show it if you lacked confidence. All the best musicians are naturally nervous people, you know. It's what makes them produce superior performances. Plus, you have me as well. I'm more than just your friend, really,' I added.

'Yes, I know.' She sighed. 'When I'm playing, I feel like I'm in another world where everyday things don't matter. But in the real world, it's not like that, is it? You and I are passing each other on different roads. I'll shortly be packed off down South and you will be up here doing your thing.'

'Well, let's take things as they come,' I replied. 'The Leadmill gig may make all the difference. I think we can win it and you never know, it might even convince your dad that there's a future in music.'

She laughed. 'No chance of that. But yes, it would be good to show him he can't be right all the time,' squeezing my hand as if in silent reassurance as we walked slowly around the lake.

To all intents we appeared as two young lovers discussing music and sweet nothings and even though I wanted to stretch out every moment of our time together, the hour quickly evaporated before she turned her head to me again.

'I've got to get back now,' she said, giving me a hug and a final kiss. 'Thanks for coming to see me,' she added, gazing into my eyes. 'It's just what I needed.'

'Me too. Good luck with your exams this week,' I replied. 'Then let's see what happens,' as I watched her walking away from me before eventually disappearing between the distant stone pillars of the park gates. She was out of sight but not out of my mind and I wondered what trouble I was getting myself into.

*

I rehearsed the band lads hard during the following week and we got a thirty-minute set together for the Woolley gig. It wasn't too heavy or demanding, just some soft rock and blues tracks that we could get through, and more important, that Rosalyn could busk along to if she turned up. Terry offered to provide his van for us free as he could claim back the expense as College activities and so we were all sorted.

At three pm on the Friday afternoon we left for the cricket ground and I warned the lads to stay off the booze and watch the match instead. It was a beautiful Summer's afternoon and the ground provided great views across the surrounding hills and open countryside. I got changed into Walter's gear inside the van and then helped the guys carry our stuff into the social club pavilion where we'd be playing later on.

Outside the building, two old blokes in shirtsleeves and cloth caps were sat together on a bench, clutching a pint of beer each and enjoying the sunshine. As I passed by them one shouted out, 'Naw then lad, 'oo tha playin' wi' tonight?'

'College,' I answered.

'Cold Edge?' he asked. 'Bloody good side, them lads.'

'No,' I said. 'It's the College. We're playing the Council, from Barnsley.'

'Barnsley?' shouted the second guy. 'Ow've they gone on then today?'

'No,' I shouted back. 'The Council, not the football team.'

'Council?' repeated the first guy. 'Them buggers never empty our bins on time. An' tha's no need to shout lad. Ah'm only deaf in one ear.'

'Sorry,' I said.

'Surrey?' shouted the second guy. 'Are they playin' 'ere tonight?'

'Enjoy the game gents,' I said, walking off and hoping that they didn't ask for requests from us later on.

Once all the cricket players had assembled, a coin was tossed and I looked at Colin, who told me that the Council team would be batting first, as our side started to make their way out onto the field.

'Will you go over to square leg?' asked the Head of Mechanical Engineering, otherwise known as our Captain this afternoon.

'What?' I said. I'd no idea what he was on about, but Colin pointed to a patch of empty grass on the other side of the ground.

'If the ball comes your way, then throw it back to the keeper,' he said.

'Who?' I asked.

'Our wicket keeper, Melvyn,' he said, pointing to the chap standing behind the set of stumps.

Play was started by an old guy wearing a white coat and I wondered if he would be coming round at half time with a tray of cockles and seafood. After sixteen overs and not much activity on my section of the field, it was time to change sides. The Council team seemed good, having scored a total of ninety-two runs and they had only used up seven of their batters.

As our team went in, or out, to bat, I couldn't remember which from Walter's instructions, I sat next to Colin on the pavilion verandah. He was batting at number seven and I was given number ten.

'Don't pay any attention to their wicket keeper,' he said, pointing to a stout, ugly-looking brute stretching his legs in peculiar angles behind the batsman's stumps. 'He'll no doubt be sledging in a bit.'

I looked at him puzzled. 'Are we expecting snow?' I asked, glancing up at the blazing sun.

'No, you idiot. It's an expression we use when one side tries to intimidate the batsmen into droppin' their concentration an' makin' a mistake.'

This game had a foreign language all of its own, I thought. No wonder we didn't have it back home where we preferred things to be a little more straight-forward and understandable.

'And watch out for that guy as well,' said Colin, pointing to a slim, good-looking guy about my age, who was limbering up to bowl his first ball.

'Why? Who is he?' I asked.

'Soapy Wrightson,' he replied. 'And a damned good cricketer, he is an' all.'

'Why's he called Soapy?' I asked.

'Because he's their clean up specialist. He's usually a slow spin bowler, but every so often he'll slip in a fast one that takes out the tail enders.' I fiddled with my genitals box whilst trying to work this out and hoped that Soapy would be all washed up by the time it was my turn to bat and thus would leave my tail end where it was, safely tucked up and out of harm's way.

I glanced around at the number of people who were watching the game. There was quite a crowd and they seemed intent on following the proceedings, applauding politely as they supped their beer in the sun. I spotted Jenny, who waved at me before adjusting her straw boater as she lolled back on a deck chair, her tanned legs seductively crossed and she looked gorgeous.

Our side chalked up fifty-nine runs which seemed good to me, but apparently wasn't and we were losing. Colin went out to bat and did well, adding a further twenty-five runs pretty quickly. Then his running mate was caught after hitting one in the air before his replacement was given out for three after being found with his leg before wicket, as I was reliably informed by a colleague. I pondered the possible meaning of this for a while as where else could his leg have been if not in front of the wicket, but I couldn't make any sense of it.

Then our Captain yelled at me to fasten up my pads and get out there.

'James Martindale,' announced a tinny voice from a tannoy speaker on the side of the pavilion and I got a cheer from the band lads and a clap from Jenny as I walked out to take my place.

I stood at the wicket as Walter had shown me and nodded at the umpire. Behind him, a tall bloke with a droopy black slug moustache seemed to be walking off the field, before suddenly turning round, charging up like a bull and windmilling his arm round as I squinted at him. I felt something rush past my ear and before I had even moved, their keeper was tossing the ball back to his fielders.

Shit, I hadn't even seen that one coming down, let alone try and hit it and as my legs started to wobble I turned round in the hope of an encouraging word from their wicket keeper.

'Waz thy lookin' at?' he growled, menacingly. 'Does tha want mi to black thi lamps for thi? We'll 'ave tha wi' this next one, just see.'

I turned back and realised it was all part of the sledge act that Colin had mentioned although I just felt like whipping round again and wrapping the bat around his neck. But then that just wouldn't be cricket.

The bowler seemed to disappear behind the umpire and I lifted my head for a better view before he suddenly reappeared and let another missile fly. I didn't see this one either but swung my bat wildly as hard as I could, only to see it fly sideways out of my hand and nearly connect with one of their fielders beyond the wicket. A cheer went up amid the ribald laughter coming from the other players at my cack-handed performance and as I retrieved my bat and settled back at the crease, I thought, right, watch this, you fuckers.

This time the bowler changed tack and tried a slower ball which I followed like a cat on a cornered mouse. I stepped forward and swung the bat like a baseball slogger, catching the ball firmly and it flew up into the sky over my left shoulder. Everyone was 'ooing' and then I heard the word 'six' and a cheer being shouted out, as I stepped backwards watching where the ball would come down to land - and promptly fell over the stumps behind me.

'How 'is 'ee?' yelled out the fat keeper as I got to my feet and then I saw the umpire pointing up at the clouds, prompting me to look up there as well, wondering what was flying overhead.

'That means tha's out, yer dozy git,' the wicket keeper roared at me.

My cricket debut was over as I slumped back to the pavilion. Only in this game could you hit a sixer and yet still be out. It would have won the game for us if only I hadn't been so clumsy, but thank God, it was now over.

We of course lost the match by a whisker, but I didn't care despite the College not regaining their respect against the Council team. Everyone seemed to be in good spirits as they milled round with a drink and a burger and I got the band guys organised on the verandah. We were tuned up and ready to start when suddenly she was there: Rosalyn came over to us whilst her mum took a seat at a table and I introduced her to the band.

Surprisingly, they were all polite and welcoming towards her. She was dressed casually in light jeans and a tee shirt top and looked stunning. I got her amped up and sound-checked then we were all set to go and kicked off with *Maggie May*.

Rosalyn took it all in her stride. She had a perfect ear for listening and recognising the chords and then improvising and putting in solo sections when I nodded to her. And all without rehearsing. We went straight into *Rock'n Me Baby* and then *Cherry Bomb* and we sounded great. Then we played our version of *Like a Fox on the Run* and as I looked over at her and sung the lyrics with the sun shining down on us, I realised they could have been written just for her. It was magical stuff for a warm Summer's evening and to hell with the cricket shit, this was more like it.

We got some pleasant applause as we played and as we took a breather, I introduced all the members of the band individually. Then as I looked around the audience, I nearly dropped the mike as I saw Jenny in deep conversation with Rosalyn's mother. Whatever they were talking about seemed quite intense from a distance and I tried not to stare. How did they know each other? Shit, I thought, this could turn out bad for me tonight.

After another couple of numbers, we were due to finish the set with *Run to You* which I thought was amusingly relevant seeing that we were at a cricket ground, before it suddenly dawned on me that the song was actually about a guy juggling his time between two female lovers. Moreover, the original artiste was also a fellow Canadian. Could I have picked a more inappropriate piece? Woody was already starting up the opening groove on the hi-hats and I had to get him to play them quietly and keep repeating the section, as I turned back to address the audience, feeling my cheeks already starting to burn red.

I tried to make a joke by saying we were dedicating this last track to the Council team in recognition of their superior performance this evening and whilst that got a few laughs, inside I was sweating and panicking in case anyone made a connection between me, Jenny and Rosalyn. Maybe it was just my guilty conscience working overtime, but there was no going back now and so off we went with the opening riffs and first verse.

When I reached the chorus lines, I sang them out with the passion they deserved, all the time looking at...Terry. He was stood alone over by the bar and it was the only way I could concentrate on the song. Rosalyn put in a blistering solo in the middle section as I shadowed her with the counterpoint theme on the guitar and boy, we sounded pretty good.

Colin came up to congratulate us as soon as we'd finished. 'That was great guys...and lady,' he said, looking straight at Rosalyn. 'You were fabulous.'

He stood with her chatting about her violin and nodding in a very scholarly fashion and I let them carry on as the rest of the lads crowded round them to share their compliments with our latest member. I hadn't actually asked them yet what they thought but it was clear that they all liked her.

Jenny came up and gave me a big hug and a kiss saying, 'Wow, I'm glad you're a singer and not a cricketer. Even though that lucky shot could have been the match winner...if you hadn't been so dopey,' she laughed.

'Thanks,' I said. 'Let me just get a beer, then we can chat.'

As I reached the bar, I said to Terry, 'You've gotta get me outa here and fast.'

However, he just laughed and looked at me instead. 'Tha's made tha bed lad, now tha's gotta lie on it,' before adding, 'but she's really bloody good sawing on that fiddle though, isn't she?' Did he know what was going on? Despite his bluff exterior, Terry had a nose for working things out and I more than suspected he had an inkling in his mind. But now was not the time to ask and so instead I decided to go and say thanks to Rosalyn for coming along this evening.

'I can't really chat now as I've got to pack up all our gear and load up with these guys so that Terry can get on with his taxi round,' I said to her. It was a miserable excuse and I knew it. 'But thanks for turning up tonight, you were great. I'll call you about the Leadmill when I've spoken with the guys.'

She smiled and said, 'Okay, don't forget. I've got to go now anyway as mum needs to be back home.'

God, she was so understanding of me and I watched her go, waving discreetly to her mum as they left together.

'So that's Rosalyn is it?' asked Jenny. 'She's good on that violin. What do you think of her?'

Shit, does she know what's been goin' on here, as well? 'Yes, she wanted, er, an audition with the band, but tonight was the only time she could make it,' I said. I desperately needed to get out of this hole. 'Who was that woman you were talking with earlier?' I asked.

'That was Doctor Carter. She's my GP,' she answered. 'I've known her for years but didn't realise until just now that she's also Rosalyn's mum, you know.'

'No, I didn't know,' I lied. 'Small world, sometimes.'

'Yes, talking of which, I need to –,' but she was interrupted by Terry as he came across to join us.

'Now then lass, how's that car o' yours?' he joked. 'Not been climbing any trees wi' it lately?'

Jenny laughed back and tapped his arm playfully. She really was great fun to be with and my guilt started to well up inside me again. I smiled and went along with things but underneath there was one thing I knew for certain.

Rosalyn was becoming part of my life but I wasn't at all sure how that would manifest itself going forward.

After tonight's stunning performance she just had to be with us, no question, when we appeared at the Leadmill.

I knew that sooner or later I was going to have to discuss the matter with Jenny, but tonight the atmosphere was enjoyable and jovial, so I opted for later. The sun was setting over the distant hills and the cricket guys and supporters from both sides were laughing and drinking and thoroughly enjoying what had been a great evening all round.

Looking at Jenny, I also tried to make a joke out of things.

'I was glad to part company with your dad's box,' I said. 'My balls are in need of some therapy after being cooped up like battery hens today.'

'Well, if you're lucky I might give them the free-range treatment tonight,' she answered, coyly. 'I'm staying at yours so get them prepared to be bowled over by your maiden.'

The thought took my mind off other things for the moment. 'Sounds like just what the doctor ordered,' I said, with a smile.

Chapter Twenty

Jenny lay in my arms as we snoozed in bed the following Saturday morning whilst the street below us slowly came to life. I heard the rattle of bottles from the milkman's float and as I became more awake, I tried to put my thoughts into some logical order. The Leadmill gig was in three weeks' time after which Jenny and I were planning to go away for a couple of weeks holiday. We hadn't decided between Scotland or Cornwall yet but either way, Walter had agreed to lending us the car and I felt certain he would sell it to me when we returned, having put some considerable mileage on the clock during the trip.

I also felt sure I could persuade Rosalyn to do the Leadmill gig with us, but what would happen if we actually won? Would she be willing to postpone her University place to join a tour? I was reasonably sure I could get some sabbatical leave from the College for a period of time, but how would Jenny react to that, if it meant I was going to be away touring with a load of rockers?

I knew that the band lads would all be game for it and would just take a break from their studies. Two of them had still got another year of their courses to do and the other two had opted to do a further year by converting their diplomas into performance-related degrees, all courtesy of the free education available to students in this Country. In the meantime, Jenny was at the hospital full time and I still had my job at the College, so we were doing okay for money and job security. Unlike some people, like Mick and his pit colleagues, whose lives were about to be turned upside down.

Beside me, Jenny stirred and stretched her limbs. 'Urgh, I don't feel too good,' she said. 'Must have been that Chinese, or something.'

We'd had our usual takeaway meal for two from Wing Lees last night after getting back from the cricket, but I noticed she hadn't drunk as much wine as usual and her unfinished glass was still on the bedside cabinet. In my normal tawdry and lazy fashion, as well as wanting to get her into bed as quickly as possible, I'd left the remains of our food downstairs and the stale odours of fried rice, garlic and chow mein which had been slowly drifting upstairs all night now became abundantly obvious to me.

'I'll go and clear away the rubbish and leftovers and make us some coffee,' I said, getting up and drawing the curtains back before opening the window slightly to let some fresh air in.

'Okay,' she answered, but as I went downstairs I heard her hurry to the bathroom and start retching.

That'll teach me to live on take-aways I thought, as I got the coffee ready but before I could return upstairs with the drinks, there was a sharp knocking on the front door.

The now-familiar delivery man was standing there as I opened the door in my undies.

'Some stuff for Mr Simms,' he said, and I nodded and turned as he followed me into the house with a large parcel in his hands.

As I went back into the kitchen, I glanced out into the yard and was startled to see a couple of blue uniforms bounding over the gate. Then there was a crashing noise and commotion going on at the front door as several more of them came rushing into the house.

'Stay where you are!' barked a police officer at the delivery man, as two others manhandled him to his knees and cuffed his hands behind his back. 'You're under arrest,' he shouted at him.

Then a familiar face was straight in front of mine, breathing stale beer and curry over me.

'You! I'm arresting you for possession,' yelled PC Fletcher. 'Anythin' you say will be taken down…and all that shite,' he said. 'Now, go an' put some fuckin' clothes on. We're tekkin' you in fo' questioning.'

I ran back upstairs as he followed me. 'I'm being nicked,' I shouted to Jenny, who was peering nervously around the bathroom door, startled by all the noise.

'Who's she?' demanded Fletcher.

'My girlfriend,' I yelled back at him. 'She doesn't live here. Whatever you are accusing me of, she has nothing to do with it,' I protested.

'Write yer details down now for me wi' full address an' phone number,' he shouted at Jenny as she emerged from the bathroom wrapped in just a robe. 'We need to know where we can find thee if we need to wi'out looking too long.'

'Here, take my house keys Jenny,' I said. 'Ring Terry and tell him what's gone on. He'll know what to do. And take my guitar home with you for safe keeping. Everything will be fine, you'll see. This is all one big mistake.'

She nodded back to me, but I could see she was worried.

'Where are you taking me?' I said to the charming Fletcher, as I grabbed some clothes and began putting them on.

'As far away from my patch as I can,' he replied. 'But for now, tha's gonna be questioned at Mexboro' station.'

Once I was dressed, he bundled me downstairs, where I was cuffed and marched into the back of a waiting van. The neighbours across the road were either on the pavement or staring through their windows at us. The delivery guy was pushed into a separate van and his vehicle was photographed before being driven off by another officer. Police cars had blocked the top and bottom of Gladstone Terrace and the whole scene looked like something from a TV cop show. Except it wasn't; it was real and I was shit-scared of what was going to happen to me next.

Down at the station I was processed in the same way as my previous visit to Rotherham nick. I handed over my wallet, before being told to wait whilst they got the photograph room ready. 'What am I being arrested for?' I asked.

The sergeant handling my charge sheet looked back at me. 'Says here, suspected possession of a controlled substance, with intent to supply. In plain terms that means drug-dealin' an' plenty of jail time to look forward to.'

That was rubbish as I already knew, but still I was worried. At first I thought I'd been raided because of the dodgy pornos from Dave's corner shop, but then dismissed it as they wouldn't have needed a dramatic operation like the one I'd just witnessed. No, it was that damned delivery driver and his suspect packages for my landlord, which I now realised were drug related and how I'd been caught up in it all. They were using my house as a drop-off point and I'd no doubt have to give some answers to the plods. Maybe if I just sat tight, kept calm and explained how I'd nothing to do with it or them, it would all blow over and I could go back home.

After mug shots and fingerprints were taken, I was kept waiting in a cell to stew for a couple of hours. Eventually, I was taken into an interview room where a fat guy with a briefcase and a weary expression was sitting at a table making some notes. He motioned at me to sit next to him.

'I'm Taylor, the duty solicitor here,' he said. 'Just say nowt at this stage, whilst they ask you some questions. You have the right to remain silent, so just keep quiet for the time being whilst we find out a bit more about things.'

'But I haven't done anything,' I pleaded. 'It's that cop Fletcher, he just doesn't like me for some reason.'

At the mention of his name, Fletcher entered the room with another more senior officer and the pair of them sat opposite me. The older guy flicked a switch on a cassette tape recorder before announcing his presence.

'I'm Detective Inspector Stockton and I gather you already know the arresting officer present here with me, PC Fletcher. Time is one fifteen in the afternoon. We 'ave some questions to ask you and how you respond to them will determine how quickly you will get out of here.'

He went through an extensive list of asking who I was and how long I'd lived at my address and despite the earlier advice from the solicitor bloke Taylor, I answered all his questions truthfully and accurately. I was careful to underline the fact that I had nothing to do with any drugs or stolen goods or any deliveries or anything connected to my landlord, other than the fact that I paid him my rent every week. 'There's a rent book and a copy of the tenancy agreement at the house,' I confirmed. 'It's in the cupboard, next to the staircase.'

As the older officer questioned me and made some notes, Fletcher remained silent, constantly turning over and studying the contents of my wallet on the table in front of him and occasionally glancing up at me. Eventually, picking up my ID card, he finally spoke.

'Says 'ere you're a bloody foreigner. From Canada.'

'Well, it doesn't say I'm a foreigner, you idiot,' I replied, losing my temper. 'But yes, I'm from Canada.'

'Well, what gives you the right to be 'ere then, in this Country? he asked.

'What do you mean? I've been here for over six years without any problems.'

'Well, you've got one now,' he replied.

'What are you talking about?' I asked. 'I haven't done anything wrong,' wondering where this was heading.

He leant back in his chair and looked down his nose at me. 'You see, wi've been doin' some checkin' up on you. Seems you entered this Country on a student visa. That means it would 'ave been time limited to tha period of study.'

I nodded without saying anything.

'So, are tha still a student then?' he asked. 'If so, students 'ave no money to speak of, so is this 'ow you fund your lifestyle, by supplying drugs?'

'I don't supply fucking drugs and never have,' I said, angrily, as Taylor tapped away at my arm but I ignored him. 'And no, I'm no longer a student. I have a job at the College at Barnsley.'

'Ah, but you 'ave no visa to work 'ere, does tha?' said Fletcher. 'That makes thee an illegal in our book.'

I stared back at him in bewilderment.

'Unless you can produce a visa sayin' you've the right to work in the UK, then tha's got a one-way ticket back to mountie-fuckin' land, matey,' he said. 'After tha's been detained here for a long while, naturally.'

'Well, if you let me go now I'll bring my passport in and show you the visa I've got,' I said, clearly worried about where this questioning was going.

'Yes, give my client the time to get the documentation you've asked for,' said the solicitor. 'I'm sure if you release him, he'll get back to you with what you need right away. He's clearly not involved in this drug dealing ring you're ludicrously accusing him of being a part of.'

'Oh, but we don't know that yet,' replied Stockton. 'We 'ave the right to search his house and will be doin' so and anything we find will be looked at carefully. In the meantime, he's going nowhere. We believe he's an illegal and that means only one thing. He'll be charged as one right away and locked up. Then 'eld over at Lindholme.'

'What's that?' I asked the solicitor.

'Jail, near Doncaster,' he replied. 'They also use it as a detention centre for illegal immigrants pending a court hearing to deport them. They have the right to do it if you don't have the documentation to prove you can work in this Country. For now, shut up, as I advised you to do earlier.'

My heart sank. Of all the things, this was not what I'd expected. Fletcher took great delight in reading out a formal charge which was just a blur of words, after which I was told I'd be held in custody, pending removal and a court appearance whenever they could get one arranged. They didn't seem to be in much of a hurry as they left me alone with the solicitor and Fletcher gave me a smug grin as he walked out of the door.

Taylor then gave me a run-down of what would take place next and I started to panic as this was looking bad. 'See if you can get hold of my friend Terry,' I said, giving him the number. 'He'll know what to do and where I'll be if I'm moved off somewhere. At least then he'll get a visit to me arranged.'

'They'll probably hold you here until Monday,' said Taylor. 'It'll give 'em time to search your house and they'll have to tell me if they find anything incriminating and wish to question you further about it. In the meantime, is there anything you want to tell me?' he asked. 'You can disclose whatever you like in complete confidence.'

'There's nothing to tell you. I've got nothing to do with any drugs or stuff,' I protested. 'Just call Terry and also let my girlfriend Jenny know what's happening,' as I gave him her number. 'She'll be worried sick about me.'

'Will do,' he said. 'For now, stay calm. There's nothing more you can do at this stage and I'll be back to see you in the morning.' He got up from the desk and signalled to the desk sergeant who came to walk me back down to the cell.

'Waz tha want for tha dinner tonight 'ere at the Mexboro' hotel?' he asked.

'Do I have a choice?' I asked.

'No. Whatever tha wants, tha won't be gerrin it,' he smirked, as he locked me up. 'But I just like to ask our guests all the same. Good customer service an' all that bollocks, yer know.'

I was eventually given some food and an evening paper to read, but it was a long and lonely night and my mind was doing cartwheels. Yes, I had an expired visa stamp in my passport. No-one had questioned it before, so I'd foolishly ignored it. The cops had probably got hold of it by now if they'd searched Gladstone Terrace. They wouldn't have found any stolen stuff or drugs, but it seemed they could send me back home because of something I didn't have, rather than something criminal that I had done and that just didn't seem right in my mind.

In the morning I was brought a breakfast tray and then told I had a visit arranged for eleven o' clock. Just before the appointed time an officer led me back down to the interview room where Terry and Jenny were sitting at the table waiting for me. My spirits rose at the sight of them, although Jenny was wiping tears from her eyes and Terry had a concerned look about him. Maybe this was going to be more bad news for me I thought, as they both put on a brave face to greet me and I joined them at the table.

'How can I get out of this mess Terry?' I asked. 'They're on about me being an illegal. But I thought as a Commonwealth citizen I could stay here for seven years at a time? Doesn't make sense.'

'I'm looking in on it lad, but we'll need a good lawyer for you,' he replied. 'Not that duty guy who called me. He's just on hand for anyone that the cops bring in. He told us we could see you today before you get moved to, er, prison. He's just in the office over yonder now, goin' through all paperwork he needs.'

Jenny began to cry and I held her hand to try and comfort her. 'Jenny, don't worry, this is all a misunderstanding.'

'I'll find out some more at College tomorrow about what we can do,' said Terry. 'But I don't suppose you know any lawyers on the off-chance, do you?'

A name came to my mind but for the moment I kept quiet and looked instead at Jenny.

'It's that dickhead cop Fletcher who's to blame for all this,' I said. 'He's been after me since…well, for ages now, for some reason. He's a vindicative bastard and he won't get away with it.'

'Maybe,' she said. 'But there's something else I've been meaning to tell you. I was going to tell you on Friday night but we didn't get the chance and then again yesterday, if all this crap hadn't happened instead.'

I wondered if she already knew about Rosalyn and me and I looked at her guiltily. If I'd been rumbled, then I'd have to own up. 'What is it?' I asked.

'I'm pregnant,' she answered. 'You're going to be a dad. Sometime in January, I think. That's, er, if I decide I'm going to keep it.'

'But I thought…' I trailed off, shocked. 'You're a nurse and all that…'

'We still get pregnant, you idiot,' she said. 'That's what I was talking about with Dr Carter after the cricket game. I'd been to see her in the morning and she'd confirmed my condition.'

'So, what did she say to you at the gig?' I asked.

'Well, she asked me how I was feeling and what my plans for the future were,' she answered. 'Plus, things like whether I had a boyfriend and was he the father and did he know about it. I said to her that's him singing up there and no, I haven't told him yet.'

God, could things get any worse for me? I was stunned by Jenny's news and even more so by the thought of her conversations with Rosalyn's mum. Unless Dr Carter was strict about her patient confidences, Rosalyn would by now know that I had a regular girlfriend, which I hadn't previously mentioned to her and even worse, that I was going to become a dad.

Professional ethics apart, I couldn't see such news being kept away from her by her mum. If anything, it would only help her parents in steering her towards the University place they had planned for her and as far away as possible from music and from me. I'd no way of finding out and stuck in here, I would have to assume the worst.

'Come on lass, I'll look after tha,' said Terry, putting his arm around Jenny to comfort her. 'Everythin' will be fine, tha'll see.'

Then turning back to me, he said, 'I'll get that Taylor bloke to sort out some visits for us during next week. Keep yer chin up, lad, we'll get you sorted out,' but he wasn't sounding convincing as I thanked them both for coming to see me.

After the visit, I was trundled back to my cell. Then a couple of hours later Taylor appeared to tell me I was going to be moved to Lindholme in the morning and needed to go through loads of paperwork with me beforehand. He told me that the police search of my house had not uncovered anything that was related to the drug bust and so I would not be charged with anything further. It was a relief, but it didn't make matters any better as far as I was concerned.

'I'll arrange a visit to you from Terry and from your girlfriend and I'll also find you a brief to handle your case,' he said. 'There's only so much I can do for you as I have to be available to all the other criminals, er, citizens, that they haul in here.'

Thanking him for his efforts, he left me in the cell and I suddenly felt weak and no longer in control of my life. My mind raced feverishly over the options, as I saw them. I could go back home, a single man. Start again, do something else, put all this down to experience and have some great stories to tell, maybe even write some songs about it. That would be it and my life could carry on regardless and be no worse for the experience.

After all, lots of professional musicians have left lovers behind in their wake all over the world and, hell, there had been dozens of songs written about lost women and unrequited love over the years. My story would be no different and it may even add to my credibility as a singer.

Or maybe I could marry Jenny, if she would have me of course. Become a family man and that may allow me to stay in this Country. Something told me it was the more honourable option to take, but it might not work out at all, particularly if she knew about me and Rosalyn.

I desperately needed a lawyer and a good one at that to dig me out of this hole. I only knew one and that was Rosalyn's father. Would he help me? And what if I agreed to marry Jenny, what about the band and Rosalyn? Our forthcoming gig at the Leadmill was now looking doubtful and I might have to forget about that.

After a sleepless night, I was put into a transit van and escorted by two police officers whilst my mind repeatedly played the song *Worried Man Blues* back to me as if in sadistic torment at my situation. There was one thing I knew for sure though, as we drove across towards Doncaster. I was going to have to make a decision and whatever I decided, it was going to have big consequences...and really big ones at that.

Chapter Twenty One

The first full day of my incarceration at HMP Lindholme passed without incident, as I learned the routine and activities to be followed as a locked-up guest of Her Majesty.

I was amongst a group of males aged between thirty to fifty I reckoned, all of whom seemed to be foreign nationals judging from the languages I heard, even though I couldn't understand them. Despite being surrounded by other people, it was a lonely and worrying time. However, the one thing I did have was no distractions; once the lights had been switched off at ten and we were all locked up for the night, I had all the time in the world to think.

A bright August moon shone through the latticed metal bars covering the small cell window and created a chessboard-patterned grey shadow on the back of the door and adjoining wall. The eerie soft light reminded me of the harvest moon as we used to call it back home in Ontario. It was around this time of the year that everyone was geared up for the busiest time of the farming calendar and my thoughts drifted back to my youth amongst the fields of corn and root crops and then returned again to the present. How the hell had I ended up in here?

My folks were both ordinary, unambitious but hard-working farmers. They were pleasant and helpful to others and made a point of going to church on Sundays, usually dragging me along unwillingly with them. Nice but dull, as I'd often say to my schoolmates, when we talked about living exciting lifestyles far away from the flat farm fields and boring routine of being married to the land.

I was an only child and despite my fondness for my parents, I didn't want to grow up to inherit the family tractors and mortgaged acres, getting up at dawn each day and working late into the evening on a never-ending list of jobs to be done.

Their routine didn't alter from one year to the next, but as I stared at the cell walls around me, I realised it was a better option than the one I was in. At least the immediate future on the farm would have been known with some certainty. Crops were planted in the Spring and taken out in the Fall and despite that sounding mundane, it took away the anxiety of not knowing what was coming next.

After high school my plan, if I could call it that, was to go to College in Toronto to study music. The city was a three hour drive away from the farm, so far enough to be away from the constraints of living at home, but still convenient to get back on the Greyhound bus if needed. Plus, in Canadian terms, three hours' drive was nothing; people would cheerfully travel that distance just to go shopping.

Then I'd heard about a scheme to study abroad and South London Poly was one of the institutions offering music to overseas students. That was it and I was sold before I'd even digested the small print details as they just didn't matter to me. London, England! Those bright lights, the thronging crowds and the music venues and I couldn't wait to become part of it.

However, I discovered that the reality failed to match my dreams, but nevertheless, the College experience had been generally good. Lots of music, parties and girls, but where were they all now? After graduation I'd sunk into a solitary rut of living from week to week, doing pub gigs and giving out guitar lessons to teenagers who fancied becoming rock stars as well as to old men who just fantasised about it.

My life was governed by a routine of sticking my contact details on four by six index cards in newsagents' windows, tucked in between the ads for visiting escorts, domestic cleaners and dog-walking services and checking in with my untrustworthy agent for any new bookings. Putting a brave face on my existence and convincing myself that one day my chance at the bigtime would come, I was instead slowly retreating into a world of isolation.

I'd become a lowly and lonely blues singer, drifting towards insignificance, bobbing about in the backwaters of modern society along with the rest of the detritus cast aside by its more ambitious and upwardly-destined members. Despite living in one of the world's most populous cities, I was short on the number of people I knew well and even shorter on those who genuinely could be called friends.

Then suddenly, I'd seen another world up here in Yorkshire, where people you'd never met before talked to you nicely on public transport. A place where people had the time for each other but didn't want to waste it on mincing their words. People were blunt yet simultaneously to the point and they couldn't care less whether you liked what they'd said or not.

But I did like it, along with their magnanimous outlook on other aspects of life, like community, laughter and fun. The place was ramshackle and down at heel in places, but it wasn't defeated and the folk seemed resilient to whatever the world decided to throw at them.

They were a great bunch of people, apart from the lousy shithead cop Fletcher. A chancer, whose uniform gave him ideas above his station, he'd made my life a misery. Yes, it might have been my fault that I hadn't been as diligent as I should have been with my paperwork, but it was his doing that had seen to me being banged up. And all because I'd not taken the time to think and plan what I needed to have in place.

It was typical of the way I'd been leading my life - no forethought, no planning, just do it. I sighed deeply at the cell door, realising that if I'd had the work visa in place then I'd now be back in Gladstone Terrace, tucked up with Jenny.

Jenny! Now she was pregnant and my heart skipped a beat again. What would she do about it? More important though, what would I do? Did I want to be a father at my age and cope with all that parenting crap that I'd seen older folk doing? It wasn't a pleasing prospect and anyhow, why was it all my fault? Surely, she was as equally to blame for her condition, if not more, I reckoned. I'd seen plenty of single mums out and about in my neighbourhood, so no doubt she'd fit in well.

Maybe we'd go our separate ways and I'd be able to hook up with Rosalyn, despite what her parents might otherwise think. But would she have me? Doubtful and there was no way I could afford anywhere near the lifestyle in which she lived.

No, all in all, the sensible thing would be to go back to the sanctuary of the farm where I could start my adult life over again. The last few years in England had been part of my haphazard and opportunistic lifestyle and I had the memories and scars to prove it. But getting out now before I got shackled was the sensible way forward. If I'd been chasing a pot of gold at the end of some rainbow then someone had beaten me to it.

As I laid back on the thin mattress and drifted between consciousness and fitful sleep, pictures of Rosalyn and hay bales intermingled with Jenny and me pushing a pram along Goldthorpe High Street and then Big Bert was yelling at me to work harder as I shovelled coal into a bottomless bunker in the alleyway behind my house. I woke in a sweat, panting and my heart racing.

My mind was working overtime, creating a nightmare that I was desperate to free myself from, but the calming reassurance of the dawn just didn't want to come and rescue me from my anxiety.

*

It was a great relief to see Terry later in the day and it cheered me up no end. He told me he was putting things in motion but to expect them to move slowly seeing that we were now in the Summer holiday season.

'So how's tha holding up?' he asked.

'Strange,' I said. 'I think I'm the only English speaker in here. The rest are all foreigners from Eastern Europe or the Middle East, but I'm not certain.'

'Aye, lots of 'em come off them big cargo vessels that put in at Immingham or Hull,' he said. 'They jump ship an' try to get to family or friends that are already 'ere or they get some work pickin' crops outa fields for a while. Then they'll get rounded up an' detained until a decision is made to send 'em back 'ome. That's when they start claimin' asylum as refugees an' the whole thing gets bloody complicated.'

'But I'm not a refugee, I'm a Commonwealth citizen,' I yelled. 'We even had a picture of the Queen at school and sang her song on her birthday. It's that bastard cop Fletcher, he's the one that's stitched me up.'

'I know, calm down lad. Shoutin' yer gob off won't help yer now, will it?' as a couple of the wardens looked over to our table. 'We're doin' what we can, believe me. Now, what's rest of this place like?' he asked, trying to distract me from my rantings.

I told him I was being housed in a unit separate from the other wings of the main prison complex and holding about thirty individual cells, although the presence of bunk beds in each one suggested the total numbers could double up at any time. Just listening to Terry, I didn't fancy the prospect of sharing my small space with a fat smelly turnip picker from Romania.

'This area here is where we have our meals as well as receive visitors. If you can smell onions it's probably from last night's dinner,' I smirked. 'Our food is prepared in the main kitchens area then wheeled over to our unit and served out at that end of the hall,' pointing to the far wall.

Then I indicated our indoor recreational facilities in the room next door. They consisted of a small set of bookshelves containing paperbacks and board games, an upright piano, a table tennis table and a TV on a wheel-based stand, with a remote control that was administered solely by the wardens.

On the opposite side next to the shower block we had an access door leading to a large outdoor yard with some baseball hoops and a small footie net, all enclosed by a twenty-five feet chain link fence and barbed wire topping. We may not have been in jail as criminals but we were definitely in prison, no doubt about that.

'Well, just keep calm and things will work out – one way or the other. Meantime, there's a bit of good news though,' he said.

'What's that?'

'I've got permission for you to have a guitar an' do a bit of 'omework, if you can call it that,' he said. 'I got these from Colin,' passing over a couple of songbooks to me. 'I 'ad to 'and in the guitar for x-ray treatment to check I'm not smugglin' in any drugs, but they said you'd get it later. We thought some music would keep you active and Colin wants to come an' see you as well. I told him I'd schedule somethin' in for him, so when are you free?' he smirked.

'Very funny,' I answered. 'But thank you all the same.' A guitar would be very welcome as would seeing the other friendly faces of the people I knew on the outside world.

'Plus, I've been onto that Taylor solicitor bloke again. He's got a meetin' booked in wi' a barrister chap he knows an' has asked me to go along to see if we can work out a strategy to get you out. So hopefully that will get things moving.'

'Thank you,' I said. It felt good to hear that people were caring for my welfare but I had more immediate concerns on my mind. 'I'm going to have to miss that Leadmill gig you know,' I said, miserably. 'It's on in a couple of weeks but I'm stuck in here. Will you let them know as well as the band lads?'

'Aye, no worries,' he said.

'That was my big chance at hitting the big time and now it's all lost,' I moaned.

'Big chance at what?' he asked, dismissively.

I was taken back by his reaction. 'Well, professionally, I mean. I may not have won, but at least I'd have got some exposure if it was being televised.'

'Aye an' you might have ballsed it up an' all,' he replied. 'It's not all about you, if tha hasn't realised it yet, nor is it about puttin' all yer eggs in one basket.' He shook his head. 'Young folk these days just seem to want everythin' right away an' life doesn't 'appen like that. There'll be other opportunities, you'll see.'

'Not whilst I'm in here,' I muttered.

Terry sensed my despondency and changed the subject. 'Now, what you goin' to do wi' that lass o' yours?' he asked. 'She's a bloody fine girl, er, young woman. Ah don't know what she sees in thee, but it's not right to just leave 'er in lurch, yer know.'

I was dreading this coming up but just knew in my heart that he would no doubt mention it.

'I know,' I answered, unconvincingly. I was also wondering how to ask him to let Rosalyn know about my dilemma with the Leadmill gig, but instead, he cut across my thoughts.

'She'll be comin' in to see thee tomorrow before her shift at th'ospital,' he said.

'Well, part of me just wants to hotfoot it outa here and England and look back on the whole experience, whilst part of me wants to be with her. But she might not want me,' I answered.

'Well, 'ave tha asked 'er yet?'

'No I haven't. For some reason I've been pre-occupied with other things just recently,' I said, sarcastically. 'Plus, I only found out she was pregnant a couple of days ago. Give it chance to sink in.'

'Seems like you've been sinkin' it in fairly reg'lar if tha asks me. Now tha's got ter face up to what tha's done an' be a man about it.'

'Well, I've given it a lot of thought,' I replied. 'I think my best bet is to allow them to send me back home to Canada,' recalling the decision I'd reached in my cell last night.

His face altered and he stared at me as I continued.

'Yes, I think it will be the easiest thing all round. Jenny will be fine, whether she decides to keep the kid or not and I'll be able to get on with the rest of my life without any hindrances.'

'Oh, so we're not good enough for tha now, is that it?' he replied, with a touch of anger in his tone. 'Don't mind if tha picks up our women for a bit o' shaggin' but when faced wi' a spot o' bother, then tha'd rather fuck off back to yer mam's?'

'No, I didn't mean it like that,' I said. 'It's just that it's not the right time.'

'Right time for what?' he asked, mocking me. 'Being a man? Only wimps an' them puffy southerners run away when the goin' gets a bit tough, an' ah thought tha were made o' better stuff than that. Even though our Mick says tha'll never mek a coil miner.'

Mick, I thought. 'How's he doing, Terry? Is he likely to lose his job at Barnstone?'

'Aye, pit's gonna shut an' there's nowt they can do abart it anymore. Mick's gonna tek redundancy money an' he's lookin' into movin' to Australia an' startin' afresh out there. Either that or he'll start his own business up doin' summat locally.'

'That'll be a big change for him whatever he decides,' I muttered. 'That coal pit was his life.'

'Aye, but he'd never let it become 'is master,' he replied. 'You see, while he loved his job he also accepted that there were bugger all he could do about it if and when it were ever gonna disappear. Nothin' lasts forever, lad, an' life is unfair. But Mick also loves 'is wife an' kids, so 'e has to press on wi summat else for their sake. That's how proper folk get by in life and it's how they've always done round here.'

I nodded back as I realised I was getting another of his philosophy of life lessons.

Terry continued. 'He doesn't go cryin' back to his mam when he can't have things 'is own way. If he did, she'd more than likely give 'im a bat round back o' fore'yed an' tell 'im to pull 'isself together an' stop bein' a mardy arse.'

Smiling, I looked at Terry and tried to picture his wife, who I'd yet to meet, slapping the strapping big lad Mick round his head and telling him to get his act together. If she was here now sitting in front of me, she'd probably be scolding me in the same no-nonsense manner. Perhaps that's what I needed instead of just wallowing in self-serving pity.

'Anyway, like I say, yon lass thinks the world o' thee an' yer shouldn't be leavin' 'er in the crap, if you want my advice,' he said.

I didn't but I'd got it anyway and Terry's words set my mind thinking away again. Despite resigning myself to my fate last night and deciding a quick escape courtesy of the British Government would resolve matters, his blunt honesty now stuck to my thoughts like cow shit on a shovel.

I'd initially thought Terry would understand my plight and side with me, but instead he was now castigating me for running away from my responsibilities. Not that I could run very far in here.

The visit was over all too soon and whilst it was good to see him and reassuring that he was doing so much for me, I couldn't let him go without telling him that I'd speak to Jenny and discuss things with her when she came to see me the following day.

As I shuffled back to my cell, one of the wardens interrupted me and handed over the guitar that Terry had brought for me. Thanking him, I then tuned it up and sat on the bunk, plucking sporadically at the strings and strumming a few chords. I started singing old classic songs that I'd heard from my youth and the radio back home and *In My Hour of Darkness* went round my head endlessly, until I remembered that the artiste had died of an overdose at an early age and perhaps I should sing something a bit more cheerful.

So instead, I decided to concoct a version of *Folsom Prison Blues* substituting *Lindholme* in the title to while away some of time. It kept me amused for a couple of hours, although several of my inmates would occasionally call out to me and I wasn't sure if they wanted a request or for me to shut up.

'Heya music man,' shouted out the guy from next door. 'My name ees Abdul. Sing me da toody song.'

'Sing you what?' I shouted back, having no idea what he was on about.

'Toody an' froody, ya know it?' he yelled. 'Like thees…I godda girl, she call Sue, she know jus' wadda do.' Then the Egyptian across the hallway joined in with, 'Yeh, ah godda girl she's Beebee, she give me heeby-geeby, yeh.'

'Ah, you mean this,' I shouted back, as I started singing *Tutti Frutti* and presently I had the whole wing clapping and hollering out the verses with me. They all struggled a bit with the whop bopa lu-ah line, so I had to keep going over it slowly as they repeated the words out loud, laughing their heads off as they did. I had to think up new girls' names and rhymes, so Sandy made me randy and Pheobe knew just how to squeeze me, as I kept the song going for my new-found audience.

'You sing pretty good lad,' said a warden, popping his head round my open cell door and whose name tag informed me he was called Reg. 'Sing us some more, it makes a change from the normal wailing we get from this lot in here.'

After our evening meal, we were allowed some outdoor exercise and I strolled round the enclosure and gazed up through the chain-link fence at the setting sun. I thought about my upcoming meeting with Jenny and about what Terry had said earlier in the day.

Would she want to have the baby or not? It was difficult to tell and even so I would have to ask her to marry me, which in itself was anything but easy. What if she said no? Well, if she did, then it was a one-way ticket to Toronto and thanks for the memories, dear old England.

But somehow, I felt that she would say yes, even though in terms of a courtship, as my folks used to call it, we'd had a relatively short one. Was I marrying her to avoid being sent back home, or because I'd made her pregnant, or because I genuinely loved her and wanted to be with her for the rest of my life? These were heavy matters to consider and no wonder my head ached.

Wandering back to my cell I lay on the bunk and started to strum the acoustic as I thought some more about things before subconsciously falling into *The River,* recalling the chords and the lyrics easily. Then I realised that they horribly foretold a likely future for me and bore an uncanny resemblance to my situation. Nevertheless, I sang away, not caring who heard me or how it sounded, but still wondering if the words of the song were a prophetic warning for what lay ahead for me.

A round of applause broke out from outside the cell and shouts of, 'Ferry good, ferry good,' came from Abdul. 'Now sing me I fide the law, an' the fugger won,' he shouted.

After I'd worked out what he wanted, even I felt a wry smile creeping across my face, despite the general lack of amusement at being confined in prison.

'Okay, here goes,' I shouted back.

After the intro chord pattern, I sang out the opening line of *I Fought the Law*, as the rest of them joined in the response and I strummed the guitar strings with all my might. I could hear the inmates tapping their cell doors or window bars with their ceramic mugs or singing the bits they knew in broken English until Reg shouted out, 'Lock up and lights out.'

As he walked past my door he said, 'We like that song in 'ere lad. The law always wins, you know.'

Chapter Twenty Two

Dressed in a light pink dress, Jenny looked stunning as she waited for me at the visitors table the following afternoon and my heart leapt at the sight of her. There was supposed to be no contact between the inmates and any visitors, but Reg was a bit more sympathetic, turning a blind eye to us briefly kissing and only once reminding us to stop holding hands.

'How are you keeping?' she asked.

'Just brilliant, as you can see. When I told you I'd like to go away during August, I didn't have a jail cell in mind,' I said. 'Plus, I wanted to go with you, not be on my own.'

'How's the plans going for getting you out?'

'Okay I think, but I need to ask you something before I get into that,' I said, taking a deep breath. 'Jenny, will you marry me?'

Of all the inappropriate places to make a proposal, this had to be the worst and I was well prepared for a refusal. Jenny was a bright, intelligent woman who could more than adequately look after herself without me being in her world. If she refused me then I'd fully understand and then at least I could honestly look Terry in the eye and say, well, I tried bud.

She was a little taken back but then her eyes lit up and she smiled broadly. 'Well, yes, of course I will,' she replied. 'And not just because I'm, well, you know…'

I smiled back with heavy relief and gripped her hand. 'Have you told your folks yet about you being pregnant?' I asked.

'Of course, I had to,' she said. As she leaned back in the chair I could clearly see that there was a slight swelling in her belly. 'Dad threatened to kill you before realising that he may have a grandson to look after and then he seemed to mellow a bit. He only threatened to castrate you after that. Mum was more understanding about my welfare, but then she was also concerned about you as well.'

That was very nice of her, I thought. 'But what about me?' I asked. 'Do they care whether I'm with you or not?' I asked.

'Frankly, at this moment in time they don't,' she replied. 'But if you are wanting to marry me then that will probably change things. At least dad will then have to accept you as his son-in-law and stop calling you that foreign yankee git.'

'I think there's a strong chance that I will be allowed to remain and work here if I'm getting married,' I said. 'And I can get good references from the College, which should help matters. If not, then the offer still stands. I want to marry you Jenny, only you'll have to come over to Ontario for it to happen if I can't stay here in England.'

'I'm not bothered where we get married,' she said. 'I love you and all I want is for you to be out of this place as soon as possible so we can be together as a proper couple.'

'What, a Yorkshire woman and a foreign yankee git?' I said, as we laughed together, enjoying the moment and briefly forgetting about our surroundings.

Jenny's acceptance had genuinely cheered me up and after our visit ended, I went back to my cell happy and relieved that at least my girlfriend would shortly become my fiancée. After that, who knew what would happen. But first things first; I picked up my guitar with thoughts of our forthcoming nuptials swirling around my mind and began strumming.

'New song for you to sing with me Abdul and friends,' I shouted out to all the inmates, as I began to play a bluesy shuffle pattern on the guitar. I sang out loud as the rest of them clapped and tapped their mugs along with me to the rhythm. Even Reg was joining in, jangling his key chain and whistling. Well, I had a captive audience and they were going to listen to me singing *Shotgun Wedding,* like it or not.

*

Colin came in to see me the following day and surprised me. 'I've had a word with the Gov'nor and they've allowed us to meet in the rec room next door, rather than at a visiting table,' he said. 'So go an' fetch your guitar.'

Puzzled, I asked him what he meant.

'There's a piano in there and I enquired as to whether we could practice together as you'll need it for College duties in the Autumn Term.'

'Thanks for your confidence,' I replied. 'But I might not be there.'

He ignored my comment and continued. 'The Gov'nor was very understanding. He likes anything that's academic and takes the minds of the inmates from worrying and causing bother. Plus, you're not a proper criminal who's serving a sentence, so he's a bit more sympathetic to your situation.'

I hurried back to the cell and picked up the guitar and followed him to the piano as he picked out some sheet music from a folder for us to run through.

'Have a go at this,' he said, handing me the guitar chart to *Against the Wind* and we played it once before going through it a second time. The words resonated deeply with me as it told the poignant and heartfelt story of the burdens we all have to face in life, describing how those who have weathered the storm become stronger as a result of their experiences.

As we played and sang together, I watched Colin closely and I realised that the pain I could detect in his eyes and hear in his voice was all about his former wife.

He never spoke about her and had only briefly outlined her tragic demise to me that afternoon earlier in the year when I'd mentioned the funeral for Mavis's son. But I could sense that his guilt and memories were still very much part of his persona. We were two completely different individuals, but here we were, singing together about our shared struggles with our own lives, separated only by our generation. Time moves on but some things never change, I guessed.

But what struck me more as we played and sang was Colin's ability on the piano. He was a brilliant musician, improvising as we went along and supporting me as I filled in the guitar licks. It made me proud to be sharing the experience with him and reinforced the fact that a performance is more than just a tune and playing the right notes.

I'd always known that the messages contained in the lyrics of some of the blues songs I liked covered a wide range of human suffering and aspiration. Whenever I'd played them in public I'd tried to express these themes as authentically as I could, but now it was clear that I was in the presence of a master when it came to the art of performing.

'Colin, that was great playing, if you don't mind me saying so,' I said. 'You're hiding your talent away and for no reason.'

'Well, I'd rather just concentrate on doing my teachin', but occasionally I get inspired an' let loose a little,' he said. 'You know that I made a promise to myself never to perform again in public. But sometimes I realise that life is short an' you've gotta make the most of it whilst you can. Maybe it's time to live it up a bit.'

'You'd be a great jazz pianist,' I replied. 'I could never switch from my basic blues and rock repertoire. It's just too difficult, you know.'

He smiled to himself. 'You think so? Music is what you make it lad, it's all related,' he said. 'Here, listen to this,' as he played three chords on the piano before repeating them continuously.

'Recognise that?' he asked.

I shook my head. 'It's nothing,' I said, dismissively. 'Just three odd chords. Doesn't mean anything.'

'It's gospel. Church music from way back,' he answered, solemnly. 'Just three simple chords,' as he played them over and over again, before looking up at me. 'Now, let's see what we can do with them.'

He altered the rhythm slightly and started to sing a lyric line over the top and I instantly recognised the Ray Charles classic song *I Got A Woman*.

'Now we got a soul song going,' he said. 'Join in with me and play these chords,' and as I did so he added, 'And put a little rhythm pattern into your strumming. That's it, now we got a blues duo,' as we played on a little more.

'Now we need a little up-tempo stuff going on,' he said. 'Let's speed up a tad and imagine we had a bass with us,' emphasising a walking bass line with his left hand on the lower keys of the piano as he improvised with the chords and melody on his right. 'Now we have a jazz trio going on.'

I nodded back as I jammed along with him, smiling and enjoying the experience.

'Now, let's add some percussion,' he instructed. 'Give me four on the floor with your right foot and I'll put the backbeats in on two and four on the piano stool with my left.'

As I tapped away, he did likewise. 'Now we got a rock and roll quartet,' and I nodded back at him.

Flicking over a lyric sheet from the music stand, he said, 'Okay, let me hear you sing the first verse.'

So I did as I was told and we played and tapped away merrily, before he added a bit more encouragement.

'Right, now imagine we've some snappy tight horn chords syncopated on the offbeats here – bap, bap, bap – bah, repeated in four bar loops,' he said, sliding his right hand up the keyboard to demonstrate what he'd just described, as we continued playing the groove pattern.

'Now we've got some rhythm and blues,' he shouted and I could hear what he meant, as he gently coaxed a fresh urgency and excitement from my playing.

Looking over at me again he said, 'Now imagine you've got your Les Paul on your arm and your violin player is soaring over the top of us, playing the supporting rhythm and then a counterpoint melody. Can you hear it?'

It was true. I could hear it in my head and I nodded back enthusiastically.

'So now we've got fusion. Gospel, blues, jazz, soul, bluegrass and rock and roll...how does that feel?' he shouted.

Colin had magically transformed this song from where we'd started it. There were only two of us playing but in my mind he'd created a powerhouse of sound and I imagined we had a stage full of lusty musicians around us giving it all they could.

'So, sing the first verse with me,' he instructed, and I sang out the melody line energetically as he harmonised the vocal part on thirds alongside me.

'Good, now this is the instrumental break section,' he announced, as I watched him improvise a perfect twelve bar solo whilst still yelling at me that it's the same three chords as I listened and played along, mesmerised by this man's talent and musicality.

'Now it's your turn. Show me what you can do,' and I fumbled my fingers clumsily around the guitar frets, bravely trying to follow his instructions. 'Louder!' he yelled. 'I can't hear you,' and I dug furiously into the strings in response.

I was trying to make up a solo on the spot, thinking about what notes I was playing and it was tough going. I didn't have the flexibility that my electric guitar could provide and I was having to force my fingers and hands up and down the neck and concentrate like mad just to get the right sound out.

But Colin was giving me no quarter. 'Again,' he shouted, as he continued playing the piano groove and rhythmic structure he had built up. 'Relax and breathe and just feel the music. Play from your heart and let your instrument do the work.'

This was like no music lesson I'd ever had before. I closed my eyes, trying to shut out the lingering doubt that I couldn't keep up with Colin's tempo and stamina. We weren't just passing time here, we were immersed in the beauty and challenge of the piece and the only way out was to play it.

My right arm ached and wanted to stop but I knew he would only yell at me more if I did. Instead, I breathed in deeply, summoned up what energy I could find and allowed my fingers to respond in rhythm and style over the basic chord structure, almost as if someone else was playing the instrument for me.

'Better,' he said. 'Now back to the top and this time sing it like you damn well mean it. Shoulders back and head up,' he ordered and I belted out the song for all it was worth.

In my head we were somewhere else and I forgot about everything except our performance. I was totally absorbed, caught up in the ecstasy of what we were creating as musicians. As we reached the end of the song, there was a tremendous cheer from all the block inmates and the wardens who'd been listening and clapping along as they watched from the far end of the room. I hadn't even noticed they were there.

'Not bad, for something you just told me was nothing but three odd chords,' said Colin, smiling. 'Another ten years and we might make something out of you.'

'Colin...' I started to say, but I was breathless and trembling and couldn't get my words out. Looking down, I now saw that the fingertips on my right hand had turned black and blistered but I hadn't even noticed any discomfort as we'd played. Instead, I felt flushed with an inner energy that I'd never experienced before and it flowed through my body like an electric current.

'You see what I'm getting at?' he asked, as he carried on with the piano vamp chords and rhythm, improvising away as he spoke. 'That song's been covered by so many different artists who have all put their own slant on it, no matter what their style of music was beforehand. It comes from just a root of three chords. They stand for heart, soul and mind,' he said, emphasising each of the words with accents on the keyboard as he uttered them.

I nodded back at him as he looked at me. 'We all have those three things in common. They are the keys to your inner creativity,' he said. 'That goes for your life as well as your music. No one is going to live your life, except you. You've got the tools to achieve a lot of things lad, so what's stopping you using them?'

It seemed a simple question, but I didn't have an answer and instead just stared blankly at him, still trying to calm my breathing.

'Lots of people never fail at anything in life,' he said. 'They're called losers. So-called because they never try to better themselves or the people around them. Their minds are already closed off to trying new things, so they lack the heart and soul needed to make things happen. Just because life isn't fair to any of us doesn't meant that you can't have a plan in place to achieve what you want.'

He stopped playing and twisted round on the stool to face me. 'So, I'll ask you again, what's stopping you?'

'Nothing,' I replied, ashamed at my weak answer and yet simultaneously relieved that I'd been given the impetus and incentive to decide on what I wanted in life and start planning to achieve it.

'You've given me a lot to think about Colin, thank you,' I said.

'Better than feeling sorry for yourself, wouldn't you say?' he smiled.

Chapter Twenty Three

My time with Colin had made me realise that even though I was stuck inside here, it wouldn't last for ever and there was the rest of my life to think about. It was ultimately my fault that I'd been locked up and blaming that cop Fletcher for my failings was not going to get me out any faster.

Some of my fellow inmates were here because they had been trying to make a new life somewhere better than in their own Country and had got caught trying. In that respect I was no different. Instead of trying to fight what I couldn't change, I now realised that I had to try and somehow turn it to my advantage and make the most of it.

As I pondered things, I thought about my blues music and how it had evolved from its simple origins in the plantations and cotton fields. Yes, it still had its roots and its core performers but it had also now evolved and moved on into other musical styles and forms.

Terry had described to me how the traditional industries in this part of the world were dying and how a whole range of other activities would eventually take their place. I guess what he was saying was that you can't stop progress – you can either go with it, or wallow in the nostalgia of what once existed. Life has a way of moving on and whilst I couldn't see anything wrong with celebrating what had gone before us, it seemed better to do so from a position of comfort rather than one of bitter regret and poverty.

Deep in my thoughts, I was interrupted by Reg leaning round my cell door. 'There's someone here to see you,' he said. 'Legal representation I think.'

I wasn't expecting anyone today and hurried to get myself looking half-presentable before I left the cell. As I walked into the hall and visitors area, I stopped with a shock. Sitting next to Terry at the table was Rosalyn's father, Richard Carter.

Despite the warm August weather, he was dressed very smartly in a grey pin-striped suit and pink shirt with a silk tie and pocket hanky set in cornflower blue. It all looked expensive stuff but none of it matched each other and I wondered if he'd got dressed in the dark this morning. As I wandered over to the table, he looked up and addressed me in his usual brusque and formal manner.

'Good morning. I've been asked if I would represent you as your legal Counsel. Before you say anything about money, my fees, which are not inconsiderable, would be paid through the Legal Aid system, so it won't cost you anything. That's the good news.'

'And what's the bad news then?' I asked.

'I haven't decided whether I wish to take up your case,' he said. 'I certainly don't have to do so and there's plenty of other work in my pipeline, as well as other matters on which I can be instructed.'

'So what are you doing here then?' I enquired.

He opened the manilla file on the desk and placed the contents in front of us.

'I've reviewed your case notes from the solicitor Taylor and at least you're not being charged with any criminal activity. Just an expired student visa, or an over-stayer, as it's technically called.'

I was relieved to hear that there were no criminal charges but not really surprised. I hadn't done anything wrong and even though my house had been used as a staging post for some dodgy stuff, it was all down to the dealings of slimy Simms.

'Mr Taylor mentions in his notes that the police didn't find any evidence to support criminal activity at your place of residence and indeed they now believe that the entire exercise had been promulgated as a decoy tactic by, er, your landlord, Simms, who no doubt stashed his goods elsewhere,' he said, looking down at the papers and turning a page. 'Apparently the delivery driver was found to be handling only stationery products, which in themselves, were perfectly legitimate.'

He paused for a moment as I digested what he'd said, before he continued.

'Now, turning to your expired visa. I've handled a few of these cases before and generally they result in a swift return back to the individuals' Country of origin, unless there are strong reasons why they should stay put here.'

'Well, if I'm not a criminal, isn't that a strong-enough reason?' I asked, but he ignored the question. 'Plus, I was under the impression that as a Commonwealth citizen I could stay here in this Country for seven years. Isn't that the case?'

'That is only a partially correct statement,' he answered, with a nonchalant air. 'To claim that you have a right to be in the UK would require you to have been living here prior to the first of January 1983. Reading through this file, it appears you were not. Your period of study commenced in the September of that year and the date of entry on your passport page confirms this as being the sixteenth of the same month. That's not good enough to support your flawed assertion and consequently your reasoning fails in the eyes of the law.'

His own eyes narrowed slightly whilst he stared at me, knowing that I couldn't find any fault in what he'd just related. My head slumped forward onto my chest. Once again, he had found me wanting. 'So what happens now?' I asked.

'Well, as the police will not be bringing any criminal charges against you, they will be in no hurry to get you in front of a Magistrates Court,' he replied. 'They will most probably ask the Immigration Service in Leeds to take over your case and that will mean you remaining in here, safely locked up, until they get themselves organised. In my experience it's likely that will take many months from now.'

I listened in desperation as he turned a page in the file and looked at it for a moment before continuing.

'Now, Terry, er, Mr Turner here, informs me that he is a friend and colleague of yours. He has also told me of your, er, personal circumstances, which in themselves, would give you a strong prima facie case for wanting to stay in this Country.'

I looked at Terry and he just nodded back to me without saying anything.

'But I also realise that I have a card to play here as well,' said Carter. 'A bargaining chip if you like,' he added, as his eyes narrowed again at me. 'So that is why I am here.'

'So what is it?' I asked.

'Simply this. If I represent you in Court, then no matter what the eventual outcome will be, I want no further contact from you with Ros,' he said. 'She has her place at Cambridge secured and I don't want her being distracted from her chosen route by anyone or anything. Do you understand?'

Whether it was her chosen route or not was very questionable in my mind, but I nodded in acknowledgement, as he continued. 'I'm reasonably sure that I can rely on my own daughter to follow my instructions of having no contact with you, but I regret that I can't take you on your own word,' he said. 'You have already broken it by enticing her to play with your band of students recently, despite my giving you specific instructions to the contrary on the last occasion we met.'

I looked up guiltily at him, realising that he was referring to the cricket match gig at Woolley.

'Yes, I got to hear of it, but what's happened can't now be undone,' he said. 'I have to consider the matter as being an isolated incident and I can only take appropriate steps for the future and for those things that I don't want to occur again.'

In a way I was glad that he knew about the gig because it just proved to me that Rosalyn was willing and capable of making her own decisions, despite what he otherwise thought was right and proper for her. No wonder she wanted to rebel against such an over-bearing parent. His intentions may have been in the right direction but his way of putting them into place seemed nothing short of brutal. Or maybe that was just how he did things in his chosen profession.

'So after reviewing your case notes, I think I can pre-empt things with the Immigration people and we can apply to get you out of here on bail later this month, pending a formal hearing on your eventual fate at some future date,' he said. 'Mr Taylor can make the necessary application today and he knows some people at the local Court office,

266

so there's a possibility we can get a hearing pushed up the list, before I, er, go on holiday.'

'Does that mean I will be free to go?' I asked, optimistically.

'You would still be on bail,' he said. 'There will be a string of conditions attached to your release which you will have to comply with, otherwise you will likely be jailed if you breach them. Then there will be a final Court hearing to determine your status and decide whether you will be allowed to remain in this Country or sent back to your place of origin.'

'Well, I think I can live with that,' I said.

'Be careful before you agree to anything,' he said. 'Mr Turner has very generously offered to provide surety and act as guarantor for your bail, should you be released. That means he will likely have to stump up a great deal of money if you abscond. He could very well lose his house as a result.'

'Terry, you've no need to do all that,' I said. 'That's way beyond being a friend. I can't agree to you doing such a thing.'

'Why not?' asked Terry. 'Do you want to get out of 'ere or not?'

I looked down sullenly as Carter pulled some more documents out of the file and spread them on the table as he continued with his lecturing.

'You will need to sign this standard retention contract for my services, but you will also need to sign this personal undertaking to me and Mrs Carter regarding you having no further contact with our daughter. And before you ask, there are financial penalties if you do so and in respect of which, I will not hesitate to enforce them against you,' he insisted. 'Mr Turner here will act as the witness to your signature…should you wish to retain my expertise, of course.'

In a way I was relieved that he was not acting for the other side as no doubt he'd want me on the next plane home or locked up indefinitely and I could just see him bullying the Court officials into having his own way. His arrogance and sense of righteous self-importance were both admirable and repulsive in equal measures and again I wondered how Rosalyn had tolerated living at home.

Terry then cleared his throat before looking at me.

'Mr Carter here is very well respected and regarded as a top brief, er, barrister, round 'ere. He'll get you sorted lad. For now, you've got a lovely woman in Jenny and a child to look forward to, so consider thi sen bloody fortunate that you have a lot goin' for you. It's a lot more than the other buggers in 'ere with you 'ave got.'

I looked at him and nodded as he continued. 'If you want my advice, I'd think mi sen lucky to 'ave what you 'ave wi' yor lass an' tha don't need to concern yourself with, er, anyone else,' as he shifted slightly in his chair, like a flea was biting his arse. I saw him blush as I realised he was drifting into his own Mavis-related territory here.

He cleared his throat again. 'Any'ow, agree to Mr Carter's terms and we can 'ave you outa here as soon as,' he said. 'He can bail you into my care so you don't bugger off, an' if tha does, I'll brek tha legs an' yer arms as well, then I'll do some serious damage. So, unless tha's grown a likin' for prison grub an 'avin' no beer or a woman to cuddle at night, I'd strongly recommend that you follow 'is advice.'

I looked at him and then again at Carter who was shuffling the contract papers on the table in front of us.

At that moment it dawned on me that I was having my own legendary highway crossroads experience by making a deal with the devil, only this time he was appearing during the daylight, wearing a pin-striped suit and sitting across from me.

Whilst I may not have been selling my soul to him in return for musical success, he was dangling a ticket to my possible salvation which had a heavy price attached to it. I would have to give up all contact with the most beautiful and gifted musician I'd ever met in return for his legal services to assist me. Carter would still get paid no matter what the outcome of my hearing and therefore he had nothing to lose and everything to gain.

It was indeed a deal from hell and as I took a moment to consider my fate, I heard the opening thumping bars from the colliery brass band piece *Journey into Freedom* rattle through my mind with astonishing clarity.

However, it was the choice that I had to make if I wanted to get out of prison sooner rather than later.

'Where do I sign?' I asked, with a combination of optimistic relief and a heavy heart.

Chapter Twenty Four

At least Carter was as good as his word. Ten days after our meeting, I was listed for a bail hearing at the Doncaster Magistrates Court and Taylor came to visit me to explain the procedure. He also informed Jenny to bring me in some smarter clothes beforehand in order to make a good impression to the Bench at my hearing. I wouldn't have to say anything other than to confirm my identity but it wouldn't do any harm by appearing to be a professional, he'd said.

On the appointed day I was whisked away in a prison van for the short journey into town and was led into a waiting room occupied by a handful of miscreants who looked at me in my shirt and tie with suspicion. Then a black-robed usher called out my name and I was led into a wood-panelled courtroom and after being told to confirm my name and age by the Court Clerk, I was instructed by him to sit in the dock.

Carter rose to his feet and explained my circumstances to the panel of three elderly individuals whom he addressed as Your Worships and who sat stoney-faced in their lofty vantage, occasionally peering down to take a closer look at me.

The other legal Counsel confirmed that the police would not be opposing the bail application as long as certain conditions were attached to it and that a formal hearing on my status was convened at the earliest possible date. After some nodding and muttering between the wise Worships, I was duly informed by the one sitting in the middle that I would be released on bail.

I was told to wait whilst the paperwork was stamped and issued then Carter handed me and Taylor a copy each to read before we all left the Court. I would be allowed to return to Gladstone Terrace, subject to complying with a long list of conditions. These including travelling only within a ten mile radius of my house and reporting my presence weekly to the local police station to get an attendance sheet signed.

Taylor said he would sort out my paperwork back at Lindholme and would bring back any personal items, not that I had many, for me to collect later at his office. A hearing had been set for the thirtieth of November to determine whether I would be allowed to stay in the Country or not. But for now I was free and as I left the Court building with Carter at my side, Jenny rushed up to hug me. She'd been waiting outside and big tears of relief were running down her face.

Carter nodded curtly to Jenny before turning to me. 'Now, stick to your bail conditions rigidly,' he instructed. 'You'll be hearing from me via Mr Taylor in due course,' before he marched off.

'Oh I'm so glad,' Jenny said, as she clung to me. 'Now we can get back to some form of normality.'

'Yes, we can,' I agreed, as I hugged her back. But what was that going to be like, I thought. Normality for me would shortly be nappies and sleepless nights instead of late music shows and heckling audiences. Was that what I really wanted?

She drove me back to Highfield and the neat rows of tightly packed houses never looked so welcoming. Even the pit stack at the back, with its patches of weeds and thistles sprouting out from amongst the grey dirt and shale, looked like a wild moorland waiting to be walked over and explored. I longed to just rush out and race up to the top of the heap, yelling my head off to anyone within hearing range. Then I realised I might get locked up again for being a nutter.

In my absence Jenny had been exceptionally helpful. Apparently after I'd been hauled off that Saturday morning, the police had wrecked the house turning it over for evidence of any stashed drugs and had just left everything piled in a mess. Jenny had returned later with her dad and they'd put everything back to normal.

'I had to hide these so that dad wouldn't see 'em,' she said, pointing to my stash of porn mags and rented vids stacked out of sight at the back of the wardrobe. 'Now I know what you get up to when you're on your own,' she smiled, as my face reddened. 'We get some right cases at work saying they've only been copying what they've seen in vids like these you know.'

'It's not like being with you though,' I said, but then realised once again that things would now be different. Very soon I'd have to show my face to her parents and said so to her.

'Come on, let's get it over with then as soon as we can,' she said. 'Dad's calmed down a bit now. At least you have a steady job at the College, as do I at the hospital. And we can always live here in Highfield, that's if you don't want to move in wi' us. For a while anyway, until we get somewhere better.'

I nodded back but in my heart I knew I didn't want to end up living with the outlaws, as Jenny continued bringing me up to speed. 'I haven't mentioned to them about us getting married,' she said, as we drove over to her house. 'But I have touched on it with mum. She's all for it of course as she wants what's best for me and the bump.'

'Why haven't you said anything to them if I've offered to marry you?' I asked, puzzled by what she had just told me. 'I thought you were happy for us to get married?'

'I am, but you'll have to be old fashioned and ask dad first for his permission to marry me,' she said. 'He's funny about things like that an' likes stuff to be done in a traditional way. Like what he had to do when he asked grandad's permission to marry mum.'

'What if he says no?' I asked. I thought for a moment that I might have a legitimate reason to get out of all this, before dismissing it almost as quickly. I'd made a commitment and now I would have to stick by it.

'He won't. If nothing else he wants his daughter to be happily married and so far at least, you are the best pick of any previous boyfriend I've had.'

Half an hour later I was about to find out. After Jenny's mum had politely enquired about my welfare following my release from detention – I don't think she could actually bring herself to use the word prison – she handed me a mug of tea and shame-faced, I took my place on the sofa at the side of Jenny and across from Walter, to face the music.

I decided to take the initiative. 'Walter, I would like to ask your permission to marry Jenny,' I blurted out. 'And not just because, you know, she's expecting. Even though we've not been together very long, I do love her, and I want to be with her always.'

'Oh, that's real romantic isn't it, Walter?' said Dorothy. 'Reminds me of when you asked mi dad for my hand all them years ago. It's just like that day all over again,' she said.

'It's nothin' of the bloody sort,' he retorted, fiercely. 'You weren't up bloody stick then for a start was tha?' before turning to look at me. Gripping his pipe between his teeth he emitted a huge cloud of smoke above his head. Evidently the severity of today's family meeting called for a lighting-up indoors, rather than outside in the back garden.

'Well lad, tha's done the deed so now at least tha's doing the decent thing an' payin' the price for it,' he preached. 'As a point of principle, I can't be angry wi' that when all's said an' done. An' at least she's not 'aving to marry a bloody lanky.'

'A what?' I asked.

'A Lancastrian. Some thieving, connivin' low life bugger from over 'ills,' he advised. 'Just tell me tha's got no lanky blood that's lurking abart anywhere in your ancestors.'

'I don't think so,' I replied.

'Well, in that case I suppose I'd better say yes,' he said. 'Now onto more important things. At least the lad will be born 'ere in Yorkshire. An' that's what matters.'

'How do we know that it's a boy?' I asked. As far as I was aware Jenny hadn't had a scan and if she'd had, then I'd not been told about it.

'It'll be a lad, I know it,' he said, lighting up the pipe again. 'I can just see him now, walking out at 'eadingley, looking tall an' proud and about to thrash 'em all round field.'

'What's he talking about?' I asked Jenny in a whisper, as I looked at her quizzically.

'What do you think? Cricket,' she replied. 'God 'elp us if it's a girl.' With that she stood up and went to help Dorothy who was preparing the table.

'I thought you might like something nice to eat after that, er, horrible jail food,' said Dorothy to me. 'So I've made us a nice roast with puddings, just as you like them.' Only in Yorkshire, on a hot Summer's day could we be eating a roast dinner, but I wasn't complaining.

'Thank you, Dorothy,' I said. 'And to you Walter for your permission and for welcoming me into your family.'

'Who said 'owt about welcomin' thee?' he replied. 'For now, just be grateful that I haven't put thi in bloody ground where tha belongs.'

'Well, there's one thing I've decided on,' said Jenny. 'I don't want to wear a wedding dress an' have photos taken with me showing a bump. So, we'll be getting wed in the Spring after the birth. Won't we Jamie?'

'Well, yes, I suppose we will,' I agreed.

'And I was wondrin' dad,' she continued. 'Can we have the concert room at the Club for free for the wedding reception?'

'Bloody 'ell,' he replied. 'Is there anything else tha both wants on cheap from me while tha's at it?'

'Well seeing that you're asking,' I said. 'I was wondering if you would sell me your car?'

Chapter Twenty Five

Back at College I had other practicalities to sort out. Fortunately, my time in detention had coincided with the Summer holidays so when the Autumn Term restarted in late September, nothing seemed to be awry on the surface. But I had to apologise first to the band lads for them missing their Leadmill chance.

They were understanding and ribbed me a little about being locked up, apart from Woody who was absent. He'd gone to Ibiza in August when he'd found out about the cancelled gig and hadn't bothered to return, sending a postcard instead to Robbie saying that he'd got a job in a nightclub and was having a fab time.

It meant that we'd have to find another drummer, but I thought perhaps we had run our natural course as a band and may have to re-emerge in a new incarnation, if at all, at some point in the future.

Mick and his colleagues at the colliery band had also been asking about me and I was pleased to see them again when I went over to their rehearsal one night. Even though the pit had now closed, they were still keeping their band going and I admired their resilience and enthusiasm. However, they had already filled my place on the percussion section for their London competition, thinking that I wouldn't be available. I was disappointed that I would now miss out on appearing with them on the Royal

Albert Hall stage, but nevertheless I understood the reasons and wished them well.

And of course, I'd made an undertaking to forget about Rosalyn. I hadn't had the chance to see her or even talk with her again to wish her well and now she would be on her way to Cambridge, joining an elite bunch of students and no doubt forgetting about her life in Yorkshire.

I'd probably never see her again but there was something about the chemistry of our music, as well as our brief time together, that still haunted me. I'd frequently wondered whether the combination of piano, guitar and violin would work as a basis for the musical fusion that Colin had talked about.

The thought recurred to me as I was sitting with him in his office and going through the list of new students enrolled on music courses for the Autumn Term.

'You know Colin, I had an idea after you came to see me in Lindholme and I've been thinking about it a lot ever since.'

'That's good to hear. Well, that you've been thinking, anyway,' he said, sarcastically, as he smiled at me. 'What's the big idea then?'

'Maybe we should open a blues or jazz club,' I said. 'We sounded good together and it wouldn't take much to add a couple more instruments to our combo.'

'Ah,' as he raised his eyes to the ceiling and extended an arm in a theatrical pose. '*Some to the lute, and some to the viol went, And others chose the cornet eloquent,*' he said. 'That comes from an ancient and revered poem you know.'

I didn't know and was unwilling to show my ignorance, so instead I continued with my theme.

'If we had our own venue then we could do our own gigs, as well as have featured artistes and bands,' I said.

'How does the Dearne Valley Blues and Jazz Club sound?'

'Well, that's not a bad idea and having a smart music club is something I've always dreamed about,' he replied.

'But you've got to pick the right location. Rents may be affordable in Barnsley, but no bugger would want to come along when they can have cheap ale an' bingo down at their own club. Somewhere like London would be much better, but the rent would be too high. Couldn't mek it pay. So whilst it's a nice idea, I can't see it workin' round 'ere.'

But I wanted to show some of my recently acquired Yorkshire resilience and grit. 'Why not, if we haven't tried it? Better to try and fail than not try at all. Isn't that what you said to me about doing new things?' I asked. 'You don't know if we don't give it a go and I am talking about real music fans here, not just the regular club punters.'

He smiled as he realised that I was throwing his own words back at him and put his pen down on the desk.

'Okay, you're correct, we haven't tried it. So, first thing is to put together a business plan. Get one of the lecturers in Terry's department to give you a hand with it. If you can get the financial projections to stack up, then there's a fighting chance you could raise some capital to make it work.'

I swallowed. 'Business plan? What's that?' I asked. 'I'm only used to looking at music sheets not spread sheets.'

'Well it's time tha learned then,' he replied. 'Very simply, you need to make enough money to cover your costs and have some left over for re-investment or profit. You need to show on paper at least that you're going to make enough money to service any debt you take on before anything else.'

'Well, how do I go about that?' I asked, picking up a pencil to make some notes.

Colin sat back in his chair, lowering his head for a few seconds before looking up at me.

'Well, for a music club, you'd need to think about holding two hundred gigs per year, or about four per week. Then there's the bar, which will make some money, but it has to be staffed and stocked and same if you're going to provide food. Aim for a capacity of about one hundred and fifty people, nicely seated at tables and you've got the right sort of ambience and intimacy about the place. Then there's the overheads to take care of, so once you factor that lot in you'll soon see if it's financially viable or not.'

I wrote furiously as he spoke and was excited at the prospect and the challenge about making this work. After all, other people had done it, so why not me?

Colin was on a roll. 'You could also look a little wider than just jazz and blues you know. If you opened a music venue that also featured other styles like folk or even some of the upcoming rock groups, then you'd have more customers and certainly on paper it could show you taking in more money.'

I hadn't thought of that before and now it made sense.

'There's a curious phenomenon when it comes to people's taste in music,' he continued. 'You need to be attracting the wealthier types who are likely to go for the narrower genres like jazz, or blues or even classics, rather than mainstream pop, which you can get for free on the radio or telly channels,' he said. 'Odd really, when you think that blues was once the poor man's music, nowadays it's only appreciated by the ones with cash to spend.'

'Why is that?' I asked. I'd never thought about music like that, but I could see he had a point.

'I dunno, I'm not a sociologist,' he replied. 'But what I do know is that it creates a kind of class boundary. That's what I was meaning about having a location in this part of the world. We're not big on upper class tastes in Barnsley.'

'But I don't want to go back to London,' I said.

I'd been there and whilst I could see exactly what he was talking about in terms of demographics and wealth, the prospect didn't appeal to me.

'How about Toronto?' I asked, half joking, but then I began to think about it more seriously.

'Don't know, never been there,' he said. 'But if there's a big enough interest in the music and plenty of folk and given that it's a large city, then it might work. What's it like as a place?'

'I'll tell you, pull up a chair,' I said.

'Well, some other time, maybe,' he replied. 'For now, work on your business plan so it can be considered seriously by a bank and do your research. There's plenty of help and grants going to be available to try and replace the lost jobs caused by the coal industry closures. If your club is operationally viable on paper then there might be a chance of getting some cheap funding towards making it happen.'

'That's a good point, thank you.'

'But also think about it personally,' he added. 'You've a wedding coming up and I understand from Terry that you'll soon be a dad. How are you going to juggle all that with opening a music club?'

That was an important issue. I'd mentioned it to Jenny in passing but I wasn't sure if she thought I was being serious or not. 'I'm sure she'll support me,' I said. 'But yes, I need to discuss it with her first.'

'It can be done but you need to think and have a plan ready. Planning is everything,' he said. 'Talking of which, I've got ten new guitar students here for you,' passing their details to me. 'Slot them into your working week please.'

There was one thing about Colin. He was unswervingly professional in his approach to work and I smiled back at him, realising that no matter what crazy scheme I was dreaming up, the day job still had to be done.

I needed to put some serious time into my new project but nevertheless I felt sure that it could work. It was a big step up from just wondering about where the next gig would come from and if we had our own venue then I could play my music whenever I wanted.

Let's just hope there were sufficient interested people around that would make it into a viable operation.

*

For the following couple of weeks I busied myself with all aspects of finance and business that I'd never come across before. A colleague of Terry's called Ernie gave me a hand with some templates and spreadsheet formats and I gradually got to grips with all the necessary accounts terminology and the sales and marketing elements needed.

It was a strange and at times forbidding task and though I was tempted to give up on several occasions, I nevertheless persevered. If nothing else, at least I'd understand a bit more about the economics of running a club and of course I just had to enlist some advice from my future father-in-law.

'Tha's lookin' at doin' what?' he asked in disbelief, nearly choking on his roast beef when I first mentioned it to him over the family Sunday lunch. 'Openin' a bluey's club?'

'No, a music club,' I said, as Jenny just giggled at us and Dorothy wasn't certain what we were talking about. 'For jazz and blues enthusiasts. Like your place at Edlington, but for music fans that want to hear certain styles of music.'

He looked doubtful, but somewhat relieved that at least it wasn't anything illegal and recovered his composure slightly.

'Well, first rule o' club business is to get 'old of people's money upfront before they step through door,' he instructed. 'Then hang onta cash like yer life depended on it.'

He paused for a moment. 'Secondly, don't buy 'owt from any bugger wi' out knockin' em down on price first an' then don't actually pay 'em until they start shoutin' an' screamin' at tha.'

I nodded at him. 'I'll make sure to build that into my business strategy Walter,' I said.

'I'll put yer in touch with our brewery rep if you like,' he replied. 'They're pretty good on credit terms. I can usually stretch 'em to ninety days before they threaten to cut me off. But they never do.'

'Well, let me wait until I've found a suitable place first,' I said. It was one thing spending time on everything financial and economical, but there was no point in trying to launch a music club if I couldn't find anywhere to house it. I had to put in some time looking for a venue.

Walter had begrudgingly agreed to sell me his car as soon as he found another one, although he didn't seem to be in too much of a rush. So, when we borrowed the car these days, Jenny and I would drive round looking at possible locations and working out whether they would work as a music club.

One thing I did enjoy was seeing the colours of the Autumn leaves which looked wonderful as we drove from village to village and it made me appreciate the changing beauty and nature of the seasons in this part of the world. When I'd first seen the landscape in the depths of Winter it was grey and miserable, but now there was an abundance of colour that matched anything we had back home at this time of year.

One Saturday afternoon we were driving through the valley and I spotted a for sale board perched on the edge of a building that seemed vaguely familiar. There were some lights on inside and the front door was open so I said to Jenny to pull into the car-park at the side. I then realised we were parked outside the former Darfield Miners Welfare Club.

Inside, the contents were being cleared out and a stout guy was supervising a couple of cleaners who were busy scrubbing the floor. I recognised him as the same chap who I'd met when I first appeared here and I recalled his name.

'Hello Len,' I shouted out, as we approached him.

He looked around at the mention of his name.

'Waz thy want?' he asked. 'Club's not open anymore, so we're not tekkin' bookings for performers.'

'No, I'm here about the building,' I said. 'I'm interested in renting it.'

'Fer what?' he asked.

'To use as a music venue for jazz and blues, stuff that, er, older people might appreciate.'

He looked at me. 'Well, shame that it's 'ad to shut down in first place, but if there's no pit then the miners can't have a welfare club. If tha's interested in premises, tha'll have to call one o' blokes in the Estate office. Their number is on the board outside.'

'But what do you think, Len?' I said to him, looking around at the lounge walls. 'It's big enough for what I need. There's good car-parking and reasonable access to get the musicians and their instruments in and out through the back door. A bit of work to make a bigger stage area and a lick of paint everywhere won't go amiss, as well as some money spending on the kitchen facilities and toilets.

And what about you?' I added. 'Fancy being the manager for me?'

'I could be interested,' he said. 'They're payin' me as a caretaker for time being, just to look after place, but ah don't know fer 'ow long. How much is tha payin'?'

'Don't know yet. Depends on how much it'll cost to get it up to scratch.'

'Well ring me when tha does know,' he said, handing me a phone number. 'This place 'as been part of me for last twenty years an' I wouldn't mind seein' out me last few 'ere as well. Plus, most o' suppliers already know me an' I'm local so ah can look after things like security and cleanin' jobs. So aye, ah might be interested, lad. Is this tha girlfriend?'

'Yes,' I said, introducing Jenny. 'Her dad is the club secretary at Edlington.'

'Walter Bentley?' he asked. 'Bloody 'ell, 'aven't seen that old git, sorry, old chap, in ages. How's he doin' these days?'

'Very well,' said Jenny. 'And pretty soon he's going to be a grandad, so I think old git is very relevant,' she laughed, sticking out her belly towards Len.

'Is tha gonna be 'avin' a lad as well?' he asked, with interest. 'Seems like he'll want a grandson to play cricket. Tell me 'bout 'im while ah mek thee a cuppa. Is he still married to Dorothy? Ah used to fancy 'er like mad back in the day tha knows...'

Len carried on chatting with Jenny as if they were old friends as I walked around the empty building, picturing how it could shortly re-emerge as my music venue.

Then Len agreed to put me in touch with a Coal Board Estates chap called Rogers and although he was initially sceptical when I called him, he did confirm that they wanted to see the building occupied rather than left empty.

He suggested we have a meeting and I took Len along with me on the following Friday afternoon.

Mr Rogers suggested first doing a kind of opening event to see if the idea would fly, and if so then he'd be willing to look at some lease terms. With Len on my side, we argued and cajoled him a bit and eventually he agreed to spending some money to smarten up the place for our gala night and if it was a success then he'd add it onto the rental at a later stage.

'Just make sure you have all the legal items in place to hold an event,' he advised us as we shook hands on the deal.

'What did he mean by that?' I asked Len, as we left the office building.

'It's to do wi' licensing stuff from Council, you know to sell alcohol an' host entertainment events. But don't worry about that. I still 'ave 'em from we had the club open so we can use them if anyone asks. Just mek sure you get some insurance cover in place though.' I made a note to contact Duggie.

Colin was also quite taken up by the idea when I told him about it on the Monday and showed him a layout drawing of the building.

'You know, we could possibly get the College to take an interest in it and run some courses on recording and sound engineering if we converted the games room to a studio,' he said.

My exciting project was taking shape and with some additional help on the business plan side of things, I was able to get some initial grant money approved from the Council to help get the venture going.

I did what Len had suggested and went to see Duggie who was delighted to have a business client on his books. He went through the details carefully and then opened a bank account for me in the name of The Dearne Valley Jazz & Blues Club at the Natwest just up the High Street, so that any grant money or receipts could be paid straight into it.

'Then tha's all set. Good luck and don't forget to invite me to your opening night in a few weeks,' he said.

'I will,' I replied. 'It's going to be on the thirteenth of December. It's a Wednesday night.'

'By the way, who's doing your decorating work?' he asked.

'Archie,' I replied. 'Although I've not asked him yet.' It reminded me that I needed to speak with him pretty soon in order to get him booked in.

'Bloody 'ell, in that case I'll put yer policy in place by end o' this week,' he smiled.

Chapter Twenty Six

October turned into the darker days of November and the onset of the Winter months as I continued with the plans for our opening night. Colin had agreed to perform with me and we were also looking for a top named artiste or band to come along as a feature. We needed someone who wasn't too expensive as well as not being already booked elsewhere, seeing that we were opening during the busy run up to Christmas.

After lunch one afternoon, I was sitting in Colin's office scanning through some suggestions, when he appeared at the door. 'Just emptied the pigeon-holes,' he said, throwing a pile of unopened junk mail into his wastepaper bin. 'There was some stuff in yours too,' dropping some items on the desk in front of me.

I glanced at the envelopes and noticed a hand-written one in a style that I didn't recognise. I opened it and pulled out a single sheet of cream paper. 'This is strange,' I said, as I read the contents.

Colin looked up. 'Problem?'

'I don't know. I can't make it out,' as I quickly scanned through the contents again.

'Well, what is it?' he asked.

'It's a note. Written on headed paper from somewhere called Downing College, Cambridge. It's not signed but I think it's from Rosalyn. You remember her, the violin player?'

'Of course, how could I forget her?' he said. 'How's she getting on?'

'That's just it, she doesn't say,' as I stared blankly at the piece of paper. 'It's just this weird message quoting the lyrics from *Dust in the Wind*. That's the song we first played together back in the summer…but the words are really about the mortality of people and the inevitability of death. Then there's some other stuff below it that I don't recognise. If it's come from her then I don't understand what she is trying to tell me,' I said, puzzled.

'Let me see,' asked Colin and I passed the piece of paper to him. 'I don't think I know the song, but...' He stopped as the colour drained from his face and he breathed out heavily. 'I do recognise this last line,' he said. '*That what has been may never be again,*' comes from a classical work. I think this note is a cry for help Jamie and an urgent one at that. When did she send it?'

I turned the envelope over. It was postmarked the twenty first. 'Two days ago,' I said. 'Why do you ask?'

'Was Rosalyn in any way spiritual or religious?'

'I don't think so, other than going to the Catholic school. Is that relevant?'

'Perhaps,' he said, as his brow furrowed tightly in concerned thought. 'From my reading of this I wonder if she is going to do something in two days' time. That's today, which is St Cecilia's Day. It's a Catholic Saint's day.'

'That doesn't mean anything to me other than her music teacher was called Sister Cecilia,' I replied. 'So what?'

'So what?' he exclaimed. 'I may be over-reacting but I'd say we've got to get to her and quickly. I can't let this happen a second time,' he muttered, grabbing his coat.

'What do you mean second time?' I asked. 'You've got me worried now.'

'Let me just re-arrange our classes this afternoon with whoever's available.'

He dashed off to the admin office as I picked up the note and read it again. The words were just lines of poetry to me and I wondered if they were meant merely as something symbolic and innocent, reflecting the fact that any contact between Rosalyn and myself had been banned by her father. But something in the message had got to Colin and his strange reaction was now bothering me.

'Colin, what's going on?' I asked, as he returned to collect his car keys.

'I'll explain on the way, come on,' he replied. 'I hope I'm wrong but I need to make sure,' as I followed him to the College car-park.

He drove aggressively through the town centre before joining the A635 and then turned south onto the A1 motorway. I was confused to say the least, but I didn't want to distract him from his driving. As we settled into the steady flow of the traffic, he became a little calmer. 'I hope we're on a fool's errand,' he said. 'At least then the worst we've done is to waste a few hours and a tank of petrol. But it's a price worth paying, if only to put my mind at rest.'

'What are you talking about Colin? You've now got me very confused as well as worried.'

'Well, let me explain my thinking,' he said. 'Firstly, St Cecilia is the patron saint of musicians. Her saint's day is today, which coincidentally is also the birthday of the composer whose work is quoted in that note. It's from a piece called *Hymn to St Cecilia* by Benjamin Britten. He was a classical composer who attended the Royal College of Music – before my time of course – but we studied him in great detail when I was a student there.'

'I still don't get the connection,' I said.

'Britten died at an early age, but he was deeply affected by two great forces all through his life. For one, he was a pacifist, or a Conscientious Objector as they used to call them back then and he had to leave England for a time during the war,' he replied.

'Secondly, he was homosexual at a time when such things were not accepted as they are nowadays. This constant anxiety about a person's individual choice being taken away from them by someone in authority and the resulting conflict it causes appeared in a lot of his works.'

This was all getting too much for me and I said so. 'That's all very well and knowledgeable, but what the hell has it got to do with Rosalyn?'

'Well, she's at a top seat of academia, no doubt coming across intellectuals and concepts that the rest of us don't see in everyday life,' he replied, quietly. 'That note is the clue. I know she hasn't signed it, but who else would send you an anonymous letter like that to your place of work?'

'Yes, it can only have come from her,' I conceded. 'And I think I can work out why it is not signed.'

'Well, my fear is that she may do something tragic on the very day that she should be celebrating her love of music,' replied Colin. 'I wonder if she feels that she's been forced into a choice through someone else's will, rather than her own? Does that ring any bells with you?'

'Loud and fucking clear it does,' I said, with horror. 'Her father has insisted on her going to Cambridge to study law. I'd always suspected it was something that she didn't really want to do. Plus, he also made sure there was to be no further contact between us. That's why the letter is unsigned.'

290

'Well, let's hope we get to her first and make sure she's alright. At least we can do that much,' he replied. 'So much talent simply cannot go to waste.'

Colin had now got me really worried. For a start I was breaking my bail conditions and I hadn't disclosed to him that I was supposed to stay local. Secondly, I realised that I should have called Rosalyn's parents to let them know, but that would have betrayed the fact that there had been some contact between us – the very thing that her father had got me to sign and guarantee that I wouldn't do. And finally, even though I loved Jenny and we were going to be married and have a family, I couldn't ignore this note that I'd just received.

It was the right thing to go and see if Rosalyn was okay and for the moment, the rest of the world could go to hell. I was having my own personal conflict with society, just as Colin's Mr Britten had no doubt experienced to a much greater degree during his life.

Once more I felt in awe at the hidden qualities of the man sitting next to me. How did he know all these things? 'I hope you are wrong Colin,' I said. 'Not because of what you've just told me but because I'm fearful of what we might otherwise find.'

'Well, at least we're doing something,' he replied. 'For the last twenty years I've silently cursed myself for not being in the right place at the right time to save my Gabriella from her untimely end. I vowed then that I'd never let that happen to anyone else if I could help it. I couldn't live with myself if we did nothing tonight and then found out that something bad had happened. At least now we'll find out one way or another, soon enough.'

I remained silent, troubled by what I'd heard and also chastened by Colin's willingness to intervene in the potential welfare of someone that he didn't really know.

Whether it was through guilt or compassion, I couldn't really tell. But whatever it was, I was now part of it. My mind worked furiously as I stared out at the road and traffic ahead of us, trying to work out the reasoning behind this mysterious note and whether there was a simple explanation for it. I hoped to God that there was, but for the life of me I couldn't see it.

A couple of hours later, we pulled off the motorway and headed into the centre of Cambridge. It was already dark and the traffic was busy on the roads as people returned to their homes for the evening from their various workplaces.

Colin pulled into a petrol station. 'See if they have an A to Z street map in the shop or if you can get some directions to the College. It'll save us some time whilst I fill up.'

I did as I was told and returned to the car. 'It's not far,' I said. 'The guy just said keep on this main road for about two miles and we'll pass it on the right.' Colin nodded as he pulled out his wallet and headed inside to pay the attendant.

Presently, we slowed and pulled up at the side of an illuminated signboard in front of a gated entrance to the College. 'There should be a porter's lodge around here,' said Colin, as I followed him out of the car and along a high stone wall before he dashed into a small building which to me looked like a gatehouse to a castle.

As I waited for him, I glanced quickly across to the vast College structure with its ancillary buildings and surrounding grounds. It was beautifully lit up in the Winter's evening and at any other time I would have stood and marvelled at the historic features and wonderful architecture of the place. But not tonight.

Colin came back out. 'They've telephoned the Welfare Officer and we're to wait here until she arrives.'

A few moments later a middle-aged lady wearing a tweed twinset suit walked up to us clutching some papers and keys. She peered at us over half-moon glasses attached to a silver chain round her shoulders. 'I'm Mrs Haslam,' she announced, without any pleasantries or greeting. 'You're asking about student Rosalyn Carter, I understand? And that she may be in some danger?'

'We don't know that for sure,' said Colin, trying to reassure her. 'We're, er, friends of Rosalyn and we're just concerned about her welfare.'

'Well, I've just called her room but there's no answer,' she replied. 'So, let's double check at her accommodation block,' glancing down at her list. 'It's over in Building Five, room nine, just across the quadrangle,' she said.

We followed her up to a second floor where she knocked loudly on Rosalyn's door, but there was no answer. A couple of neighbouring doors were opened by students who looked out curiously at us. Mrs Haslam asked them if anyone had seen Miss Carter today but received only shaking heads in response.

'I'll open it,' she announced, producing a master key from the bunch in her hand.

The room was darkened but the curtains were still open and the quadrangle lights shining in through the window revealed the limp outline of a body lying on a bed.

Mrs Haslam turned on a light-switch on the wall then looked at me and yelled, 'Call the Porter's office for an ambulance right away. Dial nine,' pointing to a telephone on a side desk.

On a table at the side of the bed was an opened bottle of pills and Colin and I looked at each other and feared the worst.

'She's unconscious but still breathing,' he said, leaning over Rosalyn's clothed and still body and gently placing a pillow behind her back to keep her supported on her side. 'She needs to get to a hospital now and quick about it.'

I did as I was told as Mrs Haslam ushered the curious student onlookers away from the door and instructed us not to touch anything.

Glancing around the room, it felt cold and uninviting as if we were intruding into an alien place. I could see a couple of empty wine bottles in the waste bin under the desk and I wondered if Rosalyn had simply fallen into a drunken slumber, as I desperately resisted the urge to try and shake her awake. But that wouldn't have explained the bottle of pills. She looked as if she was peacefully sleeping, but the pallor of her normally rosy cheeks was a ghostly white and dark half circles had appeared beneath her eyes.

Colin paced the room impatiently as the minutes ticked by, however we didn't have too long to wait. An ambulance crew appeared at the door and after doing some preliminary examinations, they transferred Rosalyn's prone body onto a stretcher. Colin pointed to the bottle saying that she may have been taking them but couldn't say so for sure and one of the paramedics put it into a plastic bag and sealed it.

'We'll follow her to the hospital and wait there until she's been examined,' said Colin to Mrs Haslam.

'Yes, of course,' she replied. Her snobby aloofness had decreased a little. 'In the meantime, I've got to retrieve her records from admin, so I will join you later on.'

To me it was all a bad dream taking place and everything seemed to be happening in a blur. We followed the ambulance through the city traffic and Colin remained quiet, no doubt in silent contemplation of things. It made me realise what he must have gone through with his own wife all those years ago and the thought sent icy shivers down my back.

At the hospital we hung around for ages in the waiting area until around eight o'clock when a doctor holding a clip board and studying some notes walked up to us. 'Are you the relatives of, er, Rosalyn Carter?' he asked, looking down at his notes and my heart sank at hearing his words.

'We're friends of hers,' said Colin. 'We called the ambulance. How's she doing?'

'Well, I think she's going to be fine, thanks to you,' he replied. 'From the bottle you handed to the paramedics, it looks like she's taken an overdose of diazepam.'

'What are they?' I interjected.

'They're commonly prescribed as sleeping pills for anxiety. We don't know when she took them but they're in her system rather than her stomach. She's still unconscious, although we've ran the usual tests and her vital signs are encouraging,' he said.

'Well, that's good news, isn't it?' Colin asked, hesitantly.

'Yes, her scans have shown no obvious damage so far, but we'll know better when she wakes up. Right now, we don't know exactly when that will be.'

I asked the question that I knew Colin feared the most. 'Does that mean she is in a coma?'

'Technically yes, but not a critical one,' replied the doctor. 'The effects of diazepam are more like a deep sleep. But we can't force her to wake up for fear of causing internal damage, particularly to her brain function, so we're monitoring her. She's receiving a drip to reverse the effects of the drugs and she's breathing satisfactorily at present and without the need for mechanical assistance. I expect her to fully recover quite soon.'

'Can we see her?' I asked.

'Yes, in a while. We're going to move her into a side room where we've got all the necessary equipment set up. Then you can sit with her and even speak to her. She won't respond but her brain may recognise familiar voices. I suggest you go and get something to eat and then come back in half an hour. There's a café on the ground floor,' he added.

We did as we were advised and whilst Colin was visibly relieved, I was shocked by what I'd just witnessed and said so to him.

'It happens sometimes Jamie,' he answered, quietly. 'When young people are forced into an environment that they don't want to be in. Even in places as prestigious as this one. Some free spirits aren't meant to be held captive, no matter how gilded the cage may be. If they're pressured to live up to something they don't want or can't cope with, there's a danger that they shut themselves away from others.'

'Do you think that is what has happened here?' I asked.

'I don't know for sure, but University, and the Law for that matter, isn't for everyone. I was lucky when I went to the RCM. It was what I wanted to do, but I also saw other students who couldn't manage or adapt to the pressures that the top-drawer institutions like mine or here in Cambridge demand.'

'But why didn't she say something or call?' I said to him. 'I know her parents stopped us from having any contact, but this – taking sleeping pills? It doesn't make any sense.'

'I don't think that she would intentionally want to do herself harm if she was thinking in a logical, calm and considered way,' he replied. 'But you never know what can trigger their reaction. Maybe the course was just too much for her and she couldn't bring herself to admit it,' he said, tilting his head to one side as he expressed his thoughts. 'All I know for certain is that it's a terrible thing when your free will is taken away in the supposed pursuit of career or ambition.'

After eating, we returned to the ward and were shown to Rosalyn's room. However, the welfare woman from the Uni was already inside, talking with the doctor and making notes on a file. She came out into the corridor when she saw us.

'I've had an update from the medical staff and I've been trying to call the parents, but there's no answer yet,' she said. 'I've brought a bag of clean clothes for Rosalyn from her room and I also now need to fill out a report on the incident.'

She looked over the top of her glasses at both of us in a condescending way. 'Now, who did you say you were, exactly?'

'We're friends,' said Colin. 'If you leave the form with us, I'll fill it in for you and put it on the side over there,' pointing to a table in Rosalyn's room.

'In the meantime, get yourself off home and keep trying her parents. They've probably gone out for dinner,' he added. 'Now, I need to ask the doctor something,' as he slipped away from us before returning a few moments later.

Handing me his car keys he said, 'There's a six string in the boot. Go and fetch it. The doctor said some gentle music will be fine and may help to stimulate her brain.'

Mrs Haslam left us and for the next couple of hours we sat in the hospital room alternating between singing and talking softly to our very special audience. But it was hard to look at Rosalyn as she lay peacefully, yet lifeless, against the pillows. She'd been dressed in a gown and her hair had been brushed by the nurse, but the assortment of tubes, monitors and electronic beepers around her natural beauty produced a distressing picture in my mind.

The hospital lighting had been dimmed for the night and eventually I told Colin to go and get a bit of shuteye on the soft seats in the waiting area. There was no one else here on the ward other than patients and the medical staff and the doctor had allowed us to stay on at least until the parents turned up.

I continued singing softly and strumming on the guitar in the strangely intimate yet sterile surroundings, going through my repertoire of ballads and any love songs that I could think of and occasionally getting a nodding smile from the duty nurse when she came in to do her regular checks.

Through the small hours I alternated between playing and singing and praying and hoping, all the time just convincing myself that somewhere in the recesses of her mind, Rosalyn could hear me. Even though I was used to performing on my own, I struggled to stop my voice from faltering through the haunting lyrics of *Helplessly Hoping* and *Landslide* before recovering slightly for *Sister Golden Hair* and *Girl from the North Country*.

When I sang *Four Strong Winds* I imagined her playing the beautiful violin counterpoint line with me, blending into my melody with effortless ease. There was no applause, no heckling and no shouting out for requests on this gig, but I still gave it my usual diligence and effort. I felt it was the most important performance of my life.

Around four o'clock I needed a bathroom break. As I got up from the chair, Rosalyn started to cough so I ran out of the room to find the nurse. She told me to stay outside as the coughing continued but then I heard Rosalyn's voice hoarsely asking for a drink of water. Relieved, I then went to the Gents. After splashing some cold water on my face, partly to wake me up and partly to conceal the tears I had just cried at the relief of hearing her voice again, I went back out eager to see and speak with her. Then I stopped in my tracks.

Down the corridor I could see the figures of Rosalyn's parents in her room. Her mother was on the side of the bed hugging her daughter whilst her father was in deep conversation with the doctor. Through the partially opened door I heard the doctor say that a couple of guys had been with her and had most likely saved her by calling an ambulance. I quietly retreated back the other way to find Colin, who was slumped over a couple of chairs.

'Colin,' I said, urgently shaking his shoulder. 'Rosalyn's regained consciousness. She's going to be alright. But her parents have arrived. They can't see me here.'

He rubbed his eyes as he sat up and looked at his watch. 'Then it looks like we're all done here. Come on, let's go home. We'll pick up some breakfast at a *Little Chef* on the way back.'

We made our way quietly down the staircase and out into the carpark. The chilly air forced me awake but then I stopped abruptly as I thought of something. 'Colin, did you fill in our details on that woman's form?' I asked.

'Must have escaped my mind,' he said, with a smirk. 'They'll just have to put us down as Good Samaritans instead. No-one we have met since leaving Barnsley can put a name to our faces now, can they?'

It was as if Colin had worked all this out from the outset and I was shocked as well as astonished. 'How did you know what to do though?' I asked. 'And dealing with these people in authority? I mean, if we hadn't had come down here, I dread to think what could have happened.' I was rambling and he just looked at me in his calm and considered manner.

'Sometimes you've got to trust your instinct Jamie,' he said. 'And what do you mean by authority? Just because we come from Yorkshire doesn't mean we can't deal with some folk who think they're a cut above the rest of us. We might be blunt at times but that doesn't mek us thick,' he smiled.

Then I remembered something else. 'Your guitar Colin, it's still in her room.'

'Forget about it,' he said. 'Small price and well worth paying. We can replace a guitar any time, but we can't replace Rosalyn.'

'No, we can't,' I agreed.

'Now, we're going to have to blag our way through a day's teaching as if nothing was amiss. So lots of black coffee and a full English should go down well. What d'ya think?'

Usually, the sight of all those greasy items mingling into one another on the plate of an English breakfast combo was enough to turn my stomach, but right now it seemed ideal. 'Anything to get the smell of this hospital out of my nose,' I replied. 'I'll even have a slice of that disgusting black pudding stuff on mine as well if you insist.'

He smiled back. 'Looks like we'll mek a Yorkshireman outa tha yet lad,' playfully over-emphasising his local accent. 'Tha's done tha good deed for today, that's fer sure.'

We headed out of Cambridge and back up the motorway as the faint grey light of dawn broke over the agricultural fields surrounding us. Maybe we had done our good deed for the day, but in the darkened interior of the car, it didn't stop me quietly shedding a few tears of relief at the culmination of the events of the past few hours.

As we drove, Colin remained silent but I could detect a faint contented smile on his face as he concentrated on the road ahead of him and I understood what it meant.

He was now at peace with himself.

Chapter Twenty Seven

A week after my unscheduled trip South, it was time for my residency hearing. Both Jenny and I had submitted written statements of our intentions and confirmation of our forthcoming marriage and I'd provided references given from the College. Mr Taylor was collating all the information and documents to pass onto Richard Carter who would again be representing me.

On the morning of my hearing, we all assembled in Mr Taylor's office, a short walk away from the Magistrates Court in Doncaster. He assured us that everything would go smoothly but I was still wary. Jenny was also feeling nervous and excused herself briefly to use the ladies room.

Moments later Carter entered the office to go through the statements with us. He looked at me curiously as he spread the documents out, taking over Mr Taylor's desk in the process.

'Now, have you been checking in with the police station as you were required to do so?' he asked. 'I don't want any surprises from the police when we go into Court.'

'Yes,' I replied, handing him the attendance sheet. 'Every week as you can see.'

I'd been making my regular visits to Mexborough Police Station to have my papers stamped and dated and thought back to the start of these, some three months ago. At the time I'd made a point of asking for Fletcher in person as I wanted to rub his face in it, but he wasn't on duty.

So instead, as the desk sergeant filled in my paperwork, I'd asked him, 'Would it be okay to put some flyers up on your notice board for my singing lessons? PC Fletcher's girlfriend was very keen on the idea.'

'Well, I don't think 'e would be very keen now seein' that she's buggered off an' left him for a fireman,' he'd replied. 'Not that it's any o' your bloody business to start off with.'

Well, maybe it wasn't I thought, but I'd detected he'd got some kind of satisfaction from learning about Fletcher's recent misfortune, although he wouldn't allow me to do any advertising.

Still, I got a sense of pleasure from walking into Fletcher's place of work each Friday evening to prove I was keeping to the bail conditions and was very much still on his patch as he would have referred to it.

Carter scanned the attendance sheet before asking, 'And the rest of your bail conditions. Have you been complying with them?'

'I've been following them,' I said, quietly.

'Where were you on the night of the twenty third of this month?' he asked.

I thought this would come up, as it was the night I'd gone with Colin to Cambridge. As far as I was aware, Carter hadn't seen me at the hospital, nor had anyone got a record of our names. I hadn't told Jenny about our trip and so I didn't need to ask her for an alibi. If there was no evidence of us being there, then Carter couldn't prove that I was. Even Rosalyn hadn't seen us – she had recovered consciousness but hadn't actually recognised me. The only thing that could connect me was the guitar which undoubtedly would have my fingerprints on it, but as it wasn't a crime scene there was no reason to have it checked. If Carter knew for certain that I was there, then I reckoned he would have asked me a different question.

'At home in Gladstone Terrace,' I replied, calling his bluff.

Jenny re-entered the office at that point and he looked up and nodded politely at her, before turning his attention back to me.

'Now I want to go through the procedure with you as to what will happen at the hearing,' and I let out a breath of relief that for the time being at least, neither my breach of bail nor my personal guarantee to him, had been exposed.

Two hours later it was all over. I was allowed an eighteen month time extension on a work visa and once our wedding had taken place, I could then go down the formal application route for official residency.

It was an immense relief to both Jenny and me and whilst I thanked Carter for his help, he just muttered something and left the Courtroom without shaking my hand or wishing us well for the future.

'He's an unsociable brute,' said Jenny, as she watched him leave. 'He was supposed to be on our side as well.'

'I know,' I replied. 'It's the way he is. Over-bearing bully, but at least he's done the job for us and I'm here to stay.'

'Yes, but even so,' she said. 'You'd have thought he'd be a little more civil with us. He's barely said two words to me all morning.'

'Do you know who he's married to?' I said, tempting fate.

'Who?'

'Your GP, Dr Carter. He's Rosalyn's father.'

'What?' she exclaimed. 'But Dr Carter is such a kind and considerate person. Whatever did she see in him? And poor Rosalyn, having to have him as a father, if that is what he's like to everyone.'

I wanted to blurt out that you don't know the half of it, but instead I bit my tongue. I was on dodgy ground here and needed to get off it as quickly as possible.

'Come on, let's go choose a ring,' I said. 'As a celebration. I haven't given you anything yet to show you how much I love you.'

'Haha,' she laughed. 'And what do you call this then, cowboy?' sticking out her large belly in front of us and we both giggled as we said our thanks and goodbyes to Mr Taylor.

At least he'd seemed more friendly and supportive towards us I thought as we wandered into the town centre. Everywhere was preparing for the oncoming Christmas season with fancy decorations and strings of coloured lightbulbs hanging down from lamp posts and along the corners of the buildings. A huge conifer tree together with a nativity scene beneath it was in the process of being erected by workmen in front of the town hall.

'Well at least I won't be having our baby in a stable surrounded by smelly cows and shepherds,' joked Jenny, as we walked by it.

'That's true, we're not in Ontario right now, otherwise you might just be doing that,' I replied, as we stopped to look at the H Samuels jewellery shop window before going inside.

We got some strange looks from the assistant when I said to her that we were looking for a wedding ring, but I ignored them. We scanned the trays and tried a few before eventually deciding on one which fitted Jenny's finger perfectly, as well as our budget, without any adjustments being necessary.

Jenny's pregnancy was coming along nicely. She'd had a scan and we now knew we were having a boy, but we deliberately didn't mention anything to Walter and Dorothy. There'd be time enough for that in due course.

We'd previously sat up for hours debating names and finally decided on Robert Walter. Jenny had been given an expected due date of the seventh of January, but she wanted to continue her nursing duties into December if she felt able to do so. I figured that at least she'd be in the right place if the little guy decided he'd been cooped up long enough and wanted to make a break for it. After my time in Lindholme I knew how he must feel.

We'd also decided on Jenny staying at her parents' home after the birth so that her mum could help out and then we'd all be at my place until we found something better.

I'd enlisted Archie to decorate the back bedroom for us in a nice pale lilac colour. He'd managed to get the four walls almost the same, but it was difficult to tell as the shadow from the pit heap made everything look slate grey.

After choosing the ring, Jenny was due for one of her ante-natal checks later in the afternoon so I left her and returned to College. However, she called me just after four o'clock, as I was bringing Colin up to speed with the outcome of my hearing and he passed the phone to me.

'Sorry to bother you,' she said. 'I'm at Dr Carter's and she's asked if you can come over to see her after she finishes her surgery hours at six tonight.'

'What for?' I asked, a little concerned. 'Is there a problem with the baby?'

'No, he's fine,' she replied. 'I think she just wants to give you the new dad lecture and stuff like, you know, how

I'm going to be physically, after the baby has arrived. The sex bits and suchlike. It's nothing unusual, but as you're not registered at her practice she doesn't know anything about you,' she added.

'Okay, what's the address?' as I wrote it down. 'I'll come along and see what she has to say.'

Colin looked over and smiled coyly. 'Careful what you say and careful what you wish for.'

His words echoed in my mind as I turned up shortly before six at Dale View Surgery and told the receptionist I had an appointment with Dr Carter, before taking a seat amongst a handful of elderly patients. Eventually a door opened and I was summoned to enter.

'Hello James,' said Dr Carter. 'Thank you for coming over. Please take a seat.'

I did as I was told as she settled back behind her desk.

'Now, you are no doubt aware that I am the family doctor to your partner Jenny Bentley and she tells me you're soon to be married, so you'll have a double celebration coming up. However, that's not why I asked to see you.'

I squirmed slightly as she cleared some papers in front of us. 'Now, I don't want you to say anything and incriminate yourself,' she announced, looking at me. 'I just wanted to say thank you for what you did for Rosalyn a week or so ago.'

I opened my mouth but she just held up her hand.

'Without your intervention and that of your friend, things could have been far worse for all of us. You saved Rosalyn's life and for that I am eternally grateful.'

Again, I wanted to say something, but she just continued to hold up her hand and looked at me. 'Just listen, please,' she said. 'Nobody at the hospital or at the College can tell us who the two males were who helped

Rosalyn that night. We didn't see you there ourselves so I have no evidence that it was you. But Ros later confided in me that she'd posted you a note. She said that she was a little drunk when she'd wrote it and that it wouldn't have made any sense to anyone. But it obviously did to you.'

I nodded silently, trying to maintain a poker face.

'Anyway, I'm pleased to tell you that she is fine and is going to stay with my younger sister in Ireland for a while. Ros always got on well with her and the change of scenery will do her good. The College have agreed to postpone her place for a year, that is, if she wishes to take it back up.'

'I'm really pleased to hear that Rosalyn is well,' I said, unable to keep quiet any longer. I wanted to know much more but realised that I was on thin ice here and as Dr Carter had been very gracious, I kept my response brief.

'Plus, there's this,' she said, standing up and walking over to a closet before pulling out the guitar that I'd left in the hospital room. 'I think this belongs to you, or if not, I'm sure you can do more with it than I can,' she smiled.

I smiled back. 'Thank you, it's not mine but I'll return it to its rightful owner,' realising that I'd just made an admission and confirmed what she already knew, as I took the guitar from her.

'There's one more thing' she said, pulling out an envelope from her desk drawer. 'I understand that my husband made you sign a personal guarantee, with strict financial penalties attached, banning you from having any contact with Ros.'

I looked at her, uncertain what to say, but she carried on. 'Well, I won't have my daughter being bartered as some form of security or collateral just to please my husband,' she declared.

She held the contract up in front of me and tore it into small pieces before placing them in her waste bin.

'Is it okay if I ask you what caused Rosalyn to, er, do what she did?' I said, hesitantly.

Dr Carter studied me for a few moments, obviously deciding whether she should share a family secret with me or not.

'Well, I don't know the full details and frankly they're no longer important. But Ros was intensely unhappy with her course and wanted to change it to something else,' she said. 'Music was a possibility as it was available at Downing and apparently after listening to her play, they would agree to a transfer. Ros discussed it with us one night in a tearful conversation over the phone, but then things went downhill when my husband over-reacted and told her in no uncertain terms to stick with what she had already chosen.'

I nodded at her, imagining the conversation that would have taken place. 'I'm sorry to hear that,' I said.

'You see, in my line of work James, I meet and help lots of families who have all kinds of social problems to work through,' she said. 'But sometimes, the more fortunate ones can also have issues to resolve as well. Richard's intentions are usually well-placed but sometimes he goes too far. He's not above being on the receiving end of some counselling and he needs to learn some humility and to let others live their life as they choose to do so.'

I nodded back again at her and smiled. I couldn't have put it better myself.

'Anyway, enough of the lecturing. Jenny is a lovely woman to have as your partner and very soon you'll both have enough to cope with looking after your new baby. So good luck James.' She stood up and stretched her arm across the desk to shake my hand.

'Thank you,' I replied, as I returned the handshake. 'And please send my best to Rosalyn, from all of us.'

'I will, but what we've spoken about remains in this room,' she said. 'As does everything I speak about with my patients. I just wanted you to know that Ros is well and that you have my heartfelt thanks for what you did. When I saw you both playing together in your band at Woolley I realised that there was more than just a musical connection between the two of you. A mother tends to pick up on these things, you know,' looking directly into my eyes.

I blushed, wondering how I could respond, as Dr Carter continued. 'At the time it bothered me slightly, but I kept my thoughts to myself. Ros was never a great one for being extrovert and making new friends and I think that was part of her problem at University, being out of contact with people she could trust. But looking back, I can see how lucky we are that you and her met each other in the first place. Without that happening…well, we wouldn't be having this conversation now, would we?'

'No I suppose we wouldn't,' I agreed. 'But I'm just really pleased that everything turned out in the right way,' I replied.

'So am I,' she smiled. 'Now go and learn about being a good husband and a father.'

I left the surgery and wandered back through the drizzle and darkened streets towards Conisbrough, thinking deeply about what had just taken place.

When I arrived at Jenny's house her mother was in the kitchen about to serve out a shepherd's pie and my mouth began watering at the delicious aroma wafting through into the lounge.

'I've set a place for you at the table Jamie,' she shouted from the side of the cooker, as I looked and smiled at the domestic scene laid out in front of me.

310

'So the Doc has told you about layin' off it for a few weeks after the birth then?' asked Walter, looking at me and folding up his evening paper.

'Dad, do you mind?' retorted Jenny. 'That's not a very nice topic for family conversation.'

'Only joshin' im, my lovely,' he said. 'Can't a man 'ave a bloody joke in his own 'ouse these days?'

'There's other things we can do you know,' she smiled back at me. 'I don't have to give you the details do I dad - and at your age as well?' gently goading him.

'No need to,' Walter replied. 'Ah've got somethin' he can get both 'is hands on an' keep 'isself occupied.' He reached down the side of his easy chair. 'Early Christmas present for tha lad,' he said, proudly holding up a new cricket bat. 'Tha'll need some practice gerrin' in before start o' new season.'

Jenny laughed and I joined in. 'Thank you,' I said.

'But if you think I'm squeezing my bollocks into your mouse bucket again, you're very much mistaken,' I added, as we took our places at the dining table.

'One scoop or two, Jamie?' asked Dorothy, as she hovered over us with a large steaming dish and a serving spoon. She couldn't understand why we were all laughing.

Chapter Twenty Eight

There was just one week to go before our Blues in the Valley opening night at the Darfield club and I couldn't stop thinking about it. At the venue, Len had taken delivery of some new tables and chairs, the stage alterations had been done and Archie was busying away with the decorating. I felt that it just had to be a success and I was excited that my dream of playing my blues music in this part of the world would finally be heard loud and clear.

It was evident from my business plan and research that we'd have to share the club premises with other musical styles in order to generate enough income, but I could live with that. If we could cover our costs from being open for maybe four nights per week, then I'd be happy.

I still had my College job to fall back on and even though Jenny would shortly be stopping work, she'd still have her maternity pay coming in, so we were doing okay for cash at the moment.

Colin had also become keen on the project and as he'd agreed to play as well, we needed to have a piano moved in to the venue. We'd worked out a set of numbers that we could play together and he'd also located a top named blues group and a jazz trio to appear, so we had a full bill of entertainment for the evening.

Terry had been busy putting up posters and selling tickets and so far he'd sold one hundred and thirty. That was a great result as we were aiming for a hundred and fifty covers and so we were nearly there with our target.

I'd been popping over to Darfield whenever I could during the working week and Len had been on hand supervising all the work on site, still in his capacity as club caretaker. It was a handy arrangement as it meant that he was still being paid by the Coal Board rather than by myself.

On this Wednesday lunchtime I'd nipped out with Terry for an hour or so and as we pulled into the carpark we were astonished to see the amount of activity taking place next door at the former coal mine site.

On the other side of the carpark fence, the old pit buildings and winding towers were being demolished. The whole site was a mass of lifting cranes, heavy machinery and excavators, with men scurrying about in hard hats and orange boiler suits. A procession of lorries queued up at the entrance to carry away the rubble and debris as the machines worked away at erasing all visible signs of the previous activity.

Even the mighty spoil heap in the background was being levelled and landscaped in preparation for it being turned into some open recreational space and a huge cloud of dust from the bulldozers crawling over its sides rose up to mingle with the grey skies above us.

'They seem to be in a rush,' I said to Len, when I'd asked him about all the work going on at the former pit. 'They weren't here last week.'

'Aye, I know,' he said. 'Plan seems to be to just totally eradicate all signs of our local coalmining industry an' do so as quickly as bloody possible.'

Terry just scratched his head. 'There must be well over a hundred years of history yonder and it's all being demolished in just a matter of weeks,' he said.

'Aye, just look at that bugger up on pit stack, for instance,' said Len, pointing to a bulldozer pushing up a mound of spoil with its blade. 'We made a big bloody hill to remind ourselves of all the stuff we'd dug out o' ground over years, then they go an' dig another 'oyle an' bury it all again. They call that regeneration, but I call it plain bloody stupid,' he declared. 'They could ha' spent 'alf as much money on keepin' our lads in their jobs for a few more years.'

I agreed that it was a sad sight to see, but I had other things on my mind. 'Well, what about our opening night?' I asked, distracting him from the bigger things taking place next door. 'Give me an update on where we are.'

'Well, the bar's fully stocked an' ready to go. Ah've got a couple o' locals comin' in to run it fer us, payin' em cash in 'and just for th'evening. Then, for catering, we've got two hundred pork pies on order from butcher's for delivery by Wednesday lunchtime an' two o' kitchen lasses from village school will see to 'em.'

He'd reliably informed me that a pork pie and peas supper was guaranteed to go down well, no matter what music people would be listening to. Terry seemed to agree by nodding at the catering arrangements as Len continued with his progress report.

'Toilets have 'ad a make-over an' I've even got a supply of new bog paper for 'em as well,' he said. 'All other stuff like lights, sound system an' staging are all good. Band lads can use the games room for changin' in so there'll be plenty o' room for everyone an' no fallin' out.'

'Great,' I said. 'Everything is coming together nicely,' nodding my approval.

'Just waiting on Archie now to finish off an' add some Christmas dec's around lounge an' then we'll be as good as new,' he said. 'Are tha sure tha don't want to 'ave a bingo session an' all? They always go down well, you know.'

'Don't think we'll have the time Len,' I said. 'But hold onto it for reserve, just in case,' as we said bye to him and headed off back to Barnsley.

*

On the Friday evening I was at home and I'd just paid my rent to Simms's collector. Jenny was doing a late shift at the hospital and would be going back to her parents' house tonight rather than coming over to mine, so I decided it was time to rent a new vid from dirty Dave. Plus, it would give me a chance to put one of our posters up in his shop window to sell a few more tickets. So I grabbed one of my tapes from the wardrobe and walked outside. The Winter darkness had brought a chill wind with it and I hurried down the street.

As I rounded the corner towards the newsagents, a small crowd was gathered on the pavement outside Dave's and they were being held back by policemen with outstretched arms. As I got closer, I could also see that two police vans had blocked the road on either end and one of them had a dog inside, which barked excitedly out of the rear window as people walked past.

I wondered if there had been an accident and as I got nearer, I caught sight of Archie and Duggie talking to each other in the group of onlookers and I went up to them to find out what was going on.

'Now then lad,' said Archie, looking very downcast. 'They're raiding Dave's for his vids. I was 'oping to change this one an' all tonight, as were Duggie 'ere, but looks like we're buggered – just as they were in this film,' he laughed, pointing to the video in his hand.

Duggie blushed, realising that his personal home viewing choices and membership of Dave's dodgy club had now been unceremoniously revealed to me.

'How did they know about them in the first place though?' I asked. 'Dave always seemed like a cautious guy to me.'

'They've been suspicious o' Dave for quite a while now,' replied Duggie. 'He tek's in some stuff now and then for his landlord bloke Simms, but 'e's not doin' anyone any harm by it.'

'Simms used to pull that trick with my place as well,' I said.

'Aye, he's well known for it locally. Always dropping off stuff at various properties that he owns an' tryin' to keep one step in front o' cops,' answered Duggie. 'And to think that he used to be a client of mine as well at one time, until he became too dodgy and no insurance company would touch him.'

'Not like Dave,' said Archie. 'He's one o' lads.'

'Aye, Dave's a different matter. He's been wi' me for a few years now ever since I first broke into his, er, well, I mean, arranged to help with his cash flow provision, you know.' I nodded, remembering how he'd first told me about his special arrangement he had with some of his clients - from time to time.

'Anyhow, I know him and his missus well,' continued Duggie. 'Only last week he told me that he reckoned the shop was being cased and thought he'd 'ad a cop go in undercover for a snoop around. Seems he were right with his instincts. They've just come back now mob-handed and they're not letting anyone in whilst they ransack the place. Don't know what I'm going to watch now this weekend,' he lamented.

'Well, you can swap me for this one,' I said, pulling my vid out of my jacket, but before we could do so we were interrupted as the front door of the newsagent opened up and a rough voice yelled out, 'Stand back and clear the way 'ere.'

A stocky guy walked out holding a large cardboard box in both of his hands and held it up at head height in front of him. It was stacked up with vids and even though the bloke was dressed in jeans and a blouson jacket and it was already dark, I could clearly make out the ugly features of PC Fletcher from the light shining out of the shop doorway behind him.

'That's the shithead cop who tried to fit me up,' I announced. 'You remember him Archie, searching my place and arresting me that Saturday morning back in the Summer?' It seemed a long time ago, but the memory and the consequences that followed that fateful event were still raw in my mind.

'Aye,' he said, lighting up a plain Park Drive. 'Fletcher. We know 'im. He's bin a pain in the bloody arse for quite a while an' is always givin' people grief for no good reason. Summat should be done about im.'

'Wait here a minute, I've got an idea,' said Duggie, quietly slipping away from us, as Fletcher began to lecture the crowd of onlookers on the pavement around him.

'This is what 'appens when people brek the law on my patch,' he yelled, with a smug grin on his face. 'You'll end up 'aving to deal with me.'

'Leave our Dave alone yer fat pig. He weren't doin' anyone any 'arm,' shouted out a woman in hair curlers and others around her cheered their approval. 'Go an' catch some proper criminals, yer piece of shite.'

'Quiet!' shouted Fletcher back at her. 'Or I'll be lockin' you an' yer big mouth up next.'

I glanced over to where Duggie had gone and saw he was at the back of the van containing the police dog. He said something to it through the window before deftly opening the door and slowly taking hold of the dog's leash, allowing it to jump down where it obediently sat by his side. Then he guided it slowly to the front of the onlookers before crouching down and leaning forward towards the dog's ear.

As Duggie stood up, the dog bolted forward across the street, its leash trailing behind him, as it made a beeline straight for its intended target and the most accessible body part on it.

Fletcher couldn't see what was happening as the height of the box in his hands obscured his line of sight. However, he soon knew about it when the dog leapt up at the soft area it was aiming for and promptly clamped its considerable jaws around his testicles. Fltecher let out a strange howling noise and doubled over at the sudden impact of several pounds of Alsatian jaw pressure being applied to his love tackle and instinctively he dropped the box onto the dog's head which only made it grip on tighter, growling furiously as it did so.

Well, it was only to be expected. Anyone would have been put out by having a heavy package dropped on their head when they were in the middle of trying to do their job.

As the videos clattered onto the pavement and were picked up by the eager punters, Fletcher rolled around on the ground and grappled with the police dog, the pair of them clinging to each other like all-in wrestlers locked in mortal combat. The crowd yelled their encouragement and cheered the dog on, thrilled at this impromptu entertainment as Fletcher's colleagues tried vainly to push them back.

Then one plucky constable caught hold of the leash and pulled on it with all his might. I feared that Fletcher was going to be separated from those parts which he'd most likely held dear all his life. Another officer yelled out a command which I didn't catch and the dog immediately released its grip and sat back, leaving the hapless plod rolling around with both hands still clutching at his groin area.

The crowd guffawed at his plight and even his colleagues couldn't resist smiling as one of them ran back to the van and re-emerged with a first aid kit.

'Hope tha's gonna give 'im a rabies shot now,' shouted out an onlooker. 'The dog, I mean, poor bugger, 'aving to bite on that rancid pig.'

There was clearly no respect for the local police force around here and as Duggie re-joined us, I asked him what he had done to get the dog to react like that.

He shrugged his shoulders. 'Ah used to be a dog trainer in the RAF back in the day,' he said, quietly. 'All them dogs they use are German Shepherd breeds and they're trained to only respond to commands given in a foreign language like Dutch or German. That way they only recognise certain words which aren't widely known,' he explained. 'Plus, it means they can easily be moved to other parts of the military or security forces wi'out having to be re-trained. Seems they're still following the same old methods,' he concluded.

'Most folk are scared of big dogs but them breeds are normally good-natured animals and they understand simple commands, so one word is all it teks.'

'Come on,' said Archie, with a knowing smile. 'Let's go whilst the goin's good an' get a pint in at the Collingwood. That Fletcher's 'ad it comin' to 'im for years, the stupid bastard, so serve 'im right. Whatever I saw in his mother, ah'll never know.'

'What did you just say?' I asked, incredulously. 'Are you his father?

'Like bloody 'ell I am,' replied Archie, defiantly. 'I only shagged 'is mother a few years back when 'e wor still in short pants. His fatha's a decent bloke, he even drinks wi' me down at Labour Club.'

'Didn't he object to you being, er, intimate, with his wife then?' I asked.

'Don't think so,' he replied. 'He were too busy shaggin' mine at same time.'

I looked over at Fletcher who was being assisted into one of the police vans by his fellow plods, whilst the rest of Dave's stash had been rounded up by the crowd of onlookers.

'Oi Fletcher, looks like you dropped a right bollock today,' yelled out the woman who'd earlier complained about him. 'Or was it the left un? Ah'd give it back to yer, but yon dog's gone an' etten it,' she shouted, as everyone around her laughed.

As we made our way up to the pub, I turned to Duggie, recalling the photograph I'd seen on the wall during my first visit to his office. 'I didn't realise you'd been in the Royal Air Force. Did you fly in the planes as well?'

'No chance lad. I used to get bad claustrophobia an' then throw up everywhere inside them,' he replied. 'They used to call me Chucky-Duggie. That's why they put me on doing dog duties instead. Spent all mi time dog-walking round the bases at Finningley and then up at Church Fenton, until I got, er, discharged.'

'Tell 'im what happened to thee,' said Archie. 'It allers mek's me smile.'

Duggie looked at me. 'Well, when I was on patrol duty, I used to slip round to the married quarters some evenings to see a woman whose husband was a cook on the camp,' he said. 'She were gorgeous and I couldn't keep away. I'd also trained this lovely young dog called Lady to keep watch on the doorstep an' she'd bark if anyone came within fifty yards of the house. That way I'd get an early warning to slip outa back door an' then I'd whistle for her to join me. Anyone who saw us would just think I was doing dog-training work.'

'Belt 'n' braces, eh, Duggie?' chipped in Archie.

Duggie continued. 'Well, one night her husband was busy doing an officers' dinner night, so I nipped round to see her. For some reason I didn't hear no barking whilst I were, er, busy inside, but when I came outa house a bit later on the dog had disappeared.'

'Having a nice pair of women's thighs wrapped round yer ears tends to affect a man's 'earing,' quipped Archie, but Duggie ignored him as he carried on with his tale.

'Unbeknown to me, the chief security officer had driven past th'ouse and noticed the dog unattended. As I couldn't be located anywhere, he'd put out a full-scale alert fearing they'd had a break-in somewhere on the base. When I got back to the guard house my Lady was there, pleased to see me, but I was in deep shit. I'd been rumbled and ended up being kicked out.'

'So was she worth it?' I asked.

'Oh aye lad,' he replied, with all sincerity. 'Love's a strange thing tha knows. I wor smitten an' still think fondly of her now, all these years later. Her gorgeous big brown eyes staring into mine, that slim and fit body and the way she used to smell. Yes, as God is my witness, I do miss that bloody dog,' before he burst out laughing.

Archie joined in the fun. 'That's Duggie's shaggy dog story lad,' he said. 'Talking of which, we need to swap these vids before we get inside. I don't want folk in pub to know I'm some kind of dirty old man.'

'Do you guys ever stop thinking about sex?' I asked.

'What and you don't?' he replied. 'Does tha think your bloody generation invented it?'

I smiled as we surreptitiously made our exchanges and then I followed them into the Collingwood tap room. 'First round is on me guys,' I announced.

'Bloody 'ell,' said Archie. 'We'll 'ave to do this more often,' as he settled into a corner table with Duggie and pulled out a box of dominoes. 'Can tha play fives 'n' threes lad? We'll teach thee, it's a pound a game,' as he emptied the contents onto the table. 'Now then Andy,' he shouted out to the landlord who was seeing to our drinks. 'How long we three bin 'ere then, tonight?'

'By my reckoning, I'd say at least a good hour Archie,' replied the landlord with a smile.

'Thought as much. Get one in for Andy whilst yer there, lad,' Archie instructed. 'And a bag o' nuts fer us as well. We know someone who might be short o' one tonight,' he chortled.

Alibis all sorted and with pints of bitter settling in front of us, I sat down to be educated in the game of dominoes. Archie swirled the tiles on the table before lighting up a cig and I sensed that we were in for a long night and figured I'd probably be out of pocket by the end of it.

But in my own mind did I feel any sympathy for Fletcher's plight? Not really.

'Good 'ealth lads,' said Archie, raising his glass and smiling broadly. 'All good things come to them that waits.'

Chapter Twenty Nine

'You've got to get over to Darfield lad an' pretty quick abart it,' announced Terry, rushing up to me as soon as I'd arrived in College on the following Monday morning. 'I've 'ad a phone call at 'ome from Len first thing this mornin'. Big problem on site to sort out.'

Oh no, this couldn't be happening just two days before our opening night and not when everything was now in place for our launch. Fortunately, I didn't have any tutorials to give until after lunchtime, so I left a message with the admin office to let Colin know that I'd had to dash out, before following Terry outside to his minibus.

'What's happened?' I asked, fearing the worst. After all the weeks of planning and preparation work that I'd put in I just hoped we wouldn't be facing a disaster.

'Dunno really,' he replied. 'Some kind of emergency on site. Len was calling me from there but the line wor cracklin' away like a bloody firework an' I couldn't hear him properly.'

Firework? Please don't say there's been a fire, I pleaded, silently. How many clubs had been notorious for having suspicious fires over the years and it'd be just like Archie to have set something ablaze with his Park Drive dog-ends. Plausible though it was, I desperately hoped that this wasn't going to be the case, yet deep down I feared that my hard work and plans were about to disappear in a cloud of smoke.

We drove into Darfield village and as we neared the site there were no obvious signs of any damage or fires. As we pulled up outside the building, everything looked peaceful and fine and I was temporarily relieved. Then I saw Len and Archie having an animated conversation and spotting the minibus, they came over to meet us.

'We've 'ad a water leak,' Len said. 'Them fuckin' contractors next door burst through a pipe over weekend,' pointing towards the men and machinery demolishing the former colliery site.

'Water Board engineers 'ad to come an' shut off the mains supply to village while they repaired it. But when they switched it back on, the pressure blew out th'inlet valves on our water tanks. I've managed to close the stop tap but it's been floodin' in for last eighteen hours by my reckoning.'

'Well, how bad is it inside?' I asked.

'Put it this way,' said Archie. 'When ah opened front doors first thing this mornin', mi paint pots came sailin' outa lobby like they were ducks on a pond. Come an' see fer yerself.'

Terry and I followed them both through the front doors and whilst any standing water had now drained away, I could see where it had left a dirty tide mark above the skirting boards and up against the freshly painted walls. The carpets squelched beneath our feet and the whole room smelled like wet, muddy dogs. The place was ruined and in despair I almost burst into tears. We were so close and yet, now, so far.

'There's no way it will dry out before Wednesday night,' said Len. 'Plus, all 'lectrics an' wirin' will now be dodgy as water has got into the fuse boxes. I was gonna say we'll 'ave to cancel th'event, but then Archie's come up with an alternative plan.'

We all looked at Archie, who cleared his throat as if he was about to make a speech.

'Ah've just come from 'avin' a word wi' Albert, who runs my Labour Club down the road,' he said. 'Wednesdays are normally a quiet night for him an' so he's prepared to rent yer the concert room if we cut him in on the takings. Plus, he'll take all booze an' barrels 'ere off yer at cost price, as well as the food tha's ordered.'

He paused for a second as he lit up a fag. 'Now, it might be a bit tight, fitting all punters in over yonder, but I think it will work. What's that sayin' you 'ave in your game, lad – the show must go on? Well now it can.'

Len came to his support. 'You know, that's not a bad idea when all's said an' done. Folk can still park 'ere and then make their way down to Club. It's only a minute's walk away. Their vehicles will be fine 'ere an' I'll put a couple o' security lads on for evenin'. Plus, if Terry has his van available, he can also ferry down anyone who can't walk.'

Terry and I looked at each other. In the circumstances, it seemed to be not a bad idea. My initial anger had subsided as I realised that the damage was not of our own doing, but I still thanked my lucky stars that we'd got some insurance in place. At least I hoped it would cover some of the outgoings that I'd already made, but I'd have to check it out later with Duggie.

In the meantime, I had a decision to make. Having raised people's expectations, it seemed to me that it was more important to have the event take place if only to get people interested in what I was trying to do. Archie was right, the show had to go on, no matter what. If we now had an alternative venue at our disposal then we might just be able to resurrect something out of this mess.

'Okay,' I said. 'I'll have to go and see Albert and check out the venue.'

'I'd better come wi' yer so that I can vouch for thee,' added Archie. 'Albert's not one who teks too kindly to, er, foreigners. Thinks they're all out to rip 'im off.'

'Well, what do you think he'll want as a fee to rent the concert room?' I asked.

'Oh, Albert's very amenable where money is concerned,' he replied. 'Fifty per cent o' ticket sales an' all o' bar takin's will be fine wi' 'im.'

'What?' I exclaimed. 'Just to rent the concert room for a few hours?' This was an extortionate amount of money. 'What about ten percent? Will he take that?'

'Only if you add another forty points on top of it,' said Archie, looking disappointed at me. 'Bear in mind that 'ere I am tryin' to do tha a big favour an' now yer quibblin' over a few bloody quid. Does tha want this gig to 'appen or not?'

I breathed out heavily, resigning myself to the inevitable.

'Okay, half the ticket sales, it is,' I said. I wondered if Archie had already negotiated a back-hander with his mate Albert on this arrangement. By my quick calculation we could be heading for a loss on this one now, but at least we'd still get the event hosted.

'Champion,' replied Archie, relieved at my change of heart. 'Now, let's get stuff organised. How many tickets have tha sold? Len says one hundred an' fifty at a tenner each.'

I nodded back in confirmation.

'Aye, then Albert will settle for 'alf of that. Oh, an' it's cash only in advance, seein' that's it not an officially sanctioned Labour Club event, if you know what ah mean.'

'Well, tell him I'll call in tomorrow evening with his seven fifty. I'll have to draw it out of the bank first.'

Archie smiled and took a deep drag on his cig.

'Plus 'e'll even lay on a couple of strippers an' all as a break from music when it's nosh time. After all, he is licensed for titillation you know.'

Terry laughed out loud. 'Now that's a job I've always wanted to apply for,' he said. 'Titillation Officer at the Council, but yer just never see it advertised,' and we all grinned at his comment.

'I don't think the girls will be necessary,' I said to Archie. 'But thank him anyway for the kind gesture.'

Archie scratched his head in that peculiar way of his when he knew he hadn't quite disclosed the whole truth.

'Well, thing is yer see, Suzi and Amy, they 'ave to practice their new fire-twirlin' routine for Sunday lunchtime. Albert lets 'em rehearse on a Wednesday as, like I said, it's normally a quiet night. They're a couple o' crackin' lookin' lasses an' think of it this way, you're gerrin' a bonus of a coupla entertainers thrown in for nowt. Plus, their fire jugglin' will go down well with the food yer puttin' on. It will be poi an' pie night - geddit?' he laughed.

'Looks like I don't have a choice then if we want the show,' I replied. 'Let's swing by the bank before we head back to College, Terry.'

Len agreed to sort out the logistics of ferrying the bar stock and Archie made his way back down to the Labour Club to confirm the details with Albert.

'What do you think?' I asked Terry, as we got back in the minibus. 'Be honest now and tell me if I'm being an idiot. Do you think I'm wasting my time here on this project?'

'Not necessarily,' he replied. 'We all used to enjoy local music events back in the day an' I don't see that things 'ave changed that much. People still prefer live music to recorded stuff. Back when ah were younger we'd queue up for hours round 'ere to see singers like Billy Fury or Ricky Valance. And them great showbands like Freddie and the Dreamers and Herman's Hermits. What a time we 'ad of it then.'

'Who?' I asked.

'Who?' he repeated, with disdain. 'Go an' do yer bloody 'omework, lad. The sixties were a great time to be young. You see, whilst all big names like the Beatles or the Stones were brekkin' into the States, we still had loads of good bands an' music goin' on here an' we went mad for it. Great songs and tunes like *Apache* and *Telstar*. You know ah can still hear that wah-wa-wah as if it was the first time. Boy, what a sound that was. We'd never 'eard anythin' like it.'

I smiled, listening to him enjoying his reminiscing about his younger years. 'Better in your days was it, Terry?'

'You're not kiddin' it was lad,' he replied. 'How about, *Tell Laura*, for instance?' as he burst into song. 'Now if tha could sing that, the girls would be queuin' up fer tha. Er, not that such things need concern thee anymore, I mean, now you're almost wed. But, aye, your lot don't know how good we 'ad it back in the day,' he said. 'Just ask yer mate Colin what we used to get up to,' as he drove us back down the road towards Goldthorpe, still singing that his love for her would never die.

Colin was unperturbed when I informed him about what had gone on and he even seemed more upbeat about the new arrangements.

'Shit happens lad, but at least the gig will go on. And the Labour Club will be furnished and well-heated, so we won't have to worry about the power goin' off an' the beer taps not working. So what more could you want? Many artistes have played in much worse conditions. Now let's concentrate on getting our set list together.'

That evening I discussed the alternative plans with Jenny and she seemed keen on us using the Labour Club. 'If you don't do it then you might not get another chance,' she said. 'Put your efforts into making it a success. The proof of the pudding will be plain to see on Wednesday night.'

'Okay,' I replied. 'Thanks for your confidence.'

'Talking of puddings,' she said, tapping her swollen belly. 'You won't mind if I don't come along, do you? It's getting close to the due date and I don't want to leave the comfort of this sofa.'

'No worries,' I replied. 'But let me know if you change your mind.'

I called in to see Albert the following evening and gave him his cash up-front. In return he graciously allowed all the musicians to have free drinks for the evening and I then wished that I'd booked Mick's colliery band to do a spot, in which case they'd probably drink the bar dry.

However, I was very pleased indeed when at seven thirty on a cold drizzly December night, we'd squeezed nearly one hundred and fifty blues and jazz fans into the concert room. They all seemed fairly relaxed with the new arrangements and keen to hear the show and that's what really mattered over whether we succeeded or failed.

Len, dressed in his trademark velvet dinner jacket and bowtie, clambered onto the stage to welcome everyone. He did the intros and explained the reasons for the last minute change of venue as Colin and I readied ourselves to open up the proceedings. We were being supported by the resident club drummer and the organist, who tonight was doubling up on a bass guitar alongside us.

I'd earlier noticed that the drummer guy had walked with a pronounced limp when he'd ambled up to sit behind his kit and I realised that he must have been the same chap whose wooden leg had been accidentally shot off at the Country and Western night here that Archie had previously told me about. Unfortunately, the experience didn't seem to affect his playing – he was still shit, but we managed to get through our set of five numbers despite him.

Then the jazz trio - an outfit Colin had organised called Three In A Bar - took over and did some nice foot-tapping numbers, not too far out and equally not too bland. For their last number Colin replaced the pianist, who instead took hold of a tenor sax, and they performed a great cover of *Take Five* leading us smoothly into the interval spot.

Len announced that supper would now be served as a batch of apron-clad dinner ladies appeared out of the kitchen and began taking plates of mushy peas and pork pies from the serving hatch to the seated punters. As they worked their way around the room, the lights were dimmed and a couple of figures dressed in full length black hooded capes took to the stage, where one of them lit a large pillar candle placed in the centre.

Then, to flashing neon lights, the capes were whipped off to reveal a couple of shapely and very scantily clad women, who I took to be Suzi and Amy, and as a pounding backing track of *Born to Be Alive* blared out through the speakers, they began their act.

After parading up and down the front of the stage, they lit up their twirling rods and batons of fire from the candle. Making their way round the room, they began juggling and tossing them to each other over the heads of the punters.

Any leery bloke trying to grab a handful of tempting fleshy backside as they sashayed past the tables was treated to a fireball blowing over their head, causing them to duck down rapidly into their dish of pie and peas, as their mates around them guffawed and cheered at the antics taking place. It provided some distraction as the main band got ready on the darkened stage and to be fair, the girls put on a good performance. They were applauded enthusiastically by the raucous crowd as they finished with a flourish by returning to the stage and lighting up their nipple tassels, twirling them round like Catherine wheels.

Watching from the bar, I had a strange fleeting vision that the Head Nun from the Sisters of Mercy school was about to appear from behind the stage curtains and berate me in front of the audience for how low I had sunk, but fortunately it was just my mind working overtime. I even managed to talk to a few of the audience, thanking them for coming along and outlining my plans for the Darfield and they all seemed very receptive and supportive.

Suitably refreshed and thankfully with no injuries or burnt scalps, we then we had a good hour or so of solid rhythm and blues. The band, called The Blue Shade Dudes, came from Leeds and they were a good crew, doing some great cover versions of blues classics together with some original stuff.

The crowd liked them, judging from the whistles and the cheers and Terry smiled at me as he joined me at the bar for a beer. Duggie waved to me from the bar corner where he was chatting up one of the half-time entertainment girls, whilst across the other side in the games room, I could see Archie busy fleecing some of his pals at dominoes.

'Listen to that groove Terry,' I said, as the band thundered through the Eric Clapton track *Further On Up The Road.* 'Can you feel how it moves in a kind of lilting, rhythmic looseness? It's allowing the guitarist to create some tension by seemingly being out of kilter, as the bass and drums behind him keep a steady beat going. Then he releases it and order is restored as he falls back into time with the rest of the band. Wonderful. These guys know their stuff alright.'

'I thought he were just showin' off,' said Terry, flatly. 'But now that you mention it, I can see what you mean, I think. Mind you, ah still prefer Joe Cocker and the Grease Band. Saw 'em 'ere once back in late sixties. Now, what performers they were.'

I looked out at our new-found blues enthusiasts nodding and smiling away at the band. We'd gathered an audience from all walks of life and from all sections of the local community who were enjoying these timeless sounds. I'd always felt that this kind of music represented that strong voice which refused to be silenced by oppression and change and instead it stubbornly communicated a sense of belonging and solidarity with clarity, honesty and simplicity. My dream of the Blues in the Dearne Valley was coming true and I was very happy with our efforts.

'What d'ya think Terry? Do you like it?' I asked. 'It's just how music should be. It's the last true voice of the human spirit.'

He nodded back as he swigged his beer. 'It's not bad, I'll give yer that,' he replied.

'You know, the messages of the Blues cover the entire range of human sufferings and aspirations, and always in authentic ways,' I said. 'They're a real reflection of how we live. Just like the ambiguity created between the minor and major keys, they convey a feeling of tragic irony which is parallel to that of our everyday existence. One minute we're fine, the next we're not, then things eventually find a way of resolving themselves.'

'Bloody 'ell,' he said. 'Tha's been spendin' too much time around that Colin. He's turned thee into a philosopher.'

Maybe he had I thought, as I took a mouthful of beer. But I could hear and see the parallels between the music, my own life and the community I was living in. We were all in a state of change, moving from what we once knew and were familiar with, to something that was uncomfortable and which created tension coupled with an emotional longing for it to be resolved.

Naturally, it would do so in time, just as the guitarist here was doing, dropping back onto the tonic note from the dominant one as he hit the first beat of the next bar, but it would only happen at the appropriate moment.

Terry would no doubt say that progress changes the material things in our lives, but for me the music was still the steady, unchanging factor, resistant to both the economic and political forces around us.

In a way it was the same with the lads at the Barnstone Colliery brass band. They were proudly and defiantly playing on, demonstrating their hard-won heritage and legacy for all to hear and see, despite the fact that their workplace had gone forever. I thought back to my time with them and how they, as well as myself, were all on our own unique journeys into freedom as I recalled the contest piece that we had played.

I decided that we would feature a brass night at the Darfield where we could include more people and maybe introduce them to other blues artists in my efforts to promote different styles of music in this part of the world.

Then the band's lead singer interrupted my intellectual musings by yelling out for me to join them on stage in a final number. So, I put down my beer and went over to retrieve my guitar as we went into *Sweet Home Chicago*, singing it as *Sweet Home in Thurnscoe*, to add some local flavour, as the crowd joined in enthusiastically with us. Having great interaction between artistes and the audience is the art of performance and these lads had it nailed.

Even Albert was very complimentary to me afterwards. 'Ah think tha might be onta summat 'ere,' he said. 'Tha's done well to bring this kind o' music to these parts. Might even catch on yer know. Let me know if you want me to host another night at any time.'

No chance of that I thought, seeing that he had made a bucketful of money out of me tonight, but I was gracious enough to say thanks for his help.

We might have to wait three months for the Darfield to dry out, but at least I had proved a point to myself. Tonight had been a success. The Blues were alive and kicking in the Dearne, even if they did come served up with pork pies and a hefty dollop of titillation. But everyone was happy and no doubt the old bluesmen would have smiled and approved of my efforts.

Chapter Thirty

After the triumph of Darfield, Christmas was also a joyous event over at Jenny's house. I'd gone over a couple of days earlier so I could spend as much time as possible with her over the holidays. She was bored stiff and housebound just waiting for junior to make his entrance known, but equally putting a brave face on her condition.

On Christmas Day Walter took me down to his club for an hour or so and I actually witnessed him buying drinks with his own money. Miracles do occur at this time of year, I thought.

Then back at the house we'd finished off the most gargantuan lunch I'd ever seen, although it couldn't be started until sometime after three, once the Queen had appeared on TV. I wasn't really sure why this ritual was followed, but nevertheless, I didn't question it and followed the convention, feeling very grateful that I was watching HM as a free man and no longer as one of her detained guests.

Jenny and I had decided to spend our Christmas present money on things for the baby, so I'd restricted myself to buying smaller gifts for Walter and Dorothy. But they had reciprocated by generously giving me their car.

'No, I won't tek any brass for it neether,' said Walter, when I'd offered to pay him for it.

'Tha'll need tha cash for little 'un now an' so that's where it's gotta be spent. We've also bought you a car-seat so you can ferry the baby around safe an' sound. My new one is due to be here next week.'

'So's mine,' said Jenny, laughing. 'At least after that, then maybe I'll be able to fit inside a car. And get back to wearing proper clothes instead of these tents,' she added.

'Will Jamie be assisting you at the birth?' asked Dorothy.

We hadn't previously discussed this aspect of parenting. Back on the farm in Ontario I'd been used to giving a hand, sometimes literally, by pulling on a new calf's leg during a difficult birthing and it was something that I hated doing. Not that I'd have to do anything like that in this case, but Jenny, bless her, intervened to save my blushes.

'No chance mum,' she said. 'You won't believe how many new dads we get in the delivery suite either throwing up or fainting an' getting in the way of things.'

'Aye, they're best kept outa way,' agreed Walter.

'Well, they do stupid things like asking if their woman is feelin' alright or trying to give reassurance when it's not needed,' continued Jenny. 'No, I just want the doc and the nursing staff looking after me,' she declared.

'Jamie and dad can stay outside, walking the corridors like normal blokes. I'll have enough trauma goin' on without 'aving to worry about them.'

'In our day, men were always told to go to the pub and wait there,' said Dorothy. 'Can't imagine what 'elp you would ha' been Walter, when I went in to have our Jenny.'

Turning to me she said, 'I'd banished him and my dad to the club for the day. The pair of them ended up getting legless and that was before Jenny had actually arrived.'

There were no objections coming from me whilst Walter just gave me a wistful look.

'Looks like tha might 'ave to tek up a pipe whilst tha's waitin' lad,' he said, pulling a wad of tobacco out of his pouch and pressing it down into the bowl of the briar with his thumb. 'Good for contemplating on things, is a pipe,' he added.

'No thanks,' I replied. 'Got my singing voice to worry about.'

'I worry 'bout it too. But a couple of bags o' this stuff might do wonders to improve it,' he muttered, before putting on his sheepskin coat and wandering out into the back garden for an uninterrupted smoke.

*

Jenny and I had decided that our plans for New Year were going to be kept simple. Walter and Dorothy would be going to his club for a party and we would have a quiet night in at her house. She didn't want to go out, not least because she hadn't got a dress that she could fit into as well as being convinced that buying another one just for the evening did not count as money well-spent. Plus, we still had a lot of things to sort out yet for the wedding and the eventual move into my place.

However, when I arrived at her house around eight on New Year's Eve, the place was in pandemonium. Walter was wandering around, half dressed in his frilly shirt and bowtie, minus his trousers and trying to brush his shoes without splashing black Cherry Blossom polish onto his cuffs.

'Bout bloody time,' he said, when he saw me. 'Jenny's gone into labour early. Ambulance has just been for 'er an' you'd better get yerself ready to go down to th'ospital pretty smartish. I'll drop tha there now on our way. Phone us at the club if anything happens,' thrusting a card in my hand.

Twenty minutes later I was at Doncaster hospital and after making some enquiries at the reception desk, I was directed to the maternity ward and told to wait before briefly seeing Jenny.

She was glad I was there with her, but I could see she was clearly in pain as she told me to stay until it was all over. I wandered around the corridors for ages looking in on her at regular intervals, but she still hadn't been moved to the delivery room, which I was told would only happen when the baby was on its way.

Eventually, I drifted over to the seating area where two other guys were already sitting and absently watching the TV. It was playing an extended mix of pop music videos from the last decade. I guessed they were also expectant dads and I wished them both a Happy New Year.

'Aye,' said one. 'And the same to thee. Wife don't half pick 'er bloody moments. Last time it wor cup final, now it's tonight. Think she's got somethin' against me spending time wi' me mates.'

'That's nothing,' said the second, older guy. 'This will be number four for us. It's the big snip for me now, so happy fuckin' new year, it's not.'

'Were you present in the delivery room for your first one?' I asked him.

'No way. Doctor had asked the missus if she preferred to have the baby's father with her when she gave birth. Not a chance, she'd told him, he doesn't get on with my husband,' he said. 'Trouble is, she'd 'ad that much gas an' air inside her I didn't know if she were jokin' or not.'

'I wor wi' mine at our one,' said the first guy. 'Well, up to the point before they threw me out.'

'Why did they do that?' I asked.

'Well, after wife gave birth I went up and thanked the doctor and pulling him to one side, I quietly asked him how soon he thought we'd be able to have sex. He just winked at me and said he was off duty in ten minutes and I could meet him in the carpark. So I lamped him instead with a bedpan.'

'Well at least it was a success, the birth part I mean.'

'Success,' muttered the older guy. 'Now there's a debatable topic.'

'What do you mean?' Either something is a success or it's not,' I said.

'Well put it like this,' he answered. 'At birth, success is about just being alive. At three years old it's not crapping in your pants. By the time tha's ten, success is 'aving friends an' at eighteen it's about 'aving a driver's licence and regular sex. And by thirty it means 'aving a good job an' a nice 'ouse.'

'So what's debatable about that?' I asked. 'Those things all seem pretty straight-forward to me.'

'Put yourself in my shoes lad,' he replied. 'I'm forty two now, so success means 'aving money, as I don't bloody have any. By the time I'm fifty-five success will be 'aving sex, which looks doubtful, then by the time I'm seventy, it'll be still 'avin' hold of a driver's licence. At seventy-five, success will be 'aving friends who are still livin' and at eighty it will be not crapping in mi pants. Then at ninety, success will be just being alive, but by then there won't be much bloody point to it.'

'You're a cheerful bloke,' I said. 'You don't know someone who drives big taxis around do you?'

'Just tellin' it as ah see it lad,' he replied. 'You've got all this to come,' as we were interrupted by a nurse holding out a surgical gown and a mask.

'Mr Martindale,' she said. 'Come and meet your new son.'

I put on the gown and mask and then followed her into the delivery room where the medical staff were clearing up and Jenny lay on a raised table, looking sweaty and radiant. She was cuddling a little bundle on her breast.

'Look what you've got,' she said. 'Happy New Year.'

I bent over and kissed her and gazed at the little guy fast asleep against the warmth of her body. 'Eight pounder as well, he is,' Jenny declared. 'Little bruiser in more ways than one.'

I was lost for words. I'd become a dad and for me at that moment there was no greater feeling on all the earth. All the celebrations taking place around the world to welcome in the new decade could not eclipse the wonder and astonishment that I felt being at her side.

My life was no longer just about me, it was about my family. The thought was over-whelming and I felt the tears roll down my cheeks as I looked down at our little creation.

'Here, take a hold of your son,' said Jenny, lifting him up. 'Say hello to Joe 90.'

'But I thought we were calling him Robert?' I asked, bewildered at what she'd just said.

'We are. It's a joke,' she answered. 'Joe 90 was a kids' TV programme a few years back. This is our little Bobby.'

'Born at one twenty-five in the morning on the first of January 1990 and weighing eight pounds and two ounces,' announced the attending nurse, as she filled in some paperwork. 'Our warmest congratulations to you both. Now sir, would you mind moving out of the way as we have to prepare the suite for the next delivery.'

'I'm gonna phone your mum and dad,' I said to Jenny. 'They said to ring them as soon as anything happened.'

'But they'll be sleeping now,' she protested.

'Good. Then I'll wake the old bugger up and give him the news,' I laughed, as the nursing staff eased Jenny onto a bed and wheeled her and little Bobby down to the ward to get some rest. 'We'll all be back here in a few hours,' I shouted after her, although I wasn't sure if she was still awake.

*

The next few weeks became a blurry and busy routine of short periods of sleep, learning to bottle feed and visiting all sorts of family relations who wanted to see the new arrival as well as meeting me for the first time. Jenny and little Bobby stayed at her parents' house as we'd agreed and I went over whenever I could, although it was more out of dutiful curiosity than to do anything useful.

Dorothy was in her element with all things maternal and even Walter knew his place by keeping out of the way and then helping out by doing something constructive, like cleaning the bathroom.

After three weeks I was even persuaded to take baby Bobby into College and so one bright day Jenny and I proudly showed off our new offspring to the department staff and to Colin and Terry. For two supposedly grown men, they both dissolved into giggling kids, cooing and making strange gurgling noises to the little guy, who didn't seem at all fazed by the attention he was receiving.

On the way back home, I had an idea. 'Let's go to visit someone you've not met yet.'

'Who's that?' asked Jenny.

'A lady called Mavis. She's the mum of the lad whose wake thing I played at, you remember? I don't have a phone number for her, but I think I can remember where she lives. We'll see if she's in.'

I was driving and so after making a few wrong turns, we finally pulled up outside Mavis's house. As I got out of the car, I was surprised to see Duggie coming up the garden path from her front door and he looked up at me.

'Now then young Jamie, what thy doin' 'ere?' he asked, looking a little embarrassed.

'Just coming to see Mavis,' I said. 'Show her our new baby. I didn't know that you knew her, Duggie.'

'Er yes, in a professional capacity, you see, insurance cover and stuff,' he said, as his cheeks flushed red.

I knocked on the door and heard Mavis shout out, 'Bloody 'ell Duggie, you've 'ad yer lot for today,' before opening the door and gasping open-mouthed at me.

'Hello there Mavis,' I said. 'Hope you don't mind the unannounced arrival. Just thought you'd like to meet my new family,' pointing at Jenny and the baby waiting in the car.

'Well of course, come on in,' she said, with a big smile. 'For a second there I thought you were, er, someone else.'

'Yes Duggie, I've just seen him leave,' I replied. 'He does my insurance cover as well.'

'Hopefully not in the same way he does mine,' she laughed, as I signalled to Jenny to bring in the carry-cot and baby. After making the introductions, we all settled down on the sofa in Mavis's front room. It brought back memories of when I was first here, almost a year ago, fleeing the wrath of Big Bert from Brodsworth.

Mavis welcomed Jenny and little Bobby like they were her long lost relatives. Any casual observer would have said they were part of the same family, but they were just being who they were: kind, friendly Yorkshire women, looking out for each other and sharing a few laughs over a cup of tea. Mavis showed Jenny the picture of Richie, still in its pride of place on her mantlepiece and I thought back to that sad day, before she looked at me and changed the subject.

'Having a child is a wonderful thing,' said Mavis. 'You get the chance to raise them the way you would like them to be,' smiling at me as she spoke.

'A son is the ultimate satisfaction of your life as a man. Not only have you continued your family name, but you can hand down knowledge, experience an' life lessons that will help him grow into a well-adjusted adult - and a Yorkshire one at that,' she added, as we laughed along with her.

'Yes, gone are the days of staying out all night with the boys,' I said. 'I've got real commitments now,' smiling back at Bobby and Jenny.

'Now, 'ave your folks back home met your young lady yet?' Mavis asked me. 'They won't have seen the baby, obviously, but when are you planning on visiting them?'

'Well, we haven't made any plans as such,' I said, sheepishly.

It was true, I hadn't yet told my folks that I was going to be married and also that I'd become a dad. It wasn't anything untoward, it was just that we didn't maintain any regular communication.

'Thought so,' she said. 'Well, let's see about that,' as she got up and went to her sideboard and opened a drawer. After a few moments she said, 'This is for you both, to help you on your way. Now, no arguments,' handing over a cheque to Jenny. 'I know what it's like to struggle as a young family. I want you to have this an' use it for your honeymoon or on the baby or whatever you like.'

Jenny held up the cheque for me to see. It was for £2,000.

'But Mavis,' I protested. 'We can't take all this.'

'Course you can,' she insisted. 'I got a big compensation pay out from the Army for Richie as I'm his only family member an' at my age I've no need for all that cash. I'd be offended if you didn't accept a little kindness.'

'Well, we could use it to go and visit my parents,' I suggested. 'They'll be thrilled to meet Jenny and their new grandson and it will be a nice surprise for them.'

'I think that's a grand idea,' she said.

We carried on chatting for a while over another cup of tea as I told Mavis about our plans for the Darfield Club and even managed to joke about how I'd been locked up for a while as an illegal. Then it was getting time for Bobby to be fed so we got our things together and promised we would keep in touch with her and call round again soon.

'She's a lovely lady,' said Jenny, as we got back in the car to drive to Conisbrough. 'How did you get to know her?'

'She was performing over at the miners' club in Darfield, when I first came up here,' I said. 'She, er, helped me get used to the locals.' Do I tell Jenny about the link between Mavis and Terry? No, better to let some things go unsaid, I reasoned.

'Well, she's very kind,' confirmed Jenny. 'I think she looks on you as a kind of a surrogate son.'

'I don't know about that,' I replied. 'But maybe you're right. She does miss her own lad, I'm sure. She's a gentle lady who's had a hard life and yet despite all that, she's very generous with her favours.'

No doubt Duggie was well placed to confirm my assessment, the dirty old sod.

Chapter Thirty One

Planning was everything Colin had said to me some time ago and, as with all his advice, he was exactly right. Jenny and I were deep into planning for our forthcoming wedding at the end of March and I was also engrossed in the opening of the Darfield which was time-tabled to happen in the following month.

Plus, with Mavis's gift we were now booked to visit my folks immediately after the wedding which would also coincide with the Easter holidays from College. It was going to be a weird kind of honeymoon although it would naturally be nice to see my parents again and introduce my new family to them.

Talk about the return of the Prodigal Son – but at least I had something to show for my wanderings and I wasn't going to rock up penniless and empty-handed. It would also be a timely visit as the worst of the Winter weather would be over by the end of March and so little junior wouldn't be at risk from the cold.

Moreover, I felt that it would be a great opportunity for Jenny to see part of my home Country where I'd been born and raised. I'd spent quite a bit of time trying to assimilate myself into Yorkshire life and culture which I'd enjoyed very much and felt that I could now reciprocate.

She'd been bombarding me with questions about what Ontario was like and very soon she'd be able to find out for herself. I could see her falling in love with the wide-open spaces and countryside and given her nursing qualifications she would have no trouble finding work if it ever came to that.

Meanwhile, remedial work on the Darfield was ongoing after the recent flooding and the Coal Board had very generously picked up the tab for the repairs, as they no doubt would be able to deduct it from the demolition contractors' bill.

This meant that I'd no need to claim anything on our insurance policy and old Archie was doubly pleased as he was getting paid twice for doing the same job. It wasn't often that he was able to boast about that.

Duggie told me we needed to set up an organising committee and publish some rules and such like and I left that bit with him as he assured me he knew someone who would assist.

As far as our wedding was concerned, Jenny's parents were traditional but not particularly religious people and so they had no objections to our plans for a low-key service at the Registry Office in town, followed by inviting friends and family to the reception at the Edlington miners' club.

Walter had begrudgingly given us the concert room for free, as long as it was on a Wednesday night. That way he wouldn't be losing any significant trade and I'd also said that I'd pay the backing musicians to play along with myself for a few requests, so he was happy with that. The things you have to do to keep the in-laws on your side.

'Who'll be your best man?' asked Jenny, one Saturday evening as we were going through the list of wedding guests.

'Don't know. Do I need one?'

'Yes, I think so, even if it's just to act as a witness to the actual ceremony,' she replied. 'My friend Steph from work will be my maid of honour, not that there's anything very honourable about her. But I've known her since we were at school together and she'll be my legal witness.'

'Well, I'll ask Terry or Colin in that case,' I replied. 'I'm sure one of them will stand up for me.'

But thinking about it, I wondered if either of them would be offended if they were not asked first? There was only one way to find out, but before that I needed to check if Colin would do a couple of numbers with me at our wedding night party.

'Yes, I'd be glad to,' he said, when I approached him about it the following Monday. 'What did you have in mind?'

'Well, something a bit light that folk can dance to if they want,' I said. 'There seems to be a hankering for some old sixties and seventies stuff from what I can gather, so not my usual repertoire of stuff. The resident band at the club will back us and they are decent guys. They worked well with me when I did my first gig there.'

Having got his agreement to performing I then tentatively asked, 'I was thinking of asking Terry if he would be my, er, witness, best man thing on the day. Do you think he'll do it?'

'Don't see why not,' he replied. 'He's a good guy and seems to like you a lot. I'm sure he'll agree.'

Terry was happy to oblige when I put the question to him later on in the day.

'Are tha gonn' be wantin' a stag night as well?' he asked. 'I'll provide the minibus for nowt if you like.'

'Thank you, but it won't be necessary,' I said. 'I've got myself into enough scrapes as it is around here without tempting fate on a stag night with a pack of boozy blokes. I can just imagine what your Mick and his band lads would be like on a night out.'

'Probably the right decision,' he agreed. 'Ah can just see tha gettin' molested by them women from the clothin' factory in town or out on a Friday in Donny, chained to a lamp an' minus yer pants. How would ah then explain that one to yer lass?'

Best man all sorted, we were now organised and ready for our nuptials.

We subsequently arranged the appointment at the Registry Office for four thirty in the afternoon, which was the last available slot and it meant that we could go straight onto the reception from town. We'd agreed that there would be around fifty guests for the evening so we'd have plenty of space for dancing and folk wouldn't feel too crowded together.

On the afternoon of twenty eighth of March, the female Registrar welcomed Jenny and me into her premises. She then warned me sternly that now I'd turned up for the ceremony, there was no escaping through the toilet windows as they were already barred and locked, before I realised she was joking. Jenny looked radiant in her bridal dress and I'd splashed out on a new Burton's suit, hoping that it would last me for several more years to come.

Walter and Dorothy took charge of little Bobby, who was very quiet for the most part and with Terry and Jenny's witness Steph by our sides, we were all set.

The ceremony was surprisingly quick and before I knew it, I was asked to kiss the bride as the Registrar legally declared us to be husband and wife. Then we posed for the photographs outside whilst the guests pelted us with confetti and rice.

When I performed later on at the club, I sung with a different voice and outlook. It wasn't me doing a gig, it was me singing to my new wife, to my new family life and for my son.

The audience of guests gave us rapt applause and cheers, especially when we did *When a Man Loves a Woman*, as a request for Dorothy, which apparently had been her favourite song at one time. It made me wonder if there had been a past rival to Walter at some point for her affections and it occurred to me that Len was the most likely candidate.

The backing lads made me sound really good and Colin and I did *Wonderful Land* as he duetted on guitar with me, followed by our version of *Walk Don't Run* before he went back to his keyboards. Together we played and sang *Mustang Sally* and *Brown Eyed Girl* belting them out enthusiastically like we hadn't a care in the world.

Even Mick was singing his head off and clearly enjoying himself and I made a mental note to wish him well for the future, as he was due to take up a new job in Australia in a couple of weeks.

We took a break for twenty minutes as some recorded Motown tracks played over the speakers and Jenny and her nursing friends took to the dance floor for a while.

Then Walter announced that the buffet was open and people began leaving their seats to get some food. I went across to the bar to get a pint and was about to speak with Terry and his wife when I was interrupted by a middle-aged guy dressed in a smart suit and tie, tapping me on the arm.

'Hello. Are you Jamie Martindale?' he asked, in a pleasant and friendly manner. 'I've just been listening to you from the games room across the bar. You sound very good.'

'Thank you,' I replied. 'And yes, I am he.'

'Then I have something here for you,' he said, pulling out an envelope from his jacket and handing it to me. 'It's

349

an invitation to audition for a new job and a very good one at that. I hope you'll take it up.'

I was momentarily stunned. 'But I already have a job,' I said. 'And I'm not looking for another one at the moment, thanks.'

He was undeterred. 'Your current job is not like this one,' he replied.

'Well, I'll shortly be going to see my folks in Canada for a couple of weeks, plus, er, this is my wedding night.' It didn't seem the appropriate time or place to be having potential career discussions with a complete stranger.

He still remained unmoved. 'No worries, the audition isn't until the end of April and the job doesn't start until May, so there's plenty of time yet,' he said. 'Plus, you've the rest of your life to be married.'

'Well, what is it?' I asked, as he'd now got me intrigued. 'And who are you?'

'The job is for a guitarist in a new music and dancing show that's being put together in Dublin, Ireland. And I'm Michael Kerry and I'm in charge of managing the band and recruiting the musicians.'

I looked at him as he continued with his patter. 'There's four months of rehearsals planned over the Summer, then the show is going to tour,' he said. 'And it's going to be a big one, very big, believe me. We've got some serious money backing this production.'

'A song and dance show? You mean like a musical?' I asked, dismissively and losing interest. Musical theatre was not my thing. 'What's it called anyway?'

'We haven't decided on a final name yet,' he said, as I opened the envelope and glanced quickly at the contents. 'The working title is called 'rivers and dances', but that will no doubt change as things get finalised and the full complement of performers join us over the coming weeks.

It's based on an earlier work from a few years back, but it's going to be completely re-vamped and made spectacular by the time we're all done.'

'You can't be serious,' I said, looking at the money section of the draft offer letter. 'This is a huge amount of cash,' as I read it again to make sure that I hadn't made a mistake.

'We are and it is,' he advised. 'That's because we want the best people we can find and that's why you'll need to pass an audition with us first. Plus, for the first four months you'll have every weekend off, so plenty of time to nip back home and see your family. Even if you only sign on for a year you'll have enough for a deposit on a nice house. And you'll be paid gross, so plenty of scope for minimising your personal taxes over here as well.'

I looked inquisitively at the charming and persuasive Mr Kerry, who now had my interest.

'Who told you about me?' I asked. 'This is a strange location and time for you to just turn up out of the blue like this.'

'Yes, it sure is,' he agreed and laughed a little. 'You did take a bit of tracking down, feller. But you were recommended by a young lady called Rosalyn Carter. She's just signed on as lead violin with us and a cracker of a player she is too.'

Rosalyn! I stared back at him, astonished.

'I don't know what to say,' I said. 'This is my wedding night and now you're presenting me with this. It's the opportunity of a lifetime.'

'Well, you don't have to say anything for the moment,' he replied. 'But obviously, you need to talk it over with your wife. Now, do you know where the Moat House hotel is, near the motorway junction?'

'Yes,' I said. It was walking distance away from where we were currently standing and talking with each other.

'Well, I'll be there until tomorrow. If I haven't got your signature on that invitation by noon, then I'll be off to London where I've got some more people to see. Everything you need to know is in the letter. The ball is in your court Jamie, so have a good evening now and I hope to see you in Dublin in due course,' he added, as he walked off and left me slightly stunned at the bar.

I studied the letter again before looking across the room to Jenny. She and I had arranged to spend our first night as a married couple at a luxury country hotel not far away and Dorothy and Walter had agreed to care for Bobby to give us some time by ourselves. I glanced across to where they were all seated at the family table, clearly enjoying the evening celebrations, as indeed I had been, up to a few moments ago.

'Jamie, they're ready for the next bit,' shouted out Colin from the stage and I wandered back in a daze as we cued up *Hurry on Sundown* with the band lads as a request from Terry. It was an ominous choice considering the conversation I'd just had.

The envelope burned hot against my chest in my inside jacket pocket as we played the classic track and Terry and his wife did some weird dancing moves on the floor in front of the band. Looking out at Jenny and our guests from the vantage of the front of the stage, I realised that my wedding night could well be a sleepless one, but not for the reasons usually given by most newly-spliced and eager young couples.

*

The taxi driver kept staring menacingly at me through his rear-view mirror as I sat quietly in the back of the cab, peering out of the side window and trying to make out any signs of life in the murky darkness beyond.

'First time in these parts, is it then?' he asked over his shoulder.

'Yes', I replied. 'I've never been to Dublin before. Only to London and Yorkshire.'

'Well, some parts are okay, some parts not, you know,' he replied. 'In the Winter time, the smoke from all the houses mingles with the smelly fumes comin' outa the tannery works an' the brewery. Then the sea air blowin' in turns it all into a foggy mess. Yer can't see nuthin' in front o' yer, so yer can't. Just like it is tonight,' as he raced along the unlit roads.

'Wouldn't it be better if you slowed down a little then?' I asked.

'What fer? Can't see nuthin' comin' the other way yet. Where ya from any roads?' he demanded.

'Ontario, Canada but I'm living in London,' I replied. 'No, I mean in Darfield, no Highfield, Yorkshire, now.' I didn't seem to be making any sense. 'I'm a musician.'

'Well, good job yer've brought a weapon wi' yer as well. Yer might be needin' it an all around here.'

'Yes, it's my axe,' I smiled. 'My guitar goes everywhere with me,' as I reached across the seat to touch the case. But it wasn't there any more, even though I was certain I'd just seen it. Frantically I looked under the back seat and then into the front. My guitar! It had been stolen or I'd gone and left it somewhere. Yes, that was it, I remembered now. It was back at Mavis's house, propped up next to the mantelpiece.

'Stop the cab,' I yelled. 'You'll need to go back. I've left my guitar and I need it. Stop and go back right now.'

'Can't do that, feller,' he replied. 'There's no going back now, only forwards.'

'No,' I yelled louder. 'Stop. Turn back. Turn back now.'

'Jamie!' shouted a female voice and I woke with a start to see Jenny looking over at me and shaking my arm vigorously. 'You were dreaming and shouting out. Are you okay?' she asked, with a giggle.

I looked back at her as I got my bearings and calmed down. We'd been on this aeroplane for several hours and whilst it had been a comfortable flight, I was ready to get off. The female attendants had made such a fuss over little Bobby, carrying him up and down the aisles in turn and they had even moved us to a row of three empty seats so that we could have plenty of room between us.

Jenny glanced out of the window and then looked down at her watch. 'Can't be too long now,' she said. 'Looks like a big city coming up. Can you see it?'

I leaned across and peered out of the plane window. 'Yep, that's Toronto,' I said. 'Nearly there.'

'I'm so excited,' she said, as she leaned across and kissed me tenderly on the side of my cheek.

At that moment the Captain announced that our descent would start shortly and that we should all return to our seats, put them in the upright position and fold away the tray tables.

'Thank you for flying with us this afternoon, ladies and gentlemen,' he said, in that reassuring and friendly Canadian accent that I'd missed for so long. 'On behalf of all of our crew onboard today, we wish you a safe and pleasant onward journey.'

The attendant handed Bobby back to us together with a small teddy bear gift toy and waved to him. I smiled across at Jenny as she got him settled into his auxillary belt across her lap.

'One final announcement to make before we land,' continued the Captain. 'I have a message for the folks sat in row twelve.'

I looked up as that was our row.

'Congratulations to Jenny and Jamie on your wedding and we hope you enjoy your honeymoon in beautiful Ontario,' he said, as the passengers around us looked over and gave a spontaneous round of applause. They all grinned at little Bobby taking pride of place, no doubt wondering which crazy Brit takes their baby on honeymoon with them.

'That message comes from the staff at the Barnsley College,' he continued. 'That's over in York-shire, folks, just to show you that I know a bit of geography. It comes in handy sometimes in my job as a pilot,' and we all laughed at his quip.

'They say keep playing them blues, Jamie. You'll go far and preferably sooner.'

Jenny and I smiled at each other and at the other passengers around us. It was a nice gesture from the people I had come to know so well over the past year and a bit and I thought about the coming months in front of us, as I reached and gently touched the audition letter that I'd earlier replaced in my inside pocket. Would it become part of my journey into freedom or would it turn into the trip to hell?

The world was a big place and yet at times also a small one and I glanced over Jenny's shoulder to see the vast Canadian landscape emerging as we descended further below the clouds. Down there on the ground my folks would be waiting patiently to welcome me and my new family, no doubt thinking I was returning to the homestead for good.

But as the words and tune of the song *Take The Long Way Home* swirled around inside my head, I knew in that moment that there was so much more of this world that I wanted to see and experience.

The blues is a mighty long river, twisting and turning as it flows into a sea of limitless musical potential and I was truly sailing on it.

****

About the Author

Tony Lawrence is a retired businessman. He was a student in Sheffield and lived in the Rotherham area during the late Eighties. He now lives in North Yorkshire with his wife, drum kit and an assortment of orphan cats. *Dearne Valley Blues* is his first novel.